I0717076

INFINITE MASS

J.K. Raymond

A Wild Ink Publishing Original

Wild Ink Publishing

wild-ink-publishing.com

Cover Design: Abigail Baia

Edited by: Brittany McMunn & Deb Lerew

ISBN: 978-1-958531-45-7

ISBN: 978-1-958531-46-4

DEDICATION

I'd like to take a moment to thank those who made this book possible.

First, my husband, Matt, who fully supported my dedication to this dream. Thanks, babe. You never doubted me for a minute.

Second, to my kids, Aidan and Jace, who have always been nothing but proud of my attempt to become an author.

Mom, thanks for buying me that first journal, it changed everything.

Rene, thanks for taking me home.

Kristin, you were my first real fan, one I desperately needed to keep going.

Cathy, thanks for helping me trudge my way through those first few drafts.

And thanks to Wild Ink Publishing for taking me on. Abby and Brittany, you made a dream come true.

Love you all,
J.K. Raymond

ONE

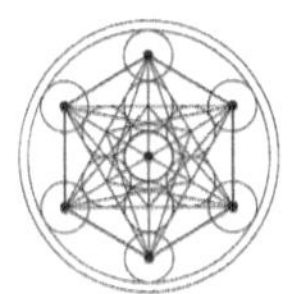

A NEW BUCKET FOR MADAME?

All Saints Day
Nov 1, 2010

Ten-year-old Morna Stahr was grumpy. She was sure another Kit Kat would improve her mood. No dice though. Sequestered in her room for an attempt to pilfer more of the goods, Morna's mood only worsened. Time always passed slowly in solitary. A stretch in the slammer was never welcomed, but with her blood sugar tanking, sour thoughts turned darker still to the bite-sized memory of sinful chocolate and crunchy wafer, smooth and crisp on teeth and tongue.

Left to her own devices, Morna glared at the empty KitKat wrapper, realizing her punishment probably would have been the same whether she'd taken one candy bar or ten.

"Play stupid games, win stupid prizes," she said, flicking the empty wrapper with her thumb and forefinger into the nearby trash can.

She knew she only had herself to blame for the lack of sugar

1

she craved. Wrong as it was, and dumb as it was, the cravings whispered new and inventive ways to land a bigger score.

If she could just find the way to get her hands on one more Laffy Taffy, it would most certainly make up for time served and at the very least, make up for the unholy fact she was up and dressed early for church on a no-school day.

"Argh!" Morna huffed, looking over at her stuffed Cheshire cat, Cradle, as she pulled against the starchy, white collar of her church shirt.

"They get you all excited for a month," she told the stuffed cat. "What are you going to be for Halloween? Do you have your joke ready? Do you think you'll get a lot of candy? Blah, blah, blah. Then you get all dressed up and do all the work. You go door to door, ALL NIGHT, and when you finally get home with your score and settle in to eat, Mom and Dad are saying you can only have two pieces...two! Seriously, what's the point?"

Morna looked at Cradle with a "Know what I mean?" look and waited for his confirmation. She held last night's discarded witch costume at arm's length before balling it up and throwing it backward over her head.

"I'm not doing this next year. It's just not worth it. I've got a ton of candy I'm not allowed to eat, a day off school, I can't sleep in, AND I'm in trouble! Grownups make no sense, Cradle. It's like they set you up to fail."

Cradle, of course, agreed with her wholeheartedly and thought she did nothing wrong by sneaking extra candy to bed last night; after all, she'd earned it. He also thought she should not feel guilty about it, which he knew she would. Not now, mind you. In the heat of the battle, Morna was nothing if not righteous. With time, regardless of her naturally rebellious stance on the unfairness of any given situation regarding her upbringing, Morna eventually felt equally guilty about everything, big or small, thought or deed. Cradle, being the good friend he was, let Morna know since she often got in far too much trouble for any actual minor infraction, admitting fault for nothing more than simple thoughts was tantamount to lunacy. If it made her feel better, she could just consider any previous time served as suitable punishment for both actual and hypothetical wrongdoings her conscience wouldn't let her off the hook about. The sin of not obeying your parents often fell into the gray area of double jeopardy, in the cat's opinion. Morna was never quite sure about the soundness of the cat's advice and often had a hard time sleeping afterward.

When Morna's mother called from the living room it was time to head to morning services, Morna groaned and placed her hand over her upset tummy. Just the thought of the extra-long drive to St. Louis from their small, rural town made her stomach lurch. She couldn't understand why her mother made such a big deal about attending the big church in the city on holy days of obligation. She would get car sick; she always did on long rides. Resigned to her fate, Morna grabbed the grinning cat and shoved it under one arm before snatching up her empty Halloween bucket, knowing it would come in handy over the next forty minutes.

After peeling herself from the floorboard of her mother's car, Morna stood green and small on the corner of Chestnut and Pine. She was tired of staring at her shoes while her mother made small talk with the other adults. Feeling brave and bored, Morna carefully lifted her eyes to the base of the stairs which marked the entryway to the towering cathedral only to quickly bring them back down, instantly regretting the attempt as her stomach rolled. Morna's mother took her hand and began their slow shuffle to the Basilica doors. Enveloped in a mass of people and surrounded by architectural perfection, Morna could only stare at her shoes, concentrating on putting one foot in front of the other.

Behind her mother's lead, Morna genuflected to one knee before entering the pew and realizing her nausea was no longer present. She thought about it for a second, making sure she really did feel perfectly well, and with great relief decided she did. Looking up without fear of vomiting, Morna took in the beauty around her. It was like a bizarre dream to suddenly feel so good surrounded by the cathedral's glory. Was it just ten minutes ago she'd been laying on a dirty car floorboard hugging a Halloween puke pail? The whole thing felt incredibly strange.

While Morna reveled in her newfound health, the rest of the congregation became silent in contemplation. Every head was bowed or turned toward the priest who had slowly begun the pageantry of making his way down the long aisle. Little Morna's head swiveled here, there, and everywhere as a wave of emotion tickled its way across every inch of her skin. A vibration akin to static electricity traveled from the bottom of her shoes to the tips of her fingers. It was as if a current of electricity flowed through her, but that was impossible. Morna inspected the rest of the crowd for any clue a single one of them might be feeling the same thing.

Nope, nada, no one, she thought to herself as the low-voltage waves increased.

The reverence, the art, and the splendor; the weight of it came upon her all at once, like a resplendent sucker punch. It seized the air from her little lungs as the silent contemplations were cut by the clearest, cleanest, most heavenly of voices.

What started soft and small had built and swirled up and outward to fill the expanse of the soaring cathedral. A musical Seraphim who seemed to have come from everywhere and nowhere. A sound not only heard but felt. As the heads of the parishioners swiveled back toward the choir, forward to the high altar, and up toward the arch vault trying to discern the source of the sound, Maude Stahr stood white as a ghost and slack-jawed as she side-eyed her ten-year-old daughter in abject fear and astonishment.

Frozen in awe, everyone listened, and everyone watched as the source of the swirling melody was identified. Morna JoAnn Stahr stood small and still, clutching an old stuffed cat to her chest as she painted a picture of heaven with her voice.

Thinking back, there had been an opus of oddities about that crisp, November morning all those years ago. But coming in at number one with a bullet would have to have been how little Morna JoAnn Stahr couldn't carry a tune in a bucket, even if her life depended on it.

TWO

BARNACLES AND BASILICAS

All Saints Day
Nov. 1, 2018

Morna stood looking into the November gale, one hand clutching the waist of her jacket, the other close-fisted around the handle of her favorite red umbrella. The umbrella didn't help much as the rain came from every possible angle while the relentless November wind constantly threatened to turn the whole damn thing inside out. Morna swore it was dusk when it was only a bit after noon.

Bracing herself against another cold blast, Morna told herself it was good she was here. Everything deep down told her she should run as far and as fast as possible. Morna just wanted to put her past behind her and purposely revisiting it didn't seem the way to go about it. All evidence to the contrary, according to every self-psychoanalyzing book she'd made herself read over the last three months.

Morna spent most of her childhood a living, breathing urban legend, and she moved to the closest big city to slip into sweet anonymity as soon as she was old enough. The important lesson she learned from her past was you could, in fact, disappear from an entire world, from all you've ever known. You could start over and create an entirely new self. Morna spent the last three years doing just that. The problem was, no matter where she went or how unwanted they were, her memories bummed a ride like barnacles on the underbelly of a boat.

Morna moved to St. Louis three months ago. She was eighteen years old and made sure no one from her hometown lived within a five-mile radius of her one-bedroom apartment in Benton Park. It wasn't the greatest of neighborhoods. In the summer it smelled of the wet, sticky hops that drifted over I-55 from Anheuser-Busch Brewery, courtesy of a Mighty Mississippi breeze. Rent was cheap enough to overlook both.

One fake ID later and every waking moment of the next few months was spent waiting tables at a local restaurant and bar in the nearby neighborhood of Soulard. Her biggest social outing included going to the laundromat and talking with her one friend from home who FaceTimed or texted almost every day. Morna did her best to keep busy by taking extra shifts, but no matter how busy she kept herself, her subconscious always found time to conjure up the past.

When one grew up in a small town, everyone knew everything about everyone. No matter how mundane a thing was, if it was a thing at all, it was chatted and shared like an old-fashioned game of telephone. And just like the game, by the time the story reached the end of the line, what little truth was left of the original story was all but buried under the embellishments it received along its travels. Morna remembered one poor girl who wet her bed one night at the ripe old age of five. The girl's seven-year-old brother enthusiastically shared the breaking news with his second-grade classmates, and his poor baby sister was forever known as Heather the Bedwetter. A ten-year-old Morna thought she might see a reference to it in a eulogy eighty years from then at Heather's funeral.

HEATHER BRANSON
BELOVED WIFE,
DEVOTED MOTHER,
AND KINDERGARTEN BEDWETTER,
DIED PEACEFULLY IN HER SLEEP.

Sympathetic ten-year-old Morna did not know she was about to forever replace Heather as the all-time, hands-down, heavyweight champion of small-town lore.

When little Morna returned home after her morning choir debut at the St. Louis Cathedral Basilica that perfect fall day eight years earlier, her mother suggested she go to her room and lie down. Morna curled up on her bed, exhausted in a way she had never felt before, cuddled Cradle close to her chest, and fell into a deep sleep. That moment was the last moment Morna remembered her home ever truly feeling like home.

She woke from her nap to muffled voices coming from the main living area of the house. As she tried to identify the individual voices, it occurred she had no idea what time it was or how long she had been asleep. What she did know was that she was hungry. She grabbed Cradle and headed to the kitchen, forgetting all about the muffled voices.

When Morna turned the corner from the hallway into the dining room, everything stopped. Every head turned and looked at her. At that moment, normal, small-town life for Morna careened off the tracks.

At her parents' dining room table sat Morna's local parish priest, pediatrician, fifth-grade parochial schoolteacher, music teacher, and grandparents from her father's side. Cradle immediately decided this was not good.

A type of small-town hysteria ensued for the next several months as word traveled of Morna's unexpected gift from God which she could not reproduce no matter the amount of overpriced vocal lessons. The hype reached epic proportions when it was determined by Father Thad and his employee, Morna's fifth-grade and Sunday school teacher, Mrs. March, that Morna must have had a spiritual experience and had been specifically chosen as a messenger of God. Looking back, only her grandparents, whom she had hardly known, had her best interests at heart. Pearl and Hayden Stahr had suggested Morna go to a faraway boarding school for a time, just until things cooled down. Cradle knew this was the one and only time Morna's otherwise absentee grandparents said anything remotely advantageous on behalf of any family member, living or dead.

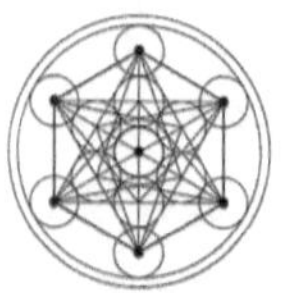

THREE

FLING 'ROUND MY CRADLE THEIR MAGIC SPELLS

Morna braced herself against another cold blast outside the Cathedral, shook her head to clear the cobwebs, and took a deep breath. She was here to careen and dehull her soul, not stand on the deck and stare retrospectively into the gale. It had been too many years with this hanging over her head. She couldn't live with the constant reminder her memories dredged up every second of the day. Her self-help books said, "Face your fears head-on," and that was exactly what she was going to do today.

"Time to get to work," she said.

As she turned toward the stairs, a wave of *Deja vu* hit like a ton of fucking bricks, knocking the breath from her lungs.

Every last hair on her body stood on end as an energy she forgot she knew shot through to her core. With one foot on the stairs, Morna's body hummed the way it had when she stood in the very heart of the cathedral all those years ago.

"Jayzus," she whispered to herself, trying to get her bearings.

Morna rubbed her arms through her coat, trying to settle herself. With a foot carefully planted on the second stair, she damn near jumped out of her skin when her cell phone vibrated against her rain-soaked thigh.

The favorite red umbrella slipped and jostled as Morna reached awkwardly into the depths of her coat pocket for her phone. With her back turned against another cold gust, she adjusted herself, tucking and retucking her wild and wet brown hair behind her ears as she looked down, finding the familiar image of Cradle's furry face had replaced the scenic fall theme she just paid two dollars and twenty-five cents for.

"What the actual f…"

Ding!

New Message: Unknown
Do not freak out.

"… uck."

Ding!

New Message: Unknown
I said, do NOT freak out.

Scouring her surroundings for any sign of life, Morna found none. It was as if she were alone in the city.

"Oh, I'm fucking outta here!" she swore, hot-stepping it off the staircase.

Ding!

Morna looked down at her cell to find it, independent of any action on her part, streaming a two-minute video of her former self.

The younger version looked serene and sang so gloriously that Morna became lost in it for a second, until the much older and wiser Morna Stahr remembered there was no video of the little "performance". If there was, she'd have seen it by now.

Ding!

New Message: Unknown
My name is Creak. We were never formally introduced.

Terrified, Morna yelled out to no one, "Where are you?" She turned in circles, eyes everywhere. "Who the hell are you?!?!"
Ding!

New Message: Unknown
Again, my name is Creak. Do NOT freak out. I am a friend, bestie, and BFF. *smiley emoji.*

Morna heard a low scratching sound behind her like a snow shovel scraping down a long concrete driveway. She turned quickly and headed back down the sidewalk, drawn toward the source of the sound, before stopping dead in her tracks. Fourteen feet above her, smack dab in her path, the metal wings of the Angel of Harmony statue loomed. The beautiful angel's wings were spread gloriously, cresting up and over three ethnically diverse, stainless-steel children, one of which had a particularly ugly dog resting its head on her little metal lap.

Morna instantly remembered her mother talking about the statue being brand new that fateful All Saints Day in 2010. She walked Morna past it and pointed, telling her all about the angel and the three ethnically diverse children, saying how lovely it was. Maude Stahr went on and on about how the statue was meant to inspire harmony among all of God's children and bring people of all backgrounds and ethnicities together. Morna vaguely remembered wanting to see what all the fuss was about and had attempted to look at the towering statue when her queasiness got the better of her, forcing her to concede without ever looking to say the statue was indeed very beautiful.

With the luring, gravelly sound suddenly gone, Morna shook her head and pulled herself from the untimely reverie as she hauled ass back to her car. Her cell dinged and vibrated from the depths of her coat pocket with every step.

"What in the seven hells?" Morna swore as she slammed her car door and plunged the key into the ignition.

Ding!

Ding!

Ding!

Morna pulled out onto the always-busy Lindell Boulevard without looking to see if the road was clear. She drove in shock and on autopilot before soon finding herself in front of her apartment, realizing she was afraid to get out of her car. She grabbed her phone to call Silla, then snatched it back fast, like the thing was sprinkled in smallpox. The vulnerable feeling didn't sit well with her. Frozen with fear hadn't been her cup of tea in quite a while, and it started to chap her ass at how easily she became paralyzed by it, again.

She needed backup. The engine roared as Morna peeled away from the curb and headed over to Silla's new place in the county, praying she'd be home. With hopes of distracting herself and clearing her head, she reached over and turned on the radio.

"This is *The Afternoon Drive* with Creak and Cradle. Hope you're buckled up out there, kiddies, 'cause it's gonna be a bumpy ride! Find your volume dial and tune in Tokyo. Here we go with one of my all-time favorites from Five Man Electrical Band with "Signs". Little caveat, Cradle would like you to know he voted for the Tesla version from 1990, but Cradle is a stuffed cat, and I am not, so my vote wins."

Morna cocked her head and quit breathing as she tried to absorb what she was hearing.

"Uh uh, no way," she said.

The song counseled her on how signs were indeed everywhere if she would just look, seconds before she flipped stations.

"Uh oh, somebody is picky about their tunes," the familiar voice blared from her low-end speakers before Morna finished hitting the next button. "Cradle, what do we do with music snobs with no heart for 1970s Canadian one-hit wonders? That's right, fat cat; hit it!"

It took one second of one note for Morna to recognize the asshole in the radio had just Rick-rolled her while Astley sang assumptions about the status of her love life.

"Nope, nope, nopity, fucking nope!" Now beyond terrified to just plain pissed off, Morna started talking back to her possessed radio like it was a normal thing to do. "I don't think so, you skeevy-ass creeper," she swore as she leaned in to flip stations, only to be interrupted by the abrasive scratching sound of a needle zipping across vinyl.

"Wow, tough crowd. Tough, tough crowd. How about you have a go, Cradle? I'm betting you have better luck. So, without further ado, here's Cradle's choice for the win! It's Verities and Balderdash, but give it a go you old, stuffed fur ball!"

Morna swerved into a grocery store parking lot and threw on the hand brake as Harry Chapin had the balls to sing "Cat's in the Cradle." It had her fighting back the tears the song always stirred up the second the first chord was struck, falling helplessly under the spell it wove around her.

The seventies hit took no mercy as it looped like it wasn't blaring from her favorite contemporary pop radio station. It could have been the fifteenth time it played, or the fiftieth, before Morna snapped out of it, repeatedly smacking at the little black knob on the radio until it broke loose and fell powerless to the floor.

She sat dead still in the busy parking lot as she stared wide-eyed at nothing, concentrating on slowing her breaths while the events of the last hour filtered through her brain, trying repeatedly without rhyme or reason to assimilate themselves into the reality she already knew. It may have been minutes or hours she sat in silence while the process looped.

Eventually, she relaxed into the headrest, closed her eyes, and took a deep breath, whispering aloud as she exhaled, "No. Fucking. Way."

Hard on the clutch, Morna threw the jeep into first and peeled off into her new reality, muttering the only thing she knew at that moment to be true.

"That cat's a fucking traitor."

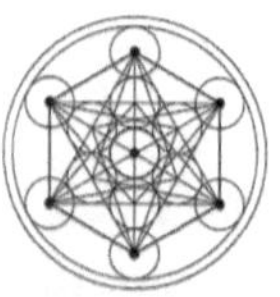

FOUR

COUNTRY ROAD, TAKE ME HOME

Thirty minutes later Morna turned onto Silla's parents' driveway out in the country after remembering Silla had said last night she was headed out that way today to help her mom with the horses.

Morna loved it here. Every single time she turned down the little one-lane gravel drive she felt instantly transported. The age-old trees lining the road were so thick they almost blocked the sky above, allowing only the tiniest shafts of sunlight to peek through the blazing tunnel of autumn leaves. She must have driven this road a thousand times and never once did it not amaze her. With a deep smile, Morna slowed her speed to a crawl, wanting nothing more than to draw out the much-needed sense of calm. The enchanted lane was beginning to work its magic as she crossed over the dry creek bed, but the peaceful feeling shattered fast as she rounded the corner to the little white farmhouse, her longtime nemesis lying in wait.

"Ugh. Asshole." Morna swore and punched the gas.

She swerved to avoid killing the demented creature who hated her with the passion of a thousand fiery suns. With spurs like daggers, the turkey she had lovingly deemed "Asshole" years ago was unfortunately still alive and gobbling to the heavens this was his turf. Three dogs ran barking alongside the berserk cretin, super stoked to either greet and/or maim her, depending on the dog.

Luckily, Silla and her mom, Ama, were in the paddock right next to the barn where Morna always parked. Ama came up fast, shooing and belittling every spurred and feathered creature who dared bludgeon her guest. The three hounds from hell continued circling and barking outside her jeep door. Ama and Silla expertly grabbed their collars and reminded the slobbering fiends they knew their guest.

"That's Morna! You know Morna! Now stop that!" Silla said sternly.

Morna cracked the door to get on with the ritual of "You know Morna." She let the hounds sniff and fuss before opening it to let their slobbering maws reluctantly approve. Now she needed to take slow, unthreatening steps toward the house, all while keeping an eye peeled for the feathered asshole with meat cleavers for feet.

Silla, her two brothers, and her Mom and Dad were watered-down descendants of the Bird Clan of the Cherokee Indian tribe and lived their lives with that in mind; well, their parents did anyway. Silla's real name, Atsilla, meant fire, and their last name, Onacana meant white owl. The Owls of the Cherokee people were often linked to medicine and being known for their wisdom. It seemed to hold pretty true in the Onacana family, at least to Morna anyway.

In no time, Morna's sentries ushered her away from the foul beasts, through the paint-chipped side door of the cozy little house, into the sanctuary of the country kitchen. Ama, who never sat still a moment in her life, cleared a fall bounty of fresh garden vegetables from the kitchen table and made room for the two mason jars. Ama's long, lean legs made quick work of crossing the kitchen to grab a pitcher of homemade sangria from the counter. She strode back to the table, matter-of-factly and efficiently filled the empty glasses. Ama gave Morna's shoulder a reassuring squeeze as she turned away, pitcher in hand. In less than a minute, after entering the kitchen, Morna sipped the finest homemade hootch in the county while looking at Silla, who in turn sipped and studied her from the other side of the table.

Ding!

Morna's hand gripped her cell which rested face down on the happy, yellow tablecloth.

"I'll leave you girls to it then," Ama said, placing the pitcher on the counter and heading back to tend to whatever chore was next.

"So, what's up?" Silla asked, genuinely curious at the unannounced visit.

Ding!

"I honestly don't know where to start, Silla. I feel like I've lost my goddamn mind."

"This have anything to do with visiting your past today?"

Silla took a drink while never taking her sparkling, green eyes from Morna's. Silla was like that. When she was in, she was all in. If you were important to her, you never needed to question it. If you weren't, well, that was a whole other thing.

Ding!

Morna's hand tightened around her cell, her eyes slowly leaving Silla's to peer down at the spooky-ass thing chirping away at her sanity with every last nerve-wracking ding.

"What's going on there, Morna?"

Silla tilted her head, shifting her emerald eyes toward the phone cradled tightly in Morna's hand.

"I honestly don't know," Morna answered softly as she brought her brown eyes up to meet her friends.

Silla slid her chair back, got up, walked to the counter, and grabbed the pitcher of Sangria. She returned as her mother had and topped off the glasses just as efficiently. Without a word, Morna's best friend plopped the pitcher between them with a look that said, "I've got all afternoon and copious amounts of alcohol". They both took a drink.

"Well fuck, Morna, let's just start with what you do know."

"I drove my happy ass down to the church, stood outside the doors, and got a feeling like someone was walking over my grave. It felt like electrical pulses rushed through every cell in my goddamn body. Then, then, I got a never-before-seen, long-lost video stream of my fucking singing miracle in 2010! It was at this point I decided it would be best if I went ahead and got the fuck up outta there."

Ding!

"Oh yeah!" Morna added with an alarming amount of sarcasm, "I almost forgot! I'm currently receiving multiple text messages from some stalkophile named Creak claiming to be my new BFF, who is apparently employed as a telepathic disc jockey at several local radio stations, and has recently started hanging out with Cradle, Covfefe?"

Morna knew she sounded bonkers.

"Cradle? Your ratty-ass stuffed cat and childhood imaginary friend? That Cradle? Is that the Cradle you're talking about?" Silla asked with genuine curiosity, a dash of disbelief, and a general look of amusement.

"Seriously, Sil?" A look of overwhelming skepticism hung heavy on Morna's face. "That's the only problem you have with that whole fucking statement?"

Ding!

Ding!

Ding!

Silla's expression dropped flat for a second or two, then lit up again as she all but dove across the table to rip the phone from Morna's hand.

"Don't, Sil!"

Too late; she swooped in and plucked the phone away like it was a nice, juicy mouse.

"Honest to God, Silla, I'm not ready for any more of this shit! Hell, I can't even get a handle on what I think I know!"

"Well, maybe that's because you need to know more to understand."

Silla flew around the table and dropped into the chair next to Morna, entering the phone's passcode as if it were her own. In seconds, the paint-chipped tips at the end of Silla's long, slender fingers were scrolling through Morna's unread messages.

"Suspended disbelief is a state I'm becoming comfortable with, Sil," Morna protested, grabbing for the phone.

Silla pulled back easily, leaning back as she opened the first unread message.

New Message: Unknown
Attachment: 1 Image
1:14 PM

The two women were confronted with a meme-generated image of Cradle dangling precariously from a tree high above the ground. The catchphrase "Hang in There!" was plastered in a bubbly font across the cuddly image.

New Message: Unknown
Audio File
1:15 PM

Silla clicked the blue play button on the audio file. Happy island music filled the kitchen as Bobby McFerrin counseled the two women in the art of being happy.

New Message: Unknown

I was going to insta or snap you, but couldn't find your profile. Are you a hermit?
1:20 PM

New Message: Unknown

If you are, it's cool. I've known a couple hermits. Craig is actually pretty awesome. I met him under...mmm, scratch that. I'm betting he wouldn't be down with me revealing his hidey holes. Anyway, super rad dude, tho.
1:21 PM

New Message: Unknown

Seriously, stop freaking out. We are going to be best buds, for real, yo! You and me, thick as thieves...well, and I suppose the creepy cat can come too.
1:45 PM

New Message: Unknown
Audio File
2:30

Silla clicked on another blue audio arrow, and four strikes of a cowbell broke the encompassing silence, followed immediately by the cheery acapella sounds of Steve from Blue's Clues, super stoked he got a letter from an unidentified source.

New Message: Unknown
Attachment: 1 Image
2:32 PM

A harmless meme-generated image of Steve, Blue, and Periwinkle was displayed on Morna's screen. The name Morna was penned across Steve's green and blue striped rugby shirt. A second later, Creak's name was deftly scribed across Blue's chest, while Periwinkle received a haphazard head transplant. In true serial-killer fashion, Periwinkle's head was ripped right off, a gaping hole artlessly stuffed with a childlike rendering of Cradle's disembodied head.

New Message: Unknown
See? Friendly, non-hostile type buddies. just hanging out looking for clues and shit. Solving apocalyptic mysteries and occasionally checking the mail.
2:45 PM

New Message: Unknown
Oooh, marked as read! Now we're getting somewhere! Ah, ah, ah. Who's the hottie reading your messages?
3:37 PM

Ding!

New Message: Unknown
Audio File/Text
3:38 PM

Another blue arrow was clicked by Silla. A tune expressly intended for Morna's hot friend inquired if she liked gettin' caught in the rain with a specific coconut drink. Just below the audio link was the simple question.

Partners in Crime?

Ding!

New Message: Unknown
Attachment: 1 Image
Found out 'hoo' you are, Silla. Nice to meet you. Any feathered
friend of Morna's is a friend of mine.
3:40 PM

Below the text was an image of an owl, wings spread in flight,
and burning like a phoenix from the ashes.
Ding!

New Message: Unknown
I'll leave you with this: I am indeed your friend, Morna. I'll be in
touch; we all have work to do.
P. S. Cradle says Hi.
P.P.S. Didn't want you to feel left out, Silla. I just checked with
Cradle; you get to come too!
3:41 PM

With a familiar ding, the Blue's Clues gang reappeared below
the latest text message with a slight modification. Magenta, the
rarely-seen spectacled sidekick of Blue, was now photoshopped
into the image with the name Silla scribbled vertically down one
long, pink ear.

Silla scrolled back to the start of the unknown messages and
clicked, reading and listening over and over again. Eventually, she
placed the phone back down on the table, her brow crinkled, eyes
unblinking and locked on Morna's. Morna grabbed the pitcher of
woefully depleted sangria and sloppily poured what little remained
into their empty mason jars.

"Well, that's fucked up," Silla said as her perfectly-coiffed
brows arched over her green horn-rimmed glasses, and a subtle, yet
curious, smile crept across her punch-drunk face.

"Ya think?" Morna asked while tipping her head toward Silla in a sarcastic "Welcome to my world" toast.

The two women looked at each other, full-on poker-faced for several quiet seconds, before breaking into a fit of uncontrollable laughter.

"Oh, my Gawd! Oh, my Gawd! Oh, my Gawd!" Silla blurted, holding her stomach as she doubled over.

"I think I'm in shock," Morna said, snorting like a wildebeest between howls.

Morna and Silla spent the rest of the evening analyzing the mysterious texts without really getting anywhere. Mostly because the information held within was little more than undesired tinder fodder, and also because they were both stink-ass drunk.

In the late hours of the evening, Morna and her bestie crept up the familiar stairs to crash in Silla's old bedroom. They chatted away the hours in hushed whispers like they had a thousand times before.

FIVE

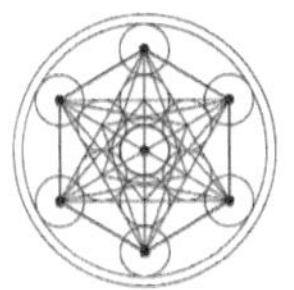

SHIFT CHANGE

M orna woke the next morning feeling better than she had a right to and headed downstairs to grab coffee before driving back to the city. In under two hours, she had to open the restaurant but still needed to snag a quick shower at home. Evidence that Ama had already been up for hours was all around her. Morna grabbed a thick slice of bacon, moaning at its smoky goodness, before pouring herself a to-go cup from the half-empty pot of coffee.

The always-busy Ama knelt in the side garden trimming back the dead leaves from this year's harvest. She looked up with a broad smile and a quick little wave. Morna waved back as she crossed the gravel drive toward her jeep, smiling to herself as she went, and happy she had a home here. Happier still it was a home that asked few questions.

Morna's cell had been eerily quiet all morning. She glanced at it after her shower and again every so often afterward. After she wiped down the bar, finished brewing iced tea, and just as the first of the lunch crowd made its way through the front door, she checked. It remained silent as a grave.

The next few hours flew by; they always did during the lunch rush. There wasn't a moment to take a pee, let alone scroll through her phone. Brewery workers from distillers to accountants made their way through the doors and ordered everything under the sun, from beer-battered fish and chips to Guinness-infused mocha ice cream. The restaurant was small but had great food; the lunch rush always reflected that.

As always, about three hours later, Morna found herself reeking of malt vinegar and beer. She poured herself a half draught from one of the thirty-two tap handles on the wall then settled herself on a stool. Just as she began to count her drawer for the day shift, her late-afternoon regular, Jeff, made his way through the front door.

Jeff was a big man by all regular accounts. He stood six-foot-three and was neither skinny nor fat. With his thick glasses and average musculature, Jeff looked like your typical brainiac, his height and width being the only physical deviations from the stereotype. Morna was pretty sure this optical illusion was the reason he didn't seem bigger to her. Well, that and the fact Zac, the head chef, was six-foot-eight, and the sous chef, Kevin, towered over all of them at just over seven feet. Because she was regularly surrounded by giants, Morna's idea of what constituted a big man was slightly skewed.

Jeff's image became clearer as he made his way to the green bar in the back of the restaurant. Morna jumped to get his usual.

"Hello there," Jeff said cheerfully as he pulled out a stool on the opposite end of the bar.

"Hey, yourself," Morna replied as she topped off his favorite beer and walked it over to him.

Jeff always came over to the bar to kill time between laundry loads. He'd have some lunch, a drink or two, and work on the daily crossword puzzle while Morna did odd jobs in preparation for the dinner rush. They passed the time easily by chatting together, and occasionally Jeff pitched in with the heavy lifting of keg changes. He was in the restaurant industry too, which was why some of his waking daylight hours were free for the mundane tasks. He always came in later than the regular lunch crowd because regular hours never applied. It was a well-known insider's joke about how vampires kept more consistent schedules. Like vampires, sometimes the days wouldn't end until the sun rose, but unlike a vampire, other days began at dawn. The money was good, and that's what kept them going when the rest of the world ate, partied, or slept.

Morna's phone gave a ding from behind the bar, grabbing her and Jeff's attention. Jeff looked back down at his crossword while Morna picked it up, saw it was a meme from Silla, and shoved it in the back pocket of her jeans. Morna leaned down and grabbed one end of a dirty rubber mat from the bar floor and dragged it toward the back door. Jeff eased wordlessly from his seat and grabbed the other end, taking a good thirty pounds of weight.

"Thanks," Morna said gratefully with a smile as she backed her plump butt into the pressure bar on the exit door that led to the back parking lot.

"Welcome," Jeff answered as he followed her into the late afternoon sun.

Together they retrieved two more sticky bar mats and hauled them outside. Morna grabbed a bottle of industrial-strength cleanser and sprayed the mats liberally while Jeff unwound a nearby hose and turned on the faucet.

"Did anything interesting happen last night?" Jeff asked casually while spraying down the first mat.

Morna, who was bent in a deep crouch, lost her balance at the mention of last night's events and fell back on her ass. The cleanser rolled from her hand to rest against a nearby wall while

Morna sat on the busted-up asphalt and laughed at herself. Jeff reached for a handout and pulled her to her feet. Morna brushed her hands on her backside and looked up at Jeff, who stared down at her utterly amused.

"That good, huh?"

"It's not what you're thinking, potty brain."

"Potty brain?" Jeff asked sarcastically, implying she could do better than that.

"I just... I'm off my game today, OK? I got some news yesterday that I'm still mulling over—it's… It's hard to explain."

Morna struggled to find words.

She unequivocally didn't want to tell Jeff what was going on, but she was a terrible liar. Whenever stuck between telling a truth she didn't want to reveal and flat-out lying about it, she always found herself frozen like a deer in headlights. It was an awkwardness she often waded through whenever someone would ask about her peculiar past. Now, it would seem an entirely different set of peculiarities set her up for more of the same social ineptitude right here in Soulard. Yippee.

"I'm sorry, Jeff. I've really got to get the bar put back together before Happy Hour." Morna turned and headed back inside, feeling like an asshole.

She trusted Jeff, she liked Jeff, and she hated she'd just made this little conversation uncomfortable. All because she couldn't say some off-hand remark and change the subject like a normal fucking person.

Morna returned to her usual way of dealing with her shortcomings. She busied herself with work while silently berating herself. Today, she chose to lose herself stocking the coolers. It wouldn't improve her mood, but it would take her mind off how pissy she'd become. In minutes, Morna was lost in the task of counting bottles of imported beer.

She heard Jeff before she saw him. From behind her, there was a familiar click followed by a slight hint of naphtha. Startled, she spun and saw him sitting back at the end of the bar.

"Hello there," Jeff said, snapping his Zippo closed and taking a pull from his Marlboro Red, smiling like the cat that ate the fucking canary.

"Hey," Morna said, unnerved she didn't hear him return through the back door.

"What's going on?" he asked, as if for the first time today.

"I thought we covered that already."

Morna was still startled at the backpedal in conversation and a little put off at his attempt at small talk. She scanned the restaurant confirming they were alone, aware for the first time Jeff made her feel a bit uncomfortable.

Without skipping a beat, Jeff returned his attention to his crossword puzzle, saying out loud, "Hold gently and protectively."

"What?" Indignant and annoyed, Morna hastily broke down empty boxes.

"Seven down. Six-letter word. Verb. Hold gently and protectively," Jeff stated plainly, never looking up from the paper.

"I don't know, Jeff. I'm not in the mood for crossword puzzles today."

A frustrated Morna responded dryly, hoping Jeff would take the hint and skedaddle. The last twenty-four hours started to weigh on her, draining her ability to humor anyone.

"Oh, come on, Morna. You're good at these."

Her patience was entirely lost. Morna looked at Jeff with daggers in her eyes.

"Seven across. Five-letter word. Noun. A harsh scraping or squeaking sound," Jeff pushed.

He raised his eyes to Morna's, delighted with the teasing.

"Out! I love you, Jeff, but you've gotta get!" Morna scooped up the crossword, rolled it into a makeshift billy club, and whacked it on the bar. "Go! Now!" she hollered, chasing after Jeff as he laughed his way out the front door.

Morna flopped the paper back onto the bar and went to clear away Jeff's forgotten, but still full, pint glass. She raised her shoulders in a why not gesture and took a long drink from the untouched pilsner. Deciding she needed a minute, she sat down at the bar with the pilfered beer and perused the crossword.

"Fuck me," Morna whispered in disbelief. The crossword lay open in front of her with only a few solved answers. The squares of seven down were filled with the letters c-r-a-d-l-e, and in the boxes directly across from it were the letters c-r-e-a-k.

Three clues were circled in the same blue pen below the unfinished puzzle. Checking the clues against the puzzle, Morna saw those were not yet solved. Pulling a pencil from her messy top knot, she read the clues out loud.

"Nine across. Noun. Eight letters. American Indian people of the southeastern US. That's easy." Morna, being friends with a half-blood Cherokee her whole life, filled in the eight letters and moved on to nine down.

"Nine down. Noun. Five letters. Large subterranean cavities. Cave, it's a cave." Morna filled in four empty blocks and added an "s" when she realized it was meant to be plural. Satisfied with her answer, she moved on to the last circled clue.

"Twelve across. Verb. Meet. Latin. Eight letters." Morna pulled from her early parochial education all the words she remembered from the endless hours of Latin lessons. She had nothing. She grabbed her phone from her back pocket and typed the word "meet" into the Latin translator. The word Congrego popped up in the translation box, and with eight letters, Morna filled in her final answer. She spent the next few minutes studying the crossword puzzle.

"Creak, Cradle, Cherokee, Cave, Congrego." She read the answers aloud several times.

Thinking hard, she picked up her glass to take another sip, but stopped mid-sixteen-ounce curl when she saw the little drops of condensation drip onto the crossword. Morna swore, setting the sweaty pint down on the bar, and started to brush away the droplets when the title of the puzzle, "Now You 'C' Me," jumped off the page.

"Now you 'C' me. Now you 'see' me. Creak, Cradle, Cherokee, Cave, Congrego."

It was clear the message was intended for her; it was also clear it was a message to meet Creak and Cradle in some dank-ass cave, but what did Silla being a Cherokee have to do with it? And what dank-ass cave, and when? And, what the hell did Jeff have to do with any of this unnerving bullshit?

"Your clues suck, buddy. I'm thinking Blue and the gang would be very disappointed, you lackluster, Dan Brown wanna be."

Morna hit the camera button on her phone, took a quick picture of the puzzle, and shot it over to Silla. She texted a quick rehash of the latest state of affairs, put her phone in her pocket, and got back to work.

Several hours later, Morna finally found herself clocking out of a twelve-hour day. It was 10:00 p.m., and she was done with a capital D. The others could handle the bar crowd. With the happy hour and dinner shift over, Morna gratefully assumed her perch at the end of the bar to count her tips and have a much-deserved drink.

Satisfied with her cash haul, she put the wad of bills in the pocket of her jeans and pulled out her cell. She took a swig of her beer, smiled at the crisp rye taste, and clicked on the message from Silla.

The message was a link to a Wikipedia page.

The Cherokee Caves of St Louis, Missouri, USA, have been important in the economic development of the city. St. Louis was built upon a complex of natural caves, which were once used for the laagering of beer by early German immigrant brewers. Underground caves are naturally cool, which was especially attractive to brewers before the advent of refrigeration.

Morna's cell vibrated, but instead of vibrating silently as she had it set for working hours, it bellowed, "Wait 'til the Midnight Hour."

New Message: Unknown

Now that Silla figured out where maybe you can figure out when genius. You think Blue would be disappointed in me? Side Table Drawer has figured out more clues than you, and he's one coaster short of a full set if you know what I mean. JK, I love ya, you crayon-eating motherfucker! *Winky emoji*

10:25 p.m.

Exasperated, Morna spun off her stool and exited out the back of the bar to call Silla. The gritty, worried notes of the Blues Band playing inside muffled as the door closed heavily behind her. Silla picked up on the first ring.

"Did you get my text?" Silla asked without so much as a hello.

"Yeah, I got it, and I got another one from our stalker friend."

"Yeah? What'd he have to say?"

"He implied I was as inept at solving mysteries as an animated accent table and that you are a regular Sherlock fucking Holmes," Morna replied in disgust.

Silla snorted a laugh, then stifled it, saying, "You gotta admit, he's funny. He's got me curious, that's for damn sure."

"John Wayne Gacy was funny, never made me wanna meet the clown in a fucking crawl space. Jesus! You're not serious, are you, Silla?"

"Well, yeah, actually, I am. We could drag this shit out or just rip off the Band-Aid and see what's underneath. It'll be an adventure."

"Silla! This dude could fall into any number of sociopathic categories. I don't think meeting an undiagnosed personality disorder in an underground bunker should be defined as an adventure. An exercise in lunacy would be a much more appropriate identifier for the escapade you're suggesting."

"Suit yourself, Morn. I already called Brick down at the Lemp Mansion, and he's going to sneak me into the caves below the restaurant. I'll let you know how it goes."

"Wait, what? You called Brick and set this all up without even telling me?"

"Well, yeah. Once I figured out where Creak wanted to meet, I needed a way to get us in there. It's not like there's a big door that says ENTER. After the attempt to turn the caves into a commercial attraction failed, all the openings were filled with rubble and sealed off."

"So, you thought, 'I'll call Brick.' Jesus, Silla, you and that guy do not have a sparkling past. Not to mention, you set all this up without even asking me if I wanted you to. That's just like you, Sil. You're always making crazy-ass plans without ever consulting me!"

"You have fun though, right?" Silla's teasing tone was getting Morna's hackles up even further than they already were.

"Yeah, like that time we went to the Lake of the Ozarks for a quick getaway, and you decided to stay with people we just met at the bar would be way better than keeping the motel room I booked. It was super fun when the DEA raided our new friends' house that night. Super fun," Morna said, super salty.

"You can't bring that up every time, Morn."

"Yes, yes, I can. I earned the right after being listed in the Tri-Lakes Gazette as a known associate of the Ozarks' largest drug cartel, thank you very much."

"Whatever. I've gotta run, or I'm gonna be late."

"Wait. What time are you meeting Brick?"

Exasperated, Morna found herself once again riding Silla's fiery tail feathers.

"11:30." Without skipping a beat, Silla said, "I'm getting in my car now. I'll swing by the bar on the way and pick you up."

Morna pressed her end, wondering once again how in the hell she always let Silla bait her into this kind of shit.

SIX

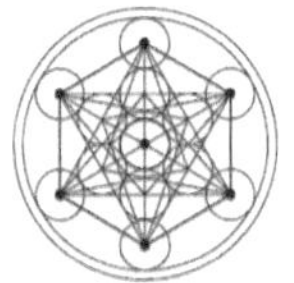

WHERE THERE'S LIFE THERE'S LEMP

It was a well-known fact the Lemps of Lemp Brewery and Mansion had used the caves below the streets of St. Louis as secret passages. It was also a great place for the Lemps to keep their massive stores of beer cool before refrigeration came along. Stored at a naturally cool temperature of about fifty-eight degrees, Lemp Beer was just about the freshest beer around.

It was also a well-known fact the caves were sealed off, but most suspected the Lemp Mansion, now a restaurant and inn, still had access. Morna and Silla were about to get a first-class education on how true local lore could be.

Silla parked a few blocks away from the mansion right at 11:30 p.m. The two women got out of the car and made their way to the back entrance where they were to rendezvous with Brick. Morna followed behind Silla like a child being dragged to a dentist appointment. It was glaringly obvious the prospect of potential pain and suffering did not motivate her pace. Silla, on the other hand, moved like a fucking alley cat in the moonlight. The thrill of the hunt oozed off her, pissing Morna off with Silla's each over-confident step.

35

Morna and Silla made their way through a dark side alley, and sitting casually on the steps with his elbows resting on his knees was Brick. He stood upon seeing them, his overly wide shoulders intensifying his leanness. Brick took a drag of his cigarette and, without a word, walked toward Silla. Starting with her face, Brick gave Silla a long, thorough look. He locked on her green eyes for a second, then lowered his gaze down to the tips of her black leather boots and back up again. He took one last step and closed the gap between them, gently grabbing her ponytail. Brick tugged on the handful of ebony and amber tresses like a handle, and eased Silla's head back as they locked eyes. He loomed over her a second longer then lowered his lips to kiss her gently on the cheek. Smiling predatorily as he pulled away.

"Hey doll, how ya been?" Brick asked, his hands still wrapped firmly in her hair.

The magnificent Silla stood there, bold as you please, easily accepting the whole encounter. She gave a mischievous smile that would have most running for the hills and shoved Brick's chest hard, ducking and twisting under the hand still wrapped in her ponytail. The whole fluid movement ended by Silla smashing the heel of her boot into Brick's instep. Now, released from his hold, she easily stepped away.

"Not bad, *doll*. You?" Silla asked all chill and casual, like the vicious meet-cute was on total par for their fucked-up course.

Brick was doubled over with his hand on his solar plexus, laughing out loud. "God, I've missed you, woman," he said, straightening to his full height while attempting to stomp the pain out of his foot.

"Aww, that's sweet. I've missed you, too, Pookey."
Silla gave him two light taps on his cheek as she walked toward the cobbled stairs leading to the cellar.
Morna shook her head in disbelief. Silla had hypnotized Brick like a snake charmer, then when her prey was completely capti-

vated, the owl swooped in for the kill. Silla was always drawn to snakes like Brick. It was like they fed a part of her soul that got bored with the mundane.

"It's not nice to play with your food, Sil," Morna whispered conspiratorially as they made their way down the stairs.

"I heard that," Brick quipped. "Do you girls want to know where the actual entrance to the caves is, or did you want a tour of the wine cellar first?" Brick asked, pulling down a sliding ladder to an otherwise invisible fire escape. He didn't wait for an answer, and without looking back, he climbed up the rickety old thing. The two women were left on the cellar stairs staring up after him as he disappeared into the dark.

"Not quite what I pictured a cave entrance to look like," Silla said as she and Morna stepped off the ladder and onto the flat tar-papered roof.

"Follow me and don't fucking fall," Brick spat.

His venomous personality returned as Silla's charms wore off.

Morna and Silla carefully followed Brick across a decorative widow's walk that couldn't have been much more than a foot in width. The spiky little arrows on the rail threatened to catch their clothes and throw them over the side with every step. When Morna and Silla finally made their way across the walk, they came upon Brick, who was bent over a closed scuttlehole in the floor of the roof.

Brick lifted the hatch with one hand and gestured toward the dark void with the other like a doorman showing guests their room at a fancy hotel.

"After you, ladies," Brick said in his most professional waiter's voice.

Morna swung her pack off her back and pulled out a flashlight. Before she could even turn it on, Brick snagged it from her hands.

"No lights until we are in the caves! Jesus Christ, Sil. I went over this with you on the phone. This could cost me my fucking job!"

"I didn't have a chance to brief Morna on your rules, Brick. No one is twisting your arm here. We made a deal, and you accepted it, so quit your bitching."

"God dammit, Sil," Brick said, exasperated as he turned toward Morna.

"Here's the rules, princess. One, no fucking lights outside of the caves. Two, you're to tell no fucking one about the fucking entrance. Three, if you are ever fucking dumb enough to come back here, and you get caught, you don't fucking know me. Understand?"

Morna moved her lips quietly while looking at her hand. She kept at it for a few seconds, ticking off a three-count gesture between her fingers and thumb.

Then, with a confounded look, stared at Brick, and asked, "What was the second *fucking* one again?" She coolly looked down like she was studying her nails, before, oh so slowly, bringing up her middle finger, "God, you're a condescending prick."

Brick hovered over Morna for a second like he was about to strike, then laughed as he turned to Silla, "Color me fucking surprised, Sil. I didn't know she had it in her."

"Jeeezus, you're *still* being a condescending prick. Where do you find these guys, Silla?"

"Who's being a condescending prick now?" Brick asked as Silla descended first into the darkness.

Brick slid the scuttlehole door back into place, completely cutting off any outside light from above while Morna and Silla stood in a pitch so black they couldn't see their hands in front of their faces. They heard Brick's shoes touch on each rung of the ladder, followed by two quick steps, and a click.

The light came on so strong they had to shield their eyes immediately. In a second or two, they found themselves in what seemed to be an old, musty-smelling cupboard. Looking around, Morna noticed no doors or windows in the small room full of empty shelves.

"You said no fucking lights until we are in the cave. This doesn't look like a cave, Brick." Morna gestured at the single light bulb glowing above them.

Brick ignored Morna's jab and pulled on one of the shelves until it opened like a door.

"I'm thinking this cupboard was closed off from the rest of the mansion when the Lemps opened the restaurant. Guess they didn't want people finding their way down to the caves and getting hurt. Hell, maybe it was closed off long before that. I honestly don't even know who knows this is here beside me. I found the scuttle-hole this summer. See, sometimes between double shifts, I like to go up to the roof and eat my lunch in peace; that's when I discovered all this."

Brick pulled a flashlight from his back pocket and turned it on while pulling the chain to the light bulb above. Silla and Morna followed suit and turned on their flashlights as Brick made his way down the rock stairwell. It was only a few steps down before they came to a landing ending in front of an old wrought iron gate. The instant temperature drop hinted they had reached the threshold of another world. Silla strode right past Brick and gave the gate a push. Looking over her shoulder, she flashed a triumphant smile to Morna.

Brick flipped a large lever on the wall to their left. A snap then a low humming sound followed by sporadic popping of ancient lights reluctantly illuminated the long-lost entrance.

"Thanks, Brick. We'll take it from here," Silla said dismissively, turning toward the gate as latent strings of light cut away the darkness like will-o'-the-wisps, revealing a myriad of deeper tunnels beyond.

"Don't you think now is a good time to tell me why you needed to get in here, Silla? I don't think leaving you girls down here alone, especially not knowing what you're up to, is such a great idea."

Silla sighed as if having to take time to talk to Brick required more patience than she had.

"First off, we aren't girls; we're women. Secondly, you're not leaving us; we're leaving you. Your part of tour guide in this adventure has come to an end. Thirdly, don't ask don't tell was the nature of our agreement, so fuck off."

Silla motioned Morna toward the gate impatiently, then turned to Brick.

"I won't thank you, and you know why. Don't worry; no one will ever know we were here. We'll cover our tracks." With a little wave of her blood-red fingertips, she said, "Good night, Brick."

Morna and Silla walked through the gate, a few feet into the wider threshold of the tunnel, when the sound of metal slammed hard. They spun to see Brick smiling like a jackal behind the closed gate, a large set of keys in hand.

"You want to play it that way, fine. You *ladies* have fun." And with a twist of his wrist, Brick locked Morna and Silla into the mouth of the long-forgotten labyrinth of dark, twisting tunnels.

"You son of a bitch!" Morna screamed, running like a bat out of hell toward the gate.

Brick pulled back just as Morna slammed into the bars, wildly throwing her arms through as she grabbed for the keys in his hands. The bastard snatched them back, jingling the oversized ring of keys over his head, and stepped left, reaching for the lever on the wall.

"No one leaves me, Silla. I leave them," Brick said darkly, killing the lights.

"Goodnight, *girls*," echoed sweetly as the cupboard door clicked closed.

"Fucking psycho!" Morna screamed from the blackness of their cavernous cell. "What the fuck are we going to do now, Silla?"

"I'm going to turn on my flashlight," Silla said as the darkness was cut by a single beam under her chin as she yelled, "Boo!"

"Jesus! You're a psycho too! You two assholes deserve each other."

"That guy? Hell no. I need my men to have a little more going on upstairs." Silla tapped her glowing temple. "The only thing that idiot has in his attic is dust bunnies. The dude couldn't find his way out of a wet paper bag. Good in bed, though," Silla said casually while looking around.

Ding!

New Message: Unknown
What a douchenozzle.
12:07 a.m.

SEVEN

PARTYIN' SOULARDIAN GUARDIAN

D*ing!*

New Message: Unknown
Also, you're late.
12:07 a.m.

"Is that the stalker?" Silla asked Morna.

"Stalker? Ladies, I've got game a stalker couldn't dream of."

A distinctive voice cut through the inky pitch.

Morna and Silla turned blindly, their flashlights cutting small shafts of light into the chasm of darkness.

"Prove it, stalker boy," Silla challenged.

"To freak them out, or not freak them out, that is the question." The voice's best rendition of Hamlet rang throughout the void. "What was it you said, Silla? It's best to rip off the Band-Aid and see what's underneath?" the quirky stalker paraphrased. "Let's go ahead and roll with that one."

The stalker's words eddied out over the cave walls in a chaotic loop as a familiar snap released a thrum of energy down the ancient, overhead wires. One after the other, the archaic fixtures protested with brilliant sprays of electrical showers before flooding the darkness in a sea of blinding light, disorienting Morna and Silla in the onslaught as they skittered backward to nowhere.

The two women stood squinting, pressed tight into the curved cave wall at their backs. Their hearts in their throats and their pulse flooding their ears, Morna and Silla lowered their arms, shielding their eyes to reveal before them an image once seen, could never be otherwise.

Inches away, right where Morna and Silla once stood, an enormous statue rested in a sphinxlike pose. Blackish-blue and textured like porous concrete from head to toe, the ominous thing was splattered helter-skelter style with dark, flinty crystals. Its boxy head looked like some sort of dragon-gargoyle hybrid, while its long body was more reminiscent of a canine.

Heavy on its front claws was an impossibly brilliant hunk of clear quartz crystal that tipped the end of a lengthy, scaled, reptilian tail curving up. From each of the things' shoulder blades were cobweb-like wings of leathery gossamer. The dark, diaphanous material cascaded like a spilled inkwell down the statue's gravely flanks to pool all around its base, creating the illusion of floating over a bottomless void in the cave floor. The scene was Hermann Rorschach meets Anselm Kiefer. In short, the physical embodiment of unnerving shit that keeps a person up at night.

A soft, low-level humming grew louder as the two women stood silently stupefied in the shadow of the impromptu artifact. Light and jolly, it was the sunny kind of humming someone does to pass the time while doing a boring task. It was as creepy as a backwoods shed chock-full of busted-up baby dolls.

"Do you hear that, Sil?" Morna asked with a shaky whisper.

A never-quiet Silla curtly nodded, her head as infinitesimal movement lured both women's gazes like a magnet. Neither of them dared a breath as they grabbed for each other's hands, confirming in silence they saw what they had just seen. The gargoyle-dragon nightmare ran its craggy nails from pinky to fore-claw across the stone floor one after the other, over and over and over.

Morna and Silla watched in fear and wonder as the nuanced mannerisms of absolute and utter tedium personified the lifeless hunk of rock. A guttural chuff and heavily annoyed sigh swirled around the mouth of the musty cave entrance as the creature's claws hastily transitioned to one lone talon, jackhammering a small gorge in the tunnel floor with every impatient strike.

"Booooooring. Can you ladies speed this up?"

Morna and Silla's eyes shot up from the statue's massive clicking claw to its fiendish face, finding an animated and very sentient expression where a lifeless one had just been.

"Freaked out?" the statue asked with one eyebrow raised and a head tilted in curiosity.

Morna and Silla scurried to nowhere. Their backs pressed firm against the mossy cave wall. Caged in from the left, and nothing but darkness in every other direction. They had no choice but to face the nightmare before them.

"Yep, you're freaked out. How can I make this easier?"

A shower of sparks rained down from the old lights in the cave's ceiling, and just like that, the demon-like statue was gone, replaced by a large flat-screen TV, a rug, and two Barcaloungers. Two frosty mugs and a pitcher of beer sat waiting on a small table between the two chairs. The TV popped on, and the big golden H from the History Channel filled the screen.

"To know history is to know life."

The statue's distinct voice echoed in a serious docudrama narration.

A large golden silhouette of the dragon-gargoyle-dog statue replaced the golden H. The words "Shit's Creak" appeared in title-style block letters in the corner of the screen, and just below that,

"New Episodes Available Now". Morna and Silla stayed frozen against the cave wall, their eyes glued to the flat screen across from them.

Narrator intonation gone, the familiar cheeky voice pumped from the TV, "What? Not girly enough for you?" A few sparkly throw pillows, two pink blankets—one covered in unicorns and the other in pugs, and a softly glowing scented candle were added to the makeshift living room.

Morna and Silla stayed put.

"Snacks! Dammit! I knew I forgot something. My mother would be horrified!" In a flash, a giant bowl of popcorn and a gargantuan martini glass full of gummy worms appeared next to the beer.

Morna broke first, cautiously walking toward the cozy little nook, and ran her hands across the back of one of the leather chairs. She clutched a handful of the fuzzy, pink unicorn blanket, kneading the soft, plushy folds between her fingers.

"It's all real, Sil," Morna said, breathless.

Silla, no longer catatonic, rounded the other chair, plopped down, kicked back, and threw the happy, pink pug blanket over her legs. She turned and filled both frosty mugs with beer, then grabbed up a handful of gummy worms.

"Comfy?" Morna asked.

"We're in this thing up to our eyeballs now, Morn. Might as well roll with it."

"Oh, for fuck's sake."

Morna bitterly conceded and plopped down, wrestling with the whimsical troop of fuzzy pink unicorns trapped under her ass. She pulled and yanked like a spaz until she freed the happy blanket and threw it over her legs.

The choppy, guttural sound of someone clearing their throat filled the air before a heavy silence and lengthy disclaimer filled the screen before them:

Disclaimer

The events that you are about to witness are true. No names or faces have been altered for anyone's protection. We at Stripey Socks Productions are not liable for any mental breakdown you may experience from being enlightened.

en·light·ened

in'lītnd,en'lītnd/

adjective

adjective: enlightened

1. having or showing a rational, modern, and well-informed outlook

We are also, now, not responsible for you not knowing what enlightened means.

No beers were harmed in the production of this program. We at Stripey Socks Productions do not condone alcohol abuse.

If you need to pee, go now.

There will be a short Q&A after the show.

The streaming episode started with the reveal of hundreds more of the rock-like statue creatures Morna and Silla had seen a few minutes before. The images started big then grew smaller and were tucked away into lesser squares until the screen was loaded with countless little cameos of varying versions of the dragon-doggie things.

"What you see in these images are Grinx," the narrator's voice began. "It is not a gargoyle, dragon, or fugly dog."

Morna and Silla watched as the screenshot zoomed in on the first square in the upper right corner, bringing it to full size. The still image of the rock-like statue moved in a way that seemed wholly impossible.

"What you're seeing is real. What you saw a few minutes ago was also real," the narrator continued.

Each little square was brought one at a time to full size as each stone creature moved as though someone had clicked off a pause button. Hundreds of images in varying versions of the statuesque creatures surreally ran, flew, and even talked.

"A Grinx is a living, breathing entity, and no, we aren't from around here. We are from a dimension called Satera. Hold onto your scientific dunce hats, ladies, while I break down everything you thought you knew about… well, pretty much everything.

Dimensions are real. There are ten of them, sort of. More like nine with fractionated, but uber-important, bits that make up the tenth. But I digress. Let's start small…ish.

Your little corner of everything lies somewhere between the third and fourth dimensions. While your planet and its people exist on a lower rung of the food chain, your survival, and evolution are imperative to all the other dimensions. Especially those fractionated, crucial bits that make up the tenth."

The screen went dark. A small, blue dot in the center slowly grew and stretched into a glowing oval that took up most of the gigantic screen.

"In the beginning," started the narrator's voice again, "there was only one dimension. In it, all things were possible. But like all good things, some greedy asshat screwed it up by wanting more. More than everything! I mean, really, what an asshat! The One— that's the HBIC—got super pissed and threw the greedy bastard out. Thing is, when The One did this, shit got real, fast."

The blue ellipse shrank into a red dot the size of a pea, then went nuclear. It blew outward across the screen, incredibly loud and fast. The whole screen went dark before bits of light formed in perfectly spaced clusters across the width of the screen. In the end, the screen was filled with nine evenly sized, green, and glowy clusters. Three much smaller, swirly, blue orbs sat beyond the green matter.

"Throwing something out of *everything* threw the whole reality of everything off. The bits and pieces fractionated off into smaller, self-sustaining bits are now known as the Ten Dimensions. You guys with me so far?" the narrator asked.

The two women, one holding a beer and the other holding a comically large bucket of popcorn, nodded their heads.

"Good. The big green ones are the first nine dimensions, and the three blue, swirly ones are the uber-important fractionated bits of the tenth I mentioned earlier. Those little buggers are big players in this game. See, The One is in this blue one here, and the greedy asshat is in that other blue one over there. The third blue one is not necessary to get into right now. Anyhoo, since the split, the dimensions have tried to pull back together and form one singular dimension again. When that goes down, there could be a new sheriff in town—so to speak. Whichever tiny, important bit has the most energy encapsulated will also house the new HBIC. That will either be The One or the asshat. If it's the asshat, well, we're all screwed. Still with me?"

Silla cuddled deeper into her snuggly pug blanket as Morna leaned forward, asking the screen, "Are you implying that God and the Devil are in a war over energy?"

"Ding, ding, ding! Tell her what she's won, Bob!" answered the interactive narrator.

An entirely different voice, sounding a lot like Bob Barker, filled the cozy little nook,

"Why, Morna, you win the opportunity to join in a battle against evil that is literally older than time."

A "The More You Know" star shot across the screen in public-service-announcement style before going completely blank. Left in an all too sudden silence, kicked back in Barcaloungers, and covered in fuzzy blankets well below the streets of St. Louis, Morna, and Silla found themselves the newest recruits in the oldest army ever.

The TV popped back on, and a Yule log screensaver crackled in the background.

"It's a lot; I know," said a low, now all too familiar voice from the floor.

Morna looked down to see a much smaller version of the statue-creature-thing curled up on the rug at her feet, peering up with a look of understanding on its grisly face.

"There is so much more to all of this than you could possibly understand right now. It truly is more than anyone has a right to ask, but we're asking anyway," said the Grinx, all traces of sarcasm gone. "We can start with the Q & A whenever you're ready. Take your time."

The statue finished, almost painfully, then lowered his craggy black head to his claws and rested it there, never breaking eye contact.

All Morna's fear of the creature had vanished at some point. She was now filled with so many questions there seemed to be no room left to fear the somber being resting at her feet. She looked down at the Grinx and considered him for the very first time without her fear riding her. It lay there, sort of curled up in the way a dog would, but not really like a dog at all. There was no fuzzy fur or wagging tail, just flat blue-black stone that moved like liquid muscle and flickered eerily in the false firelight.

Morna found herself thinking the thing was quite lovely, in a beautiful nightmare sort of way. She caught the expensive-looking collar that said "Creak" in peridot clusters, rising and falling like mossy mountains.

"So… your name is Creak? You're from another dimension and a recruiter for God's Army?" Morna asked in a getting-to-know-you kind of way.

Creak remained small and low to the ground as to not frighten them, and answered very directly with all the bells and whistles gone, "Yes, yes, and not exactly. My dimension, Satera, is a dimension of balances directly tied to yours. Grinx have always been overseers of the balances necessary for The One to remain in power. I told you earlier, energy is needed to help the dimensions come together as one, and your dimension is super important in that amalgamation.

Humanity's energy is unlike any other because it quite literally evolves as the life forces residing in it do. That's the reason why I said your dimension is somewhere between the third and fourth. Your energies have evolved you straight into a state of flux. In a nutshell, we need to get humankind's consciousness out of the primordial ooze and stand upright, ASAP. 'Cause honestly, ladies, we're not real certain what will go down if you all stay in limbo. But, we're pretty sure it's not good. I digress, back to Basic Creationism 101. When you as a people evolve collectively, so does your energy. If it's not balanced spiritually and intellectually in The One's favor, the whole thing will go to hell, so to speak."

"So, Grinx are the keepers of energy balances here on Earth, which is super important in preventing all hell from breaking loose. OK, let's assume I fully understand that impossible concept and move on to why you're here in a cave, under the streets of St. Louis, Missouri, USA, Earth, talking to me and Silla."

"I'm pretty curious about this one, too, Creak," Silla threw in.

"Hey, Sil. Glad you decided to join the Q&A. In regard to what you need to know now, I'll try to sum up an insane amount of history as succinctly as I can.

In the dimension of Satera, there were five great houses, or Domos, which were to help keep the balances of your dimension in check. My Domos, Domos Navitas, was in charge of the Mystery Ether Balances. We were the keepers of all non-human related energies in your dimension and were considered the lowest of the five Domos. No Grinx of consequence in Satera thought it was important to watch energies that did not relate to the human internal evolutionary process. We were the poor white trash of the five royal Domos. The other Domos were assigned more human-specific balances and, therefore, considered more essential to our commission from above. This is only important to know for now because it's why I'm here.

About a hundred Earthly years ago, there was a great upheaval in Satera where the great Domos were eviscerated. Because my house was so low on the food chain, there was time for my parents to whisk me away into hiding between the third and fourth dimensions."

"This is all super interesting, Creak, and I'm truly very sorry about your loss, but what does any of this have to do with me and Morna?" Silla asked, more than a little overwhelmed.

Creak gave his dark, gauzy wings a rustle, then walked his front claws backward and raised his ass in the air, and took a nice, long, cleansing breath before transitioning to upward-facing dog, "I'm getting there, woman. Jeesh, give a Grinx a minute to shower you with an overly summated version of errthang."

Now fully Zen, Creak Cirque du Soleil'ed into a happy baby pose.

"Obviously, the balances have fallen out of alignment with no Domos there to keep them in check the last hundred years or so," Creak said from his supine happy place. "Since that happened, shit has gotten a little deep in these parts. The One thinks we need a new way of keeping it from getting out of hand and turning the whole dimension into a dumpster fire. That's where you two come in. With most of the Grinx gone, The-Powers-That-Be are assembling a new set of balance keepers. So far, there's me, Cradle, those to be named later, and hopefully, you two wonder women." Creak finished in a cat pose, flashing the women a smart-ass smile from his inverted, harbinger position.

"Cradle? My stuffed cat?"

"Technically, I'm not a cat."

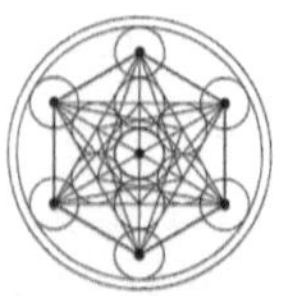

EIGHT

EVERY TIME A BELL RINGS, SAM ELLIOT GETS HIS WINGS

Morna and Silla turned lightning fast toward the rich and melodious voice, finding an eerie silhouette, blacker than pitch, moving closer as its heavy density grew in the false firelight reflected from the TV.

Scared stiff, the two women sat stock still as they stared over the backs of their chairs into a set of piercing gray eyes cutting through a darkness so thick it was like the shadowy silhouette creeping toward them wasn't anything at all. As if it somehow negated its own existence. With each step, the illusion of nothingness faded into a debatable reality, as an extraordinary framework of seraphic fan fiction stepped forward into their physical world.

A million feathers, in a thousand different hues of gray and brown, rippled and rustled in constant motion, like downy leaves stirring in a gentle, never-ending breeze.

Paralyzed, Morna and Silla stared in awe at the enormous smoke-colored wings cresting high above a set of wide mahogany shoulders easily nine feet in height. Transfixed by their hypnotic beauty, the mercurial feathers of the unheralded angel were all they could see. Neither woman could focus on anything else.

"A little dramatic there, Cradle. We are trying to keep them from pissing their pants and running out of here screaming."

"You revealed your true self like an Indiana Jones nocturnal emission, and you're going to give me trouble? We're lucky their brains haven't already dissolved," Cradle scolded the Grinx, softening his hardened features as he turned toward Morna. With piercing gray eyes heavy in concern, Cradle asked, "How you doin', kid?"

It was a voice Morna would have sworn only existed in her childhood imagination, snapping her eyes away from the trance-inducing feathers. Morna's gaze locked in hard and fast on the disturbing creature. Suspicion and disbelief burned hot in her horrified gaze.

"There's honestly no easy way to do this, Morna. I'm sorry if you're frightened," Cradle said sympathetically.

"Why in the name of fuck do you sound like Sam Elliot?" Creak interjected.

A gape-mouthed Silla rubbernecked between her BFF and the very apologetic, very beautiful angel.

"Because, you living, breathing pumice stone, when the child needed me, she had recently seen a Smokey the Bear commercial and this had been the voice she assigned to me." Turning back to Morna, the angelic giant said, "I'm sorry, Morn. I wasn't allowed to be the one to tell you, well, everything."

"Allowed? More like capable. That old furball doesn't possess the power it takes to tell you in a way that wouldn't land you in the nuthouse. For most of your childhood, you had one leg in crazy town. If he ranted to you about The One and its need of you, they'd have locked your delusional ass up and thrown away the key," Creak chided, growing bigger with every word.

"Oh, my Gawd!" Morna blurted. "You do sound like Sam Elliot. Jesus! How could I have not noticed that? *Beef, it's what's for dinner. Only you can prevent forest fires,*" Morna ran on, spewing a parade of Sam Elliot voiceovers.

"See?" Creak said, motioning toward Morna with a light toss of his nightmarish head. "We'll have to commit her in less than a week if you keep this shit up."

"The double douche... Did the Pope shit in the woods..." Morna continued to mumble from her recliner.

"I'm not entirely sure how I am the one capable of being the voice of reason in the midst of all of this bat-shit crazy, but in case you two bickering old biddies haven't noticed, Morna's losing it." Silla gestured from the angel and the Grinx toward Morna as she settled herself further into her recliner and threw back a gigantic swig of beer. "If you two don't get your heads out of your asses we're going to be checking her into Briarcliff by morning."

Silla picked up the bottomless pitcher of beer and refilled her ever-frosty mug, lifting it in a cheers-like fashion toward the two celestial beings.

"Hello, Silla. It's nice to finally meet you," Cradle said, extending his overly large hand to Morna's best friend.

No longer roofied by the hypnotizing effects of Cradle's crazy wings, Silla took in every bit of the tall, dark, and handsome creature standing in front of her.

Unbelievably tall, Cradle was the color of dark roast coffee with thick, black hair artfully twisted "devil may care" into dreads that disappeared between his trance-inducing wings. The top half of the thick black spirals were pulled up and back, secured away from a face oddly and imperfectly symmetrical. Silla considered the marvel for a moment, then lowered her eyes to take in Cradle's full, dark lips pulled to one corner on a curious smile. Silla's sparkling, green eyes lingered a brief second to think about how much fun it would be to bite at the corner of one of those lips when Creak rudely cleared his throat.

Silla mimicked the half smile on Cradle's face, while both she and Cradle ignored the impudent throat-clearer. Despite the other-worldly essence that oozed old-world propriety, Cradle was dressed like pretty much every other dude she'd ever met. The angel sported black Chuck Taylors on his large feet, wore standard American-issue loose-fitting jeans, and a not-so-loose-fitting retro 80's concert tee. The t-shirt was sort of a beige color, the black wording stretched tight over his chest and shoulders, pulled tighter still by the wings escaping the custom cut slits in the back. The artwork on the 'T' read, "Men at Work, Business as Usual," which oddly endeared Silla even more.

She reached out with the half smile still on her beautiful face and accepted Cradle's overly proper handshake in a super casual manner.

"It's nice to meet you, too, Cradle. I've heard a lot about you."

"Likewise," Cradle said as he caught himself winking at the one soul other than himself who had truly been there for Morna throughout her abhorrent childhood.

He liked this woman a lot. Probably more than he should. He found her savage, wild side, coupled with her selective bleeding heart, an appealing and rare combination. He'd seen Silla break through Morna's lonely walls and build her up time and time again, stronger and happier for the effort. For that, he would always be grateful, but winking?

Cradle pulled back from Silla's warm fingers and plunged his hands deep into his Levi's, pulling them out quickly when he realized what he'd done. Pockets? Winks and pockets! Cradle shook it off and fell back a couple of steps as he transitioned into a much more appropriate and familiar stance. Arms crossed, feet apart, wings at attention. Better.

"You're correct, Silla; we have to get this young woman back with us." Cradle reluctantly broke free of Silla's tempting gaze, turning on a heel and walking over to Morna. He knelt before her, placing a hand firmly, but gently, on her knee. "It's just me, kid. I can take any voice you'd like. Whatever you're comfortable with is fine by me."

"Is that your real eye color, or was that a lie too?" Morna asked sharply, using anger to camouflage the intimate betrayal she felt.

"Yeah kid, these are my real eyes. The same ones I've watched you with all your life."

A single tear escaped without consent.

"I want you to sound like you always have," Morna said, quickly wiping away the fugitive tear with the back of her hand.

"That's not a problem."

Morna reached out toward one of the giant, smoke-colored wings cresting over Cradle's shoulders, then pulled back, stopping quickly.

"Go ahead," he said gently, never taking his hooded eyes from hers as she reached past his considerable neck to touch a wing with the tips of her fingers.

Morna instantly recognized the texture. Soft and pliant, the feathers were indistinguishable from the touch and feel of the Cradle she'd always held so close to her heart. At that moment, she didn't need to know anything more as she clutched him tight, her head buried in his neck as she breathed him in.

"It is you," she whispered

"Yeah, kid, it is me."

"That's just greeaat," said Creak. "Now we have to spend eternity with a jumbo-sized cherub who looks like Idris Elba but talks like an Earp brother. Fan-fucking-tastic." A now much larger Creak sighed deeply and shook his head with disgust. "Can we move this reunion along, or do you two want to play dolls for old time's sake."

"I thought maybe you'd want to play fetch first," Morna said, smiling at Creak.

"That was fair. Unnecessary, but fair."

Creak smiled back at Morna, secretly delighted she now acted more like herself.

"So, what now?" An ever-efficient Silla asked the others. "Is there like a boot camp or something?"

"I'm still not entirely sure why Silla and I are here," Morna interjected. "I get you want our help, but why us?"

"Morna, there is a reason I've watched over you for most of your life," the beautiful angel said. "I was sent to look over you a few years before your singing debut, as you like to call it. See, when you and Creak over there came together in that church all those years ago, a kinship clicked into place that awoke the ethereal elements in the both of you. Creak had been placed on top of that cathedral in a comatose-like state by his sentry, Goji, in 1907. When you walked through those doors in 2010, your connection to The One Dimension woke Creak from his century-long sleep while simultaneously waking his inert paradisiacal abilities. When that happened, a series of counterbalances began to reinstate themselves, alerting The-Powers-That-Be, there were some potential heavy-hitters in the game. It was decided I would watch over you permanently until you were grown. That's why I was there when you were a child and why I am standing here asking for your help now."

"Ethereal elements? Paradisiacal abilities? I don't have any of those things, whatever they are. I think there's been a mistake, Cradle."

"Look, kid, here's the deal. You stick with me through this explanation, though, OK? I'm gonna lay it out real clear, but you've got to be willing to hear it all the way through. Don't go jumping to any conclusions about who and what you are because of what I'm about to tell you. Deal?"

Morna considered what Cradle said and gave a curt nod for him to continue.

"You are a descendant of The Ten Dimensions, technically a descendant of The One Dimension. Your ethereal lineage goes back to the beginning, Morna. Your Grandsire, Ishtar, was an angel and nephew of the most notorious angel ever known," Cradle said.

"He means the asshat. You're related to the greedy asshat, which in turn genetically gives you a shit ton of ethereal and para-disiacal abilities, even if it is watered down a bit," Creak chimed in.

"You're telling me I'm related to the Devil?" Morna asked, astounded.

"Not in a bad way, kid," Cradle continued. "Remember, he used to be The One's right-hand man. The One is not the jealous, vengeful omnipotence many make it out to be. It would never hold you, or any innocent of the asshat's line, responsible for his insolence."

"How is that possible? How can I, a human being, be related to an angel?"

"I guess that angels like to dip their wick in the human pool for variety's sake. Eternity is a seriously long time to stick with just one flavor. Am I right, Cradle?" Silla asked audaciously, wiggling her perfect auburn brows.

Creak snorted and raised his clawed paw for a high-five from Silla.

She immediately took a step back.

"Awwww, don't leave me hanging, Sil," Creak dared, a cheeky gleam in his yellow eyes.

Silla cocked her head to the side, considering the walking, talk-ing, smartass nightmare attached to the razor-sharp claws dangling in front of her, shrugged her shoulders, and gave the Grinx some skin.

"Atta girl," Creak said, satisfied.

"You nailed it, Silla," Cradle laughed. "That deed's been done so many times there's even a classification for angel and human offspring. They're called Nephilim. Some Nephilim carry ethereal abilities, some don't. Somewhere in your lineage, eons ago, Ishtar had coitus with one of your ancestors, but the child born of that union never manifested Nephilim powers, nor did any of her subsequent offspring—until you. Before your birth, there had never been a descendant of the original dimension with an active Nephilim genome sequence. You, Morna Stahr, are ethereal royalty the likes of which existence has never known, and you are currently in possession of untapped abilities that far exceed any Nephilim before you."

"You said coitus!" Creak fell, laughing on the ground like a hyena.

"But, I don't have any abilities, Cradle, and Silla's not a...a Nephilim, is she?"

"No, Silla is not a Nephilim. She is an Onacana and one with the gift of fire. The One seems to think that will come in handy."

"See, Morna, I'm special too," Silla said, giving Morna a rasp-berry. "Wait, what? I have the gift of fire?"

"Coitus!" Creak snorted, drooling a little between howls.

"Your name is Atsilla Onacana. You are a white owl of the Cherokee people, born with the call for all to see. Any medicine man or woman worth their feathers knows what it means when a Cherokee child comes into this world with streaks of red woven through their ebony hair. I'm sure your parents suspected this since the day they named you for your fiery locks. You'll be coming into your gifts directly, Silla. The Powers-That-Be are going to speed up the process a bit, so there will be a learning curve, but you're a quick study. I'm not worried."

"Shit, I'm not worried either. Bring it! Did you hear that, Morna? I get superpowers too! Hot damn! Let's get this show start-ed!" Silla sprang from her chair, ready for whatever came next.

"I don't have superpowers, Silla! You're not even a Christian," Morna said, turning from Silla to ask Cradle. "How can a Christian God go mucking around with the gifts bestowed on her by uGu?"

"Who said The One was a Christian?" Cradle asked over Creak's chortling howls. "The One is not big on the segregating of ethereal belief systems. It's all the same as The One. It's you humans who are always going around bickering about whose God is the correct God. You're all wrong, and you're all right. The One is all of them."

Creak sat up on his mammoth haunches and raised his front claws to his forehead, only to pull them away while making an exploding sound.

"Mind blown, dude," he said in his best Spicoli.

"You're a real jackass, you know that?" Cradle said. "You could help me out here."

"Fine, fine, but you're no fun...*Dude*." Creak Lebowski'ed Cradle for the hell of it, then turned toward Morna and Silla. "The feathered colossus is correct. The One is The One, The Only, and The All. It doesn't cotton to individual definitions of God, and it doesn't care that you all do. In layman's terms, it only cares that a person does the best he or she can for his or herself and their fellow humans, all the while not being too big of a dick about it. When humans follow that simple ideology, the energies within them become charged positively, and therefore are attracted to the One's dimension, making it stronger. When they don't, they are negatively charged, and the asshat gets the goods, got it?"

"I got it. You got it, Morna?" Silla asked, staring intently at the dancing flame on the candle just to her left.

"Yeah, I got it. But what about these powers of mine? The only thing I've ever done even remotely heavenly is sing like a choir of angels at the Basilica over ten years ago, and I haven't been able to do that since."

"Morna, that wasn't you. It was me. The reason you sounded

like a choir of angels is because it was a choir of angels. I'm a Seraphim, among other things, which means the voice of The One. That day ten years ago, you and Creak needed a little bump to get the celestial ball rolling in the right direction. So, I gave you one."

"That explains a lot," Morna said, astonished at how underwhelmed she felt at the closing of that particular shit show.

Turns out it was super easy to forget about scraping a decade's worth of poo off your shoe when you're receiving a code brown crop dusting, courtesy of a low-flying angel. There was just no comparison.

"Don't worry about when and where your powers will come. I promise they will manifest. They tend to arise when a series of events happen in such a way that everything just sort of clicks into place," Cradle said.

"OUCH! Goddammit!" Silla yelled, drawing everyone's attention.

She snatched her hand back fast, clutching it to her chest after having spent the last few minutes passing it back and forth over the dancing flame of the Mango Sunrise-scented candle next to her recliner.

Creak laughed so hard he rolled over, the inky jewels on his body sparkling as he shook in delight.

"Oh, my Gawd! Oh, my Gawd!" he snorted. "This is going to be so much fun!"

"You better watch that mouth, Silla," Morna said. "I'm guessing The One doesn't approve of blasphemers in his army."

Silla turned the subject back to Morna, while still cradling her burnt fingers.

"The One doesn't give a rat's ass about that blaspheming shit either. It's got bigger fish to fry," said Creak, rolling back onto his feet, and standing at his full, natural height of around four feet. "We better get these ladies under wing before someone gets hurt."

Cradle knelt before a very sheepish Silla to inspect her burnt hand.

"Roger that. Let's get to HQ and get this show on the road."

Creak padded away into the deeper recesses of the caves as the cozy living room disappeared into nothingness, landing a still-sitting Silla right on her ass, tangled up in a giant, gorgeous, ebony-colored angel.

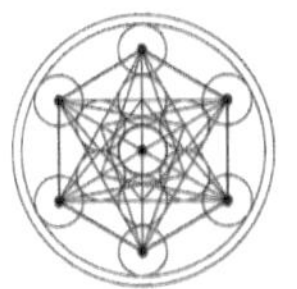

TO THE CAT CAVE

Silla and Morna followed Creak and Cradle's every turn, deep into the bowels of the Cherokee Caves. Old lights overhead magically popped on as they descended into the darkness, only to fade away when no longer necessary, leaving a chasm of weighty blackness both in front and behind them.

A massive temperature drop coupled with an increase in echoes indicated a large opening up ahead. Lights blazed from over fifty feet above as they entered an enormous underground cavern. From floor to ceiling, the quartz lining the limestone walls sparkled like diamonds. It was breathtaking, but other than a few random stalactites and stalagmites, the cavern was empty.

"HQ could use some of your decorating skills, Creak," Silla said flatly as she ran her hand along one of the damp, sparkling walls.

"Are you afraid of heights, Sil?" Creak asked, ignoring Silla's sass.

"She's an owl, Creak; it's not in her nature," Cradle fired back as a light in the far upper corner of the cavern revealed an impossible opening fifty feet above the ground. A rope ladder dropped down from its mouth like a waterfall, unrolling further and further until it reached the cavern floor.

"After you," Creak said to Morna as the group approached the bottom of the ladder.

Morna grabbed the ladder and made her way up as the other three watched from below. When she reached the top, she shouted down the all-clear to Silla, who immediately began her ascent. When the two women were safely at the top, the ladder magically rolled itself up to rest at their feet.

"Bullshit! We've already been locked in this place once tonight. I'll be goddamned if it's happening again," Silla said, bending and grabbing for the rope ladder to toss it back down.

As Silla tossed the ladder back over the ledge, a familiar scraping sound, just like the one Morna had heard the day before at the basilica, echoed off the cavern walls. Seconds later, the Grinx crested the rocky ledge.

"Cool your jets, Silla. I don't need no stinking ladder and neither does he," Creak said, casually picking pieces of loose stone out from under his claws while gesturing with his boxy, black head toward Cradle, who circled the air near the top of the cavern, his enormous smoky-gray wings outstretched in easy flight.

"Make sense?"

Morna watched in awe as her imaginary childhood friend descended toward the opening of the hidden tunnel, drawing his wings in effortlessly as he quietly stepped onto the ledge, one giant Chuck Taylor at a time.

"It's just around the corner," Creak said, waving them on with a quick jerk of his quartz-tipped tail.

When the four of them rounded the corner, they were confronted with two floor-to-ceiling Gothic-style wooden doors. Creak raised his tail and pointed its heavy, crystal tip at a panel to the side. The translucent, clear-cut stone on the end of his tail glowed a soft, pulsing green as the small screen to the right of the door mimicked the same, giving a beep. After several clicks, the reluctant sound of laboring gears groaned as the doors slowly parted.

"Welcome home, ladies," Creak said as he trotted happily into HQ.

Morna and Silla stepped through the doors to find themselves in yet another enormous cavern, but this one was anything but empty. Way off to the right looked like a modern-day NASA command center. There must have been one hundred flat screens lining the wall, floor to ceiling, all turned on, varying news stations from around the world. Below, there was one impossibly long curved desk, large enough for six workstations. A small, oriental bridge reached across a natural stream that cut right through the enormous space and cordoned off the real-life deck of the Enterprise from the rest of the open area. To the left of the bridge, the space was filled with clusters of entertainment areas. Starting at the front near the doors was a cozy living space with a fireplace and two antique sofas facing one another. Beyond that was a pool table, ping pong table, large black marble dining table with twelve high back chairs, and on the far back wall, there was a corner bar complete with tap handles and neon signs. To the right of the bar, along the far back of the cave, was a small natural amphitheater brimming with various musical instruments and sound equipment. All along the lower level were openings in the cave wall, leading to who knows where, and a myriad of staircases spiraling up to a mammoth overhead library complete with wrought iron catwalks and rolling ladders covering every inch of the soaring expanse above.

Cradle, Creak, and Silla were already halfway over the little bridge when Morna noticed she was left standing alone, staring slack-mouthed at her new surroundings. Pulling herself from her wonderment, she jogged to catch up.

"Is this your home?" Morna asked the angel and Grinx as she made her way over the bridge.

"Yes ma'am," Creak said proudly. "Well, I guess it is now," he finished, not too sure about himself for once.

The angel looked the Grinx in the eyes, saying kindly, "This is most assuredly your home for as long as you want it to be, my friend." Cradle gave Creak a quick squeeze on the shoulder and turned to Silla and Morna, saying, "It's your home too."

"Hell, yes!" Silla answered immediately.

"We'll think about it, thank you," Morna said after.

Silla looked put out but said nothing as the four made their way over to the command center.

"All right, kids. We're moving right along to intel. This here is the eyes and ears of our little operation. I don't think we need all this," Cradle motioned to the scores of flat screens, "but it makes the dog happy."

"Woof," Creak said as he raised his right hind leg over a fire hydrant that magically appeared beside him.

"Do it, and I'll rub your nose in it," Cradle warned the grinning Grinx.

"Try it, and you'll be picking feathers out of your ass for millennia," Creak fired back.

"That's not an entirely bad idea. Follow me, kids." Cradle turned and headed back over the bridge toward an open tunnel near the cozy nook of sofas.

The tunnel slanted downward gradually and gave a few snake-back turns before opening to a chamber about twice the width, but equal in height to the one they left behind. Unlike the other chamber, the rocky terrain of this floor was strewn with hazardous vent holes sending plumes of searing steam thirty feet into the air. There were razor-sharp outcroppings of rock barely visible in the gloom. The only source of light emanated from thick layers of phosphorescent vegetation clinging to the walls and ceiling, washing the whole nightmarish scene in an eerie crimson luminescence.

Morna wiped the sweat building from her brow with the back of her hand. The humidity in the cavern was so thick she found it nearly impossible to breathe. Dizzy, she reached out to steady herself on a nearby rock only to slice her hand on its jagged edges.

"Is this hell?" Morna asked, clasping her bleeding hand.

"Not even close, but you'll believe it to be soon enough," Cradle answered as he threw some sparkly dust in Morna's general direction. The particles swirled, then spiraled to settle on Morna's bleeding palm, twinkling as it soaked up the blood like some sort of first aid angel dust. "This, ladies," Cradle stretched his lengthy arms outward, "is the sparring room."

"I think I'd prefer hell," Morna said, inspecting her perfectly healed hand before shoving her head between her knees, breathing deep, hungry for air.

"You're going to be fine, kid. You'll get the knack of it in no time. You just need to acclimate."

"To hell? You want me to acclimate to hell?"

Morna looked up at Cradle from between her knees.

"You should feel right in your element here, Morn," Silla chimed in, "being that you're the devil's spawn and all."

"Yeah, it's a real home away from home," Morna responded dryly on a shallow breath. "How can you still be standing, Silla?" Morna let herself sink the rest of the way down to the cave floor. "It's sweltering in here."

"It doesn't feel that crazy hot to me. Warm, yes. Sweltering—not really," Silla looked to Creak. "How hot is it down here anyway?"

"One hundred and twenty degrees, without humidity," the Grinx answered, suddenly sounding like Alexa. The Grinx's lower half pulsed red, like the glowing embers of a campfire.

Projected from seemingly nowhere, a weather app screenshot

illuminated the Grinx's right-side flank, displaying the time, temperature, humidity, and probability of self-combustion. Probability was low at just three percent.

"What's happening there?" Silla asked, looking skeeved out as she side-eyed Creak's mind-boggling metamorphosis.

"I'm absorbing some of the heat off Morna," Creak answered like the technological modification to his anatomy was no biggie.

"From the sound of it, Silla's gifts are starting to kick in," boomed an unfamiliar voice from somewhere deep in the shadows of the cavern.

"Who was that?" Morna asked, rising to her feet, suddenly feeling much cooler.

"That would be your trainer. Well, one of them anyway. The other one can't be far. It's impossible to keep those two off each other," Creak answered, his lower half still aglow, and his personal weather app illuminating his side flank, displaying a temperature of one-hundred-twenty-five degrees and a personal combustion probability of three-point-seven percent.

"Morna. Silla. I'd like you ladies to meet Hephaestus. He's our head weapons maker and keeper of all things volcanic," Cradle said, gesturing toward the approaching behemoth.

A jumbo-sized man covered in sweat and grime padded barefoot from behind a faraway outcropping of rocks. He sported a long, industrial-style leather apron, welder's helmet, and a ginormous hammer that swung back and forth from a colossal hand at the end of an arm the size of a redwood tree trunk. Other than those few accouterments, the dude was entirely nude.

The son of Zeus casually approached the foursome, lifting his face shield to reveal one of the most handsome faces the world has ever known.

"Cradle."

"Hephaestus."

Like soldiers of old, Hephaestus and Cradle took stock of each other, making eye contact with a quick nod, and before properly shaking both hand and claw, grasping forearms in a formal show of friendship.

"Good to see you again," the giant man said, a wicked smile creeping across his face before he pulled the stoic angel in for an enormous bear hug.

"It's been three days, Heff," Cradle said.

Heff spun him round and round, gracing everyone else in the cavern with a glorious view of his perfectly bare ass.

"What can I say? I've missed you, man!"

Heff placed Cradle back on the ground with a couple of hefty shoulder pats before stooping down to give Creak a fiver and a nice long scratch behind the collar.

"Next time you miss me, could you wear pants?"

"Doubtful," Heff answered, laughing deeply as he picked up his giant hammer and swung it to rest on his shoulder before turning toward Morna and Silla. "Hello, Morna. Hello Silla. I'm Heff."

Full-on gobsmacked by the mythological smithy casually making introductions, the two women stood silent and unresponsive as the cooling Greek god extended his hand to either woman, attempting an unrequited meet and greet.

"Give 'em a minute, Heff; they've been through a lot tonight. Where's Frey?" Creak asked, ignoring the dumbfounded twosome.

"She'll be along in a minute; she's putting the kids to bed. I didn't expect you'd get this far tonight with these two. I'm surprised their brains aren't scrambled," Heff said, gesturing toward the dazed pair.

"They are looking a little worse for wear. Maybe after this, we should call it quits for the night," Creak said to Heff.

"Hey, guys!" said a blonde-haired, blue-eyed sprite of a woman cheerfully bouncing through the makeshift hell realm.

Her white-blonde hair was plaited away from her face in crazy designs, and her silvery-blue eyes were lined heavily with kohl, making her look like a punk rock Tinkerbell. The slip of a woman was rocking the latest high-end Nikes and covered head to toe in the at-home-mom gear of Lululemon, making the stunningly, brilliant amber necklace resting at the base of her throat seem ridiculously out of place. Made entirely of heavy yellow gold and seven amber stones the size of plums, the thing appeared to be as old as antiquity itself.

"Heya, Freyja!" Creak said, clearly delighted to see the pixie-sized Norse goddess.

He threw up a giant-padded, taloned claw, which Freyja eagerly hit with a slap and two bumps, pulling back while making sizzling sounds and shaking both hands and claws as if they were hot.

"Hi, Boo," Freyja said to Heff, sliding up to the big guy and giving him a quick kiss on his hulking bicep. "I liked to never got the little hellions to sleep. If they ask for one more glass of water tonight, I swear to Nott, I'm going in with the fire hose. Are these two lovely ladies, Morna and Silla?" she asked, looking over at the two gawking women.

"I'll go in next time they holler. I'm almost finished out here anyway, and yes, these two lovely ladies are Morna Stahr and Atsilla Onacanna."

Heff introduced them to his wife as if he'd known them forever.

"It's lovely to finally meet you, Morna. Silla," Freyja said, reaching out to shake the hand of each woman in turn. "We need some more girl power around here—no offense, boys."

Morna snapped from her reverie first, shaking the extended hand before her, asking, "Are you *the* Freyja?"

"The one and only," Freyja said proudly.

"But aren't you a goddess? I thought The One was the one and only? I'm sorry, but I'm so fucking confused," Morna said, all manners thrown to the wind.

"She's stuck on that secular shit again. Sorry, Frey," Creak said to Freyja. "They're getting a crash course in reality versus mythology tonight. I'm sure they don't mean to be rude." The last part said in a stern warning, aimed solely at Morna.

"Oh, that! No biggie," Freyja turned her attention back toward Morna and Silla. "I'm a Norse goddess, by human definition. I rank somewhere at the top of the angel hierarchy by Christian standards. By our standards, I'm a super-powerful and high-ranking member of The One's army. The same for my hubby. Does that help?" she asked simply.

"But, I thought you were married to Odin?" Silla threw out.

"Whew, they are behind, aren't they?" Freyja said to Creak and Cradle. "We split eons ago," she said, absently stroking her necklace.

"OK. I can roll with all this shit if you can, Morna," Silla said frankly to her BFF.

"Why the hell not?" Morna threw her hands in the air. "It's not the weirdest fucking thing we've heard in the last five minutes," she said, all but giving up on not giving in.

"Fabulous!" Freyja interjected, linking arms between both women. "I bet you two honeys are wrecked. Let's get you settled in, and we'll start fresh in the morning."

Freyja turned, leading them toward the entrance to the main living space.

"Wait!" Morna yelled, pulling to a quick stop, and jerking the other two women hard. "I can't stay here tonight!" she said to Cradle. "I have a job. A life! I have responsibilities!" she sputtered.

"Your responsibilities have been ramped up a notch or two, kiddo," Cradle said. "No one expects you to leave your life high and dry, but we've got to get you up to snuff, and there is a lot to cover. Your shifts at the restaurant are covered for the next week. Your shifts at work are covered, too, Silla."

"See? We're all good, loves. Let's get you settled; boot camp starts at 5:00 a.m., and my sweet, little assholes get up even earlier than that. Nobody likes a grumpy Freyja. It's off to bed with you, kittens, or there'll be Valhalla to pay," Freyja said, reaching her arm toward Morna with a come-hither wave.

Defeated, tired, and completely stupefied, Morna accepted her fate to follow Silla and the mother-hen goddess back through the twisting tunnels.

When they reached the main chamber of HQ, Freyja marched toward the back-left quadrant. Just as the three women approached another opening at the very back of the cave, Freyja took another hard left and marched behind the bar.

"Have a seat, ladies; the bar's open," Freyja said as she lowered the bar counter behind her.

"A-fucking-men," said Silla, pulling out a stool.

"Right?" said Freyja. "I gotta have a nightcap, or I'm never getting today to stop looping in my head. I love my kids, but damn they wear a woman out."

"How many kids do you have?" Silla asked as Freyja lined up three shot glasses on the bar.

"Two that are full-grown and out living their lives. It's the five fucking crazy little monkeys still at home that drive me to drink," Freyja said, laughing at how much she loved her litter while free-pouring a long stream of Jamison into three sturdy shot glasses, unceremoniously slamming her shot before sliding the other two amber-filled glasses toward Morna and Silla.

"*Sláinte*," Morna said, downing her shot. "Again," she said and slid the heavy glass back across the bar to Freyja.

"Same," Silla said, firing her empty glass back as well.

"Oh, we're going to get along just fine, ladies."

Freyja smiled as she lined them all up for another.

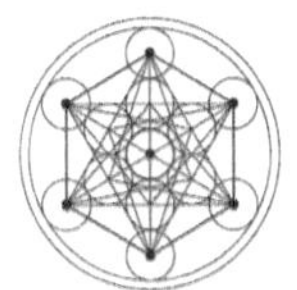

TEN

PEPPERED REFLECTION

Morna woke in a giant bedroom chamber she honestly couldn't remember settling into. A fireplace big enough to stand in blazed warmly off to the left side of the California king bed she was all nestled up in. She found herself swimming in a sea of Egyptian cotton sheets of cobalt blues and silvery-dove grays that must have had thread counts running into the thousands. Heavy and light, weighted and downy, Morna admitted, as she slid he bare legs back and forth over the heavenly linen layers, she had never been so damn comfortable in her whole life.

Rolling onto her back to settle in, Morna's breath caught at the unexpected beauty of the enormous chandelier dangling above her bed. Peppered with hundreds of dangling crystals, each perfectly cut piece caught radiant glimpses of warm light dancing from the fireplace and bent it, throwing a cosmos of rainbow-colored prisms across every surface of the otherwise pitch-black room. The result was breathtaking.

But as comfortable as she was, and as tired as she was, sleep wouldn't return. Her thoughts stirred, trying to sort out the unsortable. It tried this way and that, but in the end always went back to the start, back to when Cradle was just her imaginary friend who talked. She'd heard lots of kids talk to their imaginary friends, so she just chalked it up to normal. No one else ever heard him. How in the hell was she supposed to know he was an angel?

"Oh my God!" Morna said, mortified at all the things she told the very real being just down the hall. "Kill me now."

Morna pulled the covers over her head, embarrassed to a level she could not equate, hence the betrayal! Damned if she was going to drown in embarrassment when she'd been the one bamboozled, and as a child no less.

None of it mattered, not really. He was always there, steady as a rock, and warm as a kitten. It was more than she could say for everyone else, including her parents, with the additional exception of Silla, of course. She'd come into the picture a few years after the "miracle".

A couple of girls in middle school had set their sights on Morna. It wasn't the first time, and it wouldn't be the last, but it was the first time someone stopped the impending ass-kicking. Morna was pretty sure it was the equivalent of an early A.D. stoning. If you were different in 24 A.D., you were thrown into a hole and stoned. If you were different in the twenty-first century, your head was shoved in a throne and flushed for good measure, and Morna hadn't even been aware the swirly that day was at bat. She had been looking in the mirror at an obnoxious zit that would not go away and would not pop when she heard the sound of two heads being smacked together.

By the time Morna turned around, the two girls, Robyn Sharpe and Robin Holland, were semi-conscious on the tiles of Pacific Middle School's furthest bathroom from the overlords. Hence the repeated jumping in this perfect locale, but a girl's got to pee. If she got one more detention for using the girls' bathroom on the other side of the school, she would've gotten a call home, and well, fuck that. So, ass beating it was.

"How did you not see that coming?"

"What?" Morna asked, dazed.

"Those girls. They were right behind you. How could you not see them in the mirror coming up behind you?"

Morna didn't say anything, just pointed to what appeared to be an evil twin growing out of her chin.

"That's a doozy all right, but it's no excuse for letting the fucking Robyns sneak up on you. Their game is weak."

"Yeah, well, mine is weaker. OK?"

Morna felt like she was getting her ass handed to her yet again, but this time verbally by an unlikely savior she'd never spoken two words to before then.

That was the exact moment Atsilla Rene' Onacanna adopted Morna JoAnn Stahr. As the bell rang and the two Robyns made little effort to move, Silla dug around in her purse and pulled out a gigantic makeup bag. She dug in it until she found the perfect tool, grabbed Morna by the shoulders, and turned her toward the light. Silla talked about makeup like it was a normal thing to do, given the concussed Robyns made unholy threats as they left the bathroom door.

"Leave my girl alone, bitches, or I'll be sending you home to roost in a body bag."

"Holy shit! You can't say that!" I told her.

"I just did, and I'm still here. Sooooo."

"Your parents? Do they just throw you to the wolves every day?"

"What do you mean?"

"I mean, everyone knows about you, which makes you a walking, talking target, and you're telling me your parents never so much as got you a beginner's karate class?"

Morna just shook her head no.

"Women's self-defense?"

Again, Morna shook her head no.

Silla looked disgusted, then went on about how they were going to need to train Morna to fight for herself as Silla couldn't be there all the time. Turns out her reputation would, which dramatically cut back on the afternoon bathroom ass kickings.

"There," Silla said, turning Morna's shoulders toward the mirror.

"Holy shit. I'm beautiful." Morna remembered, looking at the five-minute makeover, she barely recognized herself. Couple that with a first and only friend, a friend who made daily ass whoopings and zits of antiquity disappear had made it the best day of Morna's life and worth the detention she'd got for being fifteen minutes late to class worth it, ten times over.

ELEVEN

BOOT CAMP

Shaking off the memories, Morna reluctantly pulled back the thick down comforter as Freyja burst through the door.

"Wakey, wakey, eggs and bakey!" Freyja said cheerfully, cranking the dimmer switch on the chandelier to full blast, and killing the enchanted atmosphere without mercy.

"What time is it?" Morna asked, rubbing her eyes.

"The crack of stupid," Freyja answered. "4:45."

"a.m.?"

"Work hard; play hard. That's the motto around here," Freyja said, bouncing to the wardrobe in about five hundred bucks' worth of canary yellow athletic gear and matching kicks. "Right now, it's time to work hard. So, up and at 'em." She threw piles of padded Under Armour at Morna. "Throw those on. The gang is already at breakfast. Chop! Chop!"

Morna inspected the pile of gear, then threw on the padded compression shirt and pants.

"Is there a bathroom in here?" she asked Freyja who dug through the wardrobe.

"Over to the right," came a muffled answer as a new pair of

Nikes flew over Freya's shoulders and landed near the bed at Morna's feet.

Morna picked up the shoes and padded barefoot to the door on the right. She was once again shocked at the size of everything. Twenty-foot ceilings held yet another crystal chandelier high over an enormous, natural bathing pool taking up the entire back left of the unconventional bathroom. A light steam rose from the glass-like surface, indicating it must be fed by a natural hot spring. There were several tall waterfalls in the farthest alcove flowing freely and making the water from below froth and foam.

"Don't take any time dolling up in there. We're going to training, not the prom," she heard Freyja yell from the other room.

Morna made a nasty gesture towward the bedroom and turned to the lengthy rock countertop, finding it littered with high-end hair accessories, make-up, and hygiene products. She threw her hair up with a tie and headband, washed her face, brushed her teeth, and headed to face boot camp. Whatever the fuck that was.

Creak and Heff were already busy training in the hell realm when Morna and Freyja made their appearance. Creak held a thick rope pulled taut between his teeth while Heff hammered metal spikes into the rock wall nearby.

"Morning, sleepy head," Silla said from high above, suspended in the air by the ropes clenched between Creak's teeth. "They're going to teach me how to fly!" Silla yelled down.

"In time, owl," Cradle's chiding response echoed to the cave floor. "We are acclimating you to heights and nasty environments for now," he tutored while hovering near an all-too-happy Silla.

Already overwhelmed with the oppressive heat, Morna wiped the sweat from her brow and pulled at the padded material covering her head to toe.

"You just about done there, Heff? Morna's gonna have a heat stroke if I don't pull her temperature down soon," Creak mumbled over the rope clenched between his jagged teeth.

"Just one more sec," Heff said, securing the last carabiner into place before giving the rope a good tug to check his work. "We're good. Drop it!"

Creak dropped the rope and trotted toward Morna, his lower half already glowing ember red as he went. "For you today, we are going to work on heat acclimation. I'm going to get you to a sustainable temperature for your current tolerance and then we'll work on you mastering this terrain. When you get comfy with the temp, I'm going to amp it up. I'll be monitoring your vitals as we go, so no worries there. Feeling better?" he asked.

"Yeah, I think I'm getting there. Where are we going that we have to train in this bullshit heat? I didn't sign up to fight The Dark Lord on his turf."

"You're not going to Hell, Morna, if that's what you're asking," Heff answered, hammering a few more spikes into the rock.

"Ever been to Egypt or the Middle East in summer? Hell, Missouri in August for that matter—same fuckin' thing," Creak shot back.

"Wait, what? This heat is to train me to acclimate to an environment I already live in?" Morna asked, pissed off.

"Yes and no. Sure, you live here, but how often do you push it to the limits in that heat? I bet your ass finds as much air conditioning and pool time as it can during dog days in the Lou."

"Summer's over, Creak," Morna said to the Grinx.

Creak huffed through his jowls.

"It's going to take you all winter to acclimate and train. Furthermore, when your little 'extras' kick in, this heat will only amplify your ability to tap into and harness them. Let's just log that in the big-ass file titled, 'Shit You Don't Need to Know Yet'. Also, stop asking so many goddamned questions and do as you're told. Now, run!"

"What?" Morna asked indignantly.

"Rrrrrrrruuunnnnnn!"

A low, demonic voice erupted from Creak as he snarled and his mouth frothed. His eyes glowed a sickly yellow, cutting through the eerie, crimson hue and scaring the living hell out of Morna. Creak peeled off after her across the craggy terrain, and pieces of black rock spewed into the air as his red-hot claws dug in for purchase.

Panicked, Morna's eyes scoured the cave for a way out. Her vision was limited in the low lighting, and together with the vented steam and jagged rocks, she barely saw three feet in front of her. The hellish huffing from behind gained on her with every step as she slammed into a wall that went straight up. There was nothing but the smooth facade stretching into the infernal abyss either way she looked. Cornered, Morna frantically ran her bare hands over the impossibly smooth surface in search of an escape. Over dents and divots too small to catch, her desperate fingers brushed against something. A shiny metal spike, just like the ones Heff had hammered into the wall for Silla, jutted from the wall above her head.

Further up were five more, spaced in three-foot increments. Morna wrapped both hands around the lowest one and pulled with everything she had, her arms buckling under the weight. Out of time, she backed up and took a running leap at the wall, grabbing hold of the spike with both hands, planting her feet, and pushing hard—using her momentum to launch past the first spike and propel her to the one above. She grabbed blindly, scrambling for the next spike, but missed by inches and fell to the floor. Her tailbone sang as it smashed into the rock.

Out of options, she picked herself up and ran. Her body screamed as she threw it at the slab of rock. Morna grabbed, planted, and launched herself up. Within seconds, she dangled from the higher spike, swinging wildly by one hand. Twisted to face the wall, she balanced precariously between the two spikes and felt for a foothold that could take her higher as Creak's rabid snarling echoed to her ears. As the Grinx closed in, she kept her body close to the wall, her muscles burning, and clambered higher.

Creak came barreling around the corner and tore vertically up the wall with fire in his eyes. Terrified, Morna threw her battered body toward a razor-sharp overhang a few feet away. Her blood-slicked hands grappled with the ragged ledge while the heat of Creak's breath seared the soles of her new shoes. Morna clutched at nothing, falling twenty feet to the cave floor.

"Gotcha, kiddo." Cradle swung in before she hit rock bottom. He swooped her up in his giant arms and tenderly held her close to his chest. The last thing Morna heard before she passed out was a low, melodic whisper, "You did good, Morn. You did real good."

Morna came to after a few minutes, still nestled in Cradle's arms. Terror-stricken, she clawed at the dark angel, cutting deep lines into his jaw with her broken and bloody nails. Cradle tightened his hold slightly, giving her enough freedom to thrash and scream out the last of her adrenaline without injuring herself in the process. She struggled a few minutes more before her panic gave way to exhaustion.

Morna breathed heavily and laid slack in Cradle's arms as he gently whispered, "I got you, kiddo. I got you."

No longer channeling the hounds of hell, a much friendlier-looking Creak made his way back to the group.

"What the fuck was that?" Silla roared down at him. When her feet touched the ground, she was already running at the Grinx with fire in her eyes. He skittered back as the ropes still tethering Silla to the wall caught tight and jerked her back, hard.

"I don't give a good goddamn what kind of zoological nightmare you are. I will fucking end you, you Cujo wannabe piece of shit!" Silla raged, pulling violently at the carabiners restraining her. "You're fucking dead!"

Creak sat back on his mammoth haunches, cautiously watching Silla struggle as her wrath turned to fire. A whoosh echoed through the chamber as Atsilla Onacana became engulfed in flames. One second she violently tugged at her bonds, the next she was pulled into an otherworldly backdraft immediately consuming, but not burning her. Silla fought like hell to break free, cursing the fire's hold. Her ire only acted as tinder for the spiraling pyre.

The flames folded and weaved together while the inferno raged on, throwing shadows of Silla's likeness on the walls all around. Then, as suddenly as it roared into being, the fire collapsed in on itself, leaving only a smoldering pile of embers.

Morna's voice broke as she bucked free of Cradle's hold. At superhuman speed, Morna ran toward where she last saw her best friend, and fell to her knees, screaming Silla's name to the heavens as the smoking pile of remnants crackled and spurted. It breathed out a red-hot heat that had Morna clambering backward.

Morna watched in both fear and awe as Atsilla Onacana burst from the white-hot ashes. Fashioned from flames, the fiery owl climbed higher and higher with every pump of her blazing wings. She crested, adjusting her wingspan like it was second nature, before diving at Mach speed toward the Grinx below.

Impossible, but there she was, glorious in all her rage. Silla stretched her talons, just short of their target, when she was suddenly blasted backward into the unforgiving cave wall by a relentless spray of high-pressured water.

"Turn it off!" Cradle yelled to Freyja who handled the professional-grade fire hose, blasting Silla with two hundred gallons of water per minute. "That'll be enough for today!"

Morna ran to her best friend who, now in her human state, lay in a lifeless, crumpled heap. The only remnant of Silla's fiery transformation was the steam rising off her rapidly cooling, naked body. Morna tentatively reached out to assess Silla's condition when she heard footsteps from behind. Seething, she turned all her confusion and fear on the group closing in.

"Get away from us!" Morna screamed at the incoming platoon of mythological creatures.

The troop pulled up short but did not back away.

Creak, Cradle, and Heff all remained still and silent as Freyja took a tentative step, saying softly, "It's all part of the training, Morna."

Freyja braved another step and bent down, placing a perfectly folded linen robe on the ground between them.

"Training!" Morna erupted and marched straight to the legendary female warrior, sucker-punching her right in her perfect jaw. "There's your fucking training!" she roared, turning on a dime to scoop up the robe and storm back to Silla.

Astonishment washed over Freyja's face, morphing quickly into something that, honest to Asgard, resembled a mother's pride. Freyja rubbed her jaw and carried on like she wasn't sucker punched by a raging, baby Neph.

"We have to do it this way, honey. There is very little time, and we need both your powers to manifest as soon as possible. The only way to do that is to put you in a situation where you perceive one, or both, of your lives are in danger. And, I have to say, it worked. At least partially, anyway."

Morna nursed Silla to her feet and gingerly draped her in the robe. She lay one of Silla's arms across her aching shoulders and wrapped her bruised and bloody arm around Silla's freezing waist, taking most of her best friend's weight onto herself.

"We're leaving," she said to no one in particular as she lugged Silla's cumbersome body toward the exit.

Cradle cautiously walked up to Morna, tenderly blocking the way.

"You can't take her from here, Morna, not now," he whispered.

With her eyes locked dead on his, Morna dared him, "Try and fucking stop me."

"Morna, she's too weak to go anywhere. She won't be strong

enough to be moved for another day or two. The first change wreaks havoc on the body. Silla needs to rest."

"She can rest at home," Morna said, pushing past Cradle.

Cradle reached out and placed a hand on Morna's shoulder.

"Would you calm the fuck down and look at her. She needs help, kid. Help, you're not qualified to give. We can help Silla, but you've got to trust us."

Betrayal fueled her exhausted body. Morna pulled her shoulder away, fast and hard, from Cradle's soft touch and lost her balance. She crumpled under Silla's dead weight into an awkward pile on the floor.

"How can we trust you? You did this to her! To me!" Morna yelled at the dark angel.

"Come on. Wake up," Morna pleaded, stroking her best friend's face. "Jesus, Sil, you're freezing," she whispered when her fingers brushed Silla's icy skin.

"What's wrong with her?" Morna pleaded.

"She needs help getting her body temperature to adjust back to normal. It's pretty standard. We can help if you'll let us. Morna, please let us help Silla. It's the best thing you can do for her right now."

Terrified for Silla, and defeated by her lack of strength and knowledge, Morna nodded. She was sickened by her inability to do anything else. Cradle bent and effortlessly scooped Silla into his arms. Morna grabbed hold of his wrist. She locked eyes with the angel, and in no uncertain terms, vowed, "She's everything to me, Cradle."

"I know, kiddo. I know," Cradle replied, with a world of understanding in his all too familiar gray eyes.

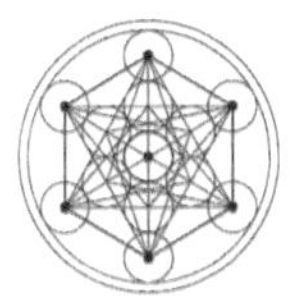

LIVE ACTION DINNER THEATER

Morna sat alone in the bed chamber where she had awakened earlier that morning. She rose from the perfectly made bed and paced to again sit for the hundredth time since sequestering herself here. She'd only left the bedroom once since Silla was taken. She'd gone to the infirmary to check on her, to see with her own eyes she was going to be OK, but she was turned away at the door. Creak told Morna she would not survive the extreme temperatures used to nurse Silla back to health. She felt useless, scared, and without Silla, totally alone. Nervous energy racked her aching body to the point she thought she might go insane. Finally, realizing there was nothing she could do for Silla at the moment but make herself sick with worry, she decided some serious scouting would serve them both better.

Morna made her way back toward Silla's room. She knew it was empty, but opened the door and found it was a mirror image of her own. The only difference was the gold, red, and orange hues reminiscent of the fire that was Atsilla Onacana. It suited Silla perfectly, and that unnerved Morna. How could these creatures know her best friend well enough to create a perfect room?

Morna walked to the bathing chamber and noticed all the products on the rock slab countertop were Silla's favorites, right down to the old-timey tin of watermelon lip gloss. She picked it up and slid the lid back, taking a whiff of the sugary-sweet scent. With the lid now closed, Morna looked at herself in the enormous mirror. Before her stood a broken person with sallow eyes and slumped shoulders. It was as if no one looked back, just an empty shell.

She placed her hands on the countertop and leaned in closer. Her hushpuppy eyes were heavier than normal, pulled down on the outside corners enough to notice a difference. It was in the eyes themselves that she found herself lost. There was no spark of laughter or hint of youth, just worry. Flat, almost black like a still pond in February. The rest of her remained the same. A little too short and a little too plump.

She liked her bubble butt, she thought, giving it a little shake in the mirror.

After several minutes of close consideration, Morna decided besides her bubble butt, she did not like what she saw at all.

"You, my friend, have to pull your shit together," she told herself out loud. "There's zero time to be broken. So, patch your shit up, and let's figure out what's next. It's time to assimilate, woman. This is your new normal. Let's get the fuck on with it already."

Morna grabbed a hair tie and pulled up her brown lob cut. It didn't all fit, the back was too short, but she liked the way the cut hung down on the sides and the front seemed a little edgy. Her muscles popped at the shoulder and bicep as she finished the messy bun. Her server's arms looked a lot like a gymnast's, too big for her body, but necessary for what they're asked to do. Just like now.

Morna walked into the main living area of the cave to look for Cradle but instead found Heff, Freyja, and five smaller versions of them gathered around an oversized dining table. Even from where

Morna stood she saw the shiny, black marble surface littered with an array of dino nuggets, applesauce squeezy-packets, and sippy cups. The elegant table for twelve had evolved into a live-action toddler war zone, and Morna found herself begrudgingly intrigued by the pre-k Ragnarök live-action dinner.

Of the twelve high-backed, silver-shield chairs, five had booster seats strapped to them. In each booster was a very unhappy tot. Morna hung back a bit and watched. Maybe she should gather a little bit more information about who and what she might be hitching her cart to.

"Eat your peas or Baboulas will come and eat you!" Heff threatened the pint-sized deities.

Every green pea scattered about the table rolled toward each other and fell in line like well-coordinated members of a green pea marching band, spelling out "NO!" in large capital letters. The room burst with giggles, all too delighted with the magic trick, which was cut short by an unexpected whirring sound.

Five toddler-sized spoons, without warning, sprouted working propellers from their tail ends as tiny wings unfolded from their colorful sides. The toddlers watched slack-jawed as the five airplane spoons flew directly to the mountains of uneaten peas. The squadron hovered a bit, dove down to the table and scooped up heaps of the unwanted vegetables, and cheerfully flew them back to the five open-mouthed ankle biters who were now ecstatic at the idea of gobbling up peas from aerodynamically enchanted utensils.

"That was a great trick, hon," Heff said to his wife. "Never seen you do that one before."

"Ha ha,"

"What do you mean 'ha ha'? I'm trying to give you a compliment, woman."

"It wasn't me, Heff. It had to be you. These little boogers can't swing that kind of mojo yet," Freyja said, gesturing to the converted pea enthusiasts.

It only took Freyja and Heff a second to look at each other before they looked around the room for another explanation.

There, hidden away in the far back corner, Morna leaned against the bar. She wore a wistful smile on her pretty, round face and watched the children happily gobble up their peas. The couple looked at each other and nodded, satisfied they'd found the explanation.

"Morna! Nice trick!" Heff hollered.

The spoon-planes crashed to the table, resuming their role as mundane tableware, much to the dismay of the rugrats, who protested immediately.

"Could you whip that up again? The kids enjoyed it!" Heff yelled.

"Whip what up again?" Morna asked, a little dazed.

"That thing with the flying spoons. Ah, never mind. It's bath time. Good trick, though," Heff replied, as he and the five itty-bitty, wailing celestials vanished from the room.

Freyja walked to Morna, placed her hand on her shoulder, and looked directly into her eyes, studying her for a minute. "You OK, nugget?"

"Yeah, I'm fine," Morna answered flatly, turning to go.

She had not forgiven her hosts yet and didn't feel like getting into it.

"Why didn't you tell us you could do something like that with the spoons?" Freyja asked as Morna walked away.

"What thing with the spoons? I didn't do anything," Morna answered, frustrated.

"Um, yeah, Sugar Bear, you did. I mean, you know you did, right?"

"I'm not your nugget or Sugar Bear, and I seriously don't know what you're talking about. I just want to be alone."

"Nope. Big nope, Monchichi. Let's hash this shit out like the ladies we are. You need to vent and not be alone. I think you've had enough time on your own in this life, and without Silla, I think you're completely lost," Freyja declared as she rounded the bar and poured a couple of shots.

Morna stood frozen, staring in utter disbelief at the balls on the chick. She braced herself against the anger boiling inside her. Going ham on a supernatural being was way out of her depth, but here she stood, getting ready to do it again anyway.

"No shit, Sherlock!" Morna spewed her rage at the legendary immortal capable of ending her existence in the time it took to microwave a Pop-Tart. "And it's your fault she isn't here. You forced this on her too fast. What if she doesn't come back from this? What if I've lost her? Fuck your girl time, Freyja. Shots and chit-chat aren't going to fix what's wrong with this situation. My best friend went up in flames like a goddamned plate of saganaki, and since then, I don't know where or how she is. So, I'm going to need you to go ahead and fuck right the fuck off!"

Morna marched behind the bar, past Freyja, and grabbed one of the shots, slamming it before picking up another and slamming it, too.

"I think I'll drink by myself tonight, Sweetums," Morna said, sugary sweet as she grabbed a bottle of wine and marched around the gaped-mouth goddess. She gave her a sturdy shoulder check as she went.

"Keep this shit up, mortal, and you'll be drinking that wine through your asshole," Freyja shot off in stern warning. Morna kept walking, flipping the goddess the bird as she disappeared around the corner.

She cleared the corner, escaping Freyja's ire, and leaned back hard into the cave wall. Her heart pounded as she swallowed huge gulps of air and tried to settle herself. She'd never been confrontational and hated when she was cornered into it. She wished people didn't push her so goddamn hard. She always did her best to never force her agenda onto others so they didn't have to feel the way she did at that moment. The conundrum followed her all her life. It was an empath thing, she guessed. There was always a little voice inside her that said, "If you don't stand up for yourself, you won't be able to live with it".

When she could finally breathe again, Morna sat the bottle of wine down on the rocky floor and did what she always did after being forced to tell someone to go fuck themselves. She ghosted, hard.

Around the corner into the main chamber, Morna saw it was empty. She crossed the vast space to the enormous, wooden sliding doors she'd entered two nights before. With her hand on one of the giant circular handles, she gave it a good yank, but it did not budge.

"Fucksticks!" Morna cursed. She placed her hand against the same glowing screened panel she had seen Creak use, and just like that, several clicks engaged as the gothic, wooden monstrosities began to part. "Well, that was way too easy,"

Past the doors, Morna made her way back through the same tunnels from thirty-six hours before. She didn't make it more than three feet before the clicks and grinding gears alerted her the doors were shut behind her. When she turned, she could have sworn the crystal-tipped tail of a Grinx disappeared behind the back of the jewel-toned sofa off the entryway to the main chamber of HQ.

"I couldn't give two shits if you opened those doors for me, Creak!" she yelled through the closing doors. "Do NOT follow me!"

Morna braced herself against the adrenaline racking her body, preparing for another fight she didn't want to have. When the final lock slid home, it echoed the finality of Creak's wordless retort off the surrounding cave walls. In the deafening silence, Morna found herself completely alone in a world that no longer made sense.

THIRTEEN

WOKE

The crackling fire warmed Creak as he lay peacefully on the velvet sofa wrapped up in his diaphanous wings like a snuggly throw. On the table next to him sat a half-drained pitcher of margaritas, complete with a giant, neon-colored bendy straw extending near his enormous maw. He turned his head to take another sip when Cradle manifested before him.

"What in the ten dimensions were you thinking? Just letting her leave like that?"

Cradle towered over Creak, his visceral fury seeped into the atmosphere creating a low-level smog that loomed heavy over the time-worn floors. Creak shimmied himself further into the soft, burgundy cushions.

Never opening his eyes, the tranquil Grinx said, "She's gotta want to be here, Cradle. The whole, 'you can lead a horse to water, but you can't make her drink' thang."

"You've made a huge mistake," Cradle seethed, the muscle in his jaw working and jumping at his tamped rage.

"You're wrong. You'll have to trust me on this one, my fine feathered friend." Creak continued, eyes still closed. "She'll come back because Silla is here, doubly so when she has time away to think and realize she can't go back to how things used to be. Morna will come back all on her own and better for it. She'll be woke, dude! You can thank me after my siesta."

Creak finished as an oversized sombrero summoned out of thin air came to rest over his cheerful face.

"Woke? That's your take on this? She'll be woke? She'll be dead, you Confucius-channeling piece of useless garden statuary!"

The giant sombrero went up in a gulf of flames. The Grinx skittered to his feet, batting at the flaming pieces of straw as soot littered the air.

"Get up! Get everyone the fuck up! We have to find Morna, NOW!" Cradle ordered and marched toward the command center of HQ, his smoky wings leaving a billowing trail of smog in his wake.

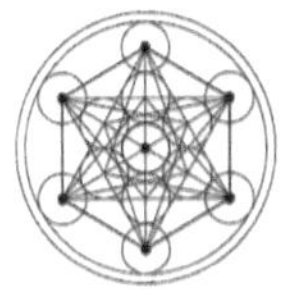

FOURTEEN

WRATH TO WRECKED

Morna made her way down the rope ladder and through the tunnels blindly. There were no magical beasties with her this time to conjure lights on a whim. When she finally made her way to the gates below the Lemp Mansion, she was wrecked. She was cold, hungry, and tired of the endless darkness weighing on her senses. She shook, pulled, and banged on the gate that Brick had locked what seemed like a lifetime ago, but it was no good.

"When I get my hands on you—o son, you're going to regret the day your momma brought you into this world," Morna vowed to the absentee prick that sealed them in.

Morna stood in the darkness, chastising herself for marching out without thinking. She acted so impulsively that her dumb ass didn't even think to grab a flashlight, backpack, or even a bottle of water for that matter.

"I could use that bottle of wine right about now. Probably would have forgotten the opener anyway. God, I'm an idiot," she said to no one, looking around in the darkness to plot her next move when the door to the pantry beyond the gate clicked open, blinding her with light.

"Brick!" Morna yelled at the figure on the other side of the gate. "I could fucking kill you, but right now, I've never been so happy to see anyone in my entire life."

"It's me, Morna. Jeff. Brick is currently unavailable to rescue you. He's far too busy trying to locate all his teeth," Jeff replied as he closed the short distance between them.

"Jeff?" Morna questioned as Jeff made his way down the stairs. "But, how?" She dropped the forearm shading her eyes as Jeff Prince's visage slowly appeared before her.

Jeff pulled out a gigantic set of keys and unlocked the gate as he answered, "I was leaving the Lemp late a couple of nights ago. I picked up a shift there to help wait on a large wedding party. Anyway, when I left, I saw you and Silla headed back behind the building, so I followed."

"You followed us? Jesus, Jeff. Stalky much?"

Jeff pulled hard on the gate, freeing her from the dark, cavernous jail.

"Ungrateful much?"

Morna's face went from wrath to wrecked in seconds. She hung her head and slowly walked into Jeff. Raising to her tiptoes, she stretched her arms upward and wrapped her hands around his neck as she buried her weary head in his chest.

Jeff bowed a bit to help Morna settle herself against him and waited. After a few minutes, Morna pulled her head back to look at her unlikely savior.

"Let's get the fuck outta here."

"Seconded," Jeff concurred, leading them toward the stairs to the world above.

Morna settled herself into Jeff's late-model, powder-blue Bronco and waited for him to start the engine when exhaustion washed over her like a slow tidal wave. She slumped against the passenger door and rested her cheek on the cool window, letting out a steady exhale as if she had been holding her breath for days.

The clear, chilled glass fogged over from her heated breath, muting the reflections of the bright streetlights above, and transforming the outside world into a medley of starbursts and shadows. Morna swiped her fingertips through the wet glaze, creating a dissonance of perceptions that resonated right down to her soul as her lashes drifted slowly closed.

"Wake up, Morna, we're here," Jeff said, giving Morna's shoulder a light squeeze.

"Hmmm? What? Where?" Morna awoke confused. Sitting up quickly, she wiped drool from the corner of her mouth and looked around for her bearings. "Where are we? What time is it?"

"It's 3:45 a.m., and we're at my apartment. I figured you might want something to eat. I don't know what you have at your place, and I knew you wouldn't want to go to a restaurant. I have bacon and coffee upstairs."

Morna could think of no reason to object. She was starving and had no food at her place. She always ate at work.

"Coffee and bacon sound great," she said, lifting the handle on the car door.

When they got upstairs, Jeff turned on a few lights to reveal the layout of his second-story flat. The stucco walls were painted in standard apartment white, and, like every traditional St. Louis flat, the hardwood floors were oak, and the ceilings were high. It was a small place, and Jeff seemed to take up too much room in it.

Morna leaned her butt against the back of his blue sofa and watched him walk to the small kitchen. Without saying a word, Jeff opened cabinet doors and gathered items to make breakfast. He looked so big in the tiny kitchen, and Morna thought to herself it was odd how gracefully he moved within the confines of the small space.

"If you want to grab a shower while I'm getting this all together, feel free," Jeff said as he pulled a carton of eggs from the fridge.

Morna didn't answer, just rocked herself off her perch, and headed down the short hallway to the bathroom.

It was a typical St. Louis bathroom. The floor was covered in tiny black-and-white octagon tiles, while the walls were tiled in peachy, flamingo-colored squares. It was hideous, but also brought a sense of familiarity that calmed her.

So much had changed, Morna thought to herself.

Nothing would ever be the same again.

"Except maybe for this God-awful bathroom," she said out loud in a fit of hysterical laughter. "I'm mental." She considered her psychological state for a millisecond and followed it up with, "Deservedly so," and turned on the white porcelain handles in the shower.

Morna thought of nothing as she stood in the hot spray. She was completely lost in the feel of the water, the emptiness of her thoughts, when a soft knock on the bathroom door pulled her back to reality.

"Yes?" Morna asked, snapping out of her catatonic state.

"I'm going to crack the door a bit and toss in one of my sweat-shirts. There's also a pair of my old girlfriend's pajama bottoms. Coffee's ready when you are. Take your time."

"OK, thanks," Morna replied, grateful for the clean clothes, but even more so for Jeff's unobtrusive manner while she mucked her way through this biblically purported, cluster-fuck of a goat rodeo.

Morna ran a brush through her tangled, wet hair, pleasantly surprised by the lingering smell of Jeff's shampoo. She put on the well-worn sweatshirt. It engulfed her so entirely that she felt ridiculous putting on the bottoms too, but it was a gentlemanly gesture on Jeff's part. She threw them on and padded out into the kitchen.

She found Jeff at a little breakfast table, doing yet another crossword. Like the perfect host he was, he folded his paper and slid it to the side, discarding his own entertainment to attend to his guest.

"There's bacon in the oven on warm, and I set out a mug for you by the coffee. There are also some leftover croissants from yesterday on the counter."

Morna looked around the kitchen to acclimate herself and found it spotless. She could smell the aroma of coffee and bacon everywhere, but there was no sign anyone recently cooked anything. His kitchen reflected the perfectly groomed and efficient server persona Jeff wore at work. Morna always thought he was acting a little when he was working, but from the looks of the perfectly tidy kitchen, he wasn't.

Morna helped herself to some fabulous-smelling dark-roast coffee from the French press on the counter. There was a tiny pitcher of cream and a restaurant-style container full of little sweetener packets and sugar; there were even three different syrup flavors. Three! Floored by all the coffee accouterments, she doctored her coffee to her liking, moaning at the first sip of hazelnutty goodness. Jeff had left an empty plate for her on the counter, and she quickly grabbed things to fill it with.

She snatched a few slices of bacon from the oven, throwing one in her mouth, and selecting a banana from a bowl brimming with fresh fruit. Morna pulled a blue, cloth napkin from a basket to find three giant croissants somehow still warm. She inhaled the scent, realizing she couldn't remember the last time she ate. She helped herself to two, smearing them with little pats of butter from a nearby glass serving dish complete with a petite, silver butter knife created solely for butter-spreading purposes. Moving around Jeff's display of adult breakfast, Morna felt like a child who had no idea what the fuck she was doing. Breakfast at her house consisted of Diet Coke and a Kind bar. How was she going to help right the balance of good and evil when a bowl of fresh fruit impressed her?

"You OK?" Jeff inquired, snapping Morna from her self-deprecation.

"Yeah, I'm good. Just tired and hungry, I think."

Morna lied as she gathered her breakfast and joined Jeff at the table.

"I've got just the thing." Jeff walked to the fridge, returning with a bottle of Bailey's Irish Cream. "Little dab will do ya," he said and poured a dram directly into Morna's coffee before following suit with his own.

He was an oxymoron. It was the casual gestures and sayings that didn't jive with the formal persona he wore and that rattled her a bit. Morna couldn't reconcile the two. But that was her problem, she guessed, not his.

"Thanks for all this, Jeff."

"Happy to do it."

They sat in silence, drinking their coffee for a few minutes while Morna popped a chunk of the buttery croissant into her mouth. Jeff seemed at ease with the whole situation, and Morna thought it odd.

Why wasn't he asking her questions about, well, everything? "Don't you want to know why I was in the caves?" Morna finally asked, breaking the silence.

"I figured you'd tell me when you were ready. I'm just glad I was in a position to help when you needed it."

Morna was transfixed by his response. She looked across the table and considered him for a long minute. His posture was straight and true, his demeanor constant and calm. He was a grown-ass man, and Morna suddenly had a feeling he'd been playing the long game.

"Are you studying me, Morna?" Jeff asked, amused.

"Yeah, I guess I am," she answered, chuckling a bit to herself with embarrassment.

It was all so casual. Morna found the whole domestic breakfast moment surreal in the wake of the shit parade that had recently become her life.

"Learn anything?"

Damn, there was the surprising, casual nature creeping in again. It made him so…accessible.

"Yeah, I guess you're a handy guy to have around when locked in a subterranean dungeon."

Morna immediately berated herself for taking the low road out of a too-personal moment. Amusement settled on Jeff's face as his eyebrows rose over his thick glasses.

"I don't think that's what you gleaned from the once over, Morn," Jeff replied, never breaking eye contact.

"I guess not. I was just thinking, as well as I know you, I'm getting the feeling I don't know you at all."

"What makes you say that?" Jeff asked, amusement still lingering on his face.

"Well, you've always been this nice guy I know from the neighborhood who I kill time with at work. We've never really hung out together outside of that, and here I am, 4:45 in the morning, wearing your sweatshirt, and drinking Irish coffee like it's a normal thing for us to do," Morna answered. "It's not a normal thing for me to do with anyone."

She hadn't wanted to add that bit there at the end. It made her feel exposed. Morna had always been a solitary person, except with Silla. Of course, she'd been with men before, but never in any capacity where they saw her as raw as this. It was always more of a mutual, physical satisfaction, and off she went. This unexpected level of intimacy with Jeff left her feeling somewhat addled.

"Nice guy from work. Well, that's fair," Jeff said, unperturbed. "Did you ever consider I was more than that, or is that something you're just now getting to?"

Morna felt a shift in the mood of the conversation.

Yep, long game, she thought to herself.

With her chair pushed back from the table, Morna walked to the kitchen, poured another cup of coffee for herself, and bought more time to think.

"Would you like another cup?" Morna asked, falling back on her server role as a crutch.

A long pause filled the space between them.

"No, I'm good," came from behind, just above her ear.

"Jeff," Morna said, more of a statement than a name.

"Morna," Jeff responded with a perfectly mirrored inflection.

Jeff's hands came to rest on Morna's shoulders, settling softly as she stood stock still. Morna didn't know how she felt or what to think at the unexpected touch.

Jeff leaned down, whispering in her ear, "Did you ever consider I'm more than that?"

Heat.

Morna's whole body was hit by an unexpected wave of it. Closer, Jeff's lips hovered above the sensitive nook where neck met nape.

"I'm waiting, Morna."

Jeff breathed a warm, hot breath, kicking off a daisy chain of depth charges that buckled her knees.

Ignition.

An abrupt blast of want blazed through her, leaving her unable to think, do, or move.

When Jeff's lips finally closed in, he said very clearly. "I'm going to need you to say yes Morna. Say you want this."

She couldn't think. Didn't want to.

"Yes."

Jeff's mouth closed over Morna's heated skin as his hands gripped 'round her waist from behind.

"Jesus." Morna breathed as her body lined up perfectly with the man standing firmly behind her; their breaths, shallow and heavy, weighted the air.

Slow and tentative, like weaving a spell. Jeff's arm crept around Morna's stomach and settled there before biting the tip of her ear as his hands traveled to her hips. The strength of his hold over her increased with every touch. Her head tilted to the side, neck lolling back as her eyes drifted up, lingering for a long moment on a tarnished silver key dangling alluringly from a worn leather cord around Jeff's neck.

Mystified.

It was so beautiful, so spellbinding, she had to touch it.

Forgetting about the man, Morna's gaze dwelled on, and solely on, the silver relic. Morna's hand traveled with purpose toward the key as Jeff's hand circled hard and fast around her wrist, squeezing tight. It didn't matter. He could break her wrist for all she cared. Morna vowed the key would be hers as Jeff's fingers pressed firm under her chin, guiding her reluctant gaze away from the trinket, forcing her eyes to lock on his.

Hunger.

Morna was looking into the eyes of hunger and its effects were staggering. Not caring how she got here or how she'd get out, Morna knew one thing. She wasn't leaving without that key.

Increasing his grip on Morna's hips, Jeff effortlessly lifted her onto the countertop.

God he was strong, she thought absently as he placed one hand on each of her knees and spread them apart while Morna sat transfixed over the dangling key.

Want burned through her veins, the key begging for her touch.

Seduction.

The closer she got to Jeff, the easier it would be to lift the key. She could play the befuddled, naive paramour for as long as it took. If a cheap roll in the hay had her leaving with that key, it was a price well paid.

Jeff looked at Morna, then, all business-like, removed his glasses and set them carefully on the top of the fridge. Within the space he'd created for himself between her legs, Jeff placed his hands on either side of her face and bent down, pulling her close.

Like magic, Morna willingly turned to putty in his hands.

His mouth parted and the space between them narrowed until his lips were on hers, ebb and flow—give, take, give, take, she mirrored every move. He moved, she moved, where his hands traveled, her hands traveled. Down, over, around, and back, laying kindling over every surface, purposely sweeping her hands closer and closer to Jeff's necklace with every labored breath.

Enraptured.

Morna used the cadence of every touch, sweep, and brush of skin to whip Jeff into a frenzy as the call of the key spiraled her further.

It was going to be hers. It was meant to be hers. She kissed her way slowly up his chest, closer to her prize, the here and now ceded to an oily blaze of heat. An apparition. A prison orrery spinning before her eyes, heliocentric, and at the speed of light around and through her. Planets and gears, galaxies and stars, redshifts, and comets, whipped her round the miniature omniverse in a surreal and dizzying tailspin.

Golden and grinding, the apparatus labored in electromagnetic waves, gnashing its metal teeth as they ground closer, snatching at the frayed threads of her soul, and folding them in one by one. Morna unraveled at the speed of light.

Riotous and hot, meteors of golden pain came in showers, burning oily and slick as she was twisted through the milling gears, the golden shower of meteors punching vacuous, massless holes through what was left of her soul.

Gilded, fragmented, vacuous, and lost.

The words looped across the emptiness of her trappings as a door slammed tight, and a key slid home, locking her away on the other side… lost. That's what she was now.

All she would ever be.

FIFTEEN

HALO, IT'S ME

Cradle was at the highest climb of the spiral staircase accessing HQ's overhead library as Creak, Freyja, and Hephaestus hauled ass into the room, loaded for war. The celestial militia was all business as they reported for Cradle's call of duty, stopping dead in their tracks when they encountered the ominous shadow laying waste to every lumen of light in the room.

"Oh shit," escaped a broken breath from Heff's lips.

The word eddied in an ethereal elocution not heard since Moses went mountain climbing.

Fifteen feet tall and crystalline in the darkest way imaginable, Cradle's presence reminded each soul he was more than a lonely child's plaything.

His halo, a six-pointed star interwoven with thirteen small circles and cross-sectioned with a rectangle rotating both counter and clockwise around and through him. Seven primitive stars pulsated at the speed of light from opposite directions through the oil-slick luminescence of the halo's geometric canals. From opposite poles, the stars accelerated within the halo's labyrinth, rocketing like bats out of hell into Cradle's empty, nebulin core, exploding in a blaze of primordial light before being snuffed out by the dark matter of Cradle's very essence. The process was infinite. After every explosion, the stars regenerated within Cradle's crown of light. Infinitely dense, infinitely hot, and growing exponentially with every explosive blaze. Cradle stood above them all. The highest of all Scribe Angels and the unheralded Governor of Relativity.

"Morna Stahr is in the hands of an enemy unknown to you," Cradle began every nebulous word frosting the room in a thin, golden layer of billowy stardust.

"His name is Tomas De Torquemada, alias Jeff Prince. He is a Rogue and, hands down, the biggest threat to existence we have ever encountered. Torquemada is in the business of siphoning energies unto himself, and in the last few years, has manufactured an army to help him do just that. Without the balance keepers on Satera, there's been no one to notice a bit of missing energy here and there. Over the last hundred years, Tomas has amassed more than enough to make him a threat across the board.

He's now in the market for a piece of dimensional real estate to solidify his place amongst the big guns, and Torquemada's got his eye on purgatory. We don't know how, but he's discovered Morna is truly universal, housing energies from both heaven and hell. Somehow, Tomas believes she's the perfect tool to help him secure dimension bit 9.333 in a hostile takeover. It would place Tomas de Torquemada's base of operations in a very exalted zip code. If he succeeds, Torquemada will have added a third power structure in a war built for two, stolen our most precious weapon, and all of humanity's limbo'd souls with it."

A three-dimensional map of the city materialized, hovering well over the heads of the troops below while cutting the darkness preying down upon them like the brightest of constellations in the night sky.

"Get her. NOW," ordered the Governor of Relativity.

The dome overhead protested with a slight heave, giving way with an otherworldly breath, and withdrawing from being as Cradle opened his nebulin wings with one powerful thrust and disappeared deep into the night sky, leaving nothing but a trail of billowing stardust in his wake.

"Da fuq was that?" Freyja asked, awestruck at Cradle's crazy change in appearance.

"I'm not entirely sure, but he would have been a hell of a lot more menacing if he hadn't sounded like he was hocking Ram, heavy-duty trucks," Creak shot back as he darted off over the bridge toward the command center.

"I'll debrief you on that particular episode of MythBusters fist and twist after we secure the package," Heff answered, looking like he'd just seen a ghost. He hefted his pack of freshly forged weapons onto his god-like shoulders and ordered, "Autobots, roll out!" just before he and Freyja evanesced to ground zero.

Creak raced over the oriental bridge as a circle-shaped platform loaded with four racks of servers rose from a subfloor beneath. The gunshot, cash register fusion of M.I.A.'s "Paper Planes" blared from seemingly everywhere in the cavernous room as Creak hopped onto the technological dais. He seated himself at the centermost point, dead center from every single rack.

"Namaste, motherfucker," Creak growled softly as he turned his consciousness inward.

Creak glowed a soft purple below his craggy, blue-black surface. The eerie essentia oozed out of him until he was fully awash in it.

"All I wanna do is—," he began to sing along with Maya as four lilac-colored prisms shot out of his bizarre visage. "Boom, boom, boom, boom," he sing-songed as each prism fired one after the other across the dais floor with laser-like precision straight into each rack of tech. North, South, East, and West, all four radii pulsed with the traffic of the information superhighway, which

Creak funneled through himself like the sentient supercomputer he was. The Grinx sang on, absently teeter-tottering his monstrous black head with the thumping bass line as he effortlessly hacked himself an all-access backstage pass into cyberspace.

Heff and Freyja landed in perfect synchronicity on the roof of the fourplex as Creak's voice confirmed in their headsets they were in the right place.

"Well, lookie there. The dingleberry left his laptop open. Dumbass," Creak said as his voice came over their headsets.

"Ready for a game of eye-spy whenever you are, Sly. Humble Phi, over," Freyja said, confirming they were a go for intel.

Creak insisted on the code names when using the headsets. They didn't need any of it, but tech made Creak happy, and a happy Creak was in everyone's best interest. So, as a group, they agreed to give in on the little shit that didn't matter to them but seemed to matter to Creak.

"Copy that, Humble Phi. I see our package on the kitchen floor. She's fucked up, guys. I can't tell visually if she's wounded. Let me do a body scan and see what we're dealing with," Creak relayed what he saw through the hijacked eye of Tomas de Torquemada's, aka Jeff Prince's, webcam.

"Copy that, Sly. Where's Waldo?" asked Heff.

"No eyes on Waldo. The package scan is reading critical. I'm getting all kinds of organ system failures. We gotta move on this. Let's see if this asshat wanna-be is dumb enough to have his phone on him. Yep, he's that fucking stupid. We got a twenty. He's in the bedroom, but he's on the move. Eyes on Waldo. He just leaned down and checked Morna's pulse, and he looked super pissed. What's wrong, cum stain, things not going your way?"

"Copy that. Lock on Waldo. Permission to proceed?" Heff asked.

"Negatory, Hammertime. Hold your position for an energy scan."

"Copy that, Sly. Standing by," Heff confirmed.

"Energy scanning Waldo. And… we have a match. Waldo is Tomas de Torquemada in a Jeff Prince suit and is, coincidentally, a loose soul. Repeat, Waldo is a loose soul. Not only is he walking around in Soulard's friendliest bartender's body, but his soul has somehow managed to have never been assigned a dimension. Since he died in 1498, wherever he has been, he's had a lot of time to plan out whatever the hell is going down."

"Copy that, Sly. Body-jacker? Confirm?" Freyja asked.

"Copy that, Humble Phi. That's a big ten-four with super-sized fries. Fenced energy is pouring off Waldo's hijacked corpse."

"Copy that, Sly. Body-jacker eight-balling on ganked energy. Go, no-go? Confirm. Hammertime, over."

"Copy that, Hammertime. No-go. This dead tweaker's amped on a solid kilo of the big E. Where he got that kind of juice is another mystery we need to solve. If this gets out, we are gonna be surrounded by reverse necromancers jumping into bodies without so much as a seance. Stand by," Creak answered.

"Confirm, Sly. Standing by for Go, no-go," Heff said.

Several minutes went by in radio silence when an impatient Freyja said into her headset, "Sly, what's a bitch gotta do to get a go around here?"

"Shut your Phi hole, Humble. Over," was all Creak said, followed by several more minutes of dead air.

Heff and Freyja took their no-go orders like any perfect soldier would. They walked sentry over the fourplex roof while being equally pissed off and hyper-alert. Freyja motioned Heff over to the east end of the roof the second she saw Jeff Prince walk out empty-handed. Creak broke radio silence in their headsets.

"You're good to go. Waldo fled the scene. Cradle's got his twenty, and the package is still on the kitchen floor. Move out. Over."

"Hammertime and Humble Phi moving out. Over," Heff confirmed.

There wasn't a single bout with fisticuffs, no lengthy chase scene, not even so much as one line from a diabolical bad guy's shitty plot reveal. The rescue was super anticlimactic until they came upon Morna's wasting body, then shit got pretty climactic, fast.

"Jesus," was all Heff said, invoking his best friend's name the second he saw the monstrosity that was once the oddly beautiful and uniquely vibrant Morna Stahr. Frozen by the wraith-like wreckage before him, the unshakable Hephaestus of Olympus stood silently by as Freyja, the Mother of All, gently scooped the diseased mortal into her fostering arms and cradled her close before evanescing them all to HQ.

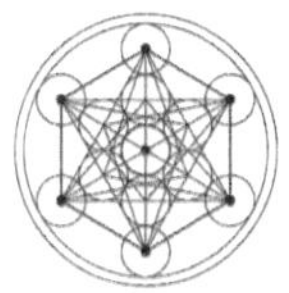

SIXTEEN

OWL FRICASSEE

"Oh shit," was all Creak said when Morna's body was laid upon her bed of blue and silver.

It lay waxy and pale, the whole of her twisted and frozen in pain.

"I've never seen anything like this before. She doesn't appear sick. It's like... like she's tainted somehow. Does anybody know what I'm saying?" Freyja asked, fiddling furiously with her necklace.

"Yeah. Like she's not even supposed to be here, shouldn't be here. Like her whole being is out of whack with the natural world. It's sorta giving me the skeeves," Creak confessed reluctantly.

"My skin crawls when I look at her," Freyja admitted, rubbing her arms.

"She can't go on like this. We have to figure out what the hell is going on. I'm going to do some research and maybe make a few calls. Standing around staring at her is not gonna get us anywhere, and from the looks of her, we don't have much time," Heff said on his way out the door, bumping into Silla outside Morna's bed chamber.

"Sorry about that," Heff said apologetically as he steadied Silla's shoulders. "That would have knocked most mortals on their ass."

"I don't think I fall under that category anymore," Silla answered confidently.

"I think you're right." Heff agreed with a wink, adding, "Looks like you're feeling better."

"Better is an understatement. That was quite a ride, but I feel better than I ever have, invincible even."

"Glad to hear it. Keep in mind, you are not invincible, Silla. None of us are. Also, there is something I need to tell you. Some pretty big shit went down while you were recuperating, and I just want to give you a heads-up."

"Shoot," Silla said, more confident than she'd ever been, as if there were nothing she couldn't handle now.

"There's a situation with Morna. It's pretty serious."

"Cut to the chase, Muscles."

He had her full attention now. Her shoulders drew back as her body straightened to its full height, her eyes sharply on his. He needed to be careful in this. Morna's well-being was a trigger for Silla, and with her new abilities so raw, telling her this was going to be like navigating a fucking minefield. A second helping of unhinged owl fricassee was the last thing anyone needed on their plates right now.

"Out with it!"

Silla's eyes flashed bits of orange and red as she burned, considering what may be wrong with her best friend.

"Cool it, Silla. I mean it, or I'm not telling you a goddamn thing," Heff ordered.

"What's cooking, good-looking?" Creak's smart-ass hyperbole had Silla turning her fiery eyes on him as he made his way up the hall.

"K..." said Creak slowly when he became the sole focus of

Silla's ire. "I thought I sensed a temperature spike out here. You feeling OK, Sil?"

Silla didn't answer. She rotated her head back toward Heff without turning her body this time. It was a super chill, owl-like thing to do. On a human, it was real-life exorcist shit, and it was disturbing as hell.

Heff looked to Creak in a, what the fuck are we supposed to do now, sort of way. One wrong move and Silla was going to go up in flames. In the small hall-like tunnel they all stood in, a backdraft would blow through HQ, devouring everything in its path. Which, while creating an unholy mess, would be survivable for the immortals. Morna, on the other hand, would undoubtedly perish in the flames.

"Ain't this a quantifiable, quixotic, quagmire of fuckery? What to do, what to do?" Creak clicked his tongue against the back of his jagged teeth, thinking. "Oh, got it! Freezer, Heff. Now!!!" Creak yelled as flames licked at Silla's feet.

Heff snapped his fingers, and just like that, the three found themselves inside a spacious walk-in freezer somewhere in the bowels of the Cherokee caves.

The temperature change on Silla's overheated body was so drastic the sub-zero freezer filled with an arctic fog as crystal lattice crept across Silla's rapidly cooling skin, coating her from head to toe.

Silla didn't skip a beat.

"What the hell is going on with Morna?"

"Chic is tenacious!" Creak said, grabbing a bottle of Goldschlager from one of the shelves with his jagged maw. "Resilient, too," he mumbled over the neck of the bottle, giving a light toss of his monstrous head, and launching the sparkly booze in Heff's direction. "It'll cool her off on the inside, too."

Heff handed the frosty bottle over to an even frostier Silla. A few of the ice crystals at the bend of her elbow shattered and floated delicately to the floor. She grabbed for the bottle and chugged down half its contents.

"I'm cool," she said on a cinnamon-flavored exhale of steam while corking the bottle. "Now, what's up?" she demanded, tossing the half-drained bottle back over to Heff.

Heff considered her and decided it was safe to answer when the twinkly, gold flecks suspended in the syrupy liquor caught his eye.

"I gotta run!" Already gone, Heff's voice echoed off the freezer walls, leaving Creak alone with Silla to explain the unexplainable.

SEVENTEEN

CRISS CROSS APPLESAUCE

Heff popped into the nursery of his and Freyja's temporary home, located beyond the sparring room of the caves. He needed to talk to Freyja stat, but what he saw in the nursery stopped him in his tracks and warmed his ancient heart to the point it almost hurt.

Shaped oddly like a star, the cavernous playroom was lined floor-to-ceiling with inlaid shelves stuffed with all manner of childlike things. From books and toys to aquariums and cages, the room was filled with varying habitats and accessories required to harbor their litter's earthly pets. Five delicate creatures would hopefully one day grow to be their children's best friends and familiars. If, and that was a big if, they could keep the kids from accidentally killing them first. It was a double-edged sword to keep the creatures near the children for the tender bonds of the familiar could form while barring their kids from loving their little critters to death with supernatural, herculean hugs strong enough to strangle a full-grown mountain lion.

It was just last night, after Freyja came back from squaring away Morna and Silla, she decided it was safest for the delicate constitutions of her children's familiars to be moved out of arm's reach. "Out of sight, out of mind," she'd said, proud of her latest idea to outsmart their brood of hellions. She performed some magic math on the mammoth inlaid shelves, resizing and reordering the whole structural layout with a quick thought. In the end, she had placed each of the giant ecosystems containing each of the very delicate familiars on the farthest ledges of the highest shelves lining the thirty-foot ceiling playroom.

Heff had just walked into the aftermath. It was Animaniacs meets Vikings with a heaping dash of Bewitched thrown in for good measure, and was the perfect recipe for a preschool revolt and petting zoo jailbreak currently in full swing.

Freyja hovered near the top of a bookshelf and caught two free-falling tots who were none too thrilled at their mother's attempt to stop them from plummeting with their recently liberated familiars at breakneck speed. The two daredevils were just beginning to wriggle free of their mother's hold when, far below, tikes number three and four backed their nanny, Hildi, into a corner with the pint-sized weapons Heff had made them for Yule.

Hildi, who was Freyja's best friend, live-in nanny, and coincidentally also her enchanted pet boar, hollered up to the frazzled, free-floating goddess, "Could I get a scooch of help down here, dear?" as rugrat number five attempted to mount and ride her into the fray.

"Crisscross applesauce!" Freyja shouted out, losing her shit.

Forced into a magical time-out, each tot suddenly sat on a star-shaped rug with their legs crossed. Each child was spaced perfectly, one tot on each point of the star. The whole brood was quiet, content, and happily sipping from golden applesauce packets. The five agent provocateurs had turned into a quinary of perfect darlings, and Freyja instantly felt like shit about it.

"Thank you, my dear. That was quite the morning, wasn't it?" Hildi asked as she tidied up the ravaged playroom. "Oh, come now, dear, are you crying? There's no need for all that hogwash, is there?" Hildi admonished the guilt-stricken Freyja as she returned the scythe, cudgel, and flamethrower to the toy bin.

Heff popped up to Freyja, gathered her in his colossal arms, and shouted down to Hildi, "Keep an eye on these little boogers while I tend to my wife," just before he and Freyja vanished.

"Oh, for fuck's sake!" Hildi swore as the temporary spell lifted in Freyja's absence, letting mob rule once again reign supreme.

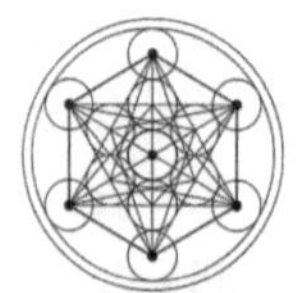

EIGHTEEN

HOW DO YOU LIKE THEM APPLES?

Back at the couple's permanent home in Sessrumnir, Hephaestus settled Freyja on his lap under the shade of her favorite apple tree in the private orchard. He held her there for longer than he should, while she let out all the stress and guilt of motherhood. He had to talk to her about his revelation, but he needed her in full-on Freyja mode to fix what he suspected was wrong with Morna.

Hephaestus placed his index finger on his wife's trembling chin and turned it upward. Her damp face was splotched red, her eyes swollen and glassy, and she was still the loveliest thing he had ever seen. This miracle of the universe, this perfectly designed warrior queen, fell to pieces whenever she fell short of some imaginary maternal golden ratio she measured herself against. An impossible feat in that a mother's love was immeasurable, but try telling her that.

"You are the perfect mother to our imperfect kids, Frey. The One himself would not fall short of using a little magical time out when faced with our litter's boundless propensity for diabolical mischief."

"But," Freya sniffed her snotty nose, "I want to be a regular mother to them. I don't want to do the monstrous things our mothers did to us. Regular moms do this shit without magical intervention all the time. Why can't I?" she asked, blowing her nose into Heff's apron.

"Because, my sweet darling, their kids aren't supernatural celestials capable of changing the nature of the world with one temper tantrum. Those lovely little terrors were entrusted to us for a reason. Nobody else can do it, woman. Even The Freyja can't if she's not fully Freyja. Be yourself, be all of her. She's powerful, good, and true, and would never hurt her kids, magic or no."

"Thanks, baby." Freyja brought the back of her delicate hand up to her runny nose and ungracefully rubbed it back and forth a few times as she sniffled. "I must look a fright," she said as her self-imposed standards of perfection recycled anew.

This tell was always a good indicator his wife was feeling better. Freyja would never not shoot for perfection; it was in her very make-up to do so. She was the original, physical embodiment of perfect proportions, and when she wore her true divine form, that golden ratio would radiate out and transpose itself mathematically onto the world around her. Her stamp of perfection was everywhere. Freya was why the whorl of a seashell could spiral to infinity, why the Mona Lisa had a secret, and why the label on a bottle of Pepsi was so damn pleasing to the eye.

Freyja kissed Heff so sweetly he forgot who and what he was, if only for a minute. When she pulled back, she was once again perfectly coiffed. There was not a hair out of place, splotches, snot, or tears to be found.

"So, what's up, chicken? I didn't expect you back at home so soon. How's Morna doing?"

"That's what I came to talk to you about. I think I have some idea of what's going on, but I'm not sure. I wanted to run something by you and see if it makes any sense, or if I'm just blowing rainbows out of my ass."

"There's a visual," Freyja said, chuckling. "Fire away, love."

"You know how you all were saying Morna looks wrong, unnatural?"

"Yeah."

"I think it's because something kicked her into angel mode."

"Nephilim don't have an angel mode, pigeon. At least, not while they're still living. I've seen a living Neph's powers kick in thousands of times, but it never turned them into an angel.

"I know what you're saying, and I agree, but hear me out. I think because Morna is so strongly linked to The One dimension, and because she's Nephilim royalty, the likes this world has never seen, the rules may not necessarily apply to her in the same way. I think the problem is existence has no idea what to do with her because there's never been a being like her before. What I'm proposing is when Morna's Neph powers kicked in, her essence did a throwback Thursday to its origins, then leveled up via the metaphysical golden ratio."

"I'm following you. What exactly is it you're suggesting Morna is then?"

"An angel born of Earth. I think Morna is a full-on angel trapped in a human body."

"And how did you come to that conclusion?"

"I was holding a bottle of Goldschlager; you know, the cinnamon-flavored liquor with the little flecks of gold in it?"

"Sure do; I love the stuff."

"Yeah, you do, kitten," Heff said happily, losing himself in the memory of the last time his wife got a hold of a bottle while the kids were having a sleepover with the aunties.

"Anyway," Heff said, shaking away the x-rated cobwebs. "I was holding the bottle of the syrupy liquor in my hand with the flecks of gold suspended in it. Then, it occurred to me that beautiful as they are, they seemed twisted, beaten, and trapped even. It's not right they are in there in the first place. I think it's the same for Morna. I think she's trapped in her human body, and if we don't get her out, or at the very least upgrade her model, she'll be consumed by it. That's when I thought of you. What if you threw a little golden ratio in Morna's direction?"

"The metaphysical golden ratio is a whole other ball game. I don't have the keys to that particular castle, schnooky lumps. I can make Morna's human body the most physically perfect version of itself, but that won't give her an ethereal body. Those things don't just grow on trees, you know."

"Well, they just might. It's a long shot, but I was thinking… what about an apple?"

"Ooooh, you've gone off the deep end now! Just went straight to it and dove right the fuck on in! Head fucking first!" Freyja roared. "You know the rules, and they aren't mine to trifle with. I'm the keeper and cultivator of those things for a reason. I know better than to go fucking around in shit I don't understand. No one knows how those things work, Heff! I'm allowed to gift one golden apple per immortal on the anniversary of their birth every hundred years. Key word being immortal. Them's the rules of the omniverse, babe."

"Then I think she'll die, and soon," Heff said sadly.

"Kiss my ass, Hephaestus!" Freyja stood and paced beneath the tree of golden apples entrusted to her and her alone. She could not remember a time she wasn't its keeper. She just always was. Freyja had no idea how she knew its rules; she just did. It was a simple cut-and-dry nine-to-five, and she was good at it. She had no idea what the tree would do if she even attempted to pick an apple from it for ill-gotten gains. She'd seen what happened when immortals, other than herself, tried to pluck one. She didn't want that for herself; she had kids to raise, damn it!

"Seriously, Freyja."

"Well, sod off! Out! Get the hell out of my orchard!" Freyja clapped back, clearly more than a little pissed.

She waved her hand in a begone manner, and poof, Heff was evicted from the premises, PDQ.

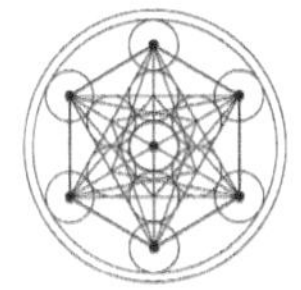

NINETEEN

FIVE FINGER DISCOUNT

Cradle was back to his standard size and sitting in a chair next to Morna's bed. The theory Heff had briefed him on two hours earlier seemed to hold water, but what if it didn't and they all ended up in the drink? Assuming they could even talk Freyja into handing over an apple, it was a serious long shot it would work on Morna the way they all hoped. No one had ever given a mortal the "food of the Gods" before, and the outcome could be direr than just Morna dying. The whole kit and caboodle they were fdoighting so desperately to right could cease to exist at all. The expansion of space and time could be thrown in reverse, and the whole damn production could collapse into nothingness. The moviephiles over at Rotten Tomatoes would have a fucking field day reviewing that particular cinematic turd. Not that a single soul would still be in existence to bitch about the ending. Further still, what if the attempt cost Freyja her immortal life, which inextricably would cost Hephaestus his? Not to mention, on the outside chance this foolhardy venture panned out, everyone lived, and the omniverse went on; what would Morna's place in it be? What in the name of the Four Horsemen would she be capable of?

"Decide anything yet?" Creak asked Cradle as he entered Morna's bedroom.

"Nope," was all he said, never taking his eyes from Morna.

Cradle rubbed the graying stubble on his cheeks with both hands. The endless worry had impossibly aged the immortal angel overnight. Cradle looked as wrecked as any parent of a terminally sick child could.

"She's got one foot in the grave, Cradle," Creak said softly.

"You think I don't know that!" Cradle thundered, standing so violently that the chair beneath him flew back into the cave wall and shattered. "I can't mess with Freyja's free will. I can't pick an apple myself. Nor can any of you! I can't make this decision about the fate of everything on my own! There isn't enough information or time to work it out."

"Ah," Creak said, "I got it now."

"Got what?"

"My friend, you are having a crisis of faith," Creak said, all Buddha on a mountaintop. "That sort of thing happens down here all the time."

"How dare you!" Cradle roared louder, marching to Creak with venom in his slate-gray eyes. "You have no clue of what you speak! Why don't you stop talking out of your craggy ass and go do something useful, like prop open a goddamn door or weigh down a stack of fucking papers, you useless, lowly, ignorant beast," Cradle seethed as he towered over the Grinx.

"Really? Project your feelings of inadequacy much? Why don't you go ahead and enlighten me then?"

"Faith has nothing to do with this, but let's assume for a singular, solitary, micro-second it does. How could I, of all beings, be accused of a lack of it? I've been sitting front-row center since opening night! I see what you can't, what mortals can't, what none of you can! I can and have seen it all! I am so intrinsically linked to the thing you accuse me of not believing that part of its blueprint has fused with my immortal soul. You know, I'm beginning to believe you might be as dumb as the fucking rock you're made of."

"Ooooh, that was a cheap shot, but Imma' let that one slide, 'cause I get it. You're having trouble understanding something, and it's probably rubbing your nerd feathers the wrong way. OK, so let's start at the peewee skill level, and I'll babystep you through Faith for Dummies. Your experiences are more like seeing is believing, not so much actual faith.

You were a scribe angel, right? The nerdiest of all angels, and your actual job was to record everything that ever happened. So, there you are, observing and recording. Watch, watch, watch, write, write, write, but you weren't ever really living. Now, here you are, sitting on the largest pile of knowledge in existence, sifting through it over and over, looking for information to help navigate your way safely through an actual, real-life shitty situation. But there are no answers in your archives, barely even a clue. Both of those things are new predicaments for you, huh? You've been tossed out of your cushy castle on high, where you watched people live their lives like it was fucking YouTube, and your ass landed in the gutter with the rest of us lowly creatures. Well, Your Highness, we ignorant gutter-dwellers figured out long ago something you desperately need a crash course in. Best pluck a quill, dork-a-dactyl, 'cause you're gonna wanna jot down this little golden nugget.

Faith means jumping in blind, cowabunga style. When we sewer rats don't have all the answers, we go with what's called a hunch or an inkling. It's the idea you know something when you have no fucking clue. Sometimes the shit works out, sometimes it doesn't, and usually it's the best any of us can do. Dude, you're Chicken Little-ing that the sky is falling, and you can't cross the road to get the hell outta the way without map-questing the best route first. If you wait for that bitch-ass app to load, Cathy, Lena, Bill, and Steve will barrel up here on their fateful nags, going seven kinds of four horsemen on mankind before you enter your starting location."

"Well, as much as I'd love to see Cathy again," Freyja said from the doorway. "I think it best we leave those four stable geniuses be, at least for another epoch or two."

"Heya, Freyja," Creak said from the awkward face-down spinal lock position Cradle had just wrestled him into.

"Hi, Creak. Is that the Boston Crab?" Freyja asked, curious as she tilted her head sideways to inspect the move.

"Reversh Boshton Crav, I fink," came a muffled answer from Creak's maw as Cradle pressed the Grinx's face further into the unforgiving cave floor.

"Nice. I would've gone with the inverted myself, but that's more of a personal choice, I think. They both do work beautifully."

"I'm happy with the results," Cradle said as he cranked up the pressure on Creak's stony bones.

"What'd I miss?" Heff asked as he saddled up behind his wife.

"Just two assholes, playing American Wrestling Federation while the world burns," Freyja answered, never taking her eyes off the assholes in question as she leaned back into her man.

"Greco-Roman. Now, that's real wrestling," Heff added his two cents, wrapping his arms around Freya's waist while he watched Cradle soar to the ceiling, preparing to deliver an ethereal pile driver to his newly self-appointed life coach.

Freyja snapped her fingers, and a golden rectangular cage appeared over Creak, encasing and protecting the Grinx just as Cradle was about to barrel in. The angel smashed so fast and hard into the magically reinforced bars that all you heard was a sickening thud.

"Frrrehayar!" Cradle mumble-yelled.

"I call that one The Fallen Angel," Freyja whispered conspiratorially to Heff, who in turn held up one of his giant mitts for a fiver she happily returned on the down low.

"Sorry I yelled at you, baby," she said on a sidebar as she kissed her favorite dent in Heff's bicep.

"Mmmumphph!"

"Oh, quit your bitching, you big baby," Freyja said to the still-impaled, moaning angel. "You'll be fine in a minute. Morna on the other hand..."

Heff turned his attention to Morna's bed. She lay twisted in pools of leaden sweat and blood, disfigured beyond any human recognition.

A disgusting, suctioning sound echoed off the walls as Cradle pried himself off the golden bars. "Is she still with us?" he asked as his form replenished entirely.

In one breath, he was seamless perfection; even the newly earned gray stubble had been erased.

"For the moment," Freyja said.

The cage over Creak disappeared as Freyja and the others walked toward Morna, leaving him free to move if he could unknot himself. Attempting to stroke his tattered chi, Creak chanted his favorite yogi's mantra. "The yoga pose you avoid most," he breathed out as he dislocated his shoulder, "is the one you need the most," he breathed in, dislocating two more key joints as he expertly executed the little-known and highly controversial Bavarian Retrograde Maneuver. "Awesome," he said to himself, cracking his thick neck while simultaneously popping his joints back in place.

Freshly realigned, Creak padded up to the threesome gathered at Morna's bedside. "What's it going to be, kids?"

"Faith," Freyja said resolutely as golden bits of mathematical magic floating in the air around her. Little snippets, hints almost, of gold-illuminated equations and theories would flash, twist, and then burn away in the atmosphere as Freyja transformed.

If a person could reach past the constraints of their mind to coalesce visually the splendor of the Sistine Chapel's ceiling with the mathematical miracles behind the pyramids of Giza, add some essence of angel, and then sprinkle the whole damn thing with numerical pixie dust, they might come close to understanding the surreal construct and fabric that was Freyja's true physical form. It was almost too much to take in, even for preternatural folk, and why she didn't dress to the nines most of the time. Well, that and the fact it royally screwed up every piece of abstract art she happened by, which by no coincidence of fate was her very favorite kind.

In turn, Freyja took one last look at each creature in the room. First Creak, then Cradle, then one last look at Heff. Only then did she look down upon the woman they all hung their hopes on. Freyja turned her consciousness inward and summoned all the good intentions behind the crime she was about to commit, converted those feelings into a string of vibrations, and released them with quantum force into the omniverse, hoping they traveled quickly to the only being in existence who could commute the sentence she knew was coming.

Satisfied, she'd tidied up any loose ends, she proceeded to execute the most exquisite maneuver The Ten Dimensions had ever known, and impossibly reached her perfect little hand into the folds of space and time.

The room was in utter silence but for the thrumming of Freyja's energies at work. Not a single soul dared breathe as Freyja stood perfectly still, waiting for the scales of Justice to catch her with her hand in the proverbial cookie jar. The goddess gave one last thought for her beautiful children, then, with an elegant twist of her wrist, plucked a piece of forbidden fruit from an entirely different space in time.

Her hand, still deep in its folds, caused the continuum to ripple and swell with the force of the broken natural laws. Freyja snatched her hand back faster than the laws of physics should allow, clearing the fold as it rippled out and slammed tight, attempting to cuff her where she stood.

Sensing the shift, Cradle leveled up at the speed of light, throwing his upgraded form over Morna's body as the rift snapped shut, releasing a subatomic boom that blew through the room, leveling everything in its path.

TWENTY

DEODAMNATUS

Pierced by shrapnel and embedded into the cave walls, Freyja and Heff turned their eyes down toward the bed where a now much larger version of Cradle was thrown protectively across what little was left of Morna Stahr. Dust and debris from the explosion settled all around them.

Cradle groaned deep and bucked off a couple of boulders the size of mini coopers before turning to look at the partially interred couple. He lifted one of his super-sized, dust-laden wings, revealing a ghastly, but still breathing, Morna.

Bloodied and broken, Freyja gave a few good bucks against the wall, holding her and her husband prisoner, rocking with all her might to dislodge her arm. Baffled at her inability to do so, she reached deep to find the well of strength she needed, releasing a cry that could only be described as the very heart of a battered woman. Raw and primitive, the roar of being married to Odin all those millennia ago lay beneath the surface of the happy, married life she clung so tight to. Harsh and loud over the sickening undertones of cracking bones and snapping tendons, Freyja tapped into the memory of how hard she'd been hit over and over by the God-like being and poured all of that vile hatred into the shattering of her arm, so she might loosen it from the unforgiving hold of the surrounding rock.

The Freyja of Sessrumnir did what all battered women do when they just can't *even*. She took a few deep breaths, swallowed down all the pain wracking her blast-worn body, and got on with life. Freyja brought forth in her tiny, mangled hand a perfectly intact golden apple, which she had, against all odds, retrieved from across space and time from her Orchards at Sessrumnir without ever leaving Morna's bedroom.

"Who's the boss, applesauce?" echoed across the rubble from somewhere deep within a Creak-shaped crevasse on the far side of the room.

"Don't need to remind me," Heff boasted. "She's always worn the pants in this family."

"That's because you never wear pants," Creak's voice spewed from the blast hole along with a shit ton of rock.

"Why is everyone hanging there like Jesus on the cross! Get down here, we're running out of time!" Cradle ordered, protectively throwing his blast-worn wings over Morna as he resurrected a jumbled patchwork of dead languages, cursing an angelic blue streak of prehistoric profanities at the incoming geyser of raining rock.

"I can't!" Heff yelled back, humbled by the fact it was true. "Must be how J.C. felt. Props, brah."

Heff sent up some love to his best friend and super famous, sin-washing bro-taganist.

"You and J.C. can hug it out on poker night, hon. We need to figure out why we can't free ourselves!" Freyja huffed, pulling and rocking with all her might to no avail. "It's like my physical strength is at human level, and I've got zero gas left for magic, ethereal or otherwise."

"Deodamnatus," Cradle whispered to himself, not a soul the wiser for what he just tried and failed to do.

Creak barreled out of his blast hole, looking happier than a pig in shit when he spotted Heff and Freyja on their prison perch.

"How's the weather up there?"

"We've got a serious situation on our hands here, Creak. Not everything is a joke," Cradle spat as he knocked a few more of the smaller boulders off Morna's bed.

"It most certainly fucking is. Everything is always a serious fucking situation, and everything is always a fucking joke. It's a paradox."

"Cut the crap and help me get these guys down," Cradle ordered the amped-up Grinx.

"Already on it." From behind a curtain of dust and debris, his long, craggy claws were already eviscerating the cave wall. Creak bored through two tons of bedrock like a rabid pocket gopher. In under a minute, Heff and Freyja were safely exhumed from their temporary tomb and carefully made their way through the mountain of rubble. "Watch your step. I made a bit of a mess," Creak warned as he did a full-on doggy shake, launching even more grit into the dreggy air.

Freyja stopped for a second to pull one last piece of shrapnel from her thigh and buckled under the pain. Heff swooped in and caught her under the arms.

"What the hell is this? Why can't we heal ourselves? Is this some sort of punishment?" Heff demanded as he cradled his broken and battered wife.

"I don't think so," Cradle said. "If and when a reckoning comes for this little stunt, I'm pretty sure we're going to know it. Right now, I think we're dealing with the physical ramifications of messing with the natural order of things. We've always been able to hop space and time, but no one has ever occupied two different points simultaneously, let alone moved something from one point to another while doing so. I'm guessing we've crossed into seriously uncharted territory, kids."

"Creak seems fine. He seems juiced up by it," Heff added.

"Dude, I'm an ethereal balance keeper of non-human energies. That explosion was rife with stuff I'm engineered to babysit," Creak explained, vibrating with the extras coursing through his rocky veins.

"And here I thought you were just an odd-looking computer geek."

"That too," Creak shot back.

"So, how do you suggest we do this?" Freyja asked Heff.

"Why are you asking me?"

"Because this whole thing was your bright idea, genius," Creak answered for Freyja.

"May I have that, my darling?" Heff gently asked his wife.

Freyja, feeling just enough better to nod her head yes, let her husband take from the crook of her arm the piece of magic that might kill her if word of this stunt got out. The foreshadowing turned his stomach and made his blood boil. Heff took the enchanted object in his gargantuan, calloused hand and considered it for a moment while pots of fire, anvils, and all the various tools of his eternal trade filled the war-torn bedroom.

"Guess you're getting your mojo back," Creak said to Heff, who wasn't listening at all.

He was too busy forging Morna a heart of gold.

THE FORGERY

Heat pounded as if the bellows of hell itself fed the raging forge. Sweat and steam poured off Hephaestus with every blow of his fabled hammer. No one had ever watched Hephaestus work before, not even Freyja. They had no way of knowing this build was different. This build was forged by the hate he held for Tomas de Torquemada and the love he held for his wife. With every blow of the hammer, a little love and a little hate poured from his heart, down his arm, and into the golden medium that would become the beating heart of Morna JoAnn Stahr. He should have known to cool himself off first and take a step back. There had been no time for all that, and if this little trick of theirs worked, he already felt responsible for the control Morna would have to fight for. The way it was being engineered held no self-control whatsoever.

It was an awesome and brutally beautiful thing to witness Heff hone himself into Hephaestus, the mythical weapons maker of the otherworld. He was colossal and foreboding, single-minded and unbending as he hammered his will into whatever adversary lay on his ancient anvil.

The mystical object fought Hephaestus every step of the way. The heat, the strikes, and the blows would make transformations seconds before the enchanted gold simply returned to its original form.

In one final desperate blow, Heff poured every bit of the golden ratio his wife had gifted him over the years into the mightiest swing he'd ever brought down, and the deed was done. Faster than the mortal eye could see, the legendary weapons maker shoved the workpiece deep into the slack tub, hardening a very reluctant heart as steam boiled madly into the atmosphere.

Heff swayed to the side, losing his balance. It had been eons since he'd last had to account for his twisted, clubbed feet.

"Creak!" Freyja roared.

"On it!" Creak came under Heff and pressed his giant, boxy head into the palm of Heff's colossal hand. "Gotcha, big guy. Lean as hard as you need," Creak said, as he took the disfigured giant's weight onto himself.

"I'm alright," Heff said, righting himself with Creak's help. "Let's get this thing somewhere it can do some good."

He tossed the precious invention to his wife who was already perfect, once again. They all looked down at the disfigured husk of the once vibrant woman on the bed. There were no moans and no haggard breaths; Morna no longer showed any signs of life. Like a tree, twisted and dark in the dead of winter. Any hope for a new beginning lay trapped below the surface.

Freyja yanked a dagger from her thigh holster as Cradle ripped open Morna's shirt. The goddess slammed the serrated blade straight down through skin and bone, angling deep. Satisfied, she tossed the knife aside and fearlessly drove her perfect hand into the gnarled opening to pull the rotten, twisted, useless heart from its shallow grave, unceremoniously shoving the new one deep into Morna's empty chest.

Freyja frantically looked left and right, not knowing what to do next. Her powers weren't back yet. Desperate, she placed her hands over the gaping hole and prayed. Prayed her powers would come back just enough to put a bit more golden ratio into the makeshift heart, make it one with Morna, make it pump, and make it beat, just once.

Creak mounted the bed and batted Freyja's praying hands away from Morna's butchered chest, then dove inward into himself. He gathered every scrap of inner energy he could find as he did that purply, oozy, glowy shit again. Within seconds, he pulsed with so much power it vibrated off the cave walls. It echoed wave on wave, orchestrating themselves into fiendishly wicked low-level hums, smacking eerily reminiscent of "Come Together" by the Beatles. The undercurrent of charged particles surrounding him swirled into an eddying tornado of raw power that entombed him in an ear-shattering crescendo.

Behind the tornado's swirling curtain, Creak was perfectly Zen in the eye of the storm. A blue river of energy carved its way down the stony surface of Creak's craggy spine, splintering off in finger-ling tributaries toward the black diamonds covering his body like dark forbidden islands. In every direction, the blue rivers crept with purpose until every last one of them became interconnected in an otherworldly web of raw power.

Creak became an open circuit. The energy ebbed and flowed, thrumming and pulsing across his surface in perfect time with the surrounding cyclone's eerily melodic hum. With each pulse, the electric currents were conducted by the interconnected gems to swell and climb, reaching higher and higher with every crackling pulse until they sparked up in white-hot arches, calling down the swirling energy in the surrounding cyclone like a lightning rod.

Connected.

Electric fire poured into the balance keeper of non-human ener-gies. The little tributaries of energy flowed across Creak's surface and swelled into rampant rivers of power. Power so wild and fast it flooded the intricate river system, spilling out and over, covering every square inch between the gems, and turning Creak's surface into a surreal hurricane of electrical storms. They raged wilder as he siphoned off the last of the surrounding cyclone, leaving him fully awash in the purest voltage this dimension has ever known and revealed himself for who and what he was.

A fully jouled Prince of Satera.

Gothically majestic and fully charged, Creak took one glorious millisecond for himself, breathed it all in, then on a wink to his baffled besties, let it all out, yelling, "Clear!" as he fired every last joule straight into Morna's heart.

The gaping mouths of his cohorts spoke volumes.

"What?" Creak said smugly with his signature cocky half-smile and raised eyebrow.

Claps echoed over the mountains of rubble, followed by, "That was the craziest fucking episode of House I've ever seen. Brav-fucking-O. I would have been here earlier, but honestly, I just wanted to kick back and see how it ended. I particularly like the bit where you ad-hocked some *Forged in Fire* and *Ocean's Eight* in a desperate attempt to save your dying patient. I gotta hand it to ya, it was a real fuckin' nail-biter."

Creak puffed out his stony cheeks then deflated them slowly as he muttered, "Busted," through jagged, bone-white fangs.

"Hi, Justice," Heff said flatly.

"Hello, Hephaestus. Nice makeover," Justice jabbed as he looked Heff up and down, from his grisly face to his grotesque feet, then turned to Heff's left, saying, "I got your message, Freyja." Hephaestus took his wife by the arm and made an awkward attempt to tuck her protectively behind him. "That won't save her from what's coming." Justice closed in on the mythological contingent renowned for their legendary powers. "It won't save any of you." Justice sneered, a look of disdain aimed solely in the direction of the very ancient, very resigned angel who stood as a quiet sentry over the deathbed of Morna JoAnn Stahr.

The closer Justice got, the more savage he looked. The dull pewter finish of Justice Gray's skin was covered in silver pox, not entirely unlike the scarification process many primitive tribes here on Earth used, but different because instead of little rocks or glass shoved under his tarnished skin, Justice kept his counterbalanced scale weights in there for easy access. Around his neck hung twelve antique, silver measuring spoons swinging and clanking as he moved, heralding with every step that Justice was near.

Clenched in the Fate's hands were two silver yardsticks used to bat and flip a silver ruler between them like a peddling street performer. The yardstick on the right measured your innocence while the one on the left measured your guilt. Justice knew that one did not necessarily negate the other. The much smaller, silver ruler, practicing ariel vaults between the two, calculated if an intention was good or bad, which, interestingly enough, was always the exact difference in measurement between guilt and innocence.

"Time to go, kids," Justice decreed.

Freyja, Heff, and Creak all looked to Cradle, not making a single move to follow Justice's orders. Justice Gray wasn't their Governor, and they would never follow his command. Damn, he was proud of the rag-tag horde. Every one of them truly deserved better from him. They deserved the truth. All of it. Cradle promised himself then and there, as soon as he was able, that's exactly what he would give them. He gave an affirmative nod of his head in consent for his crew to go peacefully with Justice.

For now.

"Let me just grab Morna," Freyja said as she leaned down to scoop up Morna's hallowed shell.

"That," Justice said, pointing one of his silvery yardsticks toward the bed, "Whatever the fuck it is, does not fall within my jurisdiction, and is therefore not my problem. On the other hand," he said, batting the spinning ruler over to balance it on the tip of the opposite stick, "You three assholes most definitely are. Let's go. NOW."

Aware

Ah, Gods. There was nothing. Nothing but emptiness. The lifeless golden heart in her chest ached with it. Its sorrow was desperate. It screamed like a banshee to be whole as it searched heaven and hell for its other half.

Lost

The scattered bits of Morna Stahr's disembodied soul echoed the gilded heart's morbid call as it careened backward through all ten dimensions like a bat out of hell, unintentionally culling grains of space and time as it ground through the locked-up gears. It shattered cogs and snapped springs as it wrestled its way free of the prison orrery. Morna's soul reassembled itself in a frenzy of reckless abandon when it reached the other side, her metaphysical fabric folding in those hijacked dimensional bits.

Found

Morna's being synthesized as her newly renovated soul poured hot and thick into her golden heart. The raw, earthy matter of her lifeless shell was instantly recast as the metaphysical bore down, creating an alchemy of all ten dimensions within her.

Bound

Morna was burning, and it felt incredibly good. The hotter it got, the better she felt. She welcomed the heat, welcomed every flame licking at the emptiness, fought it back to proper balance, and weighted it right with the color of her existence.

Morna's heart and soul were at last one within her. She was refined, and she was fucking glowing with it.

TWENTY-TWO

THE KNOWING

Morna drew straight up in bed and inhaled a lifetime's worth of oxygen in a single suffocating breath.

"Well, that's anticlimactic," she said, scanning the war-torn room for anyone and coming up short. "Just a gilded, royal angel born of Earth and nefarious, preternatural antics. Nothing to see here," she mused, somehow fully aware of how and what she'd become as she rose from her deathbed. "Some serious shit went DOWN IN HERR! Can't have anything nice, can we? Well, first things first," Morna decreed, as she dusted off her palms. "Where the fuck are you, Silla?" then instantly knew exactly where Silla was and had a feeling if she thought about being there hard enough, she would be.

"Awesome," Morna said, arriving just outside a sub-zero freezer.

Morna gave a good tug on the freezer door and tore the whole damn thing from its moorings as a tempest of arctic fog and fire bellowed out.

"Silla, it's me. Cool it, would you?" Morna batted away the raging elements as if they were an annoying fly. "I can't see a damn thing with you carrying on," she grumble-bitched and casually walked into the barrage.

"Carrying on!" Morna heard Silla fire off from somewhere deep in the flames. "I've been down here on ice for fucking days!" Silla roared her hurt and anger into the melee.

"Sorry about that. I would have been here earlier, but I was FUCKING DEAD!" Morna fired as she closed the heated distance between them.

The flames and fog vanished on a dime, leaving a very naked, crystalline Silla standing a few feet away from her recently deceased, new, and improved best friend.

"You're beautiful," Silla whispered, awestruck as steam poured off her cooling body.

"What? This old thing?" Morna joked as she tugged a little on the ripped-up, blood, and sweat-soaked shirt barely clinging to her perfect shoulders. "You're not so bad yourself, you frosty little minx... Brrrrr," she added, shivering a bit as she overtly ogled Silla's ice-capped bits.

"Stop fucking around, Morna," Silla said, clearly rattled.

"If I stop fucking around, Sil, you won't know it's me."

"You're glowing."

"You were just on fire."

"You have wings."

"Hello pot, this is the kettle. You're black," Morna mocked, crossing her arms and giving her new wings a rustle for emphasis as she gave Silla her best smart-ass smile.

Morna desperately needed this to go well. She needed to know this one thing would always remain the same—that Atsilla Rene' Onacana would always be her best friend.

"You're an angel, Morna," Silla said, bowled over at the fact.

"I'm a woman with wings. You're a woman with wings. Birds of a feather."

"We aren't even the same species anymore. I think we can throw taxonomic rank out the window."

"Ooh, fancy. Look at you, using your seventh-grade life science vocab in real life. Mrs. Yeger would be so proud," Morna teased. "What was the mnemonic for that again? Donkey Kong Plays Chess Outside For G-Sus. Silla! Snap the fuck out of it already!"

"I don't think you know what it feels like to be in your presence. I can't explain it," Silla said, heavy-hearted.

"Try."

Silla stood there silent, looking everywhere but at Morna's pleading eyes.

"Try, Silla. Please."

"You're superior, Morna. It radiates off of you. It's...it's humbling to be near you," Silla said, casting her eyes down to Morna's dirty bare feet.

"Look at me, Silla. Look me in the goddamn eyes," Morna begged, more desperate than she'd ever been.

"I can't," Silla answered softly, "I need to go, Morna."

"What do you mean you can't? Where could you possibly need to go right now?" Morna asked, shaken to her core.

"Away from you," Silla answered quietly, her eyes still focused on Morna's feet.

"Why? I don't understand. I'm still me, Silla," she pleaded, taking one step closer.

"Don't," Silla said, taking a watchful step back as little orange sparks crackled and sparked off her naked body. "Will you please let me leave?" Silla finished, uncharacteristically submissive and a razor's edge from losing her cool.

"Of course, you can leave. Why would you think you need to ask me permission? Silla, this is fucking crazy!" Morna yelled after the fiery owl who blazed past on a sizzling trail of tears.

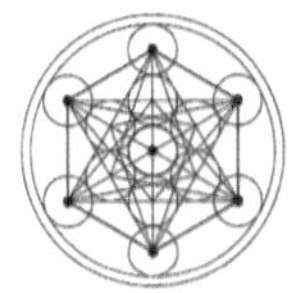

TWENTY-THREE

WELL, SHIT

Heartsick and confused, Morna somehow made her way back through the labyrinth of twisting tunnels and into the main living chamber of HQ, only to find it empty.

"Hello? Anyone home?" echoed back at her from the lofty, book-lined walls. "Where the hell is everybody?"

She scanned the vast, cavernous space. Not knowing what else to do, she walked over to the bar, grabbed a bottle of Pinot Gris to pour herself a giant glass, and immediately spit it out as if it were hellfire.

"That bottle hasn't been treated yet, dear. You'll never be able to drink it that way." Morna heard a motherly voice admonishing her attempt for a much-needed drink. "You'll have to put in a few drops of ambrosia if you want to swallow it. It's there on the end of the bar in the little purple bottle, dear."

Morna looked left and right, scanning the room. She felt the presence of something, but couldn't identify its origin.

"Down here, dear," the voice instructed. Morna looked down to see an enormous pink sow looking back up at her from the end of the bar. "I'm Hildi."

"OK."

"I'm Freyja and Heff's nanny."

"OK."

"Oh, come now, dear. I can see from the looks of you I'm not the strangest thing you've stumbled across recently," the sentient sow said as she looked Morna up and down.

"True," Morna agreed flatly. "This one here?" she asked, pointing to the luminous purple bottle on the end of the bar.

"That's the one."

Morna grabbed the glowing bottle, uncorked it, and went to pour some into her already overfull glass. "STOP!" The sow bellowed from the cave floor. "So sorry, dear. You can't go pouring that stuff willy-nilly. See, there, dear," Hildi motioned with her snout. "There's an eye dropper attached to the inside of the stopper. Just a single drop in your glass should do the trick. Any more than that and I'll be nannying you, too."

Morna put a single drop of the purple liquid into her glass and watched as its contents took on the purple color, fizzled, then restored itself to the natural, golden timbre of the wine. She considered the ethereal marvel for a whole half second before eagerly lifting the sparkling drink to her lips.

Morna smiled deeply while inadvertently rustling her new wings. The first drop of crisp, white wine was the only thing that seemed remotely familiar since her upgrade. Settled a bit now, Morna sat her glass down and headed behind the bar. Hildi watched curiously as the strange angel opened and shut every single cabinet door behind the bar.

"Can I help you find something, dear?"

"Nope, I got it!" Morna said, triumphant, as she pulled a large punch bowl up from one of the lower cabinets.

Morna made her way back around the bar, poured what was left in the bottle of Pinot Grigio into the bowl, added a drop of the purple stuff, watched it sizzle and settle, then set it down on the floor for Hildi.

"Why thank you, dear. Don't mind if I do," the sow said as she took an oddly lady-like slurp from the crystal punch bowl.

"So, Hildi…" Morna said, casually leaning into a conversation with her new drinking buddy.

"Yes, dear?" Hildi asked, pulling herself away from her sparkling trough of wine.

"You wouldn't happen to know where the fuck everyone is, would you?"

"Oh, yes, dear. They are all with Justice Gray."

"Justice Gray?" Morna questioned.

"Yes, dear. Justice Gray." Completely clueless, Morna waved her hand in small circles, encouraging the pig to give her more information. "The Spoonman?" Hildi hinted.

"Spoonman?" Morna repeated.

"The Scales of Justice, dear," Hildi explained. "He came and collected them all rather swiftly before you woke. They are probably being weighed and measured as we speak."

Hildi lowered her snout into the punch bowl of wine for another dainty slurp.

"Weighed and measured?"

"Yes, dear. Are you daft?" Hildi insulted her in the sweetest voice imaginable.

Morna picked up her glass and slid down to the floor to look the enchanted nanny right in the eyes.

"Hildi," she said, gathering the pig's undivided attention.

"Yes, dear?" Hildi answered, bringing her snout up to just inches away from Morna's angelic face.

"Who is Justice Gray, and where has he taken my friends?"

"You don't know anything, do you, dear?"

"No," Morna answered, completely deflated.

"Justice Gray is the Keeper of the Scales, dear. He is who a person's soul faces after they shuffle off this mortal coil."

"I'm going to need more than that, Hildi," Morna pressed as she continued waving her hand impatiently in circles, hoping it would somehow help the pig spill the beans on this Justice dude a bit faster.

"Have you ever heard of purgatory, dear?"

Morna impatiently nodded her head yes, hand still circling.

"Fabulous! Now we are getting somewhere. Think of purgatory as a weigh station. Everyone stops by on their way to wherever they are headed to find their next stop. Justice, of course, determines this. He balances the weight of a person's existence against his scales and then sends them on their way accordingly. In very rare cases, like the one happening with our dear friends, you get to skip the whole dying part and jump straight to the head of the line for a 'Justice is Swift' Special."

"But I thought purgatory was where you served time for minor sins before moving on," Morna challenged her unlikely tutor.

"I'll never understand how humans get that one so wrong. Serving time and suffering is what your time here on Earth is for, dear. Honestly, Morna, may I call you Morna?" Hildi asked and accepted the punchy nod of Morna's head as confirmation, then carried on without skipping a beat. "Fantastic! Anyway, I would think that one was a no-brainer. I mean, really, how big of an asshole do you all think The One is? The whole of a human's life is about learning, penance, and paying your dues. I swear on all that's kosher, I'll never understand the human condition. Honestly, dear, if a person's consciousness, coupled with mountains of heartache, and heaping doses of anxiety, doesn't set a soul to rights, a few centuries twiddling their thumbs in the borderlands on a back-burner timeout certainly won't," Hildi finished, sounding utterly exasperated.

"I'm gonna have to start writing this stuff down."

"We tried that, dear."

"Where? I've never seen it."

"You'll have to ask King James, dear."

"Ah," Morna said, raising her eyebrows and pursing her lips.

"So, they're all in purgatory being weighed and measured? Why Hildi? What crime did they commit so heinous they got a speed pass to Justice Gray's scales?"

"They saved you, my dear," Hildi said, looking her straight in the eyes.

"Well, shit."

"Indeed."

"I'm going to need some help, Hildi."

"I'd say so, my dear."

"Have you seen Silla?" Morna asked.

"She blew through here on a fit of fire about half an hour ago. Thank Goddess the kids were asleep, or they would have been imitating that stunt for hours. I swear to Hermes, I don't have it in me to deal with five flying pyros tonight," Hildi admitted, all three hundred pink pounds of her trembling at the unholy thought.

"She didn't say where she was going?" Morna questioned the quivering pig.

Hildi shook her head. "No, Silla and I haven't been formally introduced. I like to lay low until I know people won't go ham when I start talking. I believe, though, that she was heading out."

"What makes you say that?"

"Because there's an owl-shaped hole burnt into the ceiling of the dome, dear," Hildi informed Morna as she turned her snout upward toward the still-smoldering exit.

"Well, shit."

"Indeed," Hildi agreed.

"Can you help me, Hildi? Please?" Morna pleaded.

"Well, of course, dear! Why don't you doctor up a few more of those bottles of wine while I freshen up a bit? I certainly can't be expected to entertain looking like this! Chop chop, dear. Lots to do!" Hildi ordered and slowly waddled off toward Heff and Freyja's part of the caves.

Morna did as she was told and added a few drops of ambrosia to each bottle of unopened liquor. Working behind the bar gave her a sense of calm. It was such a normal thing for her to do, unfortunately, she hadn't accounted for her new wingspan while doing it. In the last five minutes, Morna had broken no less than three shelves of high-end bar glasses and two rails of pricey booze. It was a fucking disaster.

"What up, wings?" Morna addressed her new accouterments. "If you keep this shit up, I'm going to have to find a new line of work." Morna's wings gave a disgruntled huff as if they were none too pleased with her for berating them after having beaten them about every surface she happened by.

Startled by the wings' physical response to her rhetorical question, Morna turned to look in the bar mirror. She intended to watch the wings closely while asking them another question, then caught sight of her new reflection for the first time.

"Whoa," Morna breathed, mystified by the elevated likeness looking back at her. Her hair had evolved from its brown, fizzy lob into a mass of scrumptious, chocolate waves lying just over her shoulders.

Her shoulders! Her skin had an honest-to-God radiance that shimmered in the exact same tone as the golden fibers woven through her hair and her wings.

Her wings! Holy mother of Jesus, her wings crested above her dusky shoulders in amber folds of fluidic feathers that moved like whiskey in a crystal-cut glass.

"They're breathtaking," she whispered as her wings, independent of her own thoughts, expanded in pride, and made a sound like a ship's mast catching a stiff breeze. "Not humble, eh?" Morna teased the boastful extremities, which, on the fly, reacted with another lofty flap that landed her right on her ass. "Note to self: do not piss off wings," Morna went to get up and was immediately righted with another cheeky flap, landing her back where she started. "I'm sorry, OK? Jeesh," Morna conceded.

Appeased by the apology, the perceptive wings tucked themselves into the nesting folds of Morna's shoulders as she caught a glimpse of her new eyes in the lower glass cabinets. Morna raised herself to her hands and knees, crawling closer to the glowing eyes reflecting back at her from the sparkling glass. Her boring, hush-puppy browns were no more. Their color was a deep, swirling bourbon, barely a shade darker than her whiskey-colored wings. Inlaid in each were hypnotic, twisting spirals of phosphorescent gold.

The shape of her eyes was the same, but slightly turned up a bit in the corners, leaving most of the endearing sadness of the hush-puppy shape while adding a dash of hope. Her lashes, however, were completely different. Thicker, longer, and tar black as if a bit wet.

Overwhelmed, Morna fell back into the sticky darkness. She crossed her arms over her knees and lowered her head, curling herself into a ball. When she finally raised her head and opened her eyes, she was immediately confronted with a barrage of sparkles twinkling in the darkness. The same gold whirling in her irises twinkled sporadically from every spot on her arms that had previously been mottled in drab brown freckles.

"I've been fucking bedazzled," Morna said dejected, not at all thrilled about spending eternity looking like a glittery tart.

"Pretty."

Morna looked up to see a celestial tot balanced precariously on a barstool across from her.

"I like your wings," the little one said. "I think they are very pretty."

"Hello there, little one. I like yours, too," Morna said gently to the tiny winged ankle-biter as she rose from the bar floor. "My name is Morna. What's your name, sweetie?"

"I'm Nitzie. Where's my mom?" The celestial who looked the spitting image of her mother asked, rubbing sleepily at her silvery, blue eyes.

"It's nice to meet you, Nitzie. Your mom and dad had to go out for a bit. Can I help you with something?"

"Can you fix my sock?" Nitzie wiggled the offending accessory while tilting her sippy cup back.

"Yes, Nitzie. I would love to fix your sock," Morna said, smiling. "You should probably head back to bed," Morna counseled. "Better?"

Nitzie looked down at her fuzzy, pink foot and considered the sock adjustment for longer than any one person might think possible. She rotated her ankle, ruling Morna's work sufficient with a regal nod of her blonde head.

Morna watched as Nitzie, without another word, gathered up her sippy cup and blankie to toddle back from wherever she came.

"Morna?" Nitzie said, stopping mid-toddle, but never turning around.

"Yes, sweetie?"

"Justice Gray has my mom and dad, doesn't he?"

Morna didn't know what to say. Nitzie sounded forty-four and four years old at the same time.

"I'll take your silence to mean yes," the four-year-old said, much too aristocratically, even for a four-year-old.

"When you see him," Nitzie said, dead calm. "Tell Justice if he doesn't return our mother and father by morning, there will be Valhalla to pay."

Morna's blood ran cold at the menacing decree. She watched the highborn toddler turn the corner into the midnight shadows of the tunnels beyond, her satin blankie trailing behind like the lengthy train of some lofty queen's robe.

"What the actual fuck?" Morna whispered, totally skeeved out.

"Oh, and Morna?" Nitzie's regal voice boomed ominously from the dark recesses beyond. A swirl of disturbing giggles echoed, followed by an even more sweetly disturbing, "Thanks for fixing my sock."

"You're welcome!" Morna hollered. "You creepy little shit," she finished under her breath.

TWENTY-FOUR

A DISH BEST SERVED COLD

Morna pulled herself up from the cave floor for what she hoped was the last time when she heard the whispering of two gossiping females.

"Justice is such a tool sometimes."

"Well, dear. I figured if anyone could tip the scales in our favor, it would be you."

"I mean, eight millennia of serving the same old boring humble pie gets old, especially when the assholes in question don't even know why they're eating it," the flamboyant voice professed. "It's always the same, 'Why is this happening to me? I don't deserve this!' Blah, blah, blah. Um, yeah, you do. I wouldn't be serving it if you didn't order it!"

"Frosty words, my dear," Hildi said, delighted by her gossiping guest.

"I am a dish best served cold."

Morna watched as the two chattering characters came to light. The woman on the left looked barbaric, her build short, buxom, and rocking red dreads while dressed in warrior leathers. The curvaceous woman's look was completed by primitive, crimson tattoos covering every inch of her, head to toe.

"I do love getting gussied up in the leathers, Karma dear, but my goodness, do I ever chafe! There's too much of me rubbing up against the other jiggly bits of me!" the woman said as she arched back to liberally powder the underside of her woefully inadequate leather halter bra.

"Jehovah, Hildi! Is that talcum powder?" The woman on the right asked, knocking the bottle of Johnson and Johnson lavender-scented baby powder from the warrior woman's hands. "Carcinogens, be gone!"

"Carcinogens? It's baby powder, Karma!"

"Put down the cancer and step away. It's against the rules for me to tell you this in advance… Ugh, just trust me on this, Hild!"

A whole other kind of fierce; the person on the right was a good seven-foot-tall in thigh-high *Louboutin* boots. The being took confident steps on long legs, muscled to the max, and lean at the same time. A short-shorts jumpsuit made of white parachute silk, teaming with pockets clinging to all the right places. From the top of the being's bouffant-orange hair to the tips of its stiletto French manicure, the vision seemed to have stepped right off of RuPaul's runway and straight into the subterranean caves of HQ.

Morna cleared her throat, putting an instant stop to the chatter, asking, "Hildi? Is that you?"

"Why yes, dear. It's me," answered the curvy, tattooed barbarian.

"Wow! You look good!" Morna said, astounded.

"Thank you, dear. It's been a while since I got all gussied up. It does feel nice to dress up from time to time. You know how it can be; kids suck it all out of you. I honestly forget how empowering it is to put extra effort into one's appearance," Hildi said, preening as she patted her freshly powdered tidbits, adding, "Morna, this is Karma Etiam Grayness of All. Karma, this is Morna JoAnn Stahr."

Breathless, Morna stood frozen before The Fate of Cause and Effect.

"Not to worry, Morna darling." Soft but sure, Karma looked the newbie angel in the eyes and continued, "I'm very used to people not seeing me coming." Karma smiled and tenderly cupped Morna's cheek. "Let alone ever actually wanting to meet me," Karma winked and actually comforted Morna for the very first time since becoming, well, whatever the fuck she was. Karma seemed to study Morna's soul through the windows of her newly minted eyes.

Karma then cocked its head, took a deep breath, and nodded a quick confirmation to itself before saying, "You have nothing to fear from me, Morna JoAnn Stahr. True empaths rarely show up on my radar."

"I'm an empath?" Morna asked, bowled over at having her life-long suspicion confirmed by Karma itself.

"That's the nature of you beasts," Karma said to Hildi and Morna. "Always in tune, but never really knowing for sure. It's the ones who are sure they are empathic who get a frequent helping of my blue-plate special."

"And what's on the blue-plate special exactly?" Morna asked uneasily.

"Cosmic revenge," Karma decreed, coolly, omnipresent, and utterly fucking frightening. "Available breakfast, lunch, and dinner; twenty-four seven, three-sixty-five."

Morna let the fun fact wash over her for about a millisecond and filed it in the box titled "Unnerving Shit I Don't Need to Think About Right Now". Her friends needed saving, and time was running short.

"So, Hildi. Is Karma your phone a friend?" she asked casually as if an actual Fate hadn't just laid down a prophetic "reap what you sow" diner metaphor.

"Yes, dear. Karma is just what we need to halt Justice in his tracks."

"And Justice is about to be served," Karma added with a severe note of intent.

"Dine-in or catered?" Morna added darkly, falling into the subterfuge restaurant lingo.

"Catered," Karma replied coolly.

"The logistics on this delivery could prove to be a real bitch," Morna noted.

"Hildi, Morna, it's time to plan the menu," Karma said as it pulled out two barstools.

Hildi and Morna accepted the unheard-of invitation and took their seats as Karma walked round the bar and droughted each of them a pint of Guinness.

Morna and Hildi sat silent while Karma pulled a charming, silver spoon from one of the many pockets on its designer jumpsuit and placed its bent handle on the edge of each pint glass, in turn, taking special care that the brown, creamy liquid fell over the ancient utensil to settle in the bottom of each glass like a dark, muddled rain.

When it was satisfied with the long pours, Karma tilted its own pint toward its guests, "May karma run over your dogma," the unnerving Fate toasted on a thinly-veiled vow before licking the excess stout off the ancient silver spoon.

What the nanny pig and newbie angel didn't know was Karma Gray had waited its entire existence to whip up something special for its brother, which it intended to shovel down his complicit pie hole with the very utensils hanging heavy round his silver neck.

TWENTY-FIVE

GETTING THE BAND BACK TOGETHER

"Justice Gray, Fate of Scales, what in the name of The One Dimension have you done?" Cradle demanded the second they arrived on the Cliffs of Perdition.

"I redecorated. Do you like it?" Justice asked offhand, knowing the answer and not giving two shits either way.

Cradle seethed as he looked out over the meandering chaos of Purgatory proper. Left to right, as far as his perfect eyes could see, tent cities swarmed with lingering souls. Small, shoddily built concert stages littered the land. Each stage blared the various musical stylings of every recently famous and dearly departed musician known to man.

Over the din of Bowie, Cornell, Prince, and the like, vendors hawked their wares to the transient hordes of wayward souls. Swinging through on trailing swaths of fire were colossal, metal pendulums metering out the never-ending wait time. Each pendulum swung in fiery perpetuity from twenty-four sky-high grandfather clocks jerry-rigged together with scraps of rusted iron and jagged, gleaming beams of stainless steel. The monstrous keepers of time stood stoic in twenty-four raging pyres scattered throughout. The entire scene looked like a posthumous Burning Man.

"No, Justice. I do not," Cradle answered, his voice dignified, heavy, and formal.

It carried the weight of the omniverse in its strength as Morna Stahr's cuddlier version ceded into a very different persona.

"Well, I happen to think it's avant-garde," Justice said, unaffected by Cradle's answer. He juggled the silver sticks with one hand while brushing the backs of his fingernails against his bare, silvery chest. "The place lacked a certain something. Don't you think? All marble this and marble that. Velvet ropes and cue lines for as far as the eye could see. I mean, seriously, Cradle. Who wants to spend hundreds of years in line at The First National Bank of Oregon?"

"What do you mean 'spend hundreds of years in line'? Why in the name of The One Dimension are all these poor souls still here, Justice?" Cradle questioned as a gaseous smog swirled and loomed near the base of his wings.

"Poor souls? There is no need to feel sorry for them. After all, I am throwing the best after-party the ten dimensions have ever known. Folks are quite literally dying to get in here," Justice beamed at his sad joke, pausing dramatically for accolades that would never come. "Ugh. You guys suck," the fate conceded, his face falling flat with the return of his boorish nature. "Fuck the haters," he postured, more to himself than anyone else. "Get over it already. Those *poor souls,* as you call them, are having the time of their afterlives."

"Where are your brothers, Justice? I demand to know how three Moirai let this happen during a sanctioned sabbatical," Cradle pressed, shrouded in indifference as he petitioned the off-the-rails fate.

"Sanctioned sabbatical? Really?" Justice challenged. Sarcasm dripped like venom off his every word. "You've been gone for over five hundred years. Five. Hundred. Years. That's easily abandonment if not dereliction of duties. So, in conformity with ordinance number 9.001, I claim squatter's rights."

"There is no ordinance 9.001, Justice Gray," Cradle countered.

"Well," Justice decreed nonchalantly, "There should be. I'll add that to my never-ending to-do list," he added, feigning exhaustion at the perceived weight of his self-appointed position. "Nah, you know what? Let's go ahead and instate that law right the fuck now."

"What does he mean you've been absent?" Creak interjected, looking at Cradle, confused and a bit hurt.

"Your position does not entitle you to establish law, Justice," Cradle said with a dead calm, ignoring Creak. "You and your brothers are nothing but glorified babysitters here. You have no rights."

The low-level fog unfurled from Cradle's wings and diffused out and over the rock-ribbed cliffs of Perdition in a lazy, nebulin waterfall.

"True," Justice conceded, raising a hand to rub his pockmarked face. He dragged his index finger back and forth across his metallic lips. "That was true for the first hundred and fifty years or so," he concurred, losing his sticks into the air on a mighty throw. "What's a boy supposed to think, Cradle? I mean, you didn't call, you didn't write," he pandered on, catching the sticks, one, two, three. "All. That. Time," he droned without missing a beat.

"Tick, tock. Tick, tock. Tick, tock," he metered. "Without so much as a single word. So, I moved on without you."

Justice closed his argument in perfect time with the onslaught of twenty-four discordant bells ringing in the midnight hour. Below the cliffs of Perdition, throngs of forsaken clamored for safety under derelict stages and fallen marble slabs as bedlam rang throughout the wasted weigh station. Two hundred and eighty-eight thundering bells alloyed with the terrified screams of millions, making fear and time fuse in a hedonistic cacophony climbing up and over the cliffs to settle in Cradle's perfect ears.

"You've moved on? Just you?" Cradle questioned over the reigning turmoil, unaffected by the pandemonium below. "Where are the other two Fates, Justice? I left three Morai in charge, not one?"

"I was so bored, Cradle! The last thing I needed was my baby brother's bitching and moaning for all eternity about how I couldn't do this or I shouldn't do that, let alone all the incessant whining about it being their turn to weigh the souls. It was nothing but bitch, bitch, bitch, whine, whine, whine all the time! So, I made up some bullshit duties and micromanaged the little crybabies right out of my existence."

"You were bored?" Cradle questioned with a glare only familiar to the parents of teenage offspring.

"Honestly, I don't know how you did it for so long, Cradle," Justice carried on, unaware of the imminent danger behind the "you've got to be fucking kidding me" warning glare.

"What did you do with your brothers, Justice?" Cradle pressed a feather's vane from going nuclear.

"Well, let's see. It's been so long I can hardly remember," Justice answered, pretending to think on it for a long while before remembering. "Oh, that's right! I put Dorian in charge of the fun house around 1908 and haven't seen him since. Honestly, that one was just way too easy. Had a hell of a time shaking Dharma, though. I told him it was his job to keep these Tibetan prayer wheels spinning, or all the departed souls wouldn't be able to find the path to purgatory. Only seen the cosmic brown-noser once in the last fifty years or so. The sneaky son of a bitch showed up in April of '94 for a whole half second and absconded with Kurt Cobain, which was sort of a pisser. Then, I remembered I had more than enough time to locate him before Dave gets here. Oh, but mark your calendars, kiddies, 'cause we're having quite the reunion concert in forty-five years, three weeks, six days, and eight—no make that seven minutes," Justice jabbered on, sounding completely fucking bonkers as he broke into a maniacal version of "The Sky is a Neighborhood".

Creak and Freyja looked stupefied at the screwball conversation between Justice and Cradle. Hephaestus, on the other hand, looked more on edge than confused, which caught Freyja's attention pretty damn quick.

"What's going on here, brainy smurf?" Freya yelled over the clamoring bells.

"What's going on here, my dear Freyja?" Justice interjected happily, "Is the omniverse calling all four of you out for transgressions of epic fucking proportions? You've broken natural laws spanning all ten dimensions. All Ten! It borders on genius, really," he admitted, a wistful look of admiration settled over his blue-gray face. "But alas, rules are rules. Isn't that right, Cradle?"

"That's not what I meant, you pretentious pewter prick, and you know it," Freyja spat, turning her attention to the stoic angel on her left. "What the fuck is the coin purse babbling about, Cradle?"

"Ah, ah, ah, Freyja. Now is not the best time to get on my bad side."

"You have a good side?" Freyja asked, lowering her brows in concentration. She leaned her whole body to the left at first, then to the right, inspecting every tarnished inch of the man who held her fate. "Huh. Doesn't show."

"That'll be enough out of you, little apple polisher," Justice snapped, flipping the silver ruler with a bat of his yardstick, slicing her ever so slightly across a perfect ivory cheek.

Hephaestus raged, lunging for the silvered fate only to fall face-first onto the littered ground.

"Groveling, Heff?" Justice teased the mighty Olympian at his feet. "Oh, alright. If you must, but be quick about it. Justice waits for no man. Or… well, whatever the hell it is you are now," he finished with his shiny nose in the air.

Creak stooped down and worked his head between the ground and Heff's colossal hand. Without a word, the mountain of a man and the Grinx worked in tandem. Creak grew in size, bigger and taller, until he steadied the legendary smithy back to standing. He was a full eight feet five inches in height, bringing Creak's zenith to peak at eye level with the maniacal Morai.

Creak stood nose to nose with Justice. His eyes yellowed as he bared one side of his jagged, razor-sharp teeth on a low-level growl that visibly unnerved the wide-eyed fate.

"Cradle, I suggest you bring your dog to heel," Justice threatened, a weak warning, his fear of Creak's otherworldly growls peeking through his arrogance.

Cradle said nothing as Creak bared the rest of his bone white, serrated fangs, and upped his growl game to rabid hell beast before lifting a monstrous black leg to piss a runnel of steaming sulfur all over Justice Gray's overpriced playa-approved hiking boots.

Justice threw a hissy fit for the ages, that had Cradle, Heff, and Freyja caterwauling their collective celestial asses off as Creak sparked and popped, his hip working his hind leg into the ground again and again.

With a vengeful whip, Justice pierced through the sandy ground. One, two, three; his devil sticks bored swift and deep beneath the feet of Cradle, Heff, and Freyja. The gang's brief moment of levity was lost to the sudden splitting of Perdition's steadfast cliffs.

One after another, Freyja then Heff, each being fell away. The ground split and the sand came back together over the top of each hole as if it, and the being it devoured, had never been.

"Son! What are you doing?" Cradle demanded a combination

of confusion, anger, and hurt settling hard on his ancient face. "This was never part of the job, Justice. You've lost your way. Let's talk about this."

Justice just hummed happily to the tune, "The Cats in the Cradle," before sending Cradle into the cracks with a roundhouse kick.

TWENTY-SIX

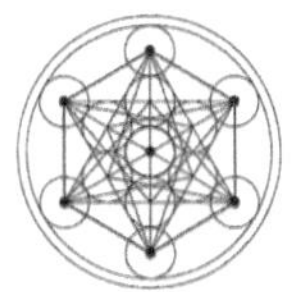

BEYOND THE PALE

Cradle found himself shackled next to Freyja, dead center on the main stage, and in the middlemost point of Purgatory proper.

"Shackles? Kid, are you off your meds?" Cradle hissed, dropping all the formal pretenses as he looked around to get his bearings.

Freyja lay helpless a few feet away, shackled, naked, and splayed face down like the Vitruvian Man. Her perfect proportions lined up exactly within the encompassing blood-red circle as every inch of her body was repeatedly branded by Pythagoras's mythical Fifth Hammer. Not seen since antiquity, the hammer was an Achilles heel in any attempt to make sense of the universe. Since math attempted to do just that, its resurfacing did not bode well for the physical personification of that attempt.

Freyja's body twisted and convulsed with each disfiguring blow, the flaming hammer, searing it deep with imperfections. The very existence of Asgard's queen was stamped out with every flaw and blemish bestowed.

The King of some Daliesque nightmare sat a good hundred feet away on a thrust stage reaching into the middle of a would-be crowd; Justice went big. There was not one, but two thrones, on the makeshift dais. The largest sat empty and was fashioned from wild, unhewn branches twisted and woven together. Savage but luxuriously padded, a crimson seat and chair back adorned the structure. In the middle of the tall, crimson back was a lowercase "t" embroidered in gold and accompanied by a sword on one side and a golden crown on the other.

The lesser throne, just to the left, was fashioned from a hollowed-out grandfather clock and currently occupied by the Fate of Scales. The chamber over Justice's head was perfectly intact, displaying a clock face reading twelve o'clock in accordance with the twenty-four monstrous timekeepers heralding the midnight hour. The clock throne reached out and over the would-be crowd with long and shining arms of silver, holding three silver chains. The chains pulled taught by the weight of ancient, silver pans swaying ever so slightly back and forth like a noose from the gallows.

"I was willing to go through with this charade of yours for the sake of Omniversal Law, but there is no longer any doubt you have become extremely unbalanced. Therefore, I must rule that you, Justice Gray-Fate of Scales, are no longer qualified to impartially weigh and measure the laws as they are written. Kid, it's past time this show of yours comes to an end," Cradle said as the fog seeped from his wings and kicked up a notch, tactically burgeoning out in finger-like feelers.

"Past time?" Justice broke out in a fit of ear-splitting laughter. The twelve spoons hanging around his neck clinked as his whole body shook. The spoons generated an eerily light, inverse accompaniment to the ongoing thunder of clamoring bells as he said, "Time is just another way to measure. Measure the seconds, minutes, hours, days, weeks, years...fucking millennia I've put in playing by the rules. Rules I had nothing to do with making. Rules that were laid down by two omnipotent pricks and a third-party negotiator. Wink. Wink. So, Rockhead, I think it's quittin' time."

"Rockhead?" Freyja yelled over to Cradle in between beatings.

"I don't know what the fuck he's going on about, Freyja! Kid's lost his fucking marbles!"

"That's you, you dumbass angel. You're Rockhead. Holy shit, you're stupid. Fucking primordial angel doesn't even get a reference to the fucking Flintstones." Justice shook his head in disbelief. "So anyway, Rockhead. I'm gonna need you to help me pull the string on that dodo bird one last time."

"I don't think I can make this any plainer, but I'll try. You're fired," Cradle said as he busted out of his shackles.

He'd only put up with the Morai's insidious ramblings to find out how and why Justice had managed to pull off this little stunt, but enough was enough. Morna was alone, possibly dead, possibly half-crazed from the change; if and when one had ever taken place. He'd solve this mystery when there was more time, and if there was a price to pay for what they had all done, they would pay it. Karma would make sure of that. But, for right now, Justice needed a serious time out.

Perhaps somewhere in a weightless environment, Cradle thought happily to himself.

"You can't fire me, dummy. Haven't you been listening? It's quitting time. I'm quitting, you're quitting, we're all quitting these bullshit, low-level, government-issue jobs."

A seraphic chord ripped from Cradle's chest, echoing across purgatory as an unidentifiable force brought the primordial angel to his knees. Neither matter nor antimatter, the mystical force brought the weight of the omniverse as it settled heavily upon Cradle's ancient shoulders. Like Atlas holding up the sky, Cradle strained against the unbearable pressure, lifting and twisting to look over his dark shoulders to find them barren.

It was unthinkable. Beyond any known law, an unidentifiable, asymmetric force negated the inverse duality which allowed and powered Cradle's specifically designed binary existence. Against every known possibility, Cradle's boundless wings had been clipped.

"Of course, there will be some growing pains while we restructure," the fate went on as if nothing were out of the ordinary. "We will have to cut some of the fat off the middle, but have heart. Many of you will be staying on, and we are offering a very special, free skills training program to get you up to speed on what will be expected during and after the rebranding efforts. For the rest of you, well, we wish you luck in your new endeavors. That's the nature of these hostile takeovers. But, if you bear with us, I think you'll find that when the dust settles, we'll all be happier for the improvements. I know I will be, but then again, *I'm* upper management."

"Someone has seriously thought this shit through!" Freyja spat through the pain, interfering with her ability to hear, let alone understand Justice's ramblings. "This isn't a Justice is Swift special." Freyja roared at the onslaught of another brand, then pressed on, "We came with Justice willingly. Why would he even think he would need all this... Arrrgh, goddammit that smarts! Heff! Heff? By Odin's beard, I'm talking to you, husband!" Freyja yelled into the dirty stage floor.

"He's not here, Freyja. Neither is Creak!" Cradle yelled through the mysterious force bearing down upon him.

"He's busy, Freyja. He's one of the chosen few who will be staying on," Justice chimed in. "Not to worry, though, you'll be in far too much pain to have any time to miss his ugly mug. I am truly sorry about all this, but I simply can't have you hanging around with all that mathematical bullshit floating about and screwing up my plans. I need it to be midnight constantly, where the veil of omniversal law is thinnest and the most easily bent."

"Why did everyone run, Justice? What are they afraid of? What happens at midnight?" Freyja roared back, ignoring her pain and heartache at Heff's absence while the Fifth Hammer continued its disfiguring blows.

Heff was a big boy; he could take care of himself. Wherever her husband was, Freyja bet her ass he was trying to figure this shit out too. It was one thing she could trust. For now, she needed to stall. Freyja needed to think between the brands and blows of the hammer fucking up her power but not her mind.

"Arrrgh!" Freyja screamed out with all she had into the derelict boards of the stage floor, hoping it would help clear away the cobwebs of pain.

She knew there were mere seconds before the next strike, and she needed every last one of them to think, to figure.

Whatever was happening with Justice went beyond a 'Justice is Swift Special', she thought to herself between savage blows.

Whatever he was doing went beyond the pale.

"Oh shit... *The Pale.*"

An entirely different set of warning bells went off in her head.

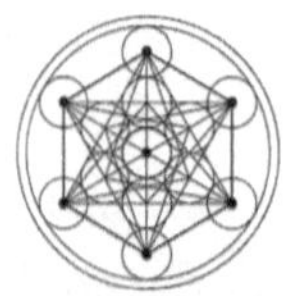

TWENTY-SEVEN

CHECK, CHECK, CHECK

"Fucking traitor," Creak spat between jagged teeth from his flight path high above Purgatory Proper.

The Grinx hid in plain sight, blending seamlessly into a narrow outcropping of rock like a sniper in a ghillie suit. Left behind when the others vanished, it was obvious whatever juice Justice wielded didn't work on him, and Justice neither seemed to notice nor care.

Underestimated.

"Fine by me, wouldn't be the first fucking time," Creak said, rustling his gossamer wings along his gravely flanks in a way that chafed roughly against the thin, translucent material.

It was a bad habit he'd broken long ago, and for good reason. Do it enough and it would rip the delicate wings to shreds.

"Trigger warning," Creak Piaget'd the not-so-subtle behavioral workings of his guilt-ridden inner child, recognizing the wing chafe for exactly what it was.

Regress and regret. It had taken him years to break the physical habit, years more to understand and corral the motivations causing the self-inflicted injuries in the first place.

"Check yo self before you wreck yo self," he mantra'ed,

invoking unto his bruised ego the lyrical stylings of his favorite modern-day philosopher, O'Shea Jackson, before looking inward to give his chakras a full-on seven-point inspection.

And just as he'd suspected when he looked under the hood. He found the third one was a bit further out of whack than the acceptable norm, and The One knows, he knew why.

Creak and his family were underestimated before. It was long ago when he'd been no more than a hatchling. Through no heroics of his own, it had played out well for him. The real heroes of that ill-fated fairy tale were his parents, the King and Queen of Domos Navitas. King Vicus and Queen Veritas had used the underestimation of their house's power to their advantage. An advantage that bought them enough time to save their hatchling's life instead of their own. Though he'd been working on it for years, the survivor's guilt still chapped his ass.

"I forgive you," he absolved the baby Grinx he used to be for the millionth time.

He sent his truth inward to set his manipura to rights. As always, his true self knew better, and his third chakra responded accordingly, which meant it lined up almost perfectly with the other six, but not quite. While he understood it wasn't his fault and had gotten in the habit of regularly forgiving the innocent baby Grinx, the adult he'd grown into at the cost of his parents' lives couldn't cut it the fuck loose and probably never would. The best he could do for now was accept the baseless guilt as part of his truth, which also meant accepting the misalignment of his third chakra as a permanent handicap bore onto him the day he lived and his parents died.

"What are you up to, you shiny shithead?" freshly realigned, Creak took careful stock of the traitorous scene playing out below.

Souls continued to run amok, "Check." Bells still clamored, "Check." Fires still raged, "Check." Pendulums still swung, "Check." Cradle was kneeling, "That's new." Heff was M.I.A.,

"The plot thickens." Freyja was being Vitruvian-ed fifty shades of fucked up with no safe word. "Not fucking cool, Mr. Gray," Creak swore on a rabid snarl as his yellow gaze fell onto Justice, who marched up and down the Perdition stage in some sort of full-on rant.

Creak couldn't quite hear what was going on, but from the looks of it, Justice was giving Cradle and Freyja a good old-fashioned dressing down.

"What an asshat."

Creak shook his head in disgust as he looked over the littered ground for potential objects he could use as weapons.

"Christ on a cracker," Creak communed in disbelief as four pinhole-sized voids appeared in the sandy ground surrounding the throne dais where Justice Gray rested his burnished ass.

Creak cocked his head, searching for a central angle as he zoomed in. The leathery part of his wings pressed forward, high, and tight around his neck as his body adjusted, altering itself to focus more closely on the four holes. Breathless, the subtle bones within his wings curved up and out, cresting just behind his jagged, black ears in a spider web of razor-sharp, fine-tipped points as he adjusted his reticle like the most skilled of snipers, landing all four of his marks perfectly in his countless crosshairs.

Creak lost himself in watching with his wings instead of his eyes while denial rode hard over what he knew in his heart to be true. His mind raced, bargaining against his fight or flight senses to stand firm and concentrate as his worst fears crept into reality. He knew those holes. He'd seen them before. Tiny portents heralded with their appearance a Nostradamic quatrain of The Four, all the while reality sieved away into nothingness grain by grain.

"You bastard," he whispered as the scene played out, a bona fide repeat performance of the beginning of the end for Satera. Creak's breath caught in his throat as a good old-fashioned dose of

PTSD washed hard and fast over his stony core, cementing him in terror to the cliffs where he stood.

"My mother would take offense to that, you low-bred mongrel," Justice spat as he tossed a lasso perfectly around Creak's thick neck, pulling tight.

"Fuc—" Creak was cut short as the rope yanked fast and hard, snaring in its noose the tiny bones of his wings that had been high and tight in attention.

"It's off to the pound with the rest of the strays, you fucking cur. If it was up to me, I'd put you down right here, but Torq says you're some sort of doggie royalty and that earns you certain considerations," he gritted through clenched teeth as he put all his weight behind another good pull, snapping all the fragile bones in Creak's wings like dried-up twigs. "Torq didn't say you had to be in one piece, though," he snarled, toppling the bound and broken Grinx with a hard kick to the solar plexus, courtesy of a steel-toed, piss-soaked boot.

TWENTY-EIGHT

ANGEL SPLAINING

"Cradle! It's The Pale! The Pale!" Freyja choke-screamed just before another blow hit her hard enough to damn near knock her unconscious.

"The Pale? Freyja, listen to me. You have to stop and listen to me right now!" Cradle yelled to the Norse warrior.

Justice had popped off somewhere, and he didn't know how long he had to talk with her alone. Freyja wasn't making any sense, and The One help them all; it was easy to understand why. The Freyja of Sessrumnir had endured a beating that would put an end to almost every immortal he'd ever known. It hurt him more than it should to watch her take the repeated blows, to watch her hold on and push through the pain as she tried to stay sane.

It was in that moment, on that stage, in the middle of Purgatory Proper, it became clear to Cradle the Freyja he had come to know was much more than mathematical perfection, more than a friend, a wife, and even more than a mother. Freyja of Sessrumnir was one badass immortal soldier, and he was proud to have her by his side.

"Freyja! Listen to me! Listen to my voice! It's Torquemada! It has to be him behind this! We know Torquemada wanted Morna.

We know Torquemada has the power to make a play for purgatory! There's no other explanation!" Cradle gritted out as the weight of the ages continued to bear down upon his shoulders.

Freyja heard Cradle's words envelop over, around, and through the haze of pain blistering her body. She heard Cradle talking, yelling over to her, but the pain reached deep, branding her charred skin to her very core. The sound of Cradle's voice swirled all around but wouldn't settle into her ears, couldn't translate through her pain. Knowing she had little time, she stopped trying to listen and focused hard on the task at hand. Cradle needed to hear *her*. She needed to be crystal fucking clear.

"Arrrgh!!! Son of bitch bucket! Judas Priest! Mother pucker! Cheese and fucking rice!" Freyja unleashed an unholy hybrid string of standard adult fare and mother-approved cuss words as she braced hard through the searing pain. She felt the fabric of her construct unravel into nothingness. "Son of a motherless goat! Fuckity, fuck, fuck, fuck! Shiitake fungrooms!" she yelled into the gritty floor as the heat seared further and further, all the way to her immortal soul. She knew she was fading away into nothingness with every destructive blow of Pythagoras's cock-sucking hammer. This was it. She only had one more chance to get through to Cradle as she poured everything she had into one last, broken cry, "Cathy's coming, Cradle! Cathy's fucking coming!"

Freyja screamed, just before her whole world went black.

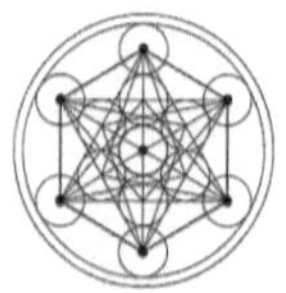

TWENTY-NINE

CATHY

The four holes in the floor of purgatory took on a life of their own. While two remained minuscule, the other two grew. The second largest was a good two feet by three feet, while the largest of the four was easily double in diameter. The next-to-largest shot upward from somewhere deep in its center, a laser beam of crimson red reaching without end into the midnight sky, while the largest of the four was somehow not really there. The very definition of what nothing might look like if it were actually possible to realize such a thing.

The nothing of The Four yawned and stretched, never settling on a shape as something ate away at its emptiness, forcing it to cede to an impossible lake of liquid smoke and viscous mirrors. The Pale barreled up and through its mercurial opening on a nag of white-hot ash.

One smoldering hoof hit hard on the line betwixt The Between and everything else, collapsing into shapeless ashes only to reclaim its fleeting form before the very last ash blew away on an eddying wind.

Collapsing, swirling, and rebuilding itself with every step into

Purgatory, the nag-chuffed plumes of soot and smoke swirl all around, specifically passing over and around, the area just above its cinder saddle, creating in its noticeable absence a very clear outline of an otherwise invisible rider.

Small and female, the rider wasn't seated, but stood firm on a white-hot saddle with reins held taut in one hand and a rapier drawn forth in the other. Resolute, the ghost rider charged up and out as she inhaled an otherworldly breath of the volatile ash, expelling it back into the atmosphere on a silent scream of inaudible power.

"Lena! Stop!" resonated out on the amplified quiver of regurgitated cinders.

A communication inaudible to the ears but rather a gritty string of vibrations traveling aloft on a charred, transcendental breath. It settled itself and its message deep in the far reaches of any soul who dared breathe it in. A soul who, once touched by its resonance, became immediately darker and forever sadder for ever having acknowledged its call.

"Jesus. The fucking Pale," Cradle swore, beating the shit out of himself for not truly hearing Freyja.

The One help him. He would never make that mistake again, given he wouldn't be around much longer to make any more mistakes. Taking in the smallest particulate of the infected air would forever change who he was on a visceral level, but fuck if he wasn't going to do it anyway. What choice did he have? It was a long shot, but it was the only way out of the shit show. If he could put a little chink in the *laissez-faire* armor worn by The Pale, he might be able to reach the Catherine he hoped still dwelled somewhere within.

Cradle thought of the beautifully conflicted woman he once knew. Thought of the way she forgave everyone for damn near anything while never letting herself off the hook for a single, solitary word or deed she'd ever dared breathe life into. In all his existence, he'd never met another being as equally torn up for being exactly who they were supposed to be. When he'd met Cathy a hundred earthly lifetimes before, he'd met his match.

Inimically singular, Cathy's smile was a one-in-a-million simper that never quite concealed the sadness in her eyes as they wasted long afternoons tangled up in sheets and meaningless, philosophical hyperbole. Each one tried to escape who and what they were, if only for a little while. He could see her now, leaning over him, her long brown hair mussed from root to tip, and glowing like a halo in the late afternoon sun as it shone through the broken, stained-glass window of the abandoned church he'd long ago called home. Transfixed, he'd stroke the backs of his fingers through those strands, losing himself in the way she allowed him to lazily explore everything about her. And when she flashed her bewitching smile down upon him, he'd reveled in it. It had all been beautifully simple, so easy. Until the day it that wasn't.

"Oh, but how lovely a creature you were, Catherine," Cradle whispered to his memories before taking in a giant's breath worth of the asphyxiating residue expelled by the anomalous rider. He held it deep, absorbing as much as he could for as long as he could. Only when his body bucked violently in rejection of the dark, foreign matter did he cry out on a broken breath the affirmation needed to make her soot his own.

"I accept this! Let it be mine!" Cradle avowed as a single human lifetime worth of ceaseless inner torment bore in perpetuity by The Pale jumped ship, transferring itself from her war-torn soul to his.

Cradle knelt against the gritty stage floor, back arched, and head thrown to the sky as the rider's pain rode hard through his broken body, stitching itself to his very marrow. Sweat poured in rivers down his naked shoulders, settling salt deep into the open wounds where his wings had been while the newly acquired inner torment cauterized the damage from within.

When the last of the burden finally settled itself deep within him, his wracked body shuddered to return the recycled essence back to The Pale. And so, he did. Using what was left of his broken breath, Cradle sent his gift. A virtual vortex of crystal-clear particulates. An Angel's breath worth of mercy, Cathy was never able to give herself.

Cleansed of self-doubt, the unburdened particulates of The Pale Rider's essence sailed back to her on a string of vibrations Cradle prayed would momentarily settle her soul, carrying with it the inaudible message, "Cathy halt! Please, Cath, it's not time!"

The rider's head snapped fast and hard, stopping her ride full tilt as she pulled up short. Dead still she stood, unencumbered by the testy, smoldering beast beneath her as she looked toward the source in heavy silence. A sentience of sorts, something akin to relief then empathy, momentarily flashed across her devoid face as a corporeally challenged version of the Catherine he knew long ago short-circuited over the current incarnation.

"I *am* The Pale," the rider countered in her vacant language. "There is no Cathy here."

Cradle breathed a sigh of relief he did not let it settle on his face. He'd gotten through. She was communicating with him.

Easy, he thought to himself, aware of how this one moment in time was the only chance he'd get to diffuse the pending apocalypse.

One wrong move and it was all over.

"My apologies," Cradle offered, bowing his head low. "I am Metatron," formally introducing himself as he ignored the weight of the ages still pressing down upon him.

"Metatron. The Voice. The Grand Communicator. Well, Meta-tron, that explains *how* you can hear and speak to me. What it does not do is explain why you would choose to do so. You should know better, angel," The Pale said, vacant of emotion as her earthly image flashed and shorted like a rogue strobe light over her ghostly form.

"Yes, Pale Rider. I do know better. Does that not beg the question why would I risk so much to do so?" He answered humbly.

He was at her mercy here. He needed her curious if nothing else. If he so much as hinted they'd known each other or how she was making a mistake, The Pale would run him down on a trail of white-hot ash, never stopping to look back.

The earthly image of Cathy settled and lingered a while over The Pale's face as she looked toward the hole emitting crimson light into the never-ending sky. It, and the two other portents, had gotten no bigger since The Pale had charged into purgatory.

"It is a dangerous game you play, Metatron. The fate of everything does not wait for a defunct angel's stamp of approval."

"No, Pale Rider. However, it does seem to wait on yours."

Cradle made a show of turning his eyes toward the three inert portents as Cathy sharply locked her empty eyes on his. Her corporeal face ceded to the wraith-like version and stayed frozen for several quiet seconds. Damnit, he'd unsettled her. She didn't like how he noticed the others awaited her call. The order he'd heard her call out to The Red was the fuel-firing his attempt to treat her in the first place. He knew when he heard her order, The Pale must have sensed something wasn't right. There was no way The Four would stop their ride before it began if something wasn't off from the very beginning.

"The Four and their business is no business of yours, Metatron. Shouldn't you be somewhere writing things down in a book? Oh, that's right. You were demoted, were you not? For sticking your nose where it doesn't belong, if I remember correctly?"

Yep, she was pissed, and becoming more corporeal by the second, which could be good... or very, very bad if memory served. The good news was she was sentient enough to talk with him, sentient enough to know the role of Metatron the angel, if not Cradle the man she once knew.

"Technically, I wasn't demoted. I was transferred."

"For being impartial, wasn't it? I was impartial, angel. Lena, Bill, and Steve were impartial. It didn't get us transferred. It got us corralled and hobbled for all eternity with nothing to do but think. What was your punishment, Metatron? Light duty as a middle management assembly-line sorter in a borderland weigh station with unrestricted leave for babysitting duties?" The Pale questioned with her emotionally vacant sound as baby blue fire stirred in her empty eyes.

At least she knew his origin story, or most of it anyway. Unfortunately, it didn't seem to endear him to her in the least.

"Pale Rider, I am humbled by your burden. I respect your office and its duties, but I think you know it is not time."

"Why do you say this, angel?"

"The dimensions have not come together, Rider. It is written the ride shall come when there is but one dimension again. It is then and only then The Four shall be called to run down every soul and quark who have no place within."

"We were called, angel. So, we answer."

"Called? That is not possible."

"Yet, here I stand."

Cradle did his best to remain suppliant as he questioned. He dared not press too hard, but he needed more intel to understand how this could have happened. Clearly, Justice was involved, but surely they didn't wield the kind of force it would take to call up The Four. Hell, no one was wielding that kind of Torque.

"Shit."

Cradle wasn't sure on the hows, but he'd become crystal fucking clear on the who.

"Yet, there you stand," Cradle countered, no longer questioning whether Cathy was in there.

This was the sort of conversation she loved; he'd almost forgotten that about her. She loved drawing things out longer than needed, dropping clues like breadcrumbs along the way. The longer she kept you hooked, the longer she could control the length of the conversation. The Cathy of old could keep you guessing about the ins and outs of her weekly trip to the Saturday market for hours on end. Because the longer she kept you talking, the fewer the minutes she had alone in her mind to think about how much she hated herself.

"Tell me, did The Four know it was Torquemada who called when you barreled out of your oubliettes, or had you all just been chomping at the bit for so long you didn't really care who the fuck called or why? Anything to take your mind off things right, Cath?" Cradle spat.

He was done with her cryptic bullshit.

"We have no choice. The whos and whys of it are not our burden. We have but one job. The whole of everything else is not up to us."

"Bullshit, Cathy. You stopped. You ordered Lena to stop. I know you know The Ride is a mistake."

"And now so do you, Metatron. You also know whose mistake it is. You're welcome."

Oooooh, there she was. The Pale Rider and his darling Catherine were not so dissimilar after all.

"Fuck you, Cathy! I know you! You're no fucking soothsayer. Don't you dare try to take a prophetic high road with me. I know exactly what you're doing."

"Careful, Cradle. If I didn't know better, I'd say you're still bitter at the way we left things," Cathy jabbed.

As a high-def technicolor image of the woman she used to be settled over her wraith-like form, letting Cradle know good and damn well the core of her remembered everything and always had, despite pretending otherwise. For a fucking eternity.

"Still playing games, Catherine? Dragging things out for your amusement? Even when the stakes are this high?"

"The stakes are always high when you're marked Unknown, Cradle. I would think that might be something you would know a little bit about," she mused lightly. Her painfully beautiful smile made light of his current situation in spite of serving eternity in her very own personal hell. "Besides, it makes the conversation that much sweeter." She eased back in the saddle, satisfied with her carefully chosen words... "The art of conversing has truly become lost, especially on the younger generation, don't you think?" Cathy asked on a forced note of sweet, tinkling laughter. Her ghost washed her ever-present pain into nothing but eddying wisps of ashen breath.

Not taking the bait, Cradle decided to step carefully over the Pandora's box of epic fucking proportions. Cathy lay casually at his feet, then aimed where it would hurt most, and fired. "What kind of creature have you become that you would run down the whole of everything and burn it all to ash simply because you can't stand the thought of being alone with yourself for one more single, solitary, goddamn second?"

"Settle down, Cradle. Contrary to what you might think, the Four are not mindless beasts," Cathy fired sharply. "We are aware the race was rigged, and we take no pleasure in riding it that way. I was calling the cavalry home when you rudely interrupted me."

"Interrupted you? Catherine Incongnita Patri, Pale Rider of The Four, how fucking dare you! I took, upon my soul, a lifetime's worth of your burden and unending self-hatred. I lifted it from your immortal soul in a desperate bet I might have but a few moments alone with you. Just YOU! A hundred years of inner peace I wagered for a few moments without your baggage getting in the way! To stop you from having to eke out an eternity alone, personally responsible for making the biggest mistake ever fucking made!"

"And it paid off. I know it stings, but that's what happens when you bet on a horse to show and it places first. Your gamble paid off, Cradle, and that's a good thing if memory serves. Besides, you would have figured it out on your own as soon as you saw the special treat The Grand Inquisitor has waiting for you," she added, making a show of turning her ghostly eyes toward the ancient torture devices the twisted bastard had employed during his lengthy reign of terror across sixteenth-century Spain.

"Goddamnit, Cathy! This isn't a fucking game! Tell me what you know! No bullshit, only facts!"

"There is no Cathy here," The Pale Rider announced, vacant of emotion.

Cradle would have fallen to his knees if he weren't already there. With his soul as broken as his body, the angel watched the empty outline of the woman he'd once loved turn cold and ride away. The image smacked hard of the last day he ever saw her alive when she'd shut him out of her heart. Her words are just as cold, and her eyes are just as empty.

"Pale Rider, wait!" Cradle pleaded, panicked at the quickly deteriorating wisps of ash and soot.

"We were summoned once before," The Pale called on the violent wind as she rode away. "You should know that, Cradle. We did not hesitate then. We were selfish and just wanted it to end. We'd eviscerated an entire species before sensing something was wrong. When we finally realized what we had done, it was too late."

The rider stopped her ashen nag at the very edge of the mercurial lake on the floor of Purgatory.

She turned slowly, locking her icy blues with Cradle's, and said in a hauntingly tangible voice, "When you are finished with Tomas de Torquemada, light a fire and toss the source of his power into the heart of it. Feed the fire with your breath, angel, and open yourself up to feel the well of my pain living deep inside of you now. Do that and I will come to collect it, and him—personally."

And with that, Cathy was gone.

181

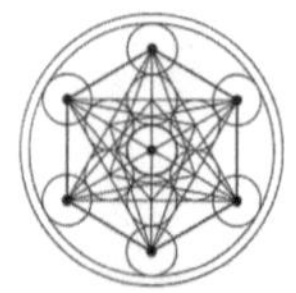

THIRTY

IRON FILIGREE AND FLEUR-DE-LIS

From where Silla sat perched on HQ's overhead dome, she saw it wasn't a dome, but a piece of grass in a well-kept, private garden of someone's remodeled Benton Park mini-mansion. The monstrous old houses were everywhere in this area of St. Louis. Most were in utter shambles, gutted for their copper, and left for dead. The others were magnificent mansions being brought back to life. Some touted glorious Victorian colors and spiraling turrets, while others were all brownstone or red brick with iron filigree and fleur-de-lis embellishments as far as the eye could see. Scattered devil-may-care among the bones of those yet to be resurrected. Silla decided she enjoyed the contrast. It seemed a perfect world the way it was, and she silently hoped it would stay that way, a dystopian days-of-future past.

Wrapped in a robe, tucked in an Adirondack chair, and munching on a small backyard picnic, Silla was about as comfy as she could be, considering… well, every-fucking-thing. She'd sat in the moody blue moonlight for the last half hour or so, eavesdropping at the hole she'd burned through the dome of HQ, not feeling the least bit guilty for liberating the clothes, goodies, and wine from the mini-mansion gourmet kitchen. Hey, it wasn't her fault the folks who lived there didn't care enough about their digs to lock the back door when they weren't home. After all, it *was* Benton Park. In her mind, she was doing the new homeowners a favor. Had it been any other sneak thief combing through their newly renovated humble abode, the lesson would have cost them a hell of a lot more than a makeshift hospitality basket.

From the topside, the owl-shaped hole looked like an odd shadow in the grass and nothing more, but it acted like the perfect spy gear mic for her snooping ears. The arc of the dome carried the softest of murmurs right up and out of the arched ceiling. In the last half hour, Silla had heard a lot.

So far, she could add a talking pig and a flying toddler to the ever-increasing list of fairytale bullshit she now believed in. The talking pig was a little much, like Mrs. Poole from FBDO, for Silla to take seriously. The dainty-winged diva who rocked pink fuzzy socks was a kindred spirit fo' sho. Silla had spent a few minutes in, honest to God, awe over the little munchkin who wasn't about to lie down like a pre-orphaned Disney character while some asshole pummeled her parents. Nope, Nitzie was a little badass, and Silla couldn't wait to babysit.

"Fuck, I suck," Silla confessed to the moon overhead. "Nitz is a hard-core card-carrying member of the Binky Badass Club, and I'm a wine-drinking, robe-wearing coward. What the hell is wrong with me?" Disgusted, Silla swept the pile of snacks off her lap, chucked the crystal-cut Mikasa stemware across the lawn, and grabbed the half-empty bottle of 2014 Prisoner Cabernet. "Whoa! whoa! whoa!" Silla came to her senses around mid-chuck. "No need to throw the baby out with the bathwater!" she counseled. "Let's not add stupid to our list of disappointing identifiers. Coward's plenty for now."

It was quiet. Too quiet. Silla had lain in silence, clutching the bottle of cab and staring up at the stars for over ten minutes, wanting nothing more than to hear her best friend's voice, when a God-awful sound escaped the owl-shaped emergency hatch. Like a hive of bees swarming a yodeling honey badger, the sound was grating… and a familiar one at that.

Onto her belly, Silla grunt-crawled to the opening and peered in to see Morna fifty feet below… tending bar? She was up top, drowning in guilt, and that bitch was down there tending bar and humming. Humming!

"What the actual fuck, Morna?" Silla whispered as she watched her bestie expertly open bottles of wine, delicately add little drops of something into each bottle, then professionally recork them, all while murdering "Steal My Sunshine".

Silla rolled onto her back and stared up at the blue moon, not knowing how to feel as she hummed along. Strange things were afoot at the Circle K.

"I don't know what to do here, kids," she said plainly to the garden gnomes to her right. "It's not like I'm afraid of her. I could never be afraid of Morna. It's just this angel vibe she's putting out; it makes me feel… less than. You know what I'm saying, don't you, Jason?" she asked, directing her question to the black and white garden gnome sporting a blood-splattered goalie mask. "Never were much of a talker, were you? Honestly, you guys, if I could just find a way around the vibes, she isn't aware she's putting out, we could get through this thing."

Silla turned toward the odd couple gnome duo on her right.

"I mean, seriously, what fun is it in being a superhero, fiery, owl thingy when I can't hang with my bestie?" Silla turned onto her stomach and looked a Miss Piggy gnome right in the eyes. "It never bothered you for a second that Kermit over there was an entirely different species, did it?" Silla shot a look of derision at the garden gnome toadstooling it on a ceramic mushroom, sporting a green face and webbed feet, looking more than a little sexually harassed by the sexy pig gnome grabbing him by his hose-enhanced cloaca. "It ain't easy being green, is it, little buddy?"

"Goddamn, motherfucking, son of a bitch!" sailed up and out of the hole on a tinkling symphony of shattering glass, followed by a cantankerous, "What up, wings?" cutting short Silla's late-night gnomeopathic therapy session.

Back over at Mach speed, Silla shoved her face down into the hole to see Morna inspecting the empty shelves behind her as her unfledged wings clumsily cleared an entire shelf of high-end barware. Silla watched, sort of horrified and sort of delighted, as Morna turned again and again, causing her inexperienced, gargantuan wings to clear entire rails of top-shelf booze. It was like watching a winged bull play Jenga in a China shop, and it was everything! She couldn't look away. Fully enraptured with the not-so-perfect angel below, a well-loved bartender made his innocuous way down the side alley on the other side of the fence. A neighborhood staple well known for walking his dog and policing the streets late at night, Jeff Prince went completely unnoticed as he entered through the side gate of the well-kept garden Silla sat ostrich ass up in.

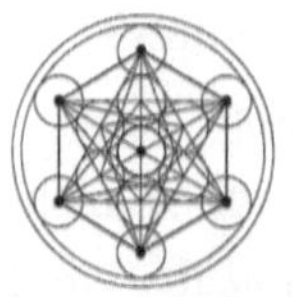

THE NETWORK

Creak woke with a headache cleaving perfectly down the center of his head. He swore on his House that a quarry master had professionally driven a wedge straight through the stone center of his skull.

Clank! Clank! Clank! Pshhh!
Clank! Clank! Clank! Pshhh!
Clank! Clank! Clank! Pshhh!

"Grrrrrrrrrrrahhhhhhhhhhh!" Creak snarled a mouthful of sulfuric, yellow foam at the incessant banging.

Each clank carved deeper, sluicing through the Grand Canyon-sized ache in his head as it traveled down his spinal cord in a river of pain, gully-washing through every mangled nerve in his busted-up wings. Cracking the slits of his reptilian eyes, his stomach rolled, and he spewed a volcano's worth of foamy sulfur.

Clank! Clank! Clank! Pshhh!
Clank! Clank! Clank! Pshhh!
Grrrrrrrrahhhhhhhhhh!

Creak growled, looking inward for the answers he was physically incapable of reaching with his eyes. He needed to know where he was and who the hell was making all the fucking noise so he could kill them.

He breathed through the pain and relaxed into his surroundings, letting one tense muscle at a time slip away from his consciousness. The slab beneath took all of his weight as he tranced into a boneless state of awareness, inviting the materials supporting him to be seen by his mind's eye as a helpful extension of his own body. Just like that, he was one with his surroundings and able to identify everything in the extended network as something kindred.

Dead to the world, Creak lay inert and stone cold as he took stock of his environment. He communed with every element in the room, right down to the very last quark. Easy enough to do if he knew how to get the hell out of your own way. Ego wasn't welcome in the Network; to join, he had to let go.

Creak inventoried chromium, nickel, molybdenum, silicon, aluminum, carbon, and iron as the main ingredients in the surrounding network. Stainless steel? Huh, he was in a stainless-steel cage. Boy, did that ever smack of treason. Someone did their homework. The question was, how? As far as he knew, Goji was the only other surviving Grinx from Satera. Though he hadn't seen his sentry in nearly a hundred years, he knew in his heart there was no way he would have shared Sateran insider secrets with anyone, let alone a weasel-like Justice Gray. Besides, it couldn't be Goji. He was from House Navitas, too, and was privy to the knowledge this little trick didn't work well on a Grinx from his House.

It didn't make sense, Creak thought as he combed through his mind for answers and came up with zip, zilch, nothing, nada.

Gah, his head hurt. He couldn't think. Creak tapped into the air flowing around the Network of his stainless-steel cage, drawing it down and through himself like a thermoelectric cooler. Acting like a heat pump, he simply forced the much cooler air back out into the Network, subsequently dropping the core temperature of the metal floor he was lying on to mercifully soothe his throbbing head like a Make-A-Wish cold compress. In the Network, there was no need for material things. Everything he could ever want was already there; he just had to know where to look and never, ever take more than what was needed. Greed in the Network would get him bounced quicker than a bill to revolutionize the American healthcare system.

The cage wasn't going to be a problem, so there was that. Whoever thought he was incapable of manipulating his way through poor conducting metals didn't know dick about the Grinx of Domos Navitas. The Balance Keepers of the other four Domos couldn't manipulate their way through alloys like stainless steel due to their inability to manipulate anything deemed "unnatural". The other houses could, of course, manipulate the non-alloy metals, but hell, even the youngest hatchlings of Domos Navitas could do that! Great conductors like the purer metals were easy. The framework was solid, a lattice structure was laid out perfectly, and all they had to do was relax, let go, and play connect the dots as they zipped down the line.

Mixed metals like stainless steel were a whole other story. It was an easy enough fix for a Navitas Grinx, but a Grinx from any other House would find it impossible to fill in the missing hunks of latticework conducive to good conductivity. Without good conductivity, you weren't going far, and it was going to hurt like hell when you finally figured it out. Sort of like traveling on a bullet train hell-bent for Tokyo, only to realize a day late and a dollar short that enormous hunks of track were missing. Shit just wasn't going to end well.

So, while the other Houses could identify unnatural alloys in a network, they couldn't manipulate them, and that's where Creak's family had the upper hand. While a Navitas Grinx could never manipulate energies solely identifiable to humans, they could manipulate the hell out of anything non-human related. All they had to do was identify gaps and fill them with elements they plucked from damn near anywhere in any given Network. If a Grinx from any other house on Satera so much as tried to patch a gateway through a metal alloy grid, they'd short-circuit and be fried out for days. Not that they would ever dare lower themselves to notice, let alone fiddle with the non-human energies they deemed so very far beneath them.

His House had always played the little-known ability close to their chest. They would have just gotten made fun of for it anyway. It would never occur to any of those self-righteous, quartz-collared snobs why anyone of consequence would want to get their claws dirty with amps, volts, joules, bytes, or bits. And it was just fine by the Grinx of House Navitas that not one of the other Royal Domos thought them more than a poor man's electrician. Their holier-than-thou derision made it that much easier for the Master Journeyman of House Navitas to go completely undetected, becoming virtual ghosts in any machine.

Clink! Clink! Clink! Pshh!

"That's it! Time to Shawshank! Alla-ka-Andy-Abra-Dufrense!"

Creak tapped into every electron in his body and started with the purple, glowy shit again.

This time, instead of washing over him, the purple glow pulsed in waves built like liquid magma, building until his rocky crust cracked from the pressure in lilac hairline fractures.

Creak quieted his id, checked his ego, then humbly reached out into the local Network and plucked the missing elements necessary to patch a solid gateway through his stainless-steel cage as his surface gave way. It released an explosion of electrons that hitched a ride across the alloy lattice like a hot current down a live wire. When he came to the end of the line, he simply unplugged from the Network, his raw energy firmly on the other side of the stainless-steel prison walls.

Pulled together by natural attraction, the stuff that made him… well, him, pooled together in a purple orb and waited patiently as he connected to the Network on this side of the prison wall and gathered up the right bits to sculpt himself a new casing. In less than a wink, Creak was on top of the stainless steel cage, freshly reassembled. His headache was gone, and his broken wings a thing of the past.

"Namaste." He bowed low, head to the side as he humbly thanked the Network of Local Energy for the hook-up, noticing before he unplugged that something was out of whack within the natural order of things. "What in the wild, wild world of sports?" he chuffed and metaphysically leaned into the Network to get a better read, checking off the fundamental components of Purgatory as he went. "Shitload of Carrara marble? Check. Metric ton of non-partisan ethereal elements? Check."

The information processed through Creak at a throughput impossible for even the nerdiest of nerds to wrap their heads around. Those little, black, flinty stones adorning his rocky hide were more than mere decoration; they were black diamonds. Those powerful gems, coupled with the mammoth hunk of quartz on the tip of his tail, made the Navitas Grinx a living, breathing super-computer powered by the rawest and purest of unfettered energies swirling beneath the rocky surface of his blue-black hide.

Perched on top of his recent prison cell, Creak huffed a bit as he filled his new body with some much-needed oxygen before opening his yellow eyes. He needed to figure out how in the name of Marie Curie there could be radiation seeping across Purgatory and also find the asshole making all the fucking racket so he could kill them.

"Heff? Hey, Heff! Up here! Man, am I ever glad to see your ugly mug!"

HERE AND NOW

Karma had spent the last hour filling Hildi and Morna in on her plan to cull Justice's larger-than-life ego. Karma planned on knocking down the out-of-touch Morai using little more than parlor tricks and guilt. Who was Morna to argue with the living, breathing, metaphysical embodiment of Newton's third law?

"Sounds like a very fine plan, Karma dear, but how can we execute any of that from here? As Morna said, the logistics on this delivery are going to be a real bitch." Hildi reached out her henna'd hand to give Morna a comforting, motherly pat. "As far as I know, every working portal to dimensions 9.333, 9.666, and 9.999 all stopped working at the end of the Mayan 'calendar'," Hildi said, making air quotes when she purposefully over-stressed the word calendar. "With no time left to use them, the originals are mostly buried in landfills with the rest of humanity's garbage. If you can find one, you'd need to be a shaman to eke out what little magic may remain in the sum of their circles, and as far as I know, Mayan priests are in short supply these days."

"No worries, ladies. We just need to make a quick stop by Gringo Jones' and we should be all set."

"Gringo Jones?" Morna questioned. "You mean the South American import store?"

"Is there another Gringo Jones? Of course, I mean *that* Gringo Jones. Where the hell else in 2018, St. Louis, would you expect to find a Mayan priest?" Karma answered, annoyed with having to explain herself as she rubbed little circles at her temples. "Honestly, it's like you've never met a Mayan holy man before."

"We knew what you meant, Karma, dear. It's been a while, you understand," Hildi said, stroking Karma's akimbo soul.

The last thing they needed was for the Fate to think they didn't know what they were doing, regardless of the fact the assumption was more or less dead-on, balls-accurate. Karma had spent an eternity wading through the aftermath of folks who blew through life like a bull in a China shop. All of them were one hundred percent sure they were doing the right thing, while one hundred and twenty percent wrong most of the time.

"Remind me, doll, would you? I was a little more than Freyja's childhood pet the last time I conversed with a Mayan about the Count of Days."

"Forget about the damn calendar, Hildi. That outdated hunk of stone is no more than a Fisher-Price See 'n Say toy to those who know what they are doing. You only need the stupid bauble if you're an inexperienced traveler, which Me'tok is most definitely not.

Morna side-eyed Hildi and rolled with it. Karma was their only shot at getting to Purgatory, and it was obvious the Fate was in no mood to be trifled with. With each passing second, Karma became testier and testier. Sort of like when Morna's mom made her and her mostly absentee grandparents spend quality time together. It was a forced cohesiveness; a necessary evil orchestrated by the outside universe which neither party involved was remotely happy about.

Karma spun slow and eloquent off her tall barstool, one supple, thigh-high, alabaster Louboutin at a time.

"Let's get this party started. My reactions are starting to back-log," she muttered, looking more green than sable.

"Are you alright, Karma dear? You look a little worse for wear," Hildi asked with concern in her very pig-like eyes.

"I'll be fine, Hildi. I'm just dealing with an early-bird and blue-plate special I gotta serve up at the same time, all while dealing with this shit show and every other self-serving asshole in the cosmos," Karma muttered.

"That's a whole lot of assholes," Morna said, empathetic to Karma's workload. In the last year, most of Morna's waking hours had been spent doing mostly the same, but on a much smaller scale, of course. "Can I help somehow?" Morna asked in earnest kinship.

"That's kind of you, sugar, but unless you can unseat a colonial highbrow hellbent on making electoral votes count equally for an overpopulated New York and a Wisconsin that doesn't exist yet simply because 'James Wilson'," she paused to air quote, "deems himself a diviner of democracy; all while simultaneously preparing a plate of 'Be Careful What You Wish For' to a Cheeto determined to watch the world burn on account of brown people in power making him uncomfortable—I think I'll have to handle things on my own," Karma said distantly, almost as if the bulk of her consciousness wasn't even in HQ anymore.

"James Wilson?" Morna questioned Hildi, lost and thinking maybe she was going daft or dying had somehow scrambled her brains. "God, I hope it's not permanent," she prayed under her breath.

"Yes, dear. One of the Founding Fathers of the United States of America," Hildi answered for the out-of-sorts Fate.

"I know Hildi, but the Founding Fathers are long dead."

Short of an evasive synchronized whistling, both Karma and Hildi puckered their beautifully glossed lips and averted their eyes to the dome of HQ like they'd both discovered the most interesting thing in the world up there.

"Aren't they?" Morna pressed, trying and failing to understand the connection.

"Is she daft?" Karma needled, wavering a bit on her sky-high boots before sinking back down on her barstool, completely deserting her attempt to dodge the question as she plopped her aching head into the folded nestle of her arms. "Hildi, I don't have time to go over everything with the newbie. Need I remind you, my time here is quite limited?"

"Hildi," Morna said, gathering the familiar's undivided attention. "Aren't they?" she pushed, feeling deep in her soul there was something really big she was missing here, daft or not.

Still looking up, Hildi shook her heavy, red dreads, blew out a kindergarten teacher's breath worth of patience, then turned to look Morna directly in the eyes as she simply gave in, "You're thinking linearly, dear. Nothing works that way."

And just like that, Morna knew it to be true. Her mind's eye tore open, shedding its linear human restrictions as her ethereal mind woke, laying out a grid of time and space in a wobbly layered framework she could see from multiple angles and inexhaustible perspectives.

"Whoa," Morna breathed as she metaphysically fell down a wormhole of truth she never knew she never knew.

"Um, Karma dear," Hildi said, clearing her throat a little to get the off-color fates' attention.

Karma groaned and turned her pallid head to the side, sighing to her run-down soul before cracking her aching, amber eyes. She sighed deeper still when she saw the befuddled, drooling, feathery mess before her.

"Ugh. You should have known better, Hildi. What the ever-loving fuck were you thinking?" Karma scolded before reaching blindly into one of the many pockets on her silk jumpsuit to pull out an old-timey silver snuff box with the word 'Opus' engraved in Latin across the lid in calligraphic script.

With a click, the Fate popped the lid and reached inside with her perfectly manicured fingers to pull out the tiniest pinch of black, sparkling dust.

"Technically, you brought it up," Hildi countered, not cowering in the least as she watched Karma prepare to administer an angel-sized dose of The Here and Now.

Karma rolled her perfectly made-up smoky eyes at Hildi and growled a warning low in her throat. She rubbed the dark, sparkly dust in circles between her index finger and thumb, working it into finer and finer granules before finally stopping to gently blow the small pile of crystals directly into Morna's gobsmacked face.

"Stay in the Ticks and Tocks too long without purpose, and hitching a ride to Purgatory will be the least of your worries, Morna darling." Then the Fate pulled the tiniest of silver spoons from yet another pocket, trenched it deep into the petite little snuff box, and scooped up a much larger dose of the crushed bits of ergo-sphere, whispering, "Here and Now," over the dusky little pile before snorting it straight up her heavily-jeweled nose.

"You need a fucking assistant," Morna swore wholeheartedly as she broke free of the vacuous continuum that clearly defined the perennial weight of Karma's work schedule. "Seriously, like a whole fucking slew of 'em."

"Ya think?" Karma asked with a sassy wink, looking and sounding more and more sable by the second as she closed the snuff box with a quiet click. "Listen, ladies. I can't stay here on just one plane for long; it's not how I'm built, and the cost is too high. Now," she said as she brushed the little blackened bits of remaining ergo-sphere from her freed-up hands, "let's call a cab and get over to Gringo Jones's before Me'tok finds a back-alley stickball tournament to make book on."

THIRTY-THREE

TINKERING WITH HUMANITY'S FAILED BULLSHIT

The outskirts beyond the Cliffs of Perdition were a virtual ghost town of closed steel plants, half-knit afghans, and failed rice cauliflower recipes. The Borderlands of Purgatory were littered to infinity with every unfulfilled and lost idea spanning the course of humanity's ability to hope and dream. Foundering constructs that were never quite actualized lay side by side in a boneyard of botched attempts and half-assed ideas never slated to make it out of the box. Basically, the Borderlands were a patent office trash heap come to life, and where there's a patent office, there's generally a clerk.

Albert had been there since April 1955, when he'd pissed off Justice after refusing to step on his scales while blasting the Fate relentlessly with questions about the universe. After about three weeks of Albert's endless toddleresque, Abu Ghraib inspired questioning the likes the childless Morai could never possibly imagine, the distressed Keeper of the Scales decided he'd had just about enough and simply tossed the soul of the man famous for saying, "Two things are infinite: the universe and human stupidity; and I'm not sure about the universe," into timeout equivalent of Albert's very own personal hell.

That was the first time Justice Gray had ever dipped his silvery toe into the pool of corruption, and the water had felt mighty fine indeed.

After about six-ish months of aimless wandering, Albert found and managed to settle into a beautiful, old college library just about thirty kilometers deep into the perimeter. Canted, sunk, and half swallowed up by Purgatory's sandy floor, only the second-story windows and roof remained above ground. Glorious in its Trinity-like architectural design, the half-assed structure was inevitably doomed to founder the day its designer failed to take into account the considerable weight of the books it was built to house.

Completely alone, isolated, and literally having nothing better to do, Albert started gathering things he could rework into usable items. Living on a diet of Wow! Potato chips, pluots, Crystal Pepsi, and Colgate Frozen Lasagna, Albert's first order of business was to create a toilet paper that didn't chafe. He'd finished loading seventy-five retooled pressure cookers with the shredded pages of seventy-five copies of *Mein Kampf* and had started to feel quite giddy about the idea of wiping his ass with Hitler's very own words when The Grand Inquisitor wormed his way through the second-story window of the half-sunken library.

Albert couldn't believe his fucking luck. Like a goddamn bad penny, these Jew-hating bastards kept turning up everywhere he went. Not particularly the Jewiest of Jews by a long shot, Albert was born in Ulm, Germany, in 1879 and raised by his not-so-Jewish parents, who saw fit to send him to a Catholic grade school. Albert, being a genius by the age of twelve, lost the ability to see a clearly defined God when the inimical religions battling for his young soul played a game of chicken during his formative years, staunchly challenging each other for the right of way. As if he was blindsided by a freight car chocked full of science, it created an unholy three-car pileup that had the unsupported and conflicting theories of an almighty, personal God thrown headfirst right out the fucking window.

Albert would have been happy to never look in the rearview as he drove off into his future sans God, but that was never to be. Turns out that whether you believe in something or not has very little effect on whether or not that something believes in you. Being born Jewish never defined Albert in the least, until the day someone else decided it was the only thing that did. He had been visiting America on holiday in 1933 and decided to stay a while when an upstart nut job back home decided Jews needed to be eradicated from the face of the earth because, well, in no uncertain terms, Adolf was nothing if not an asshat.

Albert, being a relatively quick study, had figured out long ago that in order to survive a bullshit situation of epic proportions, one should either head for the hills or learn to play two sides of the same coin. Defecting to America not being an option when Tomas de Torquemada climbed into his disheveled office in the heart of the Borderlands just over fifty years ago, he quickly learned to play both sides of the anti-Semitic pfenning that kept landing Reich side up at his feet every time he left his goddamn house.

"Berto, the information you gave me on the Grinx was incorrect."

"Well, Tom, you do understand that every bit of information I have to work within this God-forsaken place is debunked, false, or otherwise total fucking garbage? I'm doing the best I can given the circumstances. Drink?" Albert asked the ex-friar as he vigorously joggled a hollowed-out Shake Weight full of the homemade shine he'd stilled himself out back using old Edsel parts and the piles of rotted potatoes stacked outside the Wow! Potato chip factory.

Tomas de Torquemada turned up his bulbous nose at Berto's offer and swirled his time-worn, color-faded robes behind him like the pompous blowhard he was. "If I can't count on you, then I see no reason to keep you around," he threatened.

"You've tried that before, Tom," Albert answered casually while pouring his moonshine martini into a Burger Chef to-go cup. "I just end up right back here," he countered, both loving and hating that it was true. At some point over the last forty or so years, he'd learned to love tinkering with all of humanity's failed bullshit. He just hated having to be Tomas's bitch while doing it.

"I have The Four at my beck and call now. I think the outcome could be a little different this time. Shall we give it a try?" The Inquisitor threatened as he tap, tap, tapped the ancient key dangling from his neck with his thick, meaty finger.

"Look, Tom. The information I have here on Satera is limited at best. I've sifted through all three thousand, two hundred, and twenty-three piles of books scattered throughout the Borderlands and could only find four texts on the whole damn dimension, which, need I remind you, could only be translated after I spent the better part of fourteen years decoding the lexicons of no less than seventy-four dead languages."

"I have repeatedly asked you to call me Grand Inquisitor. And stop acting so put upon, you keep behaving as if you've something better to do. I've been here since 1498, so I can assure you, there's not. Do you want to get out of here or not, Berto? The trains about to leave the station and your actions over the next few days will decide whether or not you've earned a ticket to ride."

Albert knew at this point three things to be true. One: That the last living Grinx of Domos Navitas was the physical scientific equivalent of $E=mc^2$ on steroids. And two: That he would do anything in his power to protect it, even if it cost him his recently realized immortal soul. And last, but not least, three: That Tomas de Torquemada was most definitely an asshat, Albert mused, then said aloud, "When do we blow this popsicle stand, Tom?"

Silla was fucking livid—and most likely dying. In the last two hours, she'd been sprayed by some type of high-level, heat-coolant foam, was bagged and beaten, then transported to wherever the hell she was now, and left for dead.

She'd never seen a goddamn thing. From the time she was sprayed then bagged over the head to the last few dozen kicks to the gut, which she assumed were just for the hell of it because there was no way the first round wasn't going to end in her eventual death from internal bleeding, Silla hadn't seen or heard a single clue that could help her identify the son of a bitch who sprayed her down one last time for good measure before silently walking away. She couldn't breathe. The burlap sack over her head was half frozen to her face. Cold, wet, and sopping in toxic goo, it burned her throat and strangled her lungs every time she gasped for air.

She was going to die here.

She tried to stop breathing, just long enough to think of a way out, but the agony of holding her breath spiked against her broken ribs and overrode her will, forcing her traitorous lungs to steal the poisonous breath she needed to scream.

And on that one, last, fateful cry, Atsilla O'nacanna breathed no more.

WHAT IS THAT FUCKING SMELL?

"Heff! Heff! Hephaestus, I'm talking to you!" Creak hollered down to the Olympian smith, smith, smithing away over his work like he was going for broke.

Clank! Clank! Clank! Pshhhhh!
Clank! Clank! Clank! Pshhhhh!
Clank! Clank! Clank! Pshhhhh!

"What up, Hammer? What the fuck are you wearing!?!" Creak yelled louder, but Heff kept pounding; his back arched over the task at hand. "And what in the name of Durian is that fucking smell?" he growled, choking on the charred, sweet scent.

Clank! Clank! Clank! Pshhhhh!

"Dude!" Creak trotted up behind the Goliath, who had traded in his signature leather apron for a San Benito robe covered in the painted flames of hellfire. "Dude! We've got problems. Freyja's in trouble!"

Heff didn't flinch.

Clank! Clank! Clank! Pshhhhh!
Clank! Clank! Clank! Pshhhhh!
Clank! Clank! Clank! Pshhhhh!

Creak reached out, retracting his claws to nudge the legendary weapons maker with a disarmed paw, and damn near lost his head in the process.

Heff's hammering arm came fast and hard on a backswing, never breaking stride between his tireless blows to brainbox the Grinx. Creak dipped low and skittered back.

"What the fuck! Did you not hear me? Freyja's in trouble!"

Hephaestus stopped, turned from his work, and lifted the hood of his helmet to reveal hollowed-out eyes burning hellfire green. And behind that unholy nightmare was the workpiece. A necklace as old as antiquity itself, held fast to the charred remains of the woman it clung heavy sentry to since the day Odin himself had permanently bolted it there.

Made of heavy gold and seven amber stones the size of plums, the Brisingamen Torc was to be Freyja's scarlet letter. A not-so-subtle reminder to the world she was a slutty slut who had debased herself by screwing a disfigured, ostracized blacksmith in lieu of Odin's cold and lifeless marriage bed. Freyja had worn that shit like a badge of honor.

Heff had forged the Brisingamen for her the day she'd found and fallen in love with him in the heart of a primitive mountain range a million lifetimes ago. Creak knew she would never take it off. Hell, even if Odin himself showed up to break the spell that held it there, Valhalla would be in dire need of a new keeper before "open sesame" could pass the heartless bastard's bearded lips.

Creak felt sick. Bile rose, gritty and sulphuric in his throat as he physically choked at the live-action snuff scene playing out in front of his eyes.

"Sorry, dude, thought you were someone else!" echoed off the empty walls as Creak fell to pieces before the Hammer of Dishar-mony could strike home.

THIRTY-FIVE

FIGURES

Turns out, not breathing for a fiery owl thingy isn't really that big of a deal.

Silla choked out her last breath and waited for the icy hands of death to grab hold—but they never did. Or maybe they did, and she just didn't notice. Nothing changed but for the whole breathing part. Her body ached from the beating she'd taken and the frigid bag over her frostbitten head was still as cold as a penguin's ass on an ice flow.

Silla lay on the hard, wet floor for a few minutes and waited for something, anything to happen. Nothing. She figured it would probably be best to wait a bit longer before deciding her next move, just to be on the safe side. Silla had never died before, and she had no idea what to expect, but this sure as shit wasn't it. Pearly gates and radiant angels were nowhere to be found.

Funny, she thought to herself.

In the last week of her life, there had been ethereal beings around every damn corner. She couldn't even take a pee in the last forty-eight hours without running into some sort of feathery, mythological beastie.

"Fi—," Silla choked.

No air, no words. Figures, she thought the words she couldn't say.

A heavy grinding sound, reminiscent of her grandma's ancient, electric can opener, filled the empty space and cut short her inner, post-mortem monologue.

Silla felt a short burst of air blow past, followed very directly by a heavy thud accompanied by a hollowed-out, but determinedly masculine, "Ugh."

Welcome to the club, pal, Silla thought rather passive-aggressively when she heard the air rush from the new arrival's lungs. *Huh, thought I'd be a better person when I died*, she thought on an off-hand, internal tongue-lashing at her less-than-sympathetic welcome. *Guess you are who you are; leopards not changing their spots and all that.*

"I don't know, I sort of like this club."

Silla heard a voice, not her own, bounce around inside her head.

Great, now I'm going batty. Batty and dead. Frozen and hogtied. This is legit not heaven. I'm in hell. Figures, she thought from behind the biting, burlap hood.

"You're not in hell," bounced off the corners of her mind.

Well, this sure as shit ain't heaven, pal, Silla bounced back.

"We are in Purgatory, Silla."

And who pray tell are "we" exactly? She bounced back with an alarming amount of calm, considering she just died and was now tinkering with the idea part of the penance for her YOLO-inspired lifestyle could possibly include an eternal multiple personality disorder.

"It's Cradle, Sil. And you're not nuts, darlin', just dead."

I fucking knew it. Goddamnit bounced back flat.

"It's gonna be alright, Sil," she heard distantly in her mind but somehow closer than before.

Fuck off, Cradle. I'm dead. I don't wanna be dead. I can't help Morna if I'm—and her thoughts broke as the shock wore off, drowning her in waves of silent, trapped, heartsick cries she could never breathe life into.

"Sil," Cradle bounced deep, trying to reach her.

"Silla," the angel said aloud as he crawled closer.

She didn't answer.

Cradle dragged his broken body closer until he lay right next to the fiery woman he could never quite get out of his mind. He reached up, biting back the stinging in his lacerated wing muscles, and he gently pried the frozen burlap from Silla's icy cheeks.

When the fresh air hit, frosty crystals ran wild in a pattern of glacial lace, creeping up and over Silla's high cheekbones to frost the very edges of the auburn streaks woven through her jet-black hair.

Cradle watched as the wintriness of death kissed along Silla's face, leaving her more beautiful to him than she had ever been before. And, as was all too often as of late, where lamentable things were concerned, he was a day late and a dollar short, again. This time, it did something to him. It cracked something deep down, and it fucking hurt like nothing had ever hurt before.

"Enough!" he vowed. "Slated though it may be, I will not be your Angel of Death. Not today," he swore and broke from the binary dualities pulling at him like a fucking puppet on a string. "Angles may not have your gift of free will, but as of today," he spat, looking over his empty, blood-blackened shoulders, "I'm no one's angel!" and on his words, the strings binding him broke, leaving him free to do whatever he wanted.

"Goddamnit, Silla, don't you dare go dark on me," Cradle whispered as he pulled himself up and over Silla's spent shell. "Hold on, darlin', I'm comin' to getcha," he promised softly as he hovered above her icy-blue lips, pressing his warm mouth onto hers.

With a kiss, Cradle poured what was left of his being, broken as it was, into Silla, leaving his crippled carcass behind. He didn't take a moment to consider what any of it meant. He simply took a page from Creak's playbook and acted on faith, cowabunga style. His essence fell headlong down the well of Silla's dark silence, hoping somehow he'd find her and coax her back into the light before it all went dark for everyone, everywhere.

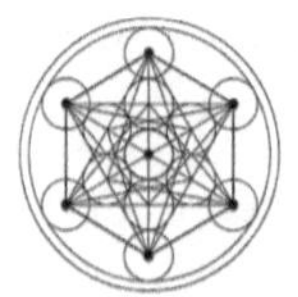

THIRTY-SIX

BODEGAS AND BLACK SHEEP

K arma, Morna, and Hildi poured out of the powder blue cab at 4740 Shaw looking like a troop of drag queens reenacting To Wong Foo. Just before they left HQ, Karma was kind enough to loan Morna some clothes. Clothes that looked like they'd jumped straight out of Serena Williams's walk-in locker room bodega. Badass as they were, the power-hitter-inspired ensemble didn't exactly mesh with Morna's less-than-badass personality. When she'd told Karma thanks but no thanks, the Fate rolled her eyes and whispered some cryptic bullshit while blowing a small pile of white, sparkling powder in Morna's general direction, making the black tulle tutu portion of the skintight, off-the-shoulder, athletic wear disappear along with her newly acquired wings.

Not thrilled with the result, nevertheless happier than before, Morna accepted the modification as a compromise on Karma's part. She was pushing her luck at best since Morna sincerely doubted negotiating terms of any kind was not something Karma did on the regular and decided to go with a simple, "Thank you," instead of the, "Oh, hell no". That Morna's inner wallflower was screaming from a megaphone from the subconscious corners of her mind.

"Where'd my wings go?" Morna asked, pressing her luck.

"Oh, I just tucked them away for a bit. They're there if you need them," Karma answered as she called a cab to pick them up from the Venice café.

She assured Hildi and Morna there was a little-known exit from the subterranean tunnels through a warded mosaic on the floor of the club's gender-neutral bathroom. Morna's shoulders felt impossibly cold as they made their way topside. She felt her wings but couldn't see them. As they shuffled through the crowded cafe, she noticed they were no longer bumping into things, which fell in the plus category considering Gringo Jones was bursting with a veritable sundry of breakable baubles, the occasional nine-foot metal rooster, and a bevy of meandering boxers who freely wandered the narrow labyrinth of aisles.

Morna took one look at Karma, Hildi, and herself as they climbed out of the cab and shook her head. There was no way they weren't going to draw a crowd. Wings or not, the three of them stood out even among the mixed-bag clientele.

"What's your problem?" Karma asked as she turned, trying to figure out why Morna had taken up residence on her shirt tails.

"Nothing. It's just crowded in there," Morna said meekly, "I figured it'd be best if we went in single file."

"Mmm hmm. Child, get your little, resplendent ass out from behind my backside."

Morna did as she was told and stepped to the front, not cowering but not waving a pride flag either.

"Are you embarrassed of me?" Karma asked straightforward.

"No," and that was true.

Morna thought Karma was magnificent.

"Hildi then? Are you embarrassed by her?"

"No, not at all," and that was true, too.

Morna thought Hildi was a wonderful creature.

"So, your problem is with you then?" Karma shot from the hip.

"I guess so."

"You guess so? Morna Stahr, you are divine. You are a radiant angel, powerful beyond all comprehension, and a smoking hottie to boot. I think it's about time you shed the human inferiority complex. It does you no honor, and you'll have no use for it where we're going."

"I don't think I know how Karma. It just sort of is. It's part of me, always has been. I wish I could be as confident and carefree as the two of you, but I don't see that happening anytime soon, wings or no wings," Morna answered, feeling like she'd somehow let Karma down.

What'd it matter anyway, she thought to herself.

They were all going to figure out when the curtain went up on this little dog and pony show, how she wasn't everything they'd cracked her up to be. Better to shit the bed now before everyone saw how underqualified she was for the starring role she suspected she was being groomed for, despite all the opening night hype.

"OK, doll. I'm going to let you in on a little secret 'cause I don't have a ton of time to school you properly in the ways of being above the fray," Karma directed as she gently grabbed Morna's hand and held it snug up to her heart. "Listen, Morna," Karma whispered. "Look and listen."

So, Morna did. She looked at the guy riding past on his bike and heard how he wished he could afford a car. If he could just afford a car, even a used-up old beater, everything would be different. She saw the young couple holding hands, totally in love. The young woman wished she were as thin as another nearby woman who checked out a colorful, life-sized metal giraffe while wondering if her lipstick was too dark for daytime wear. The thin-wisher's boyfriend wondered if he'd hit a home run in the sack last night or if his girlfriend had just been faking it again so she could get back to binge-watching The Bachelor. It wasn't only those folks. It was a fucking pandemic. Everywhere she looked, she heard. And everything she heard was doubt.

Karma gave Morna's hand a little squeeze, lowered it, and let go, but Morna could still hear everything.

"How do I turn it off?" Morna asked, overwhelmed and saddened by the reality of reality.

"In time, you'll learn to do it on your own, but for now," Karma wiped away the tear from Morna's cheek with her soft hand, "We'll just tuck that away from the 'Here and Now'," she whispered, transporting Morna back on a transcendental breath to a much quieter way of looking at things.

"Better?" Karma asked.

"Yes, much," Morna said, as she felt her wallflower petals peel and float away in the wind. Not necessarily feeling all cock of the walk, but her bah, bah, black sheep were starting to preen a bit as she asked, "Where's Hildi?"

Looking around the busy sidewalk, Morna didn't even realize she no longer gave two shits if anyone mistook them for Noxeema, Chi-Chi, or Vida as she walked through the front door of Gringo Jones, calling out Hildi's name bold as you please, scouring every corner of the store for the buxom little red-headed rocking professional grade Xena Princess Warrior livery and granny-issue BluBlockers.

"Hildi!" Morna called out as she came back down another twisting set of stairs.

"Down here, dear!"

"Where?" Morna hollered as she followed Hildi's echoing call into yet another dead-end room loaded with ceramic Day of the Dead dolls, tin lizards, and a life-sized, fully operational antique barber's chair.

"Down here!"

"Where's down here? I've seen up, but I haven't seen down,"

Morna yelled over the hordes of customers, doodads, and curiosities.

"Oh, for fuck sake!"

Hildi's voice swirled up and around, bouncing back and forth off the stacks of colorful, hand-painted flower pots.

"Dog!" Karma called out with a short whistle and a couple of quick kissy noises, "Here, dog!"

Morna about came out of her skin when a wet, slobbering tongue drug slow and rough across the palm of her low-hanging hand.

"Jesus Christ!"

"No, not Jesus Christ, Me'tok." said the boxer over the match-stick dangling out of one side of its floppy maw. "This way," it directed in a clipped, heavy Meso-American accent, giving a light toss of its cute-as-a-button head toward the center of the store.

"Well?" Karma said, halfway across the room.

Morna caught flies, frozen in place like a wax figure, seamlessly blending in with every other oddity littering the shoppe as she stared wide-eyed after the bilingual boxer shaman waddling slowly out of the dead-end room.

"... are you coming or not, Morna?" Karma scolded, double-snapping her fingers.

Morna gave a punchy nod and caught up quickly, skittering right behind Karma as the boxer-shaman dog thingy led the way toward the heart of the store, taking a hard right at a little bathroom door, before disappearing down a nearly hidden set of cellar stairs.

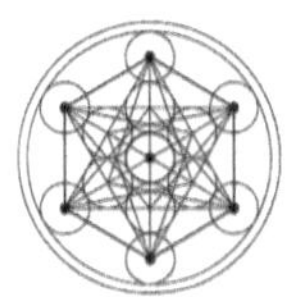

THIRTY-SEVEN

COME FOR THE PIZZA, STAY FOR THE FUN

"Your gal ain't doodly squat!" Creak wailed with the debilitated animatronic band washing down his third frosty, pitcher of Falstaff as he sat completely alone, front row center at a little red table in the eighty-sixed showbiz pizza franchise he'd tramped into over an hour before.

The fact "My Gal is Red Hot" had looped as many times as there were tracks on the White Album, and Creak hadn't noticed, did not bode well for the last living Balance Keeper of Non-Human Energies.

He'd spent the better part of two hours wandering the abandoned strip malls littering the borderlands and couldn't get the image of what Heff did to Freyja out of his mind. The neon Falstaff sign beckoned him from the dirty window of the once-happy pizza parlor. Creak opened the door and trotted inside, deciding he might do well to dunk his head in a pitcher of alcohol and physically sterilize the hellish scene from his shell-shocked eyeballs. He was surprised to hear the sounds of centipede and Pac-Man wafting across the bygone arcade and eatery of yesteryear on a doughy, pepperoni, and pineapple breeze.

He walked right up to the Falstaff tap, flipped the spigot with his claw, and stuck his big, black head right underneath. After about ten minutes, a couple of cumbersome keg changes, and really wet, but otherwise still horrified, eyeballs, Creak realized plan A wasn't going to cut it and went with plan B: Drink until you can't feel feelings anymore.

He was almost there when an old white-haired dude wearing a server's apron and looking remarkably to the drunken Grinx like Albert Einstein, walked up to his table and said, "A creature who never made a mistake never tried anything new," in a heavy German accent.

"Ever try to disinfect your eyeballs with the most refreshing beer a man can pour?"

"We are going to have to clean you up, yeah?" said the old German dude.

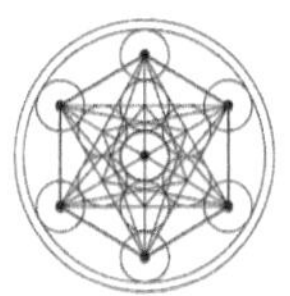

THIRTY-EIGHT

WELL... WELL... WELL... WHAT HAVE WE HERE?

Pitch black, vacuous, and with no end in sight, Cradle fell headlong down the well of Silla's soul. After a while, he gave up ever reaching the bottom and contemplated his recent detachment, what led him to it, and what it all meant.

He started with his existence as Metatron. So very long ago, he'd almost never thought of himself in that way. It was as if that life was lived by an entirely different angel. Whenever the occasion came up about those ancient times, it was almost as if he conjured information he'd read about in someone else's biography. Ironically, it would probably have been a biography he had most likely written.

Cradle had been a scribe angel since before the time of the split. He was a dork for lack of a better classification, and it had suited him just fine. The One was nothing if not a scientist, and scientists want their shit recorded, backed up, and stacked up, and that was exactly what Cradle had done for eons.

When he wasn't busy scribbling down the ins and outs of everything, he'd tinker with the implements he'd whipped up in his downtime to chart the stars. He'd peered through a pictorial glass he'd cooked up to plot the very edges of The Dimension when the blowback hit, pushing the frequencies of the split back through the glass to permanently burn the blueprint of relativity into his being, like a soul-searing tintype, upgrading his associate scribe angel status to C.E.O. of "What the Ever-Loving Fuck Just Happened".

As the only "Being" with any intel on the elevated situation, Cradle, through no fault of his own, had been given an upper hand. Neither of the two major parties was remotely happy, which congruently made Cradle both axis and ally to the two power-houses in the game of all games.

So, the powers that be did what powers that be do; they stuck the perceived threat in neutral ground, surrounded him with troops from both sides, and pretended to play nice. It unnerved Cradle so bad he'd spent his first two thousand years in Purgatory with a gnarly case of angel mange so grody the balding patches on his wings looked like the world's worst case of cradle cap.

Cradle, as he was henceforth known, was left to sort out the mess of what to do with the leftover energies swirling about after The Big Bang. For years, he pretty much did what he'd always done; he watched and wrote about nothing, until one day some-thing of note stirred on his radar. The energies swirling had evolved into something more, something sentient. Something sentient and wild.

The One and the Asshat had for years been retired to their respective corners and had been pretty much going on about their own business without giving much thought to what the other, or Cradle for that matter, was doing. It was then a single shot fired off in the primordial ooze on an otherwise unremarkable corner of the cosmos, setting off a series of simple life depth charges, O.K. Corral style. It turned an otherwise unremarkable planet into a petri dish of unforeseen possibilities, lock, stock, and two wiggling progenitors.

Cradle had watched and written, completely intrigued with the show happening on the little blue planet when the weights shifted. It hit like an eight-point-seven on the omniversal Richter scale and stirred a wave of moving volume that shifted from one dimension to another, tsunami style. Everything up to that point had been even. Every dimension had been weighted the same since the time of the split, their volumes static, until that defining moment.

Her name had been Luca, and she was the very first living, breathing, humanoid-like being who ever was. Cradle had watched her grow, play, and learn. He watched her hurt and heal, and then one day, he watched Luca die. Cradle had never seen anyone die before and wasn't sure what was happening. He knew when Luca's frail body stopped breathing, the energy powering it moved on. Out across the omniverse and straight into the One's dimension, making it quantifiably stronger and truly pissing off the Asshat.

It was right about that time, the bell rang on round one of the most notorious and preeminent heavyweight championship, brouhaha of all time. Cradle, for better or worse, had been deemed referee.

"Guh," escaped Cradle's essence when he hit the bottom of Silla's well, knocking the metaphysical wind out of his sails. Fuck that smarts!

That's whatcha get, you dumbass angel, he thought, giving himself the hell he deserved for losing consciousness to the memories of so long ago that he'd accidentally tripped into the ticks and tocks as he fell. He watched his recollections replay like a live-action documentary, completely forgetting the here and now.

"Best get your shit together," he said, righting himself to standing in the empty, black pit of Silla's soul.

Looking around, Cradle couldn't so much as see his hand in front of his face. He could barely move through the denseness of the heavily weighted atmosphere. Walking was more akin to trudging, and he stopped pretty quick after starting. Wasting that kind of energy, even in metaphysical form, was tantamount to lunacy when you didn't know where the hell you were, where you were going, and if or when you were ever going to get to recharge.

Stock still, he stood in what he assumed was the dead center of the pit. Cradle heard a muffled thumping sound, and when he concentrated hard, he heard it repeat over and over again with a high-pitched frequency that started soft, gradually getting higher in intensity, only to fall back and fade further away before swinging back up on a riotous arc. Not knowing where to start, but having a better idea than before, Cradle headed off in the direction of the din. Once he determined where it was coming from.

Everything was so echoey and dark. At first, he'd taken a few wrong turns, causing the sounds to fade further with every step. Eventually, with some trial and error, he figured out that if he placed his hand on his chest, just over his heart, he could feel the vibrations better than hear them. So, using his heart as a guide, Cradle followed the resonance pulsing through the labyrinth of darkness. Waves and tremors gave way to throbbing beats and shimmying judders of bright strobing light with every step. The closer he got, the light would hit and flash off nearby walls, and he wouldn't have known where they were if it wasn't for the whole bumping blindly into them repeatedly part.

Reaching out, Cradle ran his hand along the wall closest to him, feeling the texture drag under his fingertips. Rough and splintery, he determined with a touch that the jet-black walls were nothing more than painted plywood, covered here and there in the most brilliant neon-colored graffiti. But the strobes of light were so quick and bright against the contrasting pitch, it was all but impossible to make out what the glyphs might mean or say. The second he thought he had a read, he was blinded by the darkness and again by the light as the thumping bass line twisted down the long corridor, louder with every pulse until all of his senses were bombarded. If this was the manifestation of what Silla felt, he wasn't sure he was going to be able to get through.

Earlier, when he'd left his body behind and jumped into Silla's, hoping to chase her down before she locked herself into a corner of her mind on a much-deserved nervous breakdown, Cradle never thought he might not be able to reach her. But this was so much worse than he had imagined. It was too much. What the fuck was going on?

Cradle closed his eyes to shut out some of the sensory overload. Silent and still in the long dark hallway, he counted. He counted his breaths at first. Five seconds, in through the nose, seven seconds, out through the mouth, and repeat. When he finally settled a bit, he counted beats. When he was comfortable with that, he counted the strobing, white lights piercing through the thin skin of his eyelids on a rave-inspired pulse, lighting up the shadows behind his shuttered lashes like two desert suns eclipsing the downbeat.

Firestarter? Was the blaring breakbeat a Prodigy?

No more than Cradle asked the question in his mind, Silla's world flipped, taking him with it. In a nauseating rotation, the whole seedy, subliminal operation went belly up, landing Cradle on the ceiling. Everything rocked, side to side on a sickening wave like a tempest of wine sloshing up the sides of a rounded glass, settling quickly as fire spewed across the ceiling of the hellish corridor that had only seconds ago been the floor.

"I'm a Firestarter! Twisted Firestarter!" looped over the screaming sirens jarring in accompaniment. Thunder rang as blasts of flames shot harum-scarum from the mouth of an alcove about twenty feet down the flipside of the corridor.

Flares shot hot and wild from the mouth of the alcove, only narrow breaths of relief between each scorching blow; as if a fire-breathing dragon lay in wait in its depths, daring Cradle to enter the heavily guarded den when Silla paused for gasps of air between bellows. Cradle gathered his bearings, closed his eyes, and counted to ten. Again. When he settled himself, he opened his slate-gray eyes and looked to the graffitied walls lit by the constant barrage of fire. The glyphs, now fully visible, were an easy read but a hard pill to swallow.

"What the hell, Silla darling?" Cradle whispered on a shivering breath.

The temperature in the corridor dropped a good sixty degrees as he read his way across the graffitied wall, trudging through a blanket of snow falling across the length of the hall, now suddenly all too quiet. The soft, crystalline flakes snuffed out the fires as he read.

Amid and Among
The Betwixt and Between
The Fight Fucks You
The Fight Fucks me
Above or Below
Aloft or Afoot
Ashes on Horses
Hooves on Soot
Fire on Feather
Wing on Hook

"I'm not your *Darling*, Angel!" echoed from the alcove just up the way.

"And I'm no one's angel," Cradle whispered under his breath.

"That sucks, 'cause I could use one right about now," Silla whispered back.

Cradle took in the graffitied, lowlit walls and the all-to-sudden quiet. It was the deafening kind of quiet that came with a fresh snow. A quiet that let you know business as usual had been suspended until further notice. At first, it was peaceful, until the snow piled up to the windows, and the wolves were at your door, then the quiet quickly became unnerving as hell. If the sudden atmospheric shift reflected Silla's state of mind, which he suspected to be the case, this serene blizzardy moment was most likely the calm before the actual storm.

"Silla? Do you mind if I come down? I just want a minute to talk. I'll leave right after if that's what you still want."

Silence. Cradle waited a whole minute, then pressed again.

"Would that be O.K., Sil?"

"Fuck it! Sure! Come on!" Silla's overly enthusiastic response broke the heavy silence. "I mean, you've already come this far, I'd hate to leave you hangin'. That'd just be rude!" Silla's voice sailed entirely too happily down the blizzardy corridor.

When Cradle rounded the snowy corner into Silla's chamber, he froze dead in his tracks.

THIRTY-NINE

CENTURIAN SNACK

Odin was pissed. Loki had never heard the Chieftain so livid, not even the day Freyja marched back through Valhalla after her little mountain getaway, enthusiastically telling the big guy to take a long walk off a short pier and happily packing her bags.

Honestly, Loki never understood how Freyja could get Odin's beard in such a twist. They were never any good together, and the split had been a long time coming. Loki figured it was pride, not love, that had one-eyed Wednesday spitting runes through his teeth whenever Freya's name was so much as mentioned. He'd even gone so far as to have her name stricken from every hall he held dominion over and refused him and Freyja's sons from ever mentioning their mother's name in his presence.

Which is why today seemed such a special, special day. Odin had bellowed Freyja's name along with a various sundry of curses from his bedchamber since the clock struck midnight in Valhalla the previous evening. By Loki's count, that had been about eleven hours ago, but gods be damned if every last fucking clamoring clock and ticking timepiece lining the Great Hall wasn't still carrying on gongs on gongs that it was still fucking midnight!

"Loki! Get your ass in here! Now!"

Loki petulantly marched, hand outstretched to turn the knob to Odin's bedchamber, and paused. He shook his head and rolled his eyes at Valhalla's ornate ceilings lined with gilded swords and various spoils of war, from Christian relics to the heads of Christians themselves. The old windbag was going to send him on a mission. Odin was forever sending Loki out into the worlds beyond to spy, creep, and report. Sleuthing around for Odin was why he always came across as a jokester or trickster. Really, Loki was neither. It's just he had to make up and ad hoc most or all of the stories to tell Odin when he returned home because the old crotchety bastard couldn't take bad news straight up. Loki learned long ago, although Odin couldn't exactly kill the messenger, Loki, being immortal and all that, he could and had made Loki's rather lengthy life a veritable living Hel.

Like most of history, there was some truth in the tales Loki weaved for Odin, but there was also a bookoo of bullshit thrown in to keep the High One happy... ish. Loki didn't like to think of himself as a liar so much as a survivor, and surviving being Odin's right-hand man had required him to pull more than a few tricks from up his short sleeves over the passing millennia.

Loki had a feeling this little trip was going to be different. The Clocks were fucked, the atmosphere was thinning, and Odin was blustering a name he had banned from the Great Hall since time was told by way of sundials.

"Freyja, Freyja, Freyja." Loki said, continuing to shake his head. "I don't know what you're up to, my dear, but I'm not sure I can save you this time," Loki whispered to the winds blowing across the spacious, empty banquet hall before reluctantly turning the horned-handled knob into Odin's bedchamber.

"What's the four-one-one O' Great One?" Loki asked on the fly as he ducked under an iron shield sailing past his head with enough grace of clearance to momentarily avoid having his severed noggin added to the troupe of beheaded Christians dangling like macabre mistletoe on the other side of the bedchamber door.

"By the Gods, she's done it! And I'll have her head for it, I will!" Odin spat as he threw a polished seventh-century bowl holding a bushel of golden apples right out the fucking window. But of course, no more than he threw them out did they show right back up. Resting happily on the iron pedestal near the balcony windows, passive-aggressively glowing while soaking up the sun as they'd done for centuries. "They mock me, Loki! And I'll not have it!" Odin said, throwing his hands as he paced the room lined with furs, wood, and iron.

The flagstone floors were all but invisible beneath the layers of animal furs worn to little more than rough, bare patches of leathery skin, revealing in their nakedness Odin's preferred pacing route over the last eleven hours or so.

Loki watched Odin pace with his eyes, shifting them left to right repeatedly. He was tempted to watch the old bastard with a series of overly emphasized head swivels, but since Loki preferred his head solidly on his neck where it belonged. He decided not to exaggerate Odin's over-exaggerations.

"I want you to find that wretched whore of a woman and bring her back here. Now!" Odin ordered as he picked up the bowl of glowing fruit and chucked it out the window for the seventeenth-billionth time since Freya had not so subtly left it there.

It was basically a "fuck you very much" gift. If Freyja was going to be forced to walk around for an eternity wearing Odin's scarlet letter, then she thought it only fitting Odin should sleep next to a bowl brimming with the forbidden fruit he would never again be allowed to sink his teeth into. Since Freyja wasn't allowed in Valhalla anymore, but she still needed to gift the golden apples to a few of the folks who could never leave, she basically left the bowl of apples charmed to allow every immortal residing in Valhalla to take but one, every hundred years on the date of their birth. Everyone but Odin, that is. When her ex tried to bite into his centennial birthday gift, the enchanted fruit turned to leaden dust in his mouth. It was more or less a "How do you like them apples?" birthday present. Even Loki thought it a low blow because everyone knew without imbibing Freyja's special Centurian snack, immortals would age. Odin had been aging for quite a while now, much slower than mortals, but fast enough that he was beginning to appear a little long in the tooth.

"You know I can't do that, my most Regal Whiskered One. If she's wearing the necklace, there's simply nothing I can do. The two of you struck a bargain: as long as she wears the Brisingamen, you have no say over where she goes, what she does, or who she does. You can't touch her, Boss." Loki said casually as he brushed the tips of his fingers across the tattoos decorating every inch of his slender forearms.

Loki, for all accounts, was slim yet muscled, tall but short, and dark but fair. One would never find a way to recall his appearance if asked to do so, except for the tattoos on his arms. Loki was a shapeshifter, and his real form was unremarkable to anyone who might attempt to remember. However, if you did happen to come across the trickster in one of the many forms he took, depicted on his heavily tattooed forearms, well, those were forms one could easily recall, but would most likely never want to.

"Bullshit, Loki! She's trying to take it off! I can feel it!" Odin roared. "I knew one day her husband wouldn't be able to take looking at it anymore, while she should be his alone, all men have their breaking point! What man wants to stare at another man's mark on his woman for eternity! I always said it was just a matter of fucking time!" Odin swore over the thundering bells sailing across Valhalla for hours on end.

"Well, my Most Moist Mutton-Chopped Majesty, is it off her

or is it still on her? Halfsies wasn't in the rule book. It says right here that…" Loki pulled an aging, yellowed parchment from thin air, flipping through the crumbling, scrolled pages as he wet his fingertips with a serpentine tongue. "… It was right here… page three I think…"

"I don't give a good Gods damned what that roll of parchment says! Wipe your ass with it for all I care! Freyja's piece of shit factory worker lay is banging away at that Torc and has been for the last eleven hours! That's *intent,* Loki! And that breaks our bargain." The old man said as he cracked his neck and rubbed at his sloping shoulders with gnarled, arthritic hands.

"OK, OK. No need to get your salt and pepper fuzzies in a bunch. I'll go check it out, see what's up, and report back here in a few. We cool?"

"No Godsdammit, we are *not* cool," Odin said in a quiet calm that had steam rising in plumes from the furs layered across his hunched neck.

Odin turned his one good eye on Loki, and Loki saw fire stir behind the milky lens that had long ago smudged out the dazzling emerald greens that once sparkled there like a jewel. There was no way he was going to diffuse the situation from this side; that was clear. At this point, Loki figured it'd be best to see what the fuck Freyja and Heff were up to and to get them to knock it the fuck off before World War three got underway.

"Alright, alright. I'll go. Where is *there*, exactly?" Loki asked.

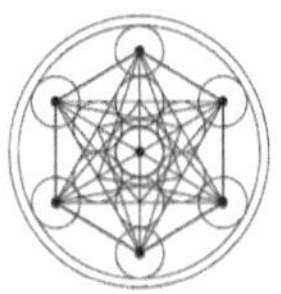

FORTY

THERE GOES THE NEIGHBORHOOD

Justice rounded the corner toward the main business office of the Chernobyl Nuclear Power Plant that Tomas de Torquemada decided to call home for the last twenty-five years of his rather lengthy stint in the Borderlands. Justice very much preferred the homeyness of the Alexandrian lighthouse, the ex-friar previously called home sweet home, but the Grand Inquisitor forever bitched it was a shitty location and had too many stairs. When Chernobyl popped up in the Borderlands in eighty-six, Tomas de Torquemada and his grubby little army moved in.

"Location, location, location," Torq had told Justice.

If he'd said it once, he'd said it a million times. Now Torq basically dwelled in Justice's back forty, which had gotten tricky for the Keeper of the Scales to keep on the down low. Souls who lay in wait for their eternal itinerary didn't regularly take to wandering beyond the Cliffs of Perdition, but they also used to shuffle through at a much quicker clip than as of late, and bored souls do stupid shit, just like bored people do.

There had been more than a dozen souls in the last month alone who decided to trek beyond the cliffs. When they found all the earthly goods, no matter how buggered those items were, they couldn't wait to trek it back and tell their friends about the wasteland chock full of the defunct earthly treasures. Which meant Justice had to step in as if he didn't have enough to fucking do already and present the wanderers with a choice which was really no choice at all. Join Torq's army or go straight to dimension 9.666; do not pass go, and do not collect two hundred dollars. As of yesterday, Torq's burgeoning Auto-de-fe' Army was stronger by a baker's dozen in these wee parts of November alone.

"We have less than twenty-four hours to pull this off, and the clocks are ticking. I want you to get the recruits zeroed in and armored to the teeth. There is no room for error. Of course, it would have been easier with a binary Nephilim, but the change was more than she could bear. Useless, just like a woman, I should have known better," Torquemada spat his disgust. "There is a right way to do things, General, and a wrong way. The Act of Faith is long overdue, and we will set things to rights, as we always believed them to be, as they should have always been. It's a calamity things have carried on this way for as long as they have. You have your orders, General. You are dismissed." Torquemada said to a body-jacked General, who, no matter how animated, still smelled like a corpse.

Dead is dead, and it will always smell that way, Justice thought as he switched to mouth breathing the fetid, dead air on the DL as he walked into the main offices of Chernobyl.

"And you!" Torquemada spun on Justice no more than he entered the room. "I need that Torc! And I need it now!"

"I have my best guy working on it right now for you, Sir," Justice said in his best brown nose.

Slightly out of practice, Justice hadn't had to suck up this much since Cradle was furloughed out to Spain just under five centuries back.

"That is what you said twelve hours ago! How fucking hard can it be to unclasp a necklace?" Torque shouted at the Keeper of the Scales, the red veins on his bulbous nose flared blue with anger. "Here!" the blustery Inquisitor yelled, tossing a Halberd recklessly close to Justice's face. "Chop her head off with that, remove the Torc, and be done with it!"

Justice barely caught the two-handled pole weapon consisting of a spike-mounted shaft with a sharp axe blade on one side and deadly pointed hook on the other. Palm on either side of the gleaming blade, Justice caught the weapon just a quarter inch from the bridge of his silvery nose and glared down the Inquisitor from either side of the razor-sharp edge.

"What a grand idea, Inquisitor," Justice said as he made a show of bowing low while dropping the handle of the long pole down to his palm. He swept back up, whipping the long-bladed into a dizzying rotation with the rest of his juggling sticks, never missing a beat as he thumbed his nose and debased himself. "Now, why didn't I think of that?"

"You'd do well to wipe that smirk off your face, Justice Gray before I do it myself. You wouldn't be the first to underestimate how serious I am. There should be a few thousand souls lying around eternity somewhere, you can question if you have pause to believe me."

"Excuse me, Inquisitor. I mean no disrespect. I am fully aware of what you're capable of. I'll go check on that Torc and be back with it in a jiffy."

"See that you do, Justice. Or there will be no place the Auto-da-fe will not find you."

Justice turned to leave the office, sneering at the ancient blowhard as he juggled his sticks, and with one hand, reached for the door handle.

"And Justice?"

"Yes, Grand Inquisitor?"

"Find Berto while you're out."

"Yes, Grand Inquisitor." Justice acknowledged the order through clenched teeth as he stepped foot into the corridor, quietly closing the office door behind him as he went.

230

FORTY-ONE

HAVE WE MET?

"Did anyone ever tell you that you look a lot like Albert Einstein?" Creak asked the old German man who joined him at his pity party for one at the little red table and was presently plying him with copious amounts of shitty coffee.

"Not in a very long time," the old German said.

"But *yoooouuuu haaaaaave* heard it? The resemblance is rather *remerkemel*," Creak slurred, closing one unfocused, reptilian eye as he leaned in closer for further inspection.

"Yes, yes, Schatz. But, it has been many, many years," the German said as he filled Creak's coffee cup with more of the heinous brew. "More important now is we get you feeling better, yeah?"

"I feel *fiiiiiiine*," Creak assured the old German, then proceeded to throw up two pitchers of Falstaff. Approximately two of the three Billy Bob's combos he'd woofed down along with a half pot of Millstone Cinnamon-Hazelnut flavored sludge and a tanker's worth of yellow, sulphuric foam.

"Yeah, you look it," Albert said in his best Americana smart-ass.

Not at all troubled by the regurgitating Grinx, Albert felt like a kid on Christmas morning! The vomit notwithstanding. He couldn't believe he was talking to a living, breathing Grinx! Albeit a drunken one, but it somehow made the unimaginable being that much more tangible. Not only did this creature he'd been reading and studying for years actually exist; it was personable, fallible, not human per se, but close e-fucking-nuff to get Albert's elbow patches in a tizzy whenever he considered the enormity of what it all meant.

"We don't have a lot of time, Schatz. We must get you sobered up and thinking straight before Torquemada comes looking for me, which by my calculations, could be any moment now. I've read a lot of things about you creatures, but there was never any mention of you being raging alcoholics. I fear I'm at a loss for what to do. It is quite a conundrum, yeah? If Torquemada finds you, he will finish you off. You are a Pagan mischief in the eyes of his religion. A belief best exterminated, yeah? The fact you exist makes him extremely uncomfortable. It screws up his limited idea of how things must be in order for the world to make sense. It is a narrow mind that cannot look at a subject from various points of view."

"Look, little old German dude, much as I'd love getting into a George Eliot quote off with you, I just watched my best friend roast his wife over an open spit, so sobering up isn't exactly high on my list of shit to do right now. Hell, I survived an apocalyptic showdown when I was two fucking years old! Two! So, tell that Porcu Tada Pants fucker to come on down! I'd love nothing more than to send about twenty-five megavolts through an asshat wanna be right the fuck now! Speaking of which, have you seen a shiny, silvery, asshat lookin' sumbitch round here?" Creak slurred, rocking back and forth before swinging low to look underneath the table as high voltage energy snapped and popped haphazardly across his rocky exterior. "Justice! Hey, Justice! Come 'ere! I gotta present for ya, ya base metal muthafucka!" Creak yelled, pounding the table with a massive, sparking claw.

"Do you mean Justice Gray? About yay high?" the German asked, holding his hand about six feet above the asbestos floor tiles.

"You're going to go with height for an identifier? On a tinman?" Creak laughed deep as his right hind claw worked round and round his hip, just cackling his craggy ass off as he sparkled and shimmered. "OK, *Einstein!*" Creak chortled, carrying on for several more seconds before falling dead sober and serious. "Yeah, we've met."

FORTY-TWO

HOL HAS

Must and damp, the smells sailed heavy with dust into Morna's nostrils about three steps from the bottom cellar area of Gringo Jones. Not a secret per se, but not exactly advertised either. The cellar was crammed full of surplus flower pots, clearance items, and broken bits of marked-down garden statuary.

Morna followed Karma, who followed the boxer, who had taken a hard right at the base of the stairs and waddled straight past a towering shelf of pots before another hard right through a doggie door within a much larger, burnt orange human-sized root cellar door, leaving Morna and Karma alone on the opposite side.

"Push!" a muffled, heavy Meso-American voice ordered from the other side of the door.

Morna thought it sounded very much like, "Woof." She kept that to herself as she ducked low, following Karma through the entryway. There was a fog wafting everywhere, and the hazy air was heavy with the smell of cigarettes, top-notch weed, and high-end alcohol. Morna batted her hand back and forth, coughing and sputtering as she traipsed through the unexpected assault on her senses when a kitschy scene, reserved for a creepy uncle's man cave by way of a bargain basement art bin, manifested right before her eyes.

A few steps further past the threshold, the absurd anthropomorphic scene solidified, making it impossible to deny the three green-felted poker tables in front of her were, in fact, full of a mixed bag of dog breeds sitting on whiskey barrel chairs, and every last one of them were, in fact, playing cards.

"What the fuck's she lookin' at?" a Saint Bernard blowing smoke rings, seated at the second table away, said with a thick Italian accent. "Tok! Yo, Tok! Da fucks 'dat broad lookin' at?"

"Calm down, Giovanni! She's with Karma," Morna heard the heavy Meso-American accent say somewhere further down the long hall-like room.

Broader than a hospital corridor, the tables were lined up one right after the other with whiteboards lining the walls. A troop of Howler monkeys, four per side, worked the dry-erase boards like clerking interns on a stock exchange floor. The monkey teams on either side worked in tandem, communicating with sign language while throwing bits of ticketed paper around as they erased and filled numbers in on numerous brackets drawn across every inch of the expansive boards.

"Hiya doll! Didn't see ya there? Lookin' good! How ya been?" The St. Bernard said to Karma.

"Giovanni! It's been ages! I'm looking good cause I'm feeling good! How's the kids?" Karma asked all flirt and glam, leaning her generous rack in ninety degrees, giving the St. Bernard something sumptuous to look at while gifting him a good, long scratch behind the ears.

She slyly waved Morna on past, toward the bar at the back of the room.

"Good, good." Morna heard the mafia-sounding mongrel answer as she slipped farther out of earshot, seeing Hildi just down the way.

"Hildi! I've been looking for you everywhere!" Morna said, delighted to see a familiar face.

Laughing at the thought, she made her way down the long room. Who would have ever thought a talking pig nanny who occasionally turned into a princess warrior would be her new normal?

"I've been right here, dear! I ran into an old friend upstairs while you and Karma were chatting outside." Hildi said, motioning toward another buxom warrior-woman sitting next to her at the bar.

The woman wore the exact same getup as Hildi, blue blockers included. As a matter of fact, the unknown woman looked remarkably like Hildi. Hell, they could've been twins.

"I was just filling him in on what was going on, and he's decided to help us out! Isn't that fabulous!

"Um?"

"Yes, dear?"

"Hildi?"

"*I said,* yes, dear."

"That guy," Morna said, pointing to the superfluous lady drinking a chardonnay to Hildi's left, "that guy looks exactly like you."

"I forget how much you don't know, dear!" Hildi laughed, "Morna, this is Loki. He's an old friend of Freyja's and mine and a shapeshifter to boot! Anyway, he's decided to help us out! Isn't that fabulous?"

Morna stared slack-jawed at the two Hildi's when Karma joined them at the bar.

"Hello, Loki," Karma said to the Hildi look-alike on the right as she walked next to Morna. "Where's Me'tok?" Karma asked the real Hildi.

"Hello, Karma." The look-alike said. "What a coincidence running into you here."

"There is no such thing as coincidence, Loki," Karma said,

unnervingly cool. "Where's the traveler, Hildi? We need to go, now. Morna's presence is stirring too many questions, and she's making the locals uncomfortable."

"He just popped off to grab some sage, he'll be right back."

"Sage?" Karma asked.

"Yes, dear. He said something about having to be purified before we get going. Said he didn't want to be responsible for grubbing up purgatory with our negative vibes or some such bullshit."

"My vibes were just fine until he showed up," Karma said, tossing her beautifully coiffed, orange hair in Loki's general direction.

"That's cool, Karma. I'll go separately. Don't wanna mess up your vibes," Loki said as he flashed into an unremarkable middle-aged man, the chardonnay in his hand suddenly a pint of dark ale.

"What does he mean 'he'll go separately', Hildi?" Karma asked.

"Oh, that. Well, see, Loki's headed to purgatory too. So, I offered him a ride with our crew."

"Nope. Nuh, uh. No way." Karma said flatly.

"I said it's cool. I'll get my own lift," Loki reassured Hildi.

"Fuck too!" said the boxer. "I'll be damned if I'm making two trips to purgatory in one day. I've got books to run, and now that the monkeys are unionized, I can't work them more than eight hours in a day, meal and smoke breaks included. Thanks a lot for that, Giovanni!" he yelled over to the Sicilian Saint Bernard, never skipping a beat.

He struck the matchstick from between his teeth along the stone floor, igniting it to light the bundle of sage he'd brought with him from somewhere in the back. Dropping the burnt match-stick, Me'tok grabbed the smoking bundle with his teeth as he started chanting in long-lost Mayan holy man while circling in and out of everyone's feet, an attempt to smudge away any lingering earthly ickiness that might hitch a ride to purgatory on their aura's.

"Hol has," Me'tok garbled over the mouthful of bundled sage.

"What?" Morna, Karma, Hildi, and Loki all said in confused unison.

Me'tok growled low in his throat, spitting out the smoking smudge stick.

"I said, hold hands."

With no time left to argue over the less-than-optimal travel accommodations, the unlikely foursome grasped each other's hands as Me'tok turned his cute-as-a-button head toward his docked nubbin tail and turned in circles.

Morna would have sworn the dog was about to drop a deuce right then and there, but as Me'tok circled, the stones of the cellar floor beneath his feet took on a life of their own. Becoming circles, within circles, within circles that spun both counter and clockwise, the room full of poker-playing dogs and number-running monkeys spiraled further and further away.

FORTY-THREE

THE SMOKY SAYONARA

Hanging upside down in front of Cradle was an offense on the senses. A bird and a woman caught transverse and between. Silla's body and head were brutalized, beaten, and still half frozen, but at least those parts of her body were still somewhat recognizably human." The feathery wings reaching out from her shattered collar bones were determinedly not. Stretched beyond their normal reach, they were broken and twisted but still crested as if caught mid-change between woman and bird, and crudely nailed to the brick-and-mortar wall of the charred, smoking alcove with metal stakes the size of railroad spikes.

Crucified chimera style, Silla hung upside down in a hell of her own making. Blackened blood and steaming ichor flowed free from feathery veins to drip down each side of her burnt human body, along the apex of fiery feathers and blistered skin. Not yet weighed or measured, this was not a toll exacted by any of the aforementioned dimensional parties for a life poorly spent. No. Silla had somehow done this to herself. Question was, why?

"Take cover, Angel!" Silla warned, coughing and spurting black goo running heavy and thick down the inverse angle of her face, flooding her nostrils, and blinding her eyes in viscera as fire licked across the tips of her broken, outstretched wings.

Cradle barely ducked out and around the alcove door before a gulf of flames blew across Silla's wings and over the floor like fire down a gasoline trail, blowing hotter and wilder as if it were fed by Silla's accompanying screams. The louder she roared, the hotter it blazed, until her screams and fire gave way to the deafening silence of heavily falling snow.

"Silla, it doesn't have to be like this," Cradle said from his crouched position on the other side of the alcove door. "Death can be beautiful. You can do anything you want. This is your world now."

"Yeah, it's a regular Bob Ross painting from where I'm hanging! Smiling fucking clouds and happy little trees every-fucking-where!" Silla choked out. "Now, can you get me the fuck down from here or what? That bitch could be back any second!" she coughed.

"Bitch?" Cradle questioned as he stood in a good foot and a half of freshly fallen snow.

"Yes! The creepy bitch who blew through on a fucking horse and nailed me here! Damnit, Cradle, this hurts!"

Cradle rounded the alcove and looked up at Silla, still crucified and choking, then thought of the words graffitied across the plywood walls.

Above and Below
Betwixt and Between
The Fight Fucks You
The Fight Fucks Me
Ashes on Horses
Hooves on Soot
Fire on Feather
Wings on a Hook

"Goddamnit, Cathy." Cradle swore under his breath.

"Yep, Cathy! That was the crazy bitch's name! And she told me to tell you, 'be sure you never forget it'! Shit! Here we go again! Take cover, Cradle!" Silla warned as Cradle dove for cover, clearing the blast zone before it was consumed floor to ceiling in another fiery manifestation of Silla's sorrow.

"We've got three minutes, then you're going to go up in flames again!" Cradle yelled from the hallway, Silla's latest temper tantrum going cold.

He'd been timing the last two bursts, and they seemed equal in pause, or at least he hoped so. It was the best he could figure, given the time constraints, because every second he waited meant another turn on the spit for the parts of Silla's body that weren't hibachi compatible.

"We've got to get you down!" he warned aloud, rounding the corner and hauling ass toward the back of the alcove.

Cradle closed in and took a running jump at the crucified wing to the right, grabbing the spike with both hands and planting his Chuck's hard against the charred brick wall, pulling with everything he had.

"You'll find no argument here!" Silla yelled back.

She braced her feet hard against the wall and pushed out in tandem with Cradle's pull, both parties ignoring the cracking bone and shredding meat. The raw urgency of the deed left no room for the feels as Silla fell heavy and crumpled, half hanging toward her center of gravity. All her weight pulled her down from the wing, still pinned to the wall.

A single "Guh" escaped breathless from Silla's lungs as the weight of her freed side pulled, shredding the crucified wing as it split under the increased burden, ripping through vein and tendon as the coracoid bone enabling flight snapped clean with a nauseating crack, releasing her broken body to slide heavy to the floor.

Dizzy and vomiting, Silla wailed between spews of bile as

spurts of flame once again licked across every inch of her eviscerated wings.

"I can't," she spewed and coughed. "Cradle, I can't."

"Just let go, Silla. You have to let go, Darlin'.'"

"I can't. I can't do it anymore," she wheezed. "Cradle, you need to run," she half choked.

"Silla, do you trust me?"

Weeping and broken, Silla nodded.

"Just let it happen, Silla. Trust me on this. Just let go, and let it burn," Cradle said as he squeezed her hand softly before slowly rising to walk away.

Cradle cleared the corner of the alcove as heat burst through the hallway. Ducking for cover, he dove into a snow drift as a surge of heat one hundred times the intensity of any previous blast blew through the hall.

When the coast was clear, Cradle rose, steaming in his own skin when he finally made his way around the corner. He smiled when he saw nothing but a small puff of smoke and a black ring of char where Silla's broken body had laid.

"Atta girl, Sil. Atta girl," was all the fallen angel said as he began his long ascent top side, solo.

FORTY-FOUR

SEVEN DEVILS

Having sobered up by the mere mention of Justice Gray's name, a very hungover Grinx, and a very expired, but otherwise intrigued, theoretical physicist spent the next hour questioning each other for intel, round robin style, almost finishing each other's thoughts like the world's most intellectually dizzying game of $25,000 Pyramid.

"Hold up! Stoked as I am, and I am starstruck. Honestly, Albert, I love your work, but I gotta get rid of this headache. Gimme a second," Creak said before starting in with the purple, oozy shit again. "Be back in a jiffy," he winked before his rocky crust fell away, releasing a bevy of floating orbs that zipped and flew around the Nobel Prize winner's head like Tinkerbell on a bath salt bender.

Albert giggled in a way he hadn't since he last wore short pants. A look of wonder and delight danced in his age-old eyes while he studied the Grinx with unbridled curiosity as he borrowed things from here and there in the surrounding atmosphere. Creak zipped, dipped, and twirled about as free as any living thing could ever possibly hope to be. Back together, freshly aligned, and sans hangover, a general look of chagrin lingered on his newly minted face.

"I'm... I'm sorry about throwing up on you. Definitely a party foul. My bad."

"Party foul? You're bad?" Albert chuckled, loving everything about the creature, right down to the strange way it spoke. "This party foul; this is alright, Schatz. It is no matter to me. I think the matter we should be concerned with right now is presently clasped around the neck of your friend's wife, yes? It seems to me this is a big piece of the puzzle. Torquemada hasn't said a word to me about a necklace, but he has intimated that whatever his full plans to take over purgatory are, they are going to happen within the next day or two."

"And he never mentioned a necklace to you? Hmmm. It doesn't make any sense, Albert. That necklace was made for Freyja by Hephaestus but bolted permanently there by Freyja's ex, Odin, as a kind of scarlet letter he estimated would shame her by its permanent presence. Odin thought Freyja would shortly come to her senses after the affair and never want anyone to know about her tryst in the mountains with a deformed, down-on-his-luck, blacksmith. But, the Wise One underestimated the connection those two found together because Freyja proudly wore that Torc like a wedding ring since the day Heff first laid it round her neck. But that's all it is. The only mystical power linked to it is some magical locksmithing by Odin and some bullshit story Loki made up about Freyja fucking a bunch of dwarves because she likes shiny shit. There's really nothing of special note about the thing other than the sheer size and market value of the seven stones inlaid in it."

"Seven stones? What color are these stones?"

"Well, they aren't really stones at all. They're beautiful chunks of highly polished amber. You know—,"

"—fossilized tree resin," Albert finished for Creak. "Creak, what mountain did Freyja and Hephaestus have their little romantic interlude?"

"Somewhere in North Dakota, I think, or maybe it was New Zealand, something with an "N," I think. I forget. Why?"

"North Carolina?"

"That's it! North Carolina."

"Sieben Teuful."

"Gesundheit."

Albert raised one fuzzy white eyebrow at the Grinx.

"You don't know German? How is this possible."

"I've been meaning to download all of the Rosetta Stone software, but so far I'm only up to the languages starting with D. If you want to chew the fat in Catalan or chit chat in Chechen, I can parlay all day. German, not so much."

"We shall have to remedy this, yeah?"

"I just did. Sieben Teufel means 'Seven Devils', but what do you mean by that? I looked up German colloquialisms on seven devils and got zilch, other than a slight honorable mention via the Florence and the Machine's 'Seven Devils' by way of German translation."

"Amazing, Schatz! You learned an entire language while we were talking. Who is this Florence, and what machine did she create? What does it do?" Albert non-equitured, then swung back around at a truly dizzying clip, "The Seven Devils are in the Appalachian mountains, Schatz. Do you think this Florence and her machine can help?"

"Help with what exactly, Albert? Dude, you're giving me whiplash."

"How did I hurt your neck? Help with the Seven Devils, Schatz. Haven't you been listening? The Seven Devils in North Carolina are where Dante's Seven hid their sins."

"Dante's Seven? Gimme a second," Creak stared off into nothingness for a good while. "Do you mean Dante's Nine Circles of hell? Because that's just a story, Albert. A good one, yes, but that's all it is."

"Nein, Schatz. It's more than a story. It's an idea, and I'm not speaking of the nine circles. It's the seven sins and the seven brothers who guarded them I'm referring to. Nothing, not even a made-up story, is ever *all* anything ever is. Things are always much more than they seem and often much less. Dante's Inferno is a work of fiction, yes, but as with all good stories, even the littlest nibble of truth will ring true with readers. They'll feel it right down to their souls. It's why the book was such a big deal. People could see the truth in it, or better yet, couldn't outright deny the probable possibilities lying within its pages. Even more so when coupled with the information drilled into their little brains on a weekly basis from the time their indoctrinated parents first brought them to church."

"Dante's Divine Comedy casually opened a door to an otherwise taboo world. A world that denied the living entry, less paid by way of eternal damnation upon pain of death. And that's a steep price to pay for curiosity, yes? Dante gave regular folks a peek into the ever-after of a soul condemned in a way that was safe. Which got large numbers of common people thinking abstractly about religion for the first time, which in turn made the powers that be extremely nervous. Up to that point, your everyday parishioner was much like a newborn baby. Often fussy and hungry, but otherwise incapable of causing any real mischief. Ah but Schatz, when those little buggers start walking and talking, curious about the alien world all around them, it's best to put the knives out of reach lest they cut off their little noses despite their curious little faces and better still to answer every question of 'Why?' with 'Because I said so,' lest the little boogers figure out how full of shit their parents actually are."

"When Dante finished that game-changing book in 1320, a

multitude of churchgoers toddled out of the unquestionable fold of mother church's hold. They became threenagers overnight, much to the dismay of the worried mother who baby-proofed everything in sight, starting with the most dangerous items and working their way methodically down the list. First and foremost were the seven deadly sins, brought to the forefront by way of a 'devil not as black as he is painted'."

"Back the fucking truck up, Albert! Are you suggesting the seven deadly sins are actual religious relics? Like tangible, actual things?"

"Yes, Schatz, of course they are! Everything is made of energy, even ideas, thoughts, and intentions. You know better than anyone that just because you can't see something per se, doesn't mean it does not exist. Energy is very tangible if you know how to harness it."

"Of course, I know that! But the energies that power thoughts, emotions, and ideas are free-form energies. They come and go at their pleasure, not ours. How the hell could you safely tuck away an idea or feeling from a group of primitive parishioners on the verge of a spiritual awakening that mommy dearest doesn't think they're ready for?"

"It's simple, Schatz. You simply childproof them and move them out of reach."

"By pouring prehistoric tree sap over the energy and rendering it inert, then burying it deep in the bowels of an unknown mountain range on the far side of the world."

"Yes, Schatz!"

"And then The Hephaestus of Mount Olympus accidentally dug it up, forged the fossilized seven most deadly sins known to man into a beautiful Torc, and unknowingly adorned The Freyja of Sussrimner with it, just before The Odin of Valhalla locked it down for eternity."

"Yes, Schatz!"

"Bad. Fucking. Luck." Creak said, full-on gobsmacked by the series of events that landed them all up shits sin-filled, amber-laden creek without a paddle, "Like, seriously. Dat's some bad juju right there. For reelz."

"Yes, Shatz. I believe this juju is what Tomas de Torquemada is after."

"But why? And how did you figure this all out anyway?"

"Let's just say purgatory is littered with all sorts of curiosities, and I've had a lot of time on my hands over the last few decades to snoop around. But I don't think the information I've gathered was ever meant for human consumption. What little I've found reads more like an old card cataloging system. I've never actually seen any books on the topic, just clues via a couple of thousand rolodex-like files that were kept meticulously by a cleric who only left the initial 'M' on the numerous logs kept.

"So, you read some old card catalogs and were able to deter-mine the seven sins have been moved to the seven hells in North Carolina, wardened by a sept of long-lost mining brothers who go by the gang tag, Dante's Seven? That's a big ass leap, even for you, Albert."

"Not really, Schatz. The records by no means seemed to be written as a secret. Each card referred to a file or book I've never seen, and those books and files are where I believe the true secrets lie. But, each card revealed just enough information to track down other cards in the catalog, referring to connecting files or books and vice versa. I don't know any of the details, but it was easy enough to put together the major bits. It seems to me those major bits and pieces have hung around your friend's wife's neck for centuries."

"And your buddy, Torquemada, needs them?" Creak asked, remembering Albert might not necessarily be on the side of the good guys.

"He's not my buddy, as you say. He holds power over me, yes, but only through Justice. Justice holds the key to my eternity, not Torquemada. He could easily have me sent to 9.666, and that would be the end for me. I have had no choice but to play both sides of the coin in purgatory, Schatz. As long as I linger in the middle ground, there is hope I can use my intellectual property, my mind, my being, for good. If I go to 9.666, I'm done for. My abilities, for better or worse, will be at the hands of a madman. There will be no hiding who or what I am from him. He will know the second I get there; me and my abilities will be his to do with as he pleases."

"You mean like you've done for Justice and Torquemada?" Creak pressed, the rose-colored glasses of meeting his idol becoming less pink by the minute.

"Nein, Creak. Justice and Torquemada have no idea who I am, or who I was."

"How, Albert? How could they not know? Justice should have known the second you set foot on his scales."

"I never stepped on Justice's scales, Creak. Torquemada's time on earth was over before mine began. They have no idea who I am."

"So, what? Justice threw you into the Borderlands because he's gerontophobic?"

"Nein. I speculate Justice simply didn't know what to do with free will. Just because the shiny shithead told me to step on his scales didn't mean I was going to. I suppose I was the first person to ever question him. When he tried to force me, it didn't work. After a few weeks-long stalemate, he sent me to the Borderlands, which appeared was something that fell within his jurisdiction to do. Honestly, he seemed as surprised as me by the way things played out. I sort of got the feeling running Purgatory wasn't his day job."

"If you didn't step on his scales, he can't weigh and measure you. If he can't weigh and measure you, he can't send you to 9.666

or any other dimension, for that matter. Your reasoning doesn't hold water, Albert." Creak hated it was true and hated he'd figured it out.

"Nein. No one has to be weighed and measured Schatz; it's a bullshit job. Energies know what they are, and they don't need someone to tell them where to go. But, if too much energy is headed in one direction at the same time, well, that could cause quite a disaster. Think about it, Creak. This place isn't a weigh station, it's a circuit breaker. Its real purpose is to keep the energy traffic moving nice and steady, so the house doesn't catch on fire."

"That sounds an awful lot like heat theory, Albert."

"That's exactly it, Creak. It's just tweaked a little to account for some previously unknown ethereal variables! You see, when a person's body dies, their energy reverts to potential energy as it makes its way to Purgatory. After it passes through the circuit breaker, it's sent into palpable motion. Hence, heat, and a shit ton of it burning its way toward dimension 9.333 or 9.666. Without Purgatory acting like a governor, too much heat would be released at one time, and the omniverse, or house, would burn through all of its potential energy too fast, and cause the clock to run down on the omniverse, stopping everything. Forever."

"Entropy? You're theorizing that Purgatory acts like a governor for the second law of thermodynamics. The basic idea that the universe is slowly running out of useful energy. Are you proposing that without Purgatory acting as a circuit breaker, useful energy would disappear at a much earlier date and time than its regularly scheduled programming, causing Heat, Death, and Chaos to over-take the Omniverse?"

"That's my theory, yes!"

"That's fucking brilliant! But, if that's true, what makes you think Justice has the power to send you anywhere? If your theory is correct, Justice is nothing more than a switch energy traffic cop."

"It's true, Justice is nothing more than a traffic cop pointing this way and that. But, Justice has recently figured out, just like a traffic cop, he can point a few energies in any direction he wants, any time he wants. Mind you, he can't do it in mass; it would cause an unholy pile-up, but a few wrong turns here and there would never be noticed. It sure as shit doesn't hurt his image to throw a few of the more annoying souls toward 9.666 to keep the other inmates in line.

"Albert, even if Justice opens the lane and directs you through, your energies will go where they are attracted, not where he says they should go."

"That was before he figured out how to flip a charge. If you've yet to be weighed and measured, you're still gathering energies. If you do something negative enough, even in purgatory, your energies will reflect that action. Justice simply tells the people who are borderline they can get a speed pass to 9.999 if they do him a little favor. That little favor is always a nasty deed that flips their charge to a negative. He then throws them on his scales in a big show and lets everyone know the measure. And Schatz, the measure is never good."

"Let's assume you're telling me the truth. It still doesn't ring true to me you would have anything to worry about. You lived a decent life, Albert. You've helped humanity evolve, that's gotta land you in the positive."

"That is true only for my professional life, but I was the most selfish in my personal life, Creak. I could have been a better father and a much better husband. So, while the good I did for humanity is definitely positively charged, the lack of attention I gave my loved ones sort of balanced it out, leaving me solidly in the median...and then, there's the Manhattan Project—"

"You didn't do it. You were a pacifist, Albert."

"It was me who inspired Roosevelt to get America involved in nuclear weapons research."

"Po-tay-to, po-tah-to. You were only trying to help."

"The road to hell is paved with good intentions, Schatz."

"Honey, if that ain't ever the truth!" declared the buxom, stallion of a woman who'd just poofed into Show Biz with a rather grumpy-looking, but otherwise adorable, boxer in an over-the-top, redonkulously expensive Louis Vuitton Doggie Bag.

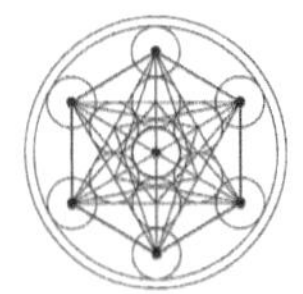

FORTY-FIVE

SILKWOOD SHOWER

About a half a millisecond later, an uninvited crowd staggered into the eighty-sixed pizza parlor, forming a wobbly kick line of vagabonds on either side of the K-9 carrying knockout. One after the other, left then right, then left again, starting with the impromptu appearance of an innocuous middle-aged man, followed by a very golden, very winged, not so Serena Williams, Serena Williams wanna be and topping the whole thing off was a possibly Charro inspired, possibly vision impaired, Princess Xena Warrior woman, all popping successively right out of thin air one, two, three, four and onto purgatory's plane like an Eye Dream of Jeannie acid trip. The four weren't there, then they were, poof, poof, poofity poof!

"Albert, am I still shitfaced or did a bunch of extras from the CW Network just drop by?" Creak asked, then turned to the extra-looking extras and said, "This isn't the commissary, guys. If you're looking for Central Perk, it's three doors down and to the left, right across from the Peach Pit."

"Greetings, King Vicus Navitas of Satera. I am Karma Etiam Grayness of All. It is an honor." The shockingly beautiful, brick house of a woman who toted the bag full of cute as a button boxer said, lowering her head and kneeling before the smart-ass Grinx in a way that could only be described as divinely majestic.

"Get the fuck outta here? Is that 'The' King Vicus?" The innocuous-looking man asked the kneeling they/them fatale.

"Yes, Loki of the Norse, Trickster of the Seven Senses, and Fifth Biggest Jackass of All Time, this—," Karma gestured their heavily jeweled hand toward Creak, "is the last living Balance Keeper of Non-Human Energies. King Vicus Navitas the Second of Satera. Karma Etiam Grayness of All answered like she was making a formal, royal introduction.

"Bitch, do I know you?" Creak snarled, glowing neon blue beneath his rocky, black hide.

"Keep up that tone, your Highness, and you'll know me better than you'd like."

"My name is Creak of the Cathedral Basilica, in St. Louis, MO. I hang out on churches and get shit on by birds for a living. You can save your curtsies for someone else."

"It's not the weirdest thing I've seen over the years. If you get your rocks off by having birds shit on you while you pretend to be a downspout, well, that's between you and the birds. That's no harm, no foul as far as the omniverse is concerned. That kind of kink doesn't even register on my radar. But, make no mistake about it, Vicus, Creak of The Cathedral Basilica, Karma knows everything, including the little-known fact you are the one and only King of All Satera, bird shit fetish notwithstanding."

Creak looked at Karma side-eyed, then turned his attention to the rest of the rag-tag horde, trying to get a read on the crowded room. Left to right, his gaze fell on one weirdo after another, until one very sparkly weirdo in particular caught his canvassing eye.

"Morna?" Creak rubbernecked it back toward weirdo number two so fast a miniature rockslide broke free beneath his studded, black leather collar, releasing a cloud of diamond dust and quartz crystals that slid and bounced in a dark, tinkling percussion of hollowed-out echoes.

"Yep. Oh gawd, I think I'm gonna throw up," the bedazzled, slightly nauseous angel muttered.

"Shut the front door! Holy shit, it worked! Are you OK? Like, how do you feel?" Creak asked as he skittered to Morna, looking her up and down while Albert hung back, soaking it all in.

"I feel like I'm gonna throw up," Morna muttered, turning her back to the crowd as she spewed the contents of her stomach into a sparkling, golden pile right next to Creak's not-so-sparkly, recently regurgitated, comfort binge.

"Of course, it worked, dear! She'll be fine, just a little motion sick. It was her first trip through The Circles."

"Hildi?" Creak turned his head toward the redheaded warrior woman with a very distinctive voice, releasing another miniature rock slide that had everyone coughing and gagging on the hazy veils of dust littering the air.

"Yes, dear?"

"But, how?"

"Really, dear? I think we have better ways to spend our time right now, don't you? First things first," Hildi said, batting at the dark, sparkling grit and coughing a few more times to clear her throat."Introductions! Seeing how you just met Karma, I'll skip them, but this fine fellow with us is Loki. He's an old friend of Freyja's and mine."

"Fine fellow, my ass," Karma knickered.

"Loki, this is Creak. My guess is there's no further explanation needed," Hildi said, ignoring Karma as she watched Loki all but drool and stare all sparkly anime-eyed at Creak.

"Are you by chance Odin's Loki?" Creak asked.

"Not by choice. I could be your Loki. I'm definitely in the market for a new Lord and Master," Loki said, rather clipped and garbled, tripping all over his serpentine tongue.

"Don't buy it, Your Highness. He'll offer to be your Loki, then vanish in the middle of the night without leaving so much as a note," Karma warned.

"Karma, I told you that wasn't my fault! Odin—"

"Odin, schmodin! Fuck off, Loki. Nobody wants to hear your excuses."

Loki sighed and looked down at his unremarkable brown leather work boots, his fanboy light fading in the dark memories of a long-ago moment he wholeheartedly wished could have gone another way.

"And who is this, dear?" Hildi asked, taking the heat off Loki as she turned toward the old man watching carefully and curious a few feet away.

"That's Albert. He works here," Creak said, giving as little information as possible.

He knew he could trust Hildi and Morna, but the others were unknowns. Sure, he'd heard of Karma and Loki. Who hadn't? But what they were doing here? Why was anyone's guess at this point.

"In a defunct Showbiz? In the Borderlands? What the fuck did you do to earn that kind of shitty eternity?" Loki asked.

"Don't answer that, Albert," Creak ordered, clipped and guarded. "It's none of his business."

"Enough!" Morna yelled.

Her voice sailed across the pizza parlor, shorting out every last video game as prize machines spewed miles of tickets into the air. The lights came down low on a powerful hum before thrumming back up to blinding, causing a waterfall of sparks to shower from the fixtures overhead. Morna was glowing rose gold with her newfound anger. Gilded filaments sparked and popped against her amber-colored, fluidic feathers in a surreal wave of power that underscored the rage and confusion of having just died only to be immediately recast as the royalist, and quite possibly the dumbest, Nephilim on earth. All this minutes before having to hitch a ride to

Purgatory by way of a metaphysical carnival ride, courtesy of a boxer bookie, while never really possessing a single clue to what the ever-loving fuck was actually happening. It was all picking this particular moment to come down on her like a rural Kansas farmhouse on a witch with a Woganowski complex.

Absolutely furious in her rage and confusion, it lit her luminous skin with an undercurrent of pink that flowed like lava, burning away every trace of earthly likeness, and leaving only a translucent apparition seething in its stead.

Hildi, Karma, Loki, Creak, and Albert stared slack-jawed as Morna Stahr levitated before them, her wings not making the slightest stroke of movement as she hovered like a reflection of endless possibilities. The holiest of unholies, or the unholiest of holies. Honestly, it was a real fuckin' tossup.

"Is, uh—Is this new?" Creak whispered out the side of his gaping maw in Hildi's general direction.

"Yep. Brand Spankin," was all the pig familiar said.

"Everybody shut the fuck up!" Morna bellowed before them, her modus operandi the same but somehow totally and inherently different.

She sounded like herself but didn't, looked like herself but didn't, and she was acutely aware her newly acquired energies were pumping her aura out and into the air. The troop of weirdos before her could not only see what she was feeling, they could feel it.

Somehow her mind's eye saw it all go down, like a slow-motion replay. Morna watched in horror as her emotions cascaded over the auras of those around her. Like a tipped bucket of tar, her emotions poured over the others' feelings and emotions in a thick, sticky layer of her own, radically shifting the entire vibe of the group to one collective mood. Her mood. Which was seriously pissed off.

"Uh oh", was all she said, because, in the blink of an eye,

everyone had, in fact, shut the fuck up and stared at her gape-mouthed and fuming, equally as pissed off as she had been. But it was different; they weren't pissed off *with* her, they were pissed off *at* her. It had become clearer and clearer by the second how not one single soul appreciated having their own feelings overridden on a raging Nephilim's whim.

Morna chanced a look to Creak who chewed wildly at the thick layer of invisible feelings Morna threw over him like a tar and feather blanket full of fleas. The others looked none too pleased themselves as they rubbed and pulled against the invisible film of unwanted feelings coating them from head to toe. The anger and disgust of being emotionally violated hung heavy in the air.

"What have I done?" Morna whispered as her rage fell away to a heavy mortification, which had her slowly drifting back to the floor.

"Don't ever do that shit to me again!" Creak coughed, gagging as Morna's emotions dissipated and fell away while her feet slowly made contact with the ground. "Gah!" the Grinx shook his big, black head hard in a way that traveled down to the sparkling chunk of quartz on the tip of his tail. "Who needs a shower?"

Every last being in the room meekly raised their hand or paw, looking violated and nauseous as Creak summoned a collective spring storm of perfectly Ph-balanced rain clouds. A variety of retired Bath and Body Works antibacterial hand soaps and a wooden crate full of scratchy loofahs, pumice stones, and indus-trial-strength scrub brushes appeared before them, gathered grate-fully from somewhere in Purgatory's rather limited Network.

Morna sat small and still on the Showbiz floor, her arms curled over her bent knees as she looked upon the aftermath of her ethere-ally charged temper tantrum. Five. Five otherworldly creatures who had seen God knows what kind of hellish nightmares in their unusual and lengthy lives were so grossed out by her accidental, emotional abuse they took a group Silkwood Shower in a Purgatory Pizza Parlor, scrubbing one another's backs and fronts with dead sea sponges while avoiding eye contact of any kind.

"I'm sorry."

Wet from head to toe and red-skinned from the abrasive decontamination, the five stood in a puddle of soap suds and emotional sludge, saying absolutely nothing in return as Me'tok circled in and out of their legs with a fresh bundle of smoking hot sage.

"Seriously, you guys. I'm really, really sorry. I didn't mean to," Morna apologized from where she sat on the floor.

Creak never looked at her as he threw a yellow flag on the play and called, "Penalty, unsportsmanlike conduct. Huddle!"

All five beings instinctively circled in as a unit and collectively moved fifteen yards away from Morna. Gossipy chatter and a couple of curses had Morna leaning sideways to eavesdrop on the preternatural pow-wow, but the group responded in kind by moving the huddle several more yards to the right until they'd shuffled through the swinging doors to the industrial-sized kitchen, leaving Morna alone on the other side.

FORTY-SIX

DA FAQ WAS THAT?

Heads in the round and arms over shoulders, the five pulled in tight and strategized.

"Da faq was that?" Loki asked the collective huddle as the swinging doors came to a slow, uneven stop behind them.

"Not kosher, that's what that was, dear."

"She just barfed her emotions all over us!" Creak blurted, dry heaving a little at the thought.

"Schatz, could she do this before?"

"I don't know, Albert. Last time I saw her, she wasn't even capable of breathing."

"What do you mean she wasn't capable of breathing?"

"I mean, she was dead, Einstein."

"Remarkable recovery," Albert noted.

"Who was dead?" Loki asked.

"Morna," Hildi and Creak said in unison.

"The angel? Nah, angels can't die, even if they want to. I've seen a few tries, but it never works out," Loki added.

"She's a Neph, dear, not an angel."

"Bullshit. That woman has wings. Nephs don't have wings."

"This Neph does," Creak countered.

"If she was a Neph and died, she'd be in 9.999. No questions asked. She doesn't look dead to me, and like I said, angels can't die."

"Loki and Albert, I'm going to need you to pay close attention, O.K.?"

Loki and Albert nodded.

"Morna Stahr is Nephilim royalty with her lineage going back to the One dimension by way of Ishtar doing the deed with one of Morna's ancestors. When Morna's Neph powers kicked in, the royal genome sequence activated and flipped her into full-on angel mode while still trapped in a human shell."

"That would never work, she'd be dead… ooooooh. Got it," Loki said. "But, how'd you get her into the angel's body?"

"Forbidden fruit, a world-class smithy, and some humble phi," Creak threw out.

"Ya lost me there, King Vicus."

"It's Creak, and it doesn't matter. Morna is a royal Nephilim by way of dimension Numero Uno. That's all you need to know."

"Humble phi? Like the golden ratio, phi? The 1.618 phi? A number or ratio, perfect or not, cannot be humble, Creak. It's just a number," Albert theorized.

"Don't say that shit around Freyja, dear," Hildi warned.

"It is when you give yours away like Freyja did for Heff, then Heff did for Morna. There's nothing humbler than gifting your most prized possession to one less fortunate and wanting nothing for yourself in return."

"Freyja and Heff of The Seven Devils, Shatz?"

"Yep."

"Seven Devils?" Hildi and Loki questioned in unison.

"Fuck this shit. I'm out," said the boxer before he disappeared in a twirling circle of smudgy red and white asbestos tiles.

"Ugh," Karma knickered, looking less sable as she reached into her jumpsuit and snorted some ergosphere straight out of the silver engraved snuff box, skipping the dainty serving spoon portion, and going for it like a coke fiend on a fresh eight-ball.

"Listen up," Karma ordered, snorting and rubbing their heavily jeweled fingers back and forth under their equine nose. "Im'a say this once 'cause we're running out of time. When I point and call your name, I want you to tell me in ten words or less what you know that immediately pertains to the goat rodeo at hand. Albert, go."

"Torquemada plans to overtake purgatory with The Brisingamen."

"King Vicus, go."

"My name's Creak."

"Go!"

"Heff's currently unlocking seven deadly sins from the Brisingamen Torc."

"Hildi, go!"

"The Brisingamen Torc is presently locked on Freyja's neck."

"Fifth Biggest Jackass of All Time, go."

"Karma, that's not fair. If you'd just let me explain—"

"Go!"

"Odin sent me. When the Torc comes off, Freyja's his."

"Well, shit," Morna said between the gap in the swinging doors.

Only one phosphorescent, twirling gold eye was visible through the crack.

"Angel, you're on the bench until we can figure out what to do with you," Karma warned.

"But—," Morna pleaded as she pushed her way through the door.

"Get!"

"No!"

Uh oh. There she went again, pissing off celestial forces of inexplicable power.

"Sweetie, have you lost your ever-lovin' mind? If I say you're benched, you're benched. Karma doesn't play. Now go!" The fate warned, pointing one beautifully manicured finger toward the dining area on the other side of the half-open doors.

"Neither do I!" Morna yelled, pissed as hell, they were trying to leave her out!

Silla was missing, Cradle was M.I.A., and from the sounds of it, Heff and Freyja were up a creek without a paddle. All because of her! No, this wasn't Karma's call. This was her shit show, thank you very much. She'd be damned if she was going to be the understudy in her own damn story, shit show or not.

Starting in with the rosy gold, apathetic wing levitation thing, Morna could feel her heels then her toes slowly peel away from the sticky kitchen floor.

"Don't you do it!" Creak warned as he grabbed for a nearby fire extinguisher with his teeth, pointing the sprayer directly toward Morna. "Cool, you're jets, angel, or I'll do it for you!"

Calm. Morna needed to calm the fuck down ASAP. Her thoughts flew through her head a million clicks a minute, and her anger turned her blood to lava as she floated further away from the dingy, red and white checked tiles lining the kitchen floor.

As one thought after another blew through her mind, she tried desperately to lock onto one, hoping it would give her some focus and quiet the crazy that had her floating light as a feather, stiff as a board, while glowing like a fucked up Himalayan salt lamp. She pumped her negative emotions into the air instead of neutralizing them.

Seconds passed as she glowed brighter, levitating higher as her flashing memories twisted themselves into her emotional effusion. She wrestled one free and locked it down, almost missing it as it sailed past her consciousness like one lone star in a shower of millions. She held on tight, keeping the lone thought firmly in the present so she could have something, anything familiar to hold on to. The thought itself was nothing of consequence. A dumbass moment randomly plucked from a gigabyte's worth of extraneous memories sailing by. For whatever reason, she'd caught this one, and she supposed it was as good as any embarrassing moment of the millions she might have selected to remind herself who and what she really was.

Morna watched, delighted and mortified, as the memory of Silla standing safely on the front porch of her parents' white farmhouse laughed and cackled at her like a berserker while Morna ran hell-bent for leather across the gravel drive and away from the murderous turkey who liked to play bludgeon Morna every time she crossed the goddamned yard. Morna lost herself in the memory of watching her best friend stand safely with her mom and dad, every last one of them screaming and caterwauling an anthology of ludicrous instructions at her on how to get the flightless beast to stand down. She jumped for her life toward a tire swing like a live-action game of Pitfall, holding tight to the swinging rope while awkwardly straddling an old tractor tire. The feathered asshole gobbled and strutted, in patient wait for her descent.

Odd as it would seem, it was there she found her peace, forgotten in memory of not so long ago when she swung mortified and giddy in the front yard of a white farmhouse chock full of the people she loved and in turn loved her, just as she was. Just like that, her ability to control her own emotions manifested as her sparkly, angel toes came into slow contact with the ground, one dazzling digit at a time.

"That was a close one," Creak said, in stern warning before awkwardly spitting out the fire extinguisher. "Are you good now or do I need to cart that thing with us?" Creak asked, tossing his head toward the canister.

"I'm good. I think. For now, anyway."

Morna felt guilty and flustered, but mostly proud she'd managed to check herself before being hosed down by a four-legged, dimensional outlier who carted expired, noxious chemicals, circa 1992.

"Now that you're back to yourself, angel, will you kindly move your ass back to the dining room? The grownups need to talk," Karma ordered coolly.

"I said 'no', Karma, and I meant it. I may not be as old or powerful as any of you, but that doesn't mean I don't have a right to be here. Besides, this is all my fault. None of this would be happening if Cradle, Creak, Freyja, and Heff didn't save me. I owe it to them to save them back. It's the least I can do."

"How very human of you, Morna darling! There you stand, a bona fide and recycled Angel, yet you still think the world revolves around you! Me, me, me, me, me! Uh, grow up!" Karma schooled the newbie. "Now, do as you're told. Go outside and sit down before you hurt yourself."

"It *is* my fault! Justice brought Creak, Cradle, Freyja, and Heff here because they helped me transition. They saved me!" Morna said, looking Creak in the eyes apologetically.

"Uh, do we really have time for this shit, dear?" Hildi asked Karma, giving her a little nudge toward the more important matters at hand.

Ones that didn't involve checking Morna's less-than-angelic ego.

"O.K. angel, you can stay, but zip it unless I point to you. Got it?"

"I thought she was a Neph, not an angel," Loki said.

"I got it."

Morna slid to the floor, deflated, in a huff of akimbo legs, black spandex, and crumpled pride at the same time Loki threw in his two cents.

"What the hell are you? Like seriously?" Loki asked, looking down at the sparkly woman sitting awkwardly in a huffy puddle of liquidus feathers and quiet dissidence.

Morna didn't say a word. She pursed her lips and shrugged her feathery shoulders in a way that could only be translated as, meh.

"Yeah, OK, that clears things up," Loki said side side-eyeing Morna before turning to the rest of the not-so-huddled huddle, saying, "So, what's the plan?"

THE RED

Justice had wanted a little time to himself to reflect and think. He'd thought a nice trip through the Babylonian gardens for old times' sake would put his mind at ease. That had been a little over three hours ago, and peace was nowhere to be found. At his wit's end and halberd still in hand, Justice used the ax portion of the pole weapon to hack and whack his way through the scenic route he'd woefully decided to take to the prison forge.

"Gah!" Justice yelled as he hacked and axed at the jungle of vines, congratulating himself on yet another less-than-stellar idea.

It never occurred to him that the Babylonian gardens hadn't been landscaped since Nebuchadnezzar split for 9.999. After he and Cradle had a tete-a-tete and realized the Book of Danielle was a somewhat skewed version of Nebuchadnezzar's spiritual belief system, visa vie secularism.

Thinking back, Justice figured it must have been somewhere around the first century A.D. when Cradle popped over to the extinct oasis for a cup of chai and nice long chat with the missing maker of The Marvel of Mankind. Thirty minutes later, the tea was cold, and the hanging gardens were forever abandoned to the wilds of the Borderlands as Neb sailed merrily on his way to 9.999, ecstatic at the idea of seeing his wife again and overjoyed to finally meet his idol, Marduk, nom de plume, The One.

"Once again, Cradle, you are solely responsible for my misery," Justice said, disgusted as he swatted at the swarms of Eocene mosquitoes buzzing 'round his shiny, sweaty head, spinning and swatting in circles until he lost his sense of direction entirely.

Looking left, then right, then up, all Justice could see was a sea of green.

"Fuuuuuccck!"

Justice's curse echoed out over the leaves, vines, and ferns in every direction, sailing and echoing back to him on an unexpected swish of rustling undergrowth.

"Who's there?" he yelled into the walls of green, turning in a circle, and scouring what little of his surroundings he could see as the rustling sound closed in.

"Creak? Creak, if that's you, I'm sorry about the whole cage thing! But, in all fairness, you did piss on my boots! Ah, never mind about that," Justice said, trying to buy enough time to figure out how to handle a Grinx with a grudge. "I'm—I'm sure we can talk things through? Let bygones be bygones? There must be something you want? Or, more to the point, someone? It's gotta be lonely being the only Grinx. Maybe I can help? I scratch your back, you scratch mine?"

"Pathetic," said a slurry, feminine voice that slithered like velvet over the leaves before they parted ways. "Negotiating with the help? My, but how the mighty have fallen."

"Oh," Justice said. "It's just you," turning his back to the voiceless, faceless woman in red who'd come forth through the jungle, seated on an enormous black destrier, and effortlessly cradling the boneless Oracle of Delphi across her lap.

"Hmm. Just me, huh?" mumbled the slurring Oracle. "I'd

thought you'd be a little happier to see me, given your current circumstances."

"That thing gives me the creeps, Lena. Couldn't you get some speech recognition software or something? Like Dragon or that thing Stephen Hawking used? Anything's gotta be better than carting around a prophetic, roofied virgin from eighth-century Greece as a mouthpiece."

"Pythia's my friend, Justice, and I'll not have you talk about her that way," said the creepily thin, roofied, eighth-century virgin as she slid down and across the neck of the gigantic black horse like a rag doll. Her ratty, long hair swung down low to the ground on one side of the enormous animal, while her dirty bare feet dangled bent and awkward over the other.

"That thing needs a bath."

"Enough about Pythia!" the Oracle commanded, her back arching and twisting over the horse in a grotesque act of puppetry. "Another word and I'll turn this war horse around and you won't see The Red again until the day you wished you didn't."

"That sounds great. Catcha later, Lena."

"You need me, Justice Gray. I have as much invested in the outcome of Torquemada's plan as you. And I know a few things that will either make or break this deal. If you're interested?" the oracle whispered, slithery and sick as Lena sat silent and still as the grave, but for the sparkling fire in her ruby eyes.

"You tracked me down in the middle of a long-lost jungle, in the Borderlands of Purgatory, because *I* need *you*? It would appear you think me as dumb as you are mute. How long has it been since you've actually spoken to someone? Ask someone a favor? One? Maybe even as much as two thousand years? You're rusty, Lena. Maybe you should go put that thing out of its misery," Justice said, pointing the hook of the halberd directly at the twisted-up thing in Lena's lap. "Then ride on over Betwixt the Between and practice your etiquette with Bill or Steve for a bit, they have plenty of time on their hands. I'm sure they won't mind," Justice turned away to resume hacking a path.

"That's where you're wrong, Justice. No one, and I mean no one, has any time left on their hands. Everyone and everything is about to end."

"Yeah, yeah, yeah, Lena, we get it. 'The Apocalypse is coming!'" Justice mimicked low in his throat. "You know, that Four Horsemen nonsense loses its luster after you threaten people with it on the regular...for a millennia."

"It's coming tomorrow, Justice Gray, for you, me, and everything else in existence."

Justice let out an enormous sigh of impatience and took a break from his landscaping trial to counter The Red. "If that's true, why did you help Torque? Why are you here? Hell, Lena, why in the name of The One who abandoned you would you even give a shit?"

Lena locked her empty red eyes on Justice as the Oracle of Delphi twisted straight up, pulled like a corpse on invisible marionette strings as the ire of loss and the desire for more that could not take shape on The Red's empty face danced awkwardly and perverse across Pythia's possessed features.

"Because I'm not done here."

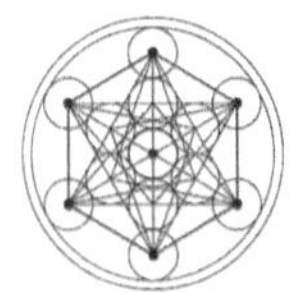

FORTY-EIGHT

YOU KNOW WE'LL HAVE A GOOD
TIME THEN

He couldn't go back the way he came; that door had been closed forever. Cradle hadn't got very far on his trek topside when the well of Silla's soul disappeared. It was a very good sign that wherever Silla was, she was whole again. Now, he needed to figure out how to do the same for himself.

Wings clipped, ethereal body cast off, and his host soul long gone, Cradle was solidly in limbo, a place he had never experienced before. He'd been near there of course, helped others find their way through when he could, and even cried for some when they couldn't manage the impossible task. Cradle had helped countless souls learn to let go of a life that no longer mattered. Lives, their souls were so attracted to they didn't understand by choosing to not let go, they allowed their energies to be swallowed whole by regret, leaving nothing for themselves.

Regret, what a greedy, greedy bastard. In all his years, in all his studies, Cradle never faced a more formidable demon. The scientific equivalent of a redshift; a fucking light thief. A supermassive black hole stopping at nothing to siphon all of a soul's energy, all of its light. The insatiable monster drains every last lumen when it can't manage to break free from the impossible pull. And for the ones who managed the task, who somehow managed to escape, regret will undoubtedly, at the very least, change the soul's trajectory. Forever.

It was his turn to let go. His turn to look in the mirrors and accept his reflection for what was and nothing more, and be OK with that. If he couldn't, well, there wouldn't be enough left of him to help himself, let alone anyone else.

When Cradle saw the trail of syrupy, silver liquid trailing behind him, he knew it was his turn to face Dorian.

"Gah. He's always been a creepy little shit," Cradle said, accepting his fate as the very last, silvery drip of days fell and sizzled into the sand. Each drip called forth a mirror, fourteen billion three hundred forty of them to be exact. Each mirror reflected one year of the fourteen-billion-three-hundred-forty he'd existed.

Cradle was about to face every last one, all the while attempting to single out one very key mirror without Dorian noticing he gave two shits, hoping and dreading its reflection would prove his reworked theory correct. A single, biographical reflection, three-point-eight-billion years old. Which, if memory served, would show himself alone in purgatory, stupefied and heartsick, peering through a pictorial glass observing the disembodied energy of the Last Universal Common Ancestor, Luca, sailing straight past purgatory and through the front fucking doors of The One's dimension on a wave of infinite mass. She would cull and burn a shit ton of energy as she went, measurably winding down the omniversal doomsday clock at one-hundred-eighty-six-thousand seconds per mile, give or take, proving the omniverse was on a crash course with heat death because a sanctioned, thirteenth-century, homogenic bigot refused to accept his fate.

Tomas de Torquemada, Grand Inquisitor of the Spanish Inquisition and asshat extraordinaire, was not so long ago denied elevated dimensional entry of any kind by The One. The Grand Inquisitor, being a small-minded yet powerful dickhead, managed to rack up a death count of over two thousand non-catholic souls because he had garnered the support of even more powerful, smaller-minded dickheads.

Being responsible for carrying out atrocities of epic proportions in one of The One's numerous names had The One itself so pissed It had Cradle furloughed out to Spain in 1498 to oversee the ending of The Inquisitor and the Inquisition, personally. Easier said than done, of course. Getting rid of the Inquisitor was one thing; ending the Inquisition itself took several hundred more years.

So it was, shortly after Tomas de Torquemada's death by Cradle's hand, the Grand Inquisitor was denied entry into an ever-after he woefully believed he was deserving of. After all, every-thing he'd done had been for the 'All Mighty's Glory'.

Hit with some hard, heretical truths he could never accept, the excommunicated friar was forced to dwell out the rest of his days as persona non grata, alone in the Borderlands until The Four came to call. And as of this moment, Cradle was about one-hundred-twenty percent certain Tomas De Torquemada had been using every last one of those endless days devising a crusade to turn the tables. If Cradle didn't get out of limbo soon, Torque and his auto da fe' Army of ungoverned souls and unstable Calvary of Four, were going to be blitzkrieging their way into 9.999 on a wave of infinite mass while Justice turned a blind fucking eye.

Encircled by his fourteen-billion mirrors, Cradle turned in the general direction of dimensional bit 9.999 and vowed, "I swear to you, Boss. I'm gonna break my foot off in that kid's ass."

FORTY-NINE

LEARNING TO FLY

Silla had burned all the way back up the well, breaking free of the darkness in a blaze of her own power. One moment all she saw was darkness. The next was all light before morphing into a ball of pure heat of her own design.

Silla blew out over a ghost town of strip malls, abandoned factories, and a half-collapsed tower that appeared suspiciously reminiscent of a long-ago buggered nuclear power plant she'd recently watched a Netflix special on. Flipping over and turning back for a better look, Silla left a miasma of flaming vapors and streaming steam in her wake.

Playing with the gas, Silla put the pedal to the metal and metaphysically leaned into the heat. She slowed her burn by simply leaning out. Every last move was brought on by a natural inclination. She'd wonder if she could fly faster, and she suddenly knew how. Wondered how to burn hotter, and she immediately knew how to do that, too!

Too good to be true, Silla thought to herself when an idea crossed her mind.

She wondered if it would work. *Surely not, but it sure would be cool if I could*, she thought.

No more than she thought it, she could breathe! Not the way she did before! No, this was better!

Cradle was right! Holy shit! He's going to rub that in, she thought to herself as she took in the air almost osmotically.

When she wanted air, needed air to fuel her burn, she simply drew it in. Not with her lungs; she didn't have lungs anymore. This was a different kind of breath entirely. This breath gave as it took. An innate symbiotic relationship that yinged and yanged with the surrounding environment. An environment that fed off her as she fed off it.

She wondered, and was suddenly filled with the fuel necessary to convert the thought into a very loud, very ecstatic, "Woohoo!" She barrel-rolled across the sky. "Woohoo! Woo-motherfucking-hoo!"

Shedding her human body was like taking off blinders, filters, pumps, and tanks. Suddenly realized you'd never needed a submarine when you were a thousand feet below the ocean waves. That you'd spent your previous days worrying about every leak, bump, and creek, while at any time you simply could have opened the door to the diving bell and become one with the ocean. It was never something to fear, but part of you. Equally integral to your well-being as you are to it.

Silla spent the next thirty minutes zipping, flipping, and burning her way back and forth over the abandoned ghost towns, gathering her bearings in more ways than one. In a little over half an hour, Silla was able to devise that she definitely wasn't in Missouri anymore. Hell, she was pretty sure she wasn't on earth anymore. The dead ringer giveaway? She was three-hundred percent sure Russian wasn't commonly used on power plant signs in the Show Me State, and the word TSCHERNOBYL written on everything around the busted-up cooling tower smacked eerily reminiscent of the word Chernobyl.

Silla had never been much of a bookworm, but she was sharp as a tack, great with directions, and could acclimate quicker than a wink. If anyone ever tried to pull one over on her, they'd better have their ducks in a row. Not unlike the four-legged fur balls floating around in a nearby cooling pond surrounding the out-of-place nuclear facility.

"Four-legged ducklings, Russian wording, and a busted-up power plant surrounded by a Burger Chef, a Dillard's department store, and the fucking Peach Pit? No way!" Silla threw on the breaks and nosedived at Mach speed, pulling up short above the cracked, weed-strewn sidewalk leading into a seriously debilitated, but otherwise wonderful-smelling Showbiz Pizza Parlor.

The doughy smells of bread and cheese bargained for a swap of energies as she morphed into a much hotter version of her former self. Looking in the dirty, dingy window, Silla smiled at her familiar reflection and fluffed her smoking hot ebony and amber hair, happy she could still exist in her previous, if somewhat higher base temperature, form whenever she wanted. She licked her lips at the idea of trading some extraneous heat for some ooey, gooey, cheesy goodness as she opened the door and walked inside, surprised as hell to see one thundering cloud pouring a centrally located spring storm just downstage from the wailing Animatronic, Rock-A-Fire Explosion Band.

"Curiouser and curiouser," Silla said as she closed in on the thundering cloud before tripping on a bucket of soapy sludge and scrub brushes.

"Son of a bitch!" sailed across Showbiz in a splash of suds and thunder of crashing tables.

A "Who the fuck is that, dear?" came from behind a set of swinging kitchen doors as they parted ways.

"Silla? Silla! I'd know that 'Son of a Bitch!' anywhere!" hit Silla's ears as the doors flew open, revealing one very relieved, very glittery, spandex-covered angel.

277

THE GOD PARTICLE

"Look, Red, I feel for ya. I really do. I gotta get over to the prison forge and get that necklace off Freyja before Torque has a spaz. It sucks you have to dwell out your days Betwixt the Between, except when Torque beckons, but calling the end of times 'cause you're not happy with the bargain you struck with the Inquisitor is like crying wolf to a bear. It's not going to instill fear, Red. All it's going to do is get you locked up, maybe permanently this time."

"Don't you wonder how he even called us in the first place, Justice? Hasn't it ever crossed your shiny, metal head he should never have been able to do that?" The Oracle asked all doom and gloom.

"He beat the system. Good for him. Good for you and me, I might add."

"Did he, Justice? Or did he break it?" the Oracle twisted, sweaty and sick, saliva drooling in long, silvery strings from the corners of her mouth.

"Get that thing a bib, would ya? And need I point out, there you stand, and here I stand and that thing in your lap is still here giving me the skeeves. If he broke the system, we wouldn't be here having this little garden party."

"Haven't you noticed that the Pale isn't around, Justice?"

"And how would I notice that, Red? Short of a stiff breeze, no one knows when that creepy wraith is lurking about. Fuck, for all I know, she's standing right next to you with her hand up Pythia's ass. It would explain all the unnecessary squirming that thing's doing," Justice half gagged.

"OK then, jackass, haven't you noticed the White and the Black aren't around either? Do you honestly think they'd stay Betwixt the Between when they have a hall pass? Think about it, Justice. None of the other Four are out and about. It's just me," Pythia whispered.

"O.K., I'll bite. Why aren't the other three runnin' around, Red?"

"Cathy's a know-it-all nerd who likes to read in her spare time, which is all the time. The last time she got out, she hoofed it straight to the library with some very overdue books, where she chatted up the librarian. A librarian who also happens to be the earth's most famous theoretical physicist and also, as fate would have it, is moonlighting for Torque in his spare time. Those little nuggets, coupled with the fact our last call to arms at your behest through Purgatory Proper a few hours ago had our darling Catherine bumping directly into a really old flame who was kind enough to gift her with an angel's breath worth of mercy. A gift that happened to carry with it some very interesting superfluous knowledge about how The Big Show really works. All of which, mind you, went down while you were off playing with a dog-thingy!"

"Yeah? And?"

"And? And!" The Red had ruby flames sparking from her eyes as Pythia levitated above the giant black horse, floating and twisting three feet above the saddle as she swore a blue streak.

"Without the God Particle, anybody and anything that's out of their assigned soul areas who are supposed to be in their assigned soul areas, and anybody and anything in but are supposed to be out are burning through all of the omniverse's energy stores at a rate of nine-point-eight-three-six E+8 feet per second."

"Come again?"

"Tachyons, you shiny shithead! Anything from mass to energy, to souls! From the fucking Horsemen to the seven inert deadly sins, Hephaestus is banging away at with that giant ass hammer! Anyone and anything jumping dimensions has to be powered by tachyons! And!" the Oracle screamed, "I don't see any tachyons in my fucking saddle bag!"

Pythia finished as Lena reached her rubied hand down the flank of her destrier, dumping the entire contents of her scarlet saddlebag onto the jungle floor, causing a dazzling waterfall of sparkling rubies in every size, shape, and color imaginable. Cascading in a glittering stream, the rubies piled into a blood-red mountain, burying Justice's jungle-rotted boots in about eight trillion karats but zero fucking Tachyons.

"Do you, motherfucker?"

FIFTY-ONE

THE FUN HOUSE

"Hey, Dorian."

"Hey, yourself, Cradle. Welcome to the Big Show!" Dorian said, making a spectacle of throwing the long tails of his blue and silver topcoat as he bowed, a formal welcome, flamboyant with all the unnecessary pomp and circumstance of nineteenth-century flair.

"No need for all the bells and whistles, Dorian. I know how this goes. Let's just get on with it already."

"Are you kidding me?" Dorian asked, his arms fully splayed out as he spun within the encircling fourteen-billion mirrors. "This is the show of all shows. As the Maestro of Mirrors, I insist we do this properly. After all, Dad, you've earned it." Dorian finished, making a show of rubbing his left ear.

The one Cradle used to grab him by when he was caught 'mistreating the reflections'. He'd only been but a sprite of a fate at the time. There was no reason for Cradle to have been so rough; they were only reflections after all.

"Maestro of Mirrors?" Cradle asked, remembering Justice saying he'd put Dorian in charge of the Fun House.

It was a slang term the tweeny bopper fates used for limbo that stuck, no matter how hard Cradle tried to correct it. Kids will be kids, but Purgatory Proper had been no place for them. That's exactly what he'd told Tina when she left them there with their Uncle Cradle for an evening out three thousand years ago. She'd never come back to get her kids, and Cradle had found himself an overnight adoptive father to one very silvery and pissed-off teen, one Dalai Lama-like middle schooler, and one very light on morality, mirror-obsessed, sociopathic toddler.

"It's got a nice ring to it, don't you think? Hell of a lot better than being monikered after a childhood dermatological condition. Now, if you would be so kind as to kneel… Cradle," the name slid off Dorian's tongue like the insult it was meant to be.

"Kid, as the… What did you call yourself again? The Malcontent of Mirrors? Yeah, that sounds right. As the Malcontent of Mirrors, you should know you'll need to use my full, formal name for the ceremony to work. Ah, you know what? You probably have your hands super full being so important these days. Honestly, I can't believe you let your brother talk you into this bullshit job just to get you out of his hair. And it worked too! Justice is spending every day at the greatest concert of fucking ever, and Dharma is somewhere off on cloud nine, high as a fucking kite, and philosophizing with Kurt Cobain about the wonders of everything earthly while driving the poor man half-mad with questions about what gravity is really like and are boobs really that great?"

And at that thought, he snapped his fingers, escalating Kurt to a nice forest cottage located next to a stream, a personal weed boutique, and some lovely forest who could talk, but only if they really needed to. Kind of like the man himself. It was the least he could do.

Dorian spewed venom from his eyes. When he realized his father wasn't even paying attention to him anymore, his anger raised a veil of twirling sand devils who twisted and danced around the mirrored desert as Cradle kept ignoring him.

"I am Metatron of the Seraphim, Archangel of the Celestial Scribe, Governor of All of Purgatory, and Keeper of the Sacred Shape."

"But! But," Dorian said as the mirrors rotated in the sands, rearranging themselves around Cradle in geometric patterns echoing the basic building blocks of all existence. "That's not fair, Cradle! Dad!"

Cradle heard Dorian whine as the mirrors closed in, folding, slapping, stacking, and twisting themselves into a complex cube complete with a six-pointed star and thirteen circles, grinding like the gears of a puzzle box as it sealed Cradle within a prison of his own light.

"Dad, I wasn't really going to put you in there! Dad, it was Justice's idea! Not really even that, it was that Asshat you hate so much."

"How many times have I told you not to call your brother an Asshat? That word is reserved for a super special piece of shit, and you know it. You're grounded!" Cradle yelled as the mirrors were almost closed completely.

"I know, Dad! I mean, The Asshat! The real one!"

"FUCKING FIGURES!" Cradle roared as the mirrors closed, the pain vibrating with the rage of his words, letting Dorian know the cat was out of the bag, and there was no putting it back.

Dorian smiled the most shit-eating grin as he imagined the just deserts headed Justice's way. If his dad somehow managed to survive the cursed mirrors. Did he want him to survive? Well, he didn't not want him to, and that was about all the time for family therapy he had today.

FIFTY-TWO

KARMA CALLS A KIKI

"Morna! Oh, thank The One! I've been worried sick about you! What's with the get-up?" Silla asked, hugging her best friend before pulling back to eye Morna's less-than-average ensemble. "Who's the old guy?" Silla added, looking over the little guy standing between the swinging doors.

"I've been worried about you, too! Where the hell have you been?"

"Long story. So, what's with the spandex and grandpa over there?"

"Silla, the last time we saw each other, you wouldn't come near me. You were afraid of me. I felt it pouring off you. You blew out of HQ with your tail feathers on fire. I haven't seen you since, and all you can think to talk about right now are my clothes and the new guy?"

"Clothes? That stretches things a bit. You look like the cover of a Spandau Ballet Album, and yeah, I'd really love to meet the person who talked you into that get-up. Bitch has gotta be something special. Hell's bells, woman! It took me five years to get you to try on a pair of beige Uggs."

"Whatever, fine, I give. You can blame the fashion choice on Karma," Morna said, turning in a little circle so Silla could get a nice, long look.

"Karma? Like you had this coming? Granted, your fashion choices have been less than stellar over the years, but I don't think you deserved this," Silla said while watching Morna clumsily pirouette for her in the soapy sludge.

Morna ignored the jab and came to a halt in fourth position while motioning toward the swinging doors with her outstretched arms.

"Grandpa over there's name is Albert," she said before dropping the campy introduction.

She really had missed Silla, and it had been way too easy to fall back into jacking around with her, but shit was serious, and she needed answers, now.

"Silla, where have you been? And how in the name of... ugh," exasperated Morna didn't know whose name to take in vain "... *whoever the fuck's in charge*, did you get here?"

"Like Albert Einstein? Are you The Albert Einstein?" Silla asked Albert, completely ignoring Morna's question. "Where is *here*, anyway?"

"Guilty," confirmed Albert, taking a slight bow. "This is Showbiz Pizza. A once very popular entertainment center and eatery for American families that had its heyday on Earth between the years 1980 and 1992 A.D."

"Yeah, Albert. I read the sign outside. I mean, where is *here*...?" Silla asked, raising her hands to the sky as she twirled for emphasis. "What do you mean had its heyday on *Earth*? Oh! I knew it!" Silla said as she connected the dots from her flight. "We're on another planet, aren't we? It's Kepler, isn't it?"

"What's Kepler?" Morna asked.

"It's an Earth-like planet," Albert answered Morna before

turning toward Silla. "Which begs the question, how would your friend here even know to ask such a question, yeah?"

"Ugh! Kiki bitches!" Karma said double snapping. "I'm calling a Kiki! Come on, children, everyone gather 'round."

She sashayed through the swinging doors, freshly dusted, elegantly rubbing the fingers of her left hand back and forth under her nose while sniffing up any excess ergosphere, savoring every gram like a fairy dust Sommelier.

"Who's that?" Silla asked.

"I'm Karma. You're Silla. Those two outliers are Loki and Hildi." Karma introduced the two eavesdroppers still lurking in the kitchen as the doors swung back open behind her. "Now, everyone grab a slice, a drink, and gather 'round. Karma's calling a Kiki."

"What the what?" Silla asked.

Karma took a deep, deep breath and said, "If everyone would be so kind as to grab some grub and put your butts in a chair, I will fill you all in on what we've missed up to this point. In other words, children, we're gonna have a Kiki, que pasa?"

"I could eat," said Silla.

"I'll grab some beers," said Morna.

"I'll grab some pizza pies from the back, yeah?" said Albert.

Everyone got busy rearranging chairs and tables, gathering up utensils, grub, and beer. In the minutes before the Kiki, the ritual of getting ready for a big family dinner did not fall short on Morna as she looked around at everyone gathering this and that for their meal together. She really hadn't known any of these beings for long, except Silla, of course. But, after her little fucked up Himalayan salt lamp trick a few minutes earlier, she really did *know* them, maybe better than any of them would like. Hence, the earlier outburst of anger and her time on the bench. Regardless, it was too late now to change the fact she had a read on everyone's intentions. Well, their feelings about their intentions, anyway, and all of those intentions were good. There was one in particular who was a confusing read, but she couldn't really blame her for that. Karma wasn't even supposed to exist on this plane. She'd been shoving the Here and Now up her nose so often to stay sane, Morna was actually worried about the fate, and couldn't fault her for putting off a less-than-steady vibe.

In the end, they'd pushed two square tables together to make a long rectangular one covered in a red and white checkered table-cloth. Pizza and pitchers of Falstaff lined the tables from one end to the other. On one side were Creak, Morna, and Silla, while on the other Loki, Hildi, and Albert. At the head was Karma, holding a particularly charming silver spoon with a bent handle in one hand and an empty beer mug in the other.

"Freaks and geeks, ladies and gentlemen, boys, and girls, you, me, shes, hes, theys, and thems! However, you choose to identify! I've called you all here today for a reading, and children, the library is open!" Karma opened her speech like she was working a drag show and she was head Queen.

FIFTY-THREE

BE KIND, REWIND

"Well, this is new," Cradle said as he looked around.

He was supposed to face the mirrors, not be swallowed whole by them. *Everyone eventually lives in a cage of their own making, but this was next-level shit*, Cradle thought as he shielded his eyes from the blinding reflections before an oil-slick luminescence slid over the mirrors, coating them and the memories they held with the blackish, mother-of-pearl shadow. Was this the sun going down on his memories? No, it couldn't be. It was too fast. He hadn't even faced them yet. It was getting darker and darker by the minute until every mirror holding his memories looked less like mirrors and more like well-polished hematite. In seconds, the brilliant hall of mirrors had gone stone-age dark.

"In the beginning, there was one dimension, and in it all things were possible," Cradle heard Creak's voice echo.

The voice wasn't live; it sounded empty and tinny, like a playback bouncing off the mirrors as they encircled him in a cylindrical carousel. Cradle stood stationary inside the spinning, mercurial carousel as pictures began to take shape within the moving walls. It was like he was inside a zoetrope. An old-fashioned toy used for seeing still, photographic sequences that looked like they moved as the cylinder spun.

The mercurial memories on the zoetrope, rewind backward in time, too fast to face, too fast to enjoy or to savor, until the images spinning were no more than an infinite swirl of smudged silver and black, creating one luminescent, oil-slick cylindrical prison. Like the canals of his one-of-a-kind halo that passed around, up, down, and through his essence. Every primordial explosion of stars gifting mass to the elemental particles swirling Willie Nillie about space.

It was so long ago; Cradle had a hard time recalling the specifics. What he did remember was when he woke up after being knocked out cold by the Big Bang, he was different. No longer a simple being who merely existed within one stable dimension. Cradle had, in an instant, become a Big Bang by-product, who, as luck would have it, possessed the unheard ability to manufacture the basic building blocks of a budding multi-dimensional omniverse.

He'd always suspected the alteration had something to do with the fact he'd been looking through a pictorial glass at the time of the explosion. The modern-day equivalent of the Hubble telescope. After an immense amount of pondering and several "What the fucks?" Cradle deduced the cosmic debris conceived from the blast must have been amplified as it traveled through the glass lenses of his telescope before exiting straight into him, elevating him to a sort of proliferous missing link status. It was the only theory he'd ever come up with that could remotely explain the unprecedented halo upgrade.

Previous to the Big Bang, his halo had been the standard-issue scribe halo, circular and golden, basically only good for powering eternal existence and illuminating texts when reading or writing late at night. But ever since The One caused the Big Bang by throwing the Asshat out of the One Dimension, Cradle's halo remained a pulsing, twisting, geometrical shape that passed in, out, around, and through him while primordial stars played chicken inside its oil slick canals.

It had taken Cradle approximately 380,000 years to figure out the collisions inside his Halo were actually not doing anything of note, but eventually, he guesstimated they were responsible for the opaque soup of protons, neutrons, and electrons which had been quietly seeping from the tip of his wings since the day of the big show. He probably would have noticed the plasma-like fog he emitted much earlier if he hadn't had to eke out his existence in the dark for the previous four hundred millennia. After the Bang, the lights went out on everything everywhere, and they didn't come back on for a very, very long time.

It was right before he got the missive from The One and The Asshat to pack his bags and head to Purgatory, he'd decided to tuck his upgraded halo away, good thing too. The powers-that-be were already pissed at him for what he saw. If they'd suspected he'd somehow leveled up or had mutated in any way because of the explosion… well, he concluded it was best never to find out. So, he turned off the luminance refractory portion of his halo, a trick all angels can do whenever they want; it's hard to sleep with those things glowing at all hours of the night. However, it's important to note, the trick only turned off the light; it never cut the power held within.

It wasn't long after he turned off his light that his feathers began to tingle in a way that felt unholy, capable of flight; a thing no scribe angel had ever known. Nerds had no use for superior flight abilities, and The One was a firm believer in the waste-not-want-not theory of energy consumption. But now, Cradle was pretty sure his wings received a very unprecedented enhancement from Scribe to Flyer. It didn't fall short on him; the modification must have been gifted by the very beings who didn't trust him further than they could throw him. But, with his bell still ringing from the blast, the missive to relocate to a very specific set of coordinates landed in his mind, compelling him to ignore all the weird happenings, except one very compulsory order: "Get to the following coordinates and stay there until further notice".

Just before the Big Yeet.

So, Cradle packed his bags and sent the coordinates to his upgraded wings, a process not much different than asking his brain to ask his hand to scratch an itch. A subliminal and oddly familiar order that resulted in a very unfamiliar take-off.

Cradle's body blasted through what would later be defined as space. Unbelievably hot and impossibly dark, Cradle's upgraded wings flew him at an unprecedented rate. Hell, he didn't even possess the measurements necessary to calculate how fast he'd arrived at the coordinates that would become his forever home.

It was there at coordinate 9.333. Cradle sat alone in the dark, pondering and studying what he knew while his Halo quietly pumped protons, neutrons, and electrons into the distant expanse. No one, not The One, not The Asshat, not even himself, was aware he had become a primordial particle accelerator, personally responsible for the slowly expanding omniverse, unwittingly gifting mass to each dimension, one tiny atom at a time.

When someone turned up the dimmer switch in the dark, about 380,000 years later, Cradle noticed the foggy soup emitting from his wings, and was given an immense amount of time with nothing better to do; eventually, he was able to theorize why. Cradle stopped looking at the spinning mirrors and turned his head toward his empty shoulders, "There will never be more," he said, sad his wings were gone, not for himself or for the lack of flight, but for the infinite mass of possibilities they had once produced and never would again.

Cradle felt hollow, for all he'd given, he'd never felt used up, but now that he had nothing to give, he felt nothing, which is exactly what there would be if he didn't get to Torquemada soon.

Interrupted, Cradle's Chuck Taylors became encircled by a floating strand of fog spiraling off the smudgy mirrors like the pulled thread of a sweater, leaving clean, shiny, and most importantly, empty reflections, where it had come away. It started at the top of the mirrors like a spool of thread that spun down in minuscule increments, the foggy thread traveling up Cradle's body, drawn to the scars on his back, like flies to a corpse.

Cradle's halo hit full shine as a horrible sound ground out. Gnashing metal and grinding teeth, the sound growled low as the ever-moving stars pulled up short, banging in protest of the halo's inner walls, creating a demonic sound that rang out across the zoetrope like a demon calling kin to vespers. Hollow and tubular, the haunting sound tolled long after the faltering stars stood still.

Cradle stood still as a statue in the quiet darkness, waiting.

Then, for the first time ever, the stars in his halo reversed course, creating an unholy backdraft that spooled off the mirrored prison into a ribbony fog, spooling like thread off the reeling mirrors straight into the scarred slits in Cradle's back.

"Oh, bloody Hell."

FIFTY-FOUR

HOLD THE FEATHERS

"Who says you can't go home again?" The Asshat asked as he twirled the Brisingamen Torc around the tip of his index talon. "Thanks, Torque. I honestly can't thank you enough. Being locked up in 9.666 really did limit my reach. Without you, I never could have gotten my hands on this little trinket.

I was like you once, too, you know? Always wanting more. More. More. More. Seems a reasonable enough request when everyone else seems to have what they deserve, and you're left wanting. Honestly, if your operation wasn't located on dimensionally neutral ground, I never would have been able to see the ins and outs of everything you were doing, wanting, coveting, and how you went about it. If you would have made your base of operations almost anywhere else in the omniverse, well… you still would have failed, of course. More importantly, I wouldn't have been able to see how childish you behaved.

Watching you run around Purgatory like a toddler hell-bent on revenge for having been sent to your room, ugh, it was such a slap in the face! A wake-up call, if you will. For years, I too ran around rattling doors and stomping on floors, swearing *my parent* would rue the day they woefully sent me there. But, watching you cry, bitch, and moan while coming up with halfhearted, half-assed plans for revenge held a mirror to my face. Do you know what I realized, Torque?" the Asshat asked as he looked upon the ex-Grand Inquisitor of the Spanish Inquisition roasting in the nearby flames.

"I realized, I'm not a child anymore! I have you to thank for that! I will concede, that 'my parent', " the Asshat stopped to air quote, "may have known what was best for me at the time, but that is no longer the case. I'm a full-grown demon now. I don't have to stay in my room if I don't want to. You know what else I realized, Torque?" the Asshat got up from the nearby breakfast nook, taking a break from his morning ritual of black coffee, a stiff Bloody Mary, and sudoku to give the roasting spit a couple of good handle cranks. "Sorry, buddy, you were looking a little well done on one side."

When the friar came back around, the Inquisitor had daggers in his eyes.

"Don't look at me that way, Tomas de Torquemada. You had this coming and then some. Your self-righteous ass played around with shit you couldn't possibly begin to understand. If I hadn't stepped in when I did, we'd all be up shit's creek without a paddle. Now, where is my basting brush?" the Demon asked, looking about for his favorite utensil. "Ah, just there." He pulled it from a nearby container of smoking tar. "Now, stop your fussing and accept your punishment like a good boy," he ordered and basted the Inquisitor head to toe in the sticky pitch. "You almost cost everyone everything, and when I say everyone, I mostly mean me. Ya fucked up Friar, and now you're gonna burn for a good long while because of it."

"Now, where was I? Oh, yes! You know what else I realized? With some good, old-fashioned hard work and ingenuity, I could build my own house, be the King of my own castle. Well, enough of that talk." The Asshat dusted off his ashy hands and headed back to the breakfast nook for a nice, long, salty sip from his Bloody Mary. "Mmm mmm mmm. Aged to perfection!" He savored the 1558 vintage aloud before turning back to the raging forge.

"Hephaestus?" the Demon called, dabbing, with the utmost decorum, the littlest trickle of blood dripping from his fangs, patting the garish and overly sensitive incisors with the delicate sleeve of Mary Tudor's impeccably preserved diamond and pearl encrusted wedding gown.

"Sire?" Hephaestus turned from stoking the forge, empty hell-fire green still burned in his hollowed-out eyes.

"Separate these into individual stones and set them into rings, would you?" the Demon continued. He tossed the Brisingamen Torc over to the stolid blacksmith. "Have your wifey there whip you up some gold to work with, and for the love of everything unholy, take off that fucking friar's robe. Shit's depressing. Jesus, Torque', good thing I stepped in when I did, you were like one step from having monks wail Enigma songs while beating themselves in the head with fucking charcuterie boards."

Hephaestus turned impassive and indifferent toward the forge, equally ignoring the Inquisitor slow-roasting like a rotisserie chicken as well as the little bits of gold illuminated magic, swirling in and about the flames like a firefly on Adderall.

The devoid giant noticed none of it as he bent, picked up a few handfuls of long cast-off children's lead-based jewelry and toys, and threw them into the melting pot, ordering, "Make gold, wife."

The little snippets of magic swirled in and out of the pot filled with lead-based children's motley as the fire grew hotter, causing the objects to melt in a golden alchemy, courtesy of what little remained of The Freyja of Sessrumnir's quickly dwindling magic.

Burned to nothing but her very essence, Freyja was now forever tethered to Heff's forge. When she'd realized she was free to leave after the necklace had finally come off, she'd also realized that no more than she left the demon's dominion, Odin would be on her like a shylock on a welsher, demanding his due for the broken bargain she'd struck so long ago.

"I'd rather burn in Hell for a millennia," Freyja's desperate thoughts had rung aloud from the forge's flames when she'd realized her fate.

"Done," said the lurking demon on the sly, accepting Freyja's personal and informal vow as a very formal and binding Oath of Allegiance. "Asylum granted."

"Oh. You. Mother. Fucking. Asshat," echoed and sparked in angry, gold-foiled expletives from the churning flames as the deal sealed with a nauseating puff of sulfur and grinding gears, tethering Freyja and her magic to the demon forge while severing them on the down low to anyone else, including Odin.

Though Freyja wasn't aware of that little extra, it was a quick look from Bloody Mary straight into the forge that caught Freyja's attention. It was the look women often shared to help each other stay one step ahead of the grave. In just under three seconds, Mary Tudor backed the truck up and dumped volumes of information to Freyja telepathically. Which Freyja returned with an oh-so-subtle gesture of sparking red flames as a thank you and a vow to return the favor when she could. Deservedly so, because Mary had just let her know she was no longer tied to Odin, meaning all she had to do was get out of her contract with the Asshat, and she would be free for the first time in a very, very long time.

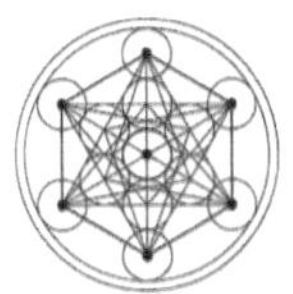

FIFTY-FIVE

NEARER MY GOD TO THEE

"Hop on! We've gotta get over to the corral and call The Calvary," The Red ordered after she'd convinced Justice the Omniverse was on a crash course with heat death, and it was somewhat his fault.

"What about that?" Justice said in disgust, pointing toward the less-than-hygienic bag of bones dry humpin' Lena's leg.

"She's riding front, hop in back," Lena said, scooting herself and Pythia forward to make room.

"Oh, I think I'd rather burn with the Omniverse than get anywhere near…that."

"Justice," The Red threatened, her eyes sparking.

"You can 'Justice' me all you want, Red. I finally got a clean bill of health from the free clinic last week. Say what you will, but I'm not getting anywhere near the typhoid Mary of STDs." Justice looked at Pythia who slid into third base with the Red's saddle horn. "Frankly, I'd rather burn down with the omniverse than contract syphilis again."

"Fine. Make a travois; she can ride behind…but be quick about it!"

"A what?"

"A travois. A sled! Book of Mormon!" The Red swore as she hopped off the horse, whipped up a quick sled, and ten minutes later, they were off to the races.

The Oracle of Delphi bounced roughly behind as Justice Gray and the Red Horseman rode hell-bent for leather through the overgrown Babylonian Gardens.

"Why go by the corral first, Lena?" Justice asked in the Red's jeweled ear. "Just what do you expect the Horseman to do about this? Saving the day is not really your schtick if you don't mind me saying."

"The Four have to be together when we're officially put back in the stocks. Our magic, science, whatever you want to call it, doesn't work unless we are unified in the field. If we are going to do this, we have to form a string quartet."

"You gonna play 'Nearer my God to Thee' while the omniverse burns, Red? I'm not sure what information gets through to the corral, but in case you missed it, that little trick's been tried before, and guess what? The Titanic still sank, and it took the band with it."

"Book of Solomon! The Four Forces must form a quartet before they can be put back in the field! Let's just put a pin in that and let it sink in a while," Pythia said as she slipped into a reverse cowboy.

"Four Forces? You are the *Four Horsemen*, Lena. You feeling O.K., Red? Have you been out of the corral too long? Need a carrot and a good brushing or something?" Justice questioned as he spat out the long, ruby-red earring that kept smacking him in the teeth every time he opened his mouth. "And when the fuck did that thing get back up here?" Justice asked, realizing the doped-up mouthpiece was looking right at him over the Red's left shoulder.

Ignoring Justice's protests over Pythia's triumphant return to the Red's saddle horn, frustrations and fears showed in Pythia's tone, "I am quite aware of what We are and what We are not. I have neither the time nor the inclination to educate you on quantum theory and its role in omniversal mythology, you fucking child."

"Whatever's clever, Red. But can you get that thing to turn back around? It's easier to hold a conversation with you when I don't have to watch it hot seat your pommel."

Lena gave Pythia a couple of light taps on the shoulder, held her index finger in the air, and motioned for her to turn around, causing The Oracle of Delphi to growl low in her throat as she eyeballed Justice before reluctantly turning around to face front.

"I pray Cathy is there. If we can't find Albert, all of this may be for naught." The Red said aloud to herself through Pythia.

"Why would we need Albert Einstein? Do we need an atomic bomb or something?"

"Yeah, I figured we could nuke our way out of this."

"Really?"

"No! Not really! You useless sideshow! We need him because M theory is above my pay grade."

FIFTY-SIX

WHAT CAN I SAY, I HATE BATHS

"Well, that escalated quickly," Loki said.

"Yeah, that really got out of hand fast," Hildi fired back.

Quoting their favorite lines from Wednesday movie nights had always been a favorite pastime, especially when they were knee-deep in shit. Which, as of late, had been so often they considered adding an additional floater night to the Netflix and chill calendar.

"It jumped up a notch," Me'tok added.

"It did, didn't it?" Loki fired back, not missing a beat at the impromptu return of the boxer shaman and movie night cohort.

People always mistook the threesome as a thruple, which didn't bother Loki in the slightest. It also couldn't be further from the truth. Hildi was in love with the local butcher, which was a long story in itself. As for himself, he'd only ever felt something for someone once, and Odin sure as shit fucked that all up the second he caught word of it. Then there was Me'tok, whose heart died the day his dad convinced the Mayans to paint his human love blue, slit her throat, and toss her carcass down a well so it would rain. All because his dad couldn't abide his son being the lowly love of a human tradesman's daughter, even if the trade was gold.

Trade was trade; her father was not only honored but delighted he would never have to pay out for the wedding his wife had been going on about since the day she was born. A girl, nothing but trouble and money. Now his family would rise even higher, having selflessly given the ultimate sacrifice of their only daughter. Now he would be the number one goldmonger in the city.

After the party, Me'tok's father chose to throw for the sole purpose of forcing him to stay, watch the whole thing, and keep his ass glued to the prince's throne as a reminder of where he belonged. Up until the last of his guests had their fill of Dionysus's offering. As all of them were strewn about the floor in states of half-dress to no dress at all, Me'tok took his final steps off the dais as his father drunkenly garbled what a lowly son he had.

"A dog", his father had said. "A dog would be a better gift bestowed on a father-to-be than the fucking disaster making his way out of the throne room."

Loki often wondered if Me'tok's father, and the father of the love of his life, had enjoyed their two days on top of the world before Me'tok went rabid on the whole damn city, including his father. Rumor has it, Me'tok's father is somewhere very cold, very wet, and the cherry on top…. he was indeed painted blue.

"I'd just about given up on you, dear," Hildi said.

"What can I say? I hate baths," Me'tok said, flashing back from the ritual cleansing done on oh so many of his people for no fucking reason.

The only rain to fall on his people's lands after a ritual cleansing and sacrifice was his tears. A misunderstanding that had circled out of control until his wrath for the continuous and very unnecessary loss of lives brought the entire civilization of the Mayans to a rather sudden and horrifying halt, something he still felt bad about.

Once the PTSD from the pizza parlor shower had worn off, it occurred to him, *maybe he could do some good here.* It was too late for his people's civilization, but it wasn't too late for their descendants, who were still very much alive and well in every corner of the world. A world that was about to end if someone didn't do something about it.

"Fair enough," Hildi said, flashing back to bath night with Freyja and Heff's five little hellions before quickly shaking off a little PTSD herself.

"So, what's the four-one-one?" Me'tok asked as the threesome made their way across the desert portion of the Borderlands, somewhere halfway between Showbiz and the not-so-mezzanine library.

"Ya missed a lot, but in a nutshell, your dad is really, really good at math," Loki said, pulling a calendar conversion chart out of thin air, pointing his finger at the scroll, and moving it down one row at a time until he got to the day's date. "If this guesstimate is correct," Loki pointed directly at one of three thousand possible dates, "Today is the Big Show."

"I'll take those odds," Me'tok fired, knowing exactly what Loki was referring to.

That fucking calendar. If there ever was a time to show that old bastard time was up on the old regime, it was right about fucking now.

Loki and Hildi didn't miss a beat.

"Couldn't agree more," they said in unison.

The Wednesday night movie-watching trio fell in step like the scarecrow, the lion, and the Tin Man, seconds away from breaking into "We're Off to see the Wizard" as they crested a sand dune that had them looking over the largest oasis anyone had ever seen.

"Am I hallucinating, dears?"

"If you are, I am too."

"Ditto," said Me'tok as they stared slack-jawed at the jungle before them.

"Is... is that... is that Justice Gray?" Hildi asked, side-eyeing the horse and riders who barreled out of the luscious, green oasis.

"Yep," said Loki.

"Yesthir," confirmed Me'tok.

Believing beer and pizza were indeed a bad idea before trekking across the desert of the Borderlands, Hildi reached beneath her enormous blue blockers and rubbed at her dry, tired, dehydrated eyes before adding, "... And The Oracle of Delphi?"

"Yep," said Loki.

"Yesthir," confirmed Me'tok.

"And... and um... is that... are they," Hildi stopped to clear her overly dry throat, "are they ride-sharing with the Red Horseman of the apocalypse?"

"Yep," said Loki

"Yesthir," confirmed Me'tok.

"We're gonna need a bigger boat," the moviephiles said in unison as the Black Ryder and the Green, in that order, barreled out of two holes that opened in the sand, falling in line behind the Red.

FIFTY-SEVEN

PIZZA AND WINGS

"Really wings?"

Morna scolded her accouterments with a peppering of curse words that would make a sailor proud as she flew past Silla inverted and tilted off center.

"And I thought I was bad at learning to fly!" Silla snortled and coughed a bit on the puff of smoke escaping her mouth in an unexpected laugh. "Note to self, giggle sounds make cute little puffy, puff balls of smoke. I'll just go ahead and add that to the weird list of shit that happened today, up to and not including both of our deaths. It's weird, don't you think, Morn?" Silla asked when Morna zoomed back up after a seventy-foot free fall.

"What's weird?" she asked, flying past Silla like someone had picked her up by the ankles.

The humiliating position had her feeling like the newborn Nephilim she was. All she needed was someone to slap her bare ass, and all would be right in this jacked-up world.

"That we died on the same day. Well, not so much we died on the same day as we died separately on the same day...I just always thought we'd Thelma and Louise it together, you know?"

Silla hollered at her, but Morna barely made out what she was saying over the rustling of her wings that had just caught the wind all wrong, like a sailing ship whose winds caught before the ropes snapped clean through.

"Bad fucking luck!" Silla said as she watched Morna fly back in the direction of Showbiz.

Silla hadn't told Morna she was running out of steam. It was hard enough on Morna to worry about learning to fly without killing herself for the second time today. Morna was pretty sure they had indefinite health for reboots at this point, but honestly, who the fuck knew anything about anything in this place?

"Waste not, want not." It was something her grandmother had always said, and Silla never gave it much thought until now. *Smart old bird*, Silla thought to herself as she laughed a bit at her choice of words. "Bird... bet that old bat knew the whole time," she said aloud as she placed one foot on the ground after the other in a landing so graceful it felt like she'd done it a thousand times, not two.

She realized how hungry she was getting as she quickly inspected her perfectly unbroken toes and untwisted ankles. And just like that, she went from light thoughts about broken toes to famine. She'd never been so hungry in her life. It had to be the flying or the burning, or both, but either way, she needed fuel, and she needed it now. Not knowing what else to do, she headed in the direction of Showbiz and Morna. Two birds, one stone.

"Ha." She was hungry, not dead.

She laughed about it and laughed again, beginning an even-paced run toward the pizza parlor of days gone by. She'd better remember to take some fuel with them before her and Morna headed back toward the Cliffs of Perdition, a place they were supposed to get to ASAP and act as a lookout, seeing how they could fly. Well, mostly anyway.

FIFTY-EIGHT

OH, HELL

"You rang?" The Asshat's words echoed off the spinning mirrors, no more than the words left his mouth.

An unlikely savior, but whatever.

"You're the last person I expected to come to my rescue, but it's been a weird day," Cradle said, looking up at the Asshat who had been his best friend so long ago he wasn't even sure if the era ever actually happened.

The walls of the zoetrope still spun, and the trippy fog still tried to do its rewind trick straight into the scars on his back. But since his wings had been seared shut by a horseman, the fog wasn't getting into the slits on his shoulder as easily as someone had planned. Though the floor wasn't spinning, the dark, swirling matter caught the low-level breeze put out by the spinning mirrors, leaving Cradle dead center and unmoving as he reached for the unlikeliest of helping hands. Honestly, he'd rather burn in Hell. Since the Asshat would be there too, it didn't make much sense to let time rewind to the beginning so he could spend what was left of it with this fucker.

"What?" the Asshat said, one eyebrow raised in genuine curiosity.

"What? You know what! Stop fucking around and help me get out of here."

"Now, why in 9.666 would I want to do that? I've got you right where I want you." That Asshat laughed a perfect, villainous laugh. "I thought you were a scribe angel. Were you the worst of them? Is that it? Did you get kicked out for being too dumb?"

"Stop fucking around, Peter. You know good and damn well why I was sent here, and we don't have time to go down memory lane. Your little plan isn't working. I don't have an actual ethereal body right now. I'm nothing more than a hologram, one that doesn't contain anything, let alone the tachyons you counted on helping you rewind time to the beginning so you could rewrite the stars, specifically your own."

"Fucking scribe angels, think they know everything. You lot are just alike," The Asshat said before coughing on a bit of the fog escaping through the hatch.

With a flick of his wrist, three bolts of blue shot into the zoetrope, restoring Cradle's body exactly the way the Asshat remembered him. Which was pretty badass for a scribe angel. Looking down at his much more muscular body, the wing upgrade was chef's kiss. Cradle wondered if Peter had a bit of a crush on him?

Wings. The thought hit him a second time, and that was all it took.

"FUCK!" the Asshat cried, forgetting to leave him without wings so the fog had slits to feed into. "I guess if you want something done right, you've got to do it yourself."

Peter pulled a blade from nowhere and jumped into the zoetrope. The floor swirled about his boots as it brimmed with sorted pieces of the omniverse like a primordial soup getting bitchy at having nowhere to be. It sizzled and sparked, looking doubly menacing as reflections popped milliseconds later off the spinning, murky mirrors.

"Where are you, nerd? I will cut those wings off you myself, and I'll take it slow. These things need never be rushed, and I've got all the time in the world… for now."

"Cool. Let me know when you're finished and I'll call the Riders to escort you back home," Cradle said, cool and collected, before he slammed the escape hatch closed with his boot.

There was a time for Chuck Taylors, and there's a time for Docs, Cradle thought after a quick change of couture; light goth meets The Matrix.

With a whirl, he leaped from the zoetrope, the split and shredded tails of his sleeveless trench fluttered in perfect protection over each feather of his newly dawned wings, and damned if he wasn't going to take better care of them.

"It's too late. You can't stop it. It's already started, and I have the god particles. Without those, you have nothing, quite literally," The asshat chuckled from his prison.

Cradle looked down at the seven rings in his hands, plucked from the Asshat's pockets, while Cradle flew up and Peter jumped down.

"You have nothing, Peter, not even a way to get home," Cradle answered.

He put the key away, the one that had lived on a long leather cord around Peter's neck for a time in memorium. A key now nestled into a pocket on the underside of a wing and was immediately sealed by chainmail-like feathers that had sewn their way over and under each other. The chainmail spun about like an orrery and came to an unwanted stop, protesting with a few growls and grinds. As if the magic itself had just begun to have fun.

"Those don't belong to you. You have no idea the powers you're messing with!"

"For real, Bro? You gave 'The Key' to Tomas De Torquemada so he could zip all over here, there, and everywhere with an omniversal pass, burning through energy to alert Dad something was off, all while collecting an auto de fey army by backing up souls in purgatory. Thinking what? If you raised enough Hell, you could get time to stop long enough to really grab Dad's attention? Get him to come see what you were doing, personally? You banked on it! You knew he'd just blame the bad kid for yet another prank and come well under-protected. Completely unaware when he jumped over to your neck of the woods, The One himself would be run into the ground by your little auto de fay army. You were going to proceed to do what with the most powerful being in existence? Throw him in a Horseman's oubliette while you played heat death with the omniversal clock? All kicked off course by you and Justice's little army burning into 9.666 all at one time with not one single tachyon among the myriad of hijacked souls? And all this before releasing the Four? I'm sure convincing them was no big deal."

They'd been chomping at the bit to really stretch their legs and put an end to their suffering, regardless of the bargain they struck. That's why he'd seen them running around outside of the corral, letting them get a taste of freedom here and there while silently speeding up the heat death. Like a frog boiling in a pot. The temperature got a little hotter with every move, enough to get the ball rolling, to get the clocks to stop. Hence, the fucking bells ringing in the midnight hour, until… that's weird.

Cradle didn't remember when they stopped ringing. Probably when he lost his body in Chernobyl trying to save Silla. And on that thought, he took a sudden inhale that reminded his new lungs of his new heart.

"But did you tell the Horseman it really wasn't the end? Did you tell them about the new beginning? The one with you in charge. The one where my wayward silver nephew thinks he's in charge of Purgatory and it's gonna be a real banger? When the Horseman started throwing souls this way and that without a tachyon among them to balance the omniversal energy trade, was it then you planned on, simultaneously but ever so quietly, rewinding the omniverse? By hooking up my old telescope to flash its memories through mirrors, and a zoetrope that would trip me bad enough, I'd be caught in them as the blueprints made their way back into the factory through my wing slits, for a very expedient rewind? You thought you could take this back to the Big Bang, but in this version, you throw The One out instead of the other way around. And you fucked the whole thing up by giving me back my wings right before kickoff?"

Cradle howled a laugh that echoed off the endless mirrors in the sand.

The howling shriek of the demon locked away inside the zoetrope shattered every last standing mirror in the sands, turning the Fun House into a mercurial lake of sand and razor-sharp glass. Cradle immediately decided he quite liked it. It reminded him of Cathy.

"Oewh!"

There it was, that breath, reminding him of his lungs, reminding him of his new heart. Guess it remembered everything just fine.

"You think a child's toy can hold me! I am the ruler of 9.666!"

"And I'm the ruler here," Cradle said, cool as a mountain breeze.

Cradle snapped his fingers in a manner that had the zoetrope flipping and folding in on itself until it found the perfect shape to keep the Asshat in for as long as Cradle needed. As if watching history play out before his very eyes, one shiny new Metatron cube made by the myth itself, shone in the sun before it patina'ed under the onslaught of razor-edged, teeny, tiny mirrored sand storms kicked up by the Metatron's wings. Already covered three-quarters in a sand dune, the cube was left behind like a tired artifact, no longer of consequence to anyone.

FIFTY-NINE

UNTWISTY TWIST

You could almost hear Freyja giggle from the fire as Nitzie untwisted the curse before it broke. Although she would no longer be tied to Odin, and the giant turd deserved nothing from her, she'd reached out to Nitzie and let her know she might be late and everything was fine.

"You're lying, Mother," came out entirely too regal, even for a four-year-old.

Sweetie, Mommy needs to send out an untwist within an untwisting. Do you think you could do that for Mommy? Freyja thought through her and Nitze's private telekinesis line.

"Well, that depends, mother. Are you really OK?"

Nothing more was said, letting the silence fill the airspace between them like an age-old sheriff who had seen and heard it all and had absolutely no place better to be.

"…" said Nitzie for thirty-three minutes.

No, godsdamnit, you little shit. Everything is not OK!

"There it is," said Nitzie. "Now was that so hard? So, what's the untwisty twist?"

Freyja could telepathically hear Nitzie's excitement at doing a "no-no spell" and at having broken her mother... again. This time, she wasn't even in the room. This kid was getting stronger by the second, like scary strong.

Yeah, yeah, peanut. Get it all out.

The squeals of the four-year-old made Freyja pull her head back and away as if she were talking to her wee one on a phone.

Are you done? Freyja asked the berserker who was definitely going to be the death of her, only to hear belly laughter.

Cool, a few more of those and two snorts, and she could finally talk to her daughter.

Ten minutes passed, and Nitzie had worked a fine deal with her mother, negotiating things that would only be on Hildi's time. More importantly, Freyja was freed from the forge, which was a freebie on Nitzie's part, but getting Odin's good looks back mattered not to the little one, and that's when negotiating got touch-and-go. See, Nitzie didn't care about Odin, but she did care about other things, like watching something called South Park because Primus was her favorite band.

"Mommy, are you sure you don't need help?" The tiniest hint of fear was finally heard in her little voice.

No, sweetie. Mommy and Daddy can handle it from here.

"OK, but I'll tell you the same thing I told the strange babysitter who fixed my sock. If you're not back by morning, Justice Grey is fu (click)."

Freyja disconnected from her daughter before the dirty word landed. If she didn't hear it, it didn't happen, at least not during the apocalypse. She'll watch a Ted Ed or something later to make up for her bullshit parenting skills.

For now, if there would ever be more than now, Odin would have his looks back for longer than a year. It's the least she could do to have Nitzie refill the bowl of apples Karma knicked, mostly for the others in Valhalla that needed them, but also to keep him off her and Loki's asses in the meantime.

"Are you sure you're OK? You were in that forge a long time," Heff said to his wife, who suddenly appeared beside him in a swirl of gold dust from the forge's hottest mound of ashes.

"I'm fine, chicken. Look, not even a tan," Freyja turned her perfect body for inspection. "Are you O.K.? I had to survive the beating, but you were the one who gave it."

"No, I'm not OK. If a man does that to the love of his life and says he's OK, put him down immediately. There's nothing there but evil."

"Aw, I love you too, ducky."

"Freyja!" Heff half yelled. "We just called our four-year-old to get you out of a deal with the devil!"

"I'm just trying to lighten the mood."

"Yeah, well, don't," Heff grumbled. "I really thought we'd lost control of the situation there. That was close."

"Yeah, me too," Freyja conceded.

"Well, where to now?"

"Look, I don't want to sound like the needy basic bitch in the middle of the apocalypse, but I smell pizza. Let's head that way," Freyja said, looking ravenous in a way Hephaestus hadn't seen in approximately six years.

"You smell pizza?"

"Did I fucking stutter?"

"Yep."

"That yep better be to smelling pizza and not the stuttering part," Freyja all but snarled.

"It was yep, you're pregnant," Heff said, then waited.

"Did I ask you if I was pregnant? NO! I asked if I stuttered, jackass! Oh, my goddess. I'm pregnant," Freyja whispered as she fell to her knees. "Nope!" she said, then stood back up.

"Are you OK?"

"Nope, but first pizza, then apocalypse, then nuthouse, in that order. We can strike number three if number two pans out."

"Pans out? So, we are rooting for the apocalypse now?"

"We? I have no idea what 'we' are doing, but I'm going to go get pizza, and if I can find Me'tok, I'm putting the quint's college fund down on four."

"As in the Horseman?"

"Yep, 'cause they've got nothing on what Hildi's going to do to me when she finds out about Nitzie's recent negotiations."

"Freyja," Heff said with a mountain of love in his eyes.

"Pizza, now!" was all Freyja yelled as she snapped her fingers, giving Heff his perfect body back. "You'd be too slow on crutches and I don't wanna carry you 'cause I'm mad."

"Come 'ere, Momma. Let Daddy handle it," Heff said as he swooped Freyja up in his once again tree trunk-sized arms.

The best part, having both arms to hold her with. He didn't care how big his arms were, but he preferred not having to use one of them to lean on a crutch when he could be doing much better things with it.

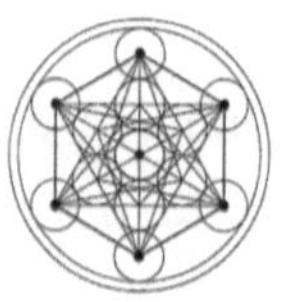

THE LITTLE CAREFREE CAR

Creak and Albert had been outside the demon's forge for a solid twenty minutes and had gotten nowhere. With time, a thing they didn't have to waste, Creak found himself closer and closer to the truth. He'd rather spend eternity on Joe Rogan's podcast than actually go through with dismantling his best friend. But he had to. All it was going to take was leaning into the network to offer it a gift. This time, the gift would be Hephaestus. The network was always willing to give when need was truly there, but it also asked in its kinship an offer which was no longer needed. A societal grab-bag of elements, protons, neutrons, and electrons. Because there was always a but, once a donation of a whole person, place, or thing was made, it could never be whole in the same way again. Not necessarily like the old story, *The Monkey's Paw*. That was about death, rot. What the network did was accept the offering and send it straight to the chop shop.

Think *Gone in Sixty Seconds*. Except it was more like a femtosecond, but po-tay-to, po-tah-to. Point being, someone could immediately reach back into the network, and if it truly saw a need and what was offered was in dire need of resurrecting, it would have no trouble doing so. But the frickin' buts in the network ruined everything, even if it was only a second later.

In a network of everything, serving all who know how to use it, shit gets picked over pretty quickly. That is to say, some things were going to be a little different with your person, place, or thing. Some people were fine with it; others, eh… it slowly drove them mad as a hatter. Since Creak wasn't asking for Hephaestus back, there was zero problem of Freyja going batshit that Heff was acting off again. Nope, now she'd just have to live with the fact he was straight up fucking gone, forever.

"I can't."

"You have no choice, my friend. If we let him go on, he will surely kill Freyja to get that necklace off. You know you cannot allow that to happen. Even if you did, what kind of monster would be left of Hephaestus if he ever broke free of the Asshat's, "as you like to call him," powers or hold he has over him? This could create a situation as bad, or worse than we are already in.

Whether Hephaestus knows it or not, he was put in charge of watching over those stones, the sins. It would be too much of a coincidence for the blacksmith of legend to be off on a pity party in the Seven Brothers' mountains while neutralizing the seven deadly sins of the human realm all by his lonesome. The coincidences that would have to take place are mind-boggling."

"Well, shit."

"Yeah. There's seven brothers somewhere who are about to be pretty pissed if the universe doesn't end. You can bet they aren't going to let Heff, his wife, and kids walk away from that."

"There'd be Hell to pay of some sort. This thing keeps getting bigger and bigger."

"Best get started where we are before another problem presents itself."

And there it was, a couple of hairs, rocks, whatever stood up under his collar. Sometimes Albert gave Creak second doubts. That thing that made him stop for a second before brushing it off. But, he didn't have time for it. Creak had to do the big, bad, and terrible. He had to notify the network Hephaestus would be an unwilling donation. Something Creak would stand trial for later. If they didn't find his once-in-a-lifetime reason for the forced donation acceptable, Creak's fate would be the same as Heff's. Which right at this moment seemed more than fair.

"Enough!" Creak growled low in his throat.

He snuck up to the dirty windows of the Ford Pinto manufacturing plant, where last time anyone checked, Heff rotated a screaming Freyja on a forge while trying to remove the Brisingamen Torc Odin himself locked there. Now, the fire was out, and not a soul was around. No tools, no leftover heat, nothing.

"Mumpff," came an unknown voice.

"Are you OK, Schatz? This is good, yah? If they are not here, maybe this could turn out another way, so you don't have to dismantle your best friend."

"Mumpff," came the voice again.

"That's not me!" Creak yelled back across the forge floor to Albert, who was on the other side of some industrialized shelves.

"It is I, mumpfff."

Creak was on it like a bird dog on a quail. It wasn't that hard to pin something so life-threateningly ill, but rich assholes and their hunting dogs did the same shit every day for sport.

"It is I—," but she was too weak to get it out.

Without another word, Creak tapped into the network for a bit of O-negative for a very frail and ironically named, Bloody Mary. It wasn't really O-negative. No bodies, no blood, but souls needed energy, and in purgatory, everybody's body had a plasma-like liquid running through it, sort of like blood, but not really.

Anyway, that's what Mary needed because some Asshat wanted to play.

"Lunchtime tour at the Voltaire."

When souls ran out of energy, poof, they're gone. Unless, of course, you're Metatron. More power, more benefits, even in the afterlife, especially in the afterlife, Creak thought to himself while he carefully monitored how much O-neg Bloody Mary was receiving.

"Where did you get this cat piss?" the Queen demanded as she pulled and slapped at the glowing square on her wrist to no avail.

"You can't rip out a Network I.V. There's nothing physically big enough to rip out, and even if it were, you can't grab it with greedy, grubby hands."

Creak finished as Bloody Mary looked at her wrist and turned her head at Mach speed to lock in on the matching, glowy tattoo on the sparkly dog thing, before reaching out to dig her nails deep into her own arm.

"Lady, have you've gone feral?" Creak yelled before biting down on her stubby arm, letting her know by the right amount of pressure she wouldn't have anything left to worry about anymore if she kept this attitude up.

"Better women than you have tried to take me down!" Bloody Mary snarled like a rabid, trapped beast.

"If you're referring to your sister, Elizabeth, the one responsible for the Golden Age, I would have to agree," Albert interjected. "But, she never really tried to have you killed, did she? The truth is up here for you to find it. My lady, it looks as though you have been the Asshat's plaything for some time. I must say, you and your gown have held up beautifully. I wish I knew this little parlor trick!" Albert chuckled as he rubbed at what was left of his wild, white hair.

"Well, Albert, the truth is up here if you want it," A much rosier Mary said, sounding less bitchy and more regal by the second. Straightening her skirts and her full head of hair, she stood and walked past Albert and Creak, calling each of them out in turn, "Mr. Einstein, congratulations on your Nobel Prize. King Vicus, your "kind" have such a kind, yet cool, nature. It's quite endearing and annoying," then paused before looking down a second in a not so formal bow, as she said, "I'm very sorry about—"

"My Queen," Creak said in a snarl, low to the ground. "I've got a lot of people, souls, whatever around here I prefer not know my name, let alone the title that just fell from your mouth like diamonds from the sky. I can assume you feel the same, and if you don't, your nickname is rather famous around here. Dare I say why Tomas de Torquemada gifted you to the Asshat as a neutral energy bag to suck on whenever his negative energies show on a radar or two, alerting folks of his unapproved holiday from 9.666."

"Silly, doggie. Surely you know The One would never allow me a spot in 9.999 alongside him. After all I did for him, after all I'd given," Bloody Mary pouted.

"Listen, lady. If you use that dog title on me one more time, I'll be slapping a town crier in front of you for the rest of your time in purgatory, letting folks know exactly who, and what, you are. A Queen who burns her people because God wanted her to. That's a hard sell, even around this joint, but let's give it a go."

"No, no, no, puppy."

Creak snarled. All finery, poise, and voice gone.

"Well, what the fuck should I call you then?"

This is "Bert," Creak said, nodding his head in Albert's direction, "and you can call me Ernie."

"These names are acceptable to me if you will call me Catherine de Medici."

"No, and nice try," shot from Bert and Ernie's mouths in a type of guffawed synchrony.

"We don't have time for this. Your cover is Elmo."

"Elmo?" Bloody Mary rolled it around her mouth, searching

for phonetic dignity. "Is this a quite famous name of marvel and renown?"

"In Elmo's World, it is," Creak said, as he turned to inspect a noise.

A rickety, rusting Pinto swung precariously from an assembly line high above his head.

"She has her own world? Marvelous. This will do nicely, Ernie. Thank you."

"No problem. Now, if you could just tell me where you think the Asshat was headed, we can get underway."

"I can tell you where he went, but I will not go with you. I have been forced to play this game. Asked, but not given a choice. Promised things I'd never asked for. I was quite happy to accept my fate. And in time, I'm sure I would be forgiven. Torquemada convinced me if I met the demon, or Asshat as you like to call him, there would be no need for punishment at all. When I protested, I was assured my time in 9.666 would be given the limelight and attention no soul could survive intact. What choice is no choice? I can find my way to the library from here. It's this way, is it not, Bert?" Lady Elmo said, with an eyebrow that said she knew a hell of a lot more than she was letting on.

"My home is your home, Lady Elmo. Please, see yourself ahead, and we will join you when and if we are able."

"So many beings associated when this was this and that was that, and who is right and who is wrong, all in the name of a being none of us knows and most certainly never will. It's almost laughable." Lady Elmo said, turning a corner off to the Borderlands, singing, "Lala lala lala lala, no man's land."

"She knew the whole time. Huh, weird. Like cereal killer weird," Earnie said, as he and Bert headed out the other side of Ford Motors.

The Pinto's claim to fame was for trapping and burning to death its human transports, twenty-seven to be exact. Upon which the Pinto's factory found its way to the Borderlands as the Ford Escort became the shiny new guy in town, everybody loved him.

Creak made a reminder to himself this was yet another thing associated with the number twenty-seven that gave him the heebee jeebees. But hell, maybe all Grinx fucking hated the number twenty-seven. There was only one of him, no way to know for sure.

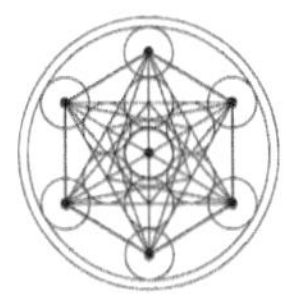

JUSTICE IS SERVED

It wasn't two seconds after the Asshat sent Odin back to Valhalla for attempting to take what was his, that he screamed Loki's name in lieu of Freyja's across the Omniverse. He didn't have to take it well, but facts were facts, deals were deals, and Odin knew it. A much younger version of him found himself screaming Loki's name with the need to take his pain out on someone. You could bet your ass it would be his right-hand trans.

Odin would never have control of Loki again, Karma thought from behind the curtain next to the bowl of apples she'd just helped herself to three more of.

Rules are rules for a reason, but some are meant to be broken. While the ergosphere she'd been shoving up her nose was necessary, at this point, it was only keeping her on the edge of the Ticks and Tocks. It wasn't keeping her tied to the places in time she needed to be.

So, while she'd waited for Odin to make it back home, Karma noticed a delicious-looking bowl of apples and got busy eating six or seven. It seemed Freyja's apples really sorted out the problem of staying put. So, she helped herself to what was left of the bowl, pouring every last one of them into one of the silken pockets in her jumpsuit that looked big enough to hold a handful of change. Pockets, portals, same difference.

Anyway, they seemed to help keep her in one place longer before popping off to goddess knew where. The most recent of those pops off landed her right here in this room, behind a curtain. Waste not, want not is what her three aunts always said when she was an ankle biter at their heels as they spun their threads. Listening to those three was about the wisest thing a being could do, which was the other thing she learned.

So, help herself she did, then waited for Odin. When he did return, man, was he seething to find the bowl of apples empty. Sure, he was young again, but if he didn't figure out what happened to those fucking apples, he'd be aging again in just under a year!

"Loki!" madder than a hatter, Odin screamed Loki's name to the ceilings of Val Hall, which really pissed Karma off.

Was this the way Odin treated her love all these years? Could he have been telling the truth about the night he popped out of her bed without so much as a kiss goodbye? At first, she got a bit jealous, then raging mad, before realizing this was something neither of them should have to exist with.

She whispered an idea that floated over like a silvery thread to land in Odin's ear, "Why would you want that useless liar, not when there was Justice to be served?"

And just like that, Karma freed her love; not that the shithead would ever know. She knew she was being unfair, but her heart ached in a way it never had before, and for that, she thought she might never forgive him.

Regardless of whether things ever worked out between her and Loki, she'd tied her jackass brother to Odin in Loki's stead. It had her laughing like a jackal as she poofed away, knowing Odin would hear it, but not recognize where the teasing laughter came from, which made her laugh harder. That and the thought she'd mixed up the old guard by moving chess pieces among pantheons, which was a big no-no, made her day in a big way.

It meant no one would look for Justice here, she thought, cackling louder still as she turned up the volume so it sounded as if the laughter came from behind Odin's perfect ear.

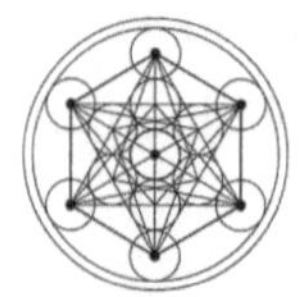

SIXTY-TWO

GIVE IT AWAY, GIVE IT AWAY, GIVE IT AWAY NOW

Going on what little information he had, Dorian popped over to the corral. Sure, as shit, two of the Four Horsemen were all who remained in the field. Well, at least it was the brothers. They'd been mahjong partners forever, and when they caught him showing interest in the game, the brothers broke a little rule about never conversing with anyone ever and taught Dorian. The three had been playing on Wednesdays ever since.

Being a Tuesday had him encountering, and barely surviving, two boobie traps before Steve and Bill realized it was just the kid.

"What the fuck did we tell you about coming over here on any other day of the week but Wednesdays?" Steve and Bill asked in unison.

"To not to," Dorian replied.

"Spill it," Steve and Bill said in unison, again.

It was creepy, but what was Dorian going to do, ask half of the bringers of the Apocalypse to stop talking in tandem because it gave him the skeeves?

"Oh, fuck," was all Steve and Bill said, in fucking unison,

before letting go of the ear-piercing whistle it seemed only folks born prior to 1950 knew how to do.

Like most things before 1950, something might be entertaining, but nine times out of ten, you could bet your ass it was going be useful too, Dorian thought as the black and green destriers barreled out of the stable, not slowing a beat as Steve and Bill ran before the horses broke from the stables.

The Four ran side by side in an awesome and terrifying sight before the Horseman. Each grabbed a pommel and swooped themselves up, defying the laws of physics in a way that looked perfectly natural.

Somehow, Dorian's stomach knew better as it lurched up everything he'd eaten since 1986. He knew because the quarter he'd dared swallow on his birthday no less, September 10, 1986, had come up with everything else in a pile that definitely did not portent wonderful things to tell.

"Fuck."

"Are you OK, kid?"

"Dad?" Dorian turned from the pile of fortune-telling puke when his eyes saw, and all but refused to see, exactly what it was that they saw. "I don't think so, because I threw up the thing I was told never to throw up, or it would be the end of the world. And now you, the First Horseman of the Apocalypse, who I've only ever seen a shadow of once, stand in front of me in the corrals, asking if I'm O.K., in a tone implying I have a Tums if you need one. But no, you wouldn't know that because you have no tone on account of you never speaking and all."

"Watch *your* tone when you're speaking to a Rider boy," came from somewhere to the left.

As both The Pale and Dorian Gray looked over their shoulders to find Cradle, leaning his arms akimbo on the top fence rail, one badass new boot on the bottom rung like he was on the universe's last Top Model for a pre-apocalyptic fragrance ad.

"Holy shit," said Dorian and the Pale, in unison.

The weird part was the Pale, A., had been talking, and B., its voice sounded exactly like Cradle's. Not only was it confusing, it was giving him the heebee geebees.

"Nope, this is too weird," Dorian said and turned to go, making it mid-turn before his dad had him pinned to the ground by the scruff of his neck.

"You, my wayward son, are going to go over to that pile of barf, dig through it bare-handed, and pick out every last important bit. Then, you're going to the stables to wash it all off and bring it back to me. All clean and shiny," Cradle finished, pushing his son's face into the dirt for a quick rub, before letting him up to do his chore.

Dorian said not a word, drug himself up, and walked in the most awkward, ashamed, mad, proud, and broken, petty walk of shame that ever did stumble back to clean up their own puke.

Cradle looked down at the ground, not that he couldn't look into her eyes, he just, his stomach seemed to drop from place whenever he thought to do so. Something was different. She felt… she felt too human.

"Cradle."

It wasn't a statement or a question. It was more than that. It almost sounded like an apology.

"Where'd the three go, Catherine? We have no time for this."

"The clocks have stopped, if you haven't noticed. We have all the time in the world, Cradle."

"Stop it!"

"Stop what?"

"Stop saying my name with my voice, Catherine. I can't, it's too much."

"Dad? Where's the hose?" Dorian whispered from behind like a child who knew they shouldn't interrupt, but if they didn't finish their chores, they were going to get in just as much trouble as if they didn't.

A conundrum as old as time itself.

"It's around back," the Pale answered.

Off he went, happy to take cover during the apocalypse of all meet-cutes.

"Don't you have work to do? Wouldn't want to be late on your first day."

"Funny. You always were funny, Cradle," she laughed at that, fading to and fro as she did.

Worth it, she thought, as in seconds she'd seen Cradle's gaze go from punishing to delighted, to terrorized at the thought of her disappearance.

Noticing his hand made a quick, but guarded motion as he reached from his hip as if to grab her. Keep her here. As if he could. Angels didn't lie; it was why she loved him so much. People lie; it's one of the things about humanity, Cathy couldn't stand. The biggest of those being "I don't love you anymore". You can't stop loving someone. You either did and therefore always did, or you do not and therefore never had. There are gray areas, as with all things, like for those who told someone they weren't in love, but were, which didn't make the love they felt or imagined any less real. It was one of many reasons humanity was her least favorite species to deal with.

Lies.

Cathy got into a huge fight about the topic once. When she mentioned she still loved Alexander, her first love, even before Cradle.

"How could you still love someone who hurt you so?"

"It's not something you turn off, Mother. It just keeps going, like the sun. Even if you never walk outside to see it again, you know it's there. You still love it for the times you had together, the way it made you feel, and how you looked forward to seeing them like dawn's first light. Tell me, Mother, how could you ever stop loving that?"

"You're a silly girl, Catherine. This talk of lovers and the sun and love eternal. Be glad you're a woman and your use was sealed the day you were born, not left to sort out love stories, or worse, philosophies from the great bread plains of Hamsfield."

Her mother wasn't a simple woman for the times they had lived in; otherwise, she never would have let Cathy dabble in these talks while kneading the day's dough. But her mother was not of the lover's ilk, to be sure. Did she love? Yes, with every labor and chore that was for her to do, and she'd minded not a bit. It was for the love of them all, her brood, she'd called them.

Cathy almost felt sorry for her, to never really know love. Her story was like many. She met a nice boy and married him. Where her story veered was the nice young man remained a nice grown man, and for that she was grateful. She told her daughters that so many times, it ought to have been a psalm.

"It's not something every woman in town could say," her mother would have said for the hundredth time.

If Pa so much as walked around the corner, she'd stop her "hennin" with the girls, as Pa called it, so as to not sound like a silly maiden. Imagine being grateful you weren't being beaten, but still never quite sure judgment wasn't lying around the corner, which Cathy learned the hard way.

Anyway, it was all lies. Lies, it was a good day when it wasn't. Lies of how James Edward Worth from across the field would make a fine husband for Catherine. She couldn't marry him. She loved Cradle, but how do you tell your parents you spent your afternoon in an old, run-down church, turning it into sheer heaven? Wasting away the late afternoon hours in a house of God. She'd be on a pyre by that very evening.

Looking back, burning would have been the better choice, with hindsight being fifty-fifty and all that.

Love.

Now, love was something Catherine held for Jamie, too. From the time they were old enough to trot the fields back and forth to each other's houses. They had been thick as thieves, but she didn't love him like that. When she said it to her parents, they looked at her like she had three heads.

It made perfect sense, their lands ran side by side and even shared a brook! And a giving well, that had been giving good, clean, cold, spring water for generations.

"That's as good as gold, Catherine! And you love him! And don't say that you don't, we won't hear it, you've lit up like a firefly every time that boy is within fifty feet of ya."

And he was right, she did. His laugh, the sparkle in his eyes, and his kindness to the animals on the farm. Men especially weren't supposed to look at animals as having souls, but Jamie would have none of that, which, being on a farm, did take a bit of the sparkle from his eyes with every damned chore required of him. Damned chores, he called them. One after another took something of his heart, but it was a big heart. He would be O.K. Whoever found themselves lucky to marry that good-time, hard-working, ale-drinking man, was in for a wonderful partner. Cathy knew that in her heart to be true.

One morning, her parents roused her at dawn, and outside was James Edward Worth, the Second of his name, on one bent, shaking knee, and it damn near broke her.

She could see it in his eyes; this was a *damned chore,* and that was something she would not be. So, she politely agreed and went on about planning the celebrations before going on her afternoon walk.

That was the day she left. Left Cradle, left Jamie, left her mother and father, brother, and sisters.

And now here she was, giving it away, all over again. If she could do it again, she would have done it another way. She would have at least aged out her years beside Cradle for as many as she had. But those luxuries she threw away left her nothing to bargain with.

She heard Jamie got to marry whom his heart had been set on, and that no stray dog ever happened by his house with a missed meal or a place to put their heads. At least there was that, and that was definitely something.

"Cathy—,"

"Shut up, Cradle."

You could have knocked the angel over with a feather.

"Look, I know you'll always love me, and taking in that part of you showed me so much more than you could ever wish to know. Don't ask. We don't have time."

"Bu—"

"SHUT UP!" Cathy faded in and out on the yell. "I know you have Peter's key. I'll be taking it now. It works the corrals. I figured it out over time. Pieces of this and that went everywhere during the Big Show. I'll be keeping it. We can't trust the other three, and when this borrowed bit of humanity is gone, no one will ever get close enough to me to know it exists.

"Cathy, if—"

"Oh, my goddess, Cradle. If you don't shut the fuck up, I'll let them burn it all to ash! I can't give you back the bit of humanity you bestowed on me. I've already given it to someone else."

Cathy side-eyed the furious angel, but he neither moved nor said a word. He was too pissed.

"I gave it to Atsilla Rene' Onacanna. When you left the alcove and she began to burn, she wasn't strong enough to make it through. I saw how you felt about her. I felt it. So, I breathed life back into a soul that could make you happy, if you let it. That's entirely up to you this time," Cathy said, fading further and further away with every word.

"I'll gather the other three. You put Albert on ice, we won't be playing M theory today… much… well, anymore. We will need him for later. He will be allowed to stay at the library. The One would like you to encourage the relationship between Him and the Grinx; it's his favorite channel," she said, like The One watches everyone's livestream.

"Like YouTube?" Cradle asked and broke into a fit of laughter. "I'll see what I can do."

"Good."

"Cradle, we know you love Morna. You're like a father to her, but she's from Peter's stock."

"Shut up, Catherine. Now would be an excellent time for *you* to shut up."

And she did.

"What's going on, Cathy? Where's Lena? Where's Bill and Steve?"

Cathy slipped into sign language, trying to hold onto as much of the gift Cradle gave her. It was indeed the most precious thing anyone had ever given to another, and it was so finite for now.

Cradle didn't skip a beat as he talked with her. He didn't give a shit how she talked to him, as long as she did.

"Dad. Dad? This is cute and all, but I don't think we have time for a first date."

This time, both Cathy and Cradle looked at the interloper like a bug they'd love nothing more than to squish under their boot heel.

Fucking kids, they both signed in unison before breaking into a fit of silent laughter.

"What the fuck is going on?" Even Dorian could admit the silent laughter thing was weirdly fucking adorable.

Helllloooo apocalypse check, he thought to himself as Cathy washed away to nothing at the exact time Cradle popped off the plane, forgetting in their banter to hand the key over.

"Good," Dorian said out loud, pulling out the shiny quarter to look at his reflection. "It would be a shame to waste these good looks."

334

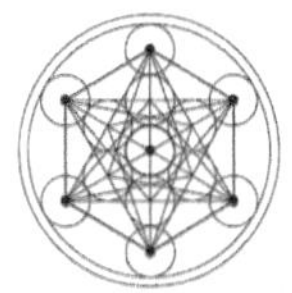

SIXTY-THREE

SEND ME AN ANGEL

Cradle was passing the library when someone who looked a lot like Mary Tudor dove headfirst into the window, the billowing skirts following like a magic trick as they squeezed through the tiny window. It was like the world's oddest burlesque show.

"Whatcha doin'?"

"Jesus Christ!" Silla yelled.

"Nope, just Cradle," he barely eked out before his lips were on hers, and damned if it wasn't getting hotter on the sidewalks of the Borderlands.

"Forgive me," he said, and then he was gone, or further away.

Before Silla could help herself, she reached out a hand and stepped forward as Cradle stepped back, again.

"Stay," Silla ordered the angel.

She closed the distance between them, taking Cradle's hand in hers, and kept her eyes locked on their entwined fingers, exactly where he was looking too.

"Listen, Cradle. I don't know what this is, but it's something. With everything going on, it's no wonder emotions are running hot. I'm not going to forgive you for the kiss because there's nothing to forgive. I wanted it, you wanted it."

"The end," Cradle summed up and dropped Silla's hand.

"Oh, bullshit! This is the beginning... once we deal with the end. Have we dealt with the end? I'm trying to find Morna, who got caught in a strong wind, but I don't know where anyone is other than that. Has there been any success? A lot of us met at Showbiz, but that was a long time ago in an apocalypse trope. Where is everybody?"

"Well, then, if that's how things are going to be," he pulled Silla in a bit closer, leaned slowly down, and whispered in her heavily pierced ear, right where a stunning stripe of cardinal red twisted with ebony before it fell tucked away. "I look forward to discussing whatever this is when we figure out where everyone is. I will put my lips on yours and know that you know you're making my world blow up."

They both broke into a lover's giggle with piss-poor timing.

"Who was headed into the library?" Silla asked as she looked around Cradle's new wings.

"Mary Tudor, I believe."

"Mary Tudor? Huh. Never would have pegged you for a misogynist, but then again, you certainly are old enough.

"I am not a misogynist."

"OK, riddle me this then, Batman. Why was one of the most powerful women in history, known primarily for killing people for worshipping a different sky daddy than hers, just allowed to wriggle into the library in the Borderlands during mid-apocalypse with the exact same plot?"

"Because your tongue was in my mouth?"

"Would you ever like for it to be there again?"

"Yes." This one hurt. "It appears I'm a bit of a misogynist," Cradle confessed.

"Excellent, now we can move on. Next question, have you seen Morna anywhere around?"

It was somewhere near the very end of Silla's question it became pretty damn clear all on their own. Morna screamed from inside the library, and there was suddenly no sign of Silla, but a cindering, smoky mess of ashes all over Cradle's new Docs.

Lena flew by with the oracle of Delphi riding front and... Justice Grey riding back? Bill was on her right flank, and Steve to her left. While seeing all Cradle had seen in his existence, he thought he knew what the definition of Hell hath no Fury like The Four might look like. He did not, because on their tails was the Wild Hunt, a sight not seen in so long it had become lore.

SIXTY-FOUR

WHEN WHAT TO MY WONDERING EYES SHOULD APPEAR

"Crazy, right?"

"Loki?" Metatron asked the nondistinct man standing next to him, drinking a mug of ale, casually watching the show.

"Why has Odin rigged up the Wild Hunt?"

"Is that what that was? It looked like the cast from Little House on the Prairie and Michael Jackson's *Thriller* were asked to play Santa and his helpers at the last minute, like right after they did some bath salts and Redbull. Any guesses as to what the reindeer are supposed to be?" Loki asked so coolly you'd swear they were already locked up in Briarwood.

"I'm going to go for the obvious for the sake of time, but I was thinking, Stephen King's *Pet Cemetery*? I'm not proud of that and reserve the right to retract my statement at a further date for a better reaction."

Loki bellowed from low in his gut. A distinct laugh, the kind the coolest kid, really the coolest, the kind who talked to everyone, the kind that wouldn't abide a bully, and always had your six, would have the confidence to laugh.

"You know you're going in there, don't you?" Cradle asked.

"Yeah, I know, but it's because I want to, not because I have to." The trickster raised his cup before bowing his head to some unknown entity, slammed the rest of his ale, threw the cup to the ground, and turned to Cradle, "Are we doing this or what?"

As they took off at lightning speed behind The Hunt, and in through the magic window that seemed to widen enough for anything that wanted through it, the war had started inside. Hildi and Karma had backed Bloody Mary into a corner as she raised her fists in the air, something shiny clutched in one hand, slightly curtained by the blood-stained lace cuff of her wedding gown. Cradle would bet a new feather it was a key.

"Don't you think you've done enough harm, Mary, my love?" a heavy German accent said, as Albert Einstein tried his luck at placating his girlfriend's, slash librarian's, assistant.

You could have heard a pin drop as every last head in the room slowly swiveled to Albert, questioning his sanity.

"Eternity is long, and she is a beautiful woman, yes? I thought she had changed her ways?"

Heads nodding, they moved in on Einstein, now questioning his loyalty. Cradle reached to feel at his inner wing. Yep, still there. So how could the key be over there?

"I have it on good authority, Albert is cool," Cradle assured the group.

"You sure, you're sure?" Creak double-checked, thinking back on how Albert and Mary pretended to be strangers in the Pinto Factory.

"One hundred percent," Cradle confirmed

"No, no, you fool," Mary carried on. "I do not think I've started enough trouble. I've never started trouble. Yet, that's what I've been since the day of my birth. Trouble for my father, my bastard sister, all the while my heart was with Spain, my mother, Queen Isabella, and with God."

"Oh, I get it! You and Torq were playing with the universe like it was a game of D&D! Right? And whoever wins the campaign gets to be God."

"Um, yes, doggie, that is how games are played from finishing school to foreign lands, are they not? And besides, we have the power of righteousness on our side."

Creak leaned over into the Green Horseman's horse's ear, "Oooooooh, she's about to be surprised."

Five little ankle biters quietly repelled off the ginormous bookshelves behind Mary Tudor, their familiars holding their ropes taught in their teeth. Albert said not a word of warning. Good guy check, you could almost hear it as every head swiveled back toward Mary Tudor, trying with all their might not to notice the preschool black ops team still in their pajamas.

"They have been practicing to show their parents. Aren't they marvelous?" Hildi whispered to Creak, "On my mark," she finished with a head nod.

"Stop that whispering or I'll blow outta here with this God key, the auto de fey army leading the way to 9.999, and you'll see Torquemada and I were right the whole time. The power I alone now hold as I burn twelve thousand souls will use up so much stored energy the universe can send me back. I'll rewind it to the perfect time. I can do it all again. Get it right this time."

"O.K. Listen, lady. You're off your rocker if you think The One takes sides. Further still, that trick with taking over The One dimension could only have happened with surprise and tactical maneuvering, something that is no longer at your disposal. But please, give it a try."

"I think I will," Bloody Mary said, turning to pluck one of the five babes on the shelves, attempting to add kidnapping to her long list of offenses.

The force of which brought the first of twenty-seven bookshelves down upon Queen Mary Tudor. For these were no regular babes, and you weren't taking them anywhere they didn't want to go. The force instead pulled the first of a line of bookshelves down upon her, stopping her in her tracks with shelves and shelves of ideas, just as broken and stupid as she was. Which, of course, didn't kill her. She wasn't going anywhere.

Especially without the key little Nitzie tossed into the crowd, yelling, "Catch, sparkly babysitter!"

Like the perfect angel she was becoming, Morna popped to the correct spot and caught the key before popping right out of the library like she'd done it a thousand times before. She didn't even have to try.

Little Nitzie would have been cut in half by the force of those twenty-seven shelves, so heavy they sank a library if it weren't for Beauregard. Beau, for short, was her familiar and boa constrictor, who twisted his body into a suspension coil that absorbed the shock, saving Nitzie's life... again.

His eyeballs went oddly spiral-shaped as he absorbed her impending death with his coil that transformed instantly into a soft and comforting hug right before Nitzie said, "Good boy. Slide?"

Beau shook his head no.

"Beau! Slide!" Nitzie ordered about two seconds from tantrum time.

Beau looked over at Hildi for consent, for which the warrior woman did a slight hand movement that said, good job, with a pinky curl, which meant great promise of a giant treat later should he bring his charge home alive. The next thing you know, Nitzie slid down the arched body of a seventy-foot python, her blankie flapping in the wind like a cape, and it was at this point her father or mother would usually catch her, but since they were out having Pizza, she instead barreled head first into a very charred, still smoking, Tomas De Torquemada himself, who had just arrived over the top of some very tall, very toppled bookshelves, making his secret return from the Asshat's spit known to everyone in the room.

The little brat and her pets were just like her goddamn mother. She was a pain in his ass during the Spanish Inquisition, and her daughter was a pain in his ass now.

"Go check on the troops. Their out back," Torq ordered Justice from his supine smoking position.

"It was the best of times, it was the—" Justice quoted quite on point for a predicament as old as time itself.

Time, something that still wasn't in full swing, and may never be again, thanks in part to his shenanigans over daddy issues. Best he played the part of Torquemada's faithful servant and went to check on the auto de fey outback, lest Torquemada figure out there was more than one traitor among his crew.

When Justice stepped outside, he saw a sight woe to anyone who should ever have to bear it with their own eyes. An auto de fey army moaning and clutching their bellies, each holding a "Party Size" bag of "Wow" potato chips. "With Olestra" was boasted proudly on the front of each bag.

Oh, he needed to act quickly. This was going to be grand, he thought before ordering the belly-aching crew to attention, threatening their afterlives to eternity as little more than stardust should they not quit their bitching and fall in line before heading back into the library.

"It's now or never, Sir," Justice said to Torquemada.

Loki moved for the door.

"Let him go." Creak sent a nonverbal message to the good guys.

What, the crew thought while somehow picking up on Creak's thoughts without headsets, something everyone of them planned to discuss with the Grinx the first moment they had a chance.

How far did this little trick go? Could he always do this? Could he hear all their thoughts, All THE TIME?

"Attention."

Creak, and the very nervous good guys, heard Justice call the army to order outside the back doors of the library. The army was going to blow through a quarter of the omniverse's infinite energy with a one-way trip to 9.999.

"Fuuuuck, kid. I'll be sticking those sticks where the sun doesn't shine should you fuck this up."

Justice heard Creak's warning loud and clear inside his head.

I'm aware, Justice thought in his head before ordering the troops to get in position for takeoff to 9.999, a slight change of trajectory from the original plan, but the cat was out of the bag, and with any luck, it wouldn't matter where they went as long as they went soon.

SIXTY-FIVE

HORSE MATH

"What the hell, Creak? You're just going to let him walk outta here?" The entire host of warriors shouted one way or another.

"Yep."

"Are you crazy, Shaz?" Albert asked with all his heart.

He was quite concerned for the little guy. Outside, you could hear Torquemada call "Charge" like a real Asshat from behind his army.

"I did not ride all this way to watch the world end on my watch," Odin said.

He turned with the Wild Hunt in tow, egging on the three of The Four Horsemen that were present with whinnies and chuffs. The Wild Hunt got to go for a ride, and the three were being forced to remain inside as Odin made his way through the back doors on Torquemada's heels.

"Oh, shut it," said Pythia for Lena to the Red's Horse, who pouted the absolute biggest pout of all pouts. "You're a big baby," Pythia added before the Oracle of Delphi was bucked right the fuck off.

"Are we? Are we gonna go get them? What the actual fuck is going on? What is your plan?" Cradle asked Creak in the most threateningly unnerving way the General of Relativity could.

While the absolute grandest entrance since Glenda popped down in a bubble began. Karma stepped one long, lean Lou Boutin at a time down a "now you see it, now you don't" gold staircase. It was spectacular. The second step showed up as if they were always there, and then disappeared after each like they never were. Karma was grace incarnate on her descent. While at the very same time, a fiery, rose gold set of stairs came from nowhere as Morna JoAnn Stahr lifted one Himalayan salt lamp pink Doc Martin, stepping neither too heavy nor too light, each step landing in a way that said there had been some changes around here.

No one was quite sure where Morna had gone when she popped out, but she sure as Hell made an entrance of it when she popped back in.

Morna emerged in a cropped, sequin top camouflaged to move like peach fire and rose embers. Hanging from her nicely rounded hips, the kind that could raid a village, hung a pair of cargos inspired by palazzo pants, with ginormous pockets here, there, and everywhere over the Army Green and peach linen. It was perfectly Morna, right down to her socks by The Awesome Sock Club, that in no way matched the rest of the outfit in the most perfect fucking way.

Morna's doc landed on the library floor the exact moment Karma's Lou Boutin touched down like a feather. There was a whistling that sat in loud enough to blow out eardrums. It was the old-time whistling thing.

"Oh, gross," Nitzie said to Bill and Steve, who were catcalling a baby Neph and the prophetic Fate from the back on their Black and Green mounts.

"What have I told you about objectifying women?" Pythia

scolded the Horsemen for Lena, as each Horseman received a twenty-seven-carat ruby to the head.

"Get your horses and get out of here," Cradle ordered the three horsemen.

"I beg your pardon," said Pythia. "We are house-trained, thank you very much," she said without a single slur as the horses nodded regally to show good manners and grace.

Even if Cradle did deserve it this time, he was mostly cool, so they thought best to let him live and do the nodding thing instead. Besides, Pythia liked the angel; over the years, he'd brought the horses the most apples. So, in apocalyptic horse math, Cradle got to live.

"Oh, dear gawd! Do NOT go out there!" Justice said, covering his mouth and nose with his elbow.

Not a stick or trick to be found as he made his way through the back library doors.

SIXTY-SIX

THE SHIT SHOW

"Just a second. I will turn on the telescope and we can see what all this hubbub is about, yeah?" said Albert, who no more than lowered the lights to see and gave everyone an eyeball of the most unholy of holies.

Tomas de Torquemada's very own auto de fey army of high-jacked souls were having their very first meet and greet with Olestra, and it was going swimmingly for Torquemada. He could only absorb so many hits before the rest of the shots fired, hit, and slipped off around him to cover The Wild Hunt and Odin with every possible liquidus warning on each bag of the low-fat potato chip side effect warning label, not a single soul in the auto de fey army bothered to read.

"Turn it off!" came from here, there, and everywhere.

From the soldiers to Torquemada, to the Wild Hunt, to Odin, then to every last being in the library, once the unholy mess started hitting the telescope lens like chemical warfare.

The three Horsemen's destriers chuffed plumes of smoke, sending out an indescribable noise meant to call The Four to the field and form a string quartet. Their animal, and otherworldly nature of the beasts, instantly realized the God key was suddenly right under their noses.

"I don't think the shit show shut this thing down, kids," Cradle said before turning to his nephew and adopted son. "It was a good try, kid, but Torquemada still has St. Peter's key. The Asshat's key, that is. Once it opens the doors to heaven's gates and allows Torquemada and the auto de fay army entry, it's over. He'll dethrone The One, rewind time to the Spanish Inquisition, and this time the Inquisition won't stop until the omniverse is in Torquemada's grubby little hands."

"Wrong," Morna said with a look of sass and relief on her face. "Tomas de Torquemada doesn't have the God key," Morna said, giving a quick wink to Karma. "It's the key he made to open 9.666's doors when the God key and his title of St. Peter were taken from him before the Big Bang. All that key will do is let you in and out of 9.666. It possesses no tachyons, and it definitely isn't letting you into 9.999. The Asshat was that much of an Asshat he had to still have the key to show for his power, so he made a bogus one. The one Tomas De Torquemada is wearing right now," Morna finished as the Pale blew through the back doors of the library, not a single feature to show for it, but the ashen hooves, swirling and stomping before they disappeared, again and again. The hooves were headed singularly in one direction.

UNDERSTANDABLE

Morna never stood so perfectly still in her whole life, or afterlife, or both, as the ashen hooves made their way to her and stopped, which had her choking on the dusty ash.

"Don't breathe, Morna! Do not breathe that in!" Cradle yelled across the library, but it was too late; whatever she wasn't supposed to breathe in was already in.

To be on the safe side, she thought it best to heed Cradle's advice and stop breathing from this point on, until her tet-a-tet with The Pale ended. Goddess let her come out of this alive, or, you know, whatever, she thought as the hot, ashen breath of the Pale's horse inched from her throat. Then, just like that, the necklace was gone. The key now in the mouth of the leader of the apocalypse, and all on her watch.

"Well fuck," she said aloud to no one but herself as the hot breath of the invisible horse cooled.

It backed further and further away, the gold key and chain swinging in the air as if held between a horse's teeth, without the horse. With an invisible flick of his head, the necklace flew back and was caught by an ashen glove that disappeared with the necklace.

"Fuck, fuck, fuck," Morna said to no one but herself.

Two seconds ago, she had a big hand in helping save the omniverse. Now she was personally responsible for letting the God key fall into the hands of the leader of the Four Horsemen!

"It's OK, Morna darling," Karma tried to settle her soul.

How could she when she just ended the Omniverse?

Some fucking angel she was, she thought, breaking down in bedazzled tears while the entire crew laughed.

"Ha. Ha," Morna said flatly. "You've all gone loony," Morna paused to catch her breath before bellowing into another breakdown, this one being quite epic as she cry-slash-yelled, "That's understandable!"

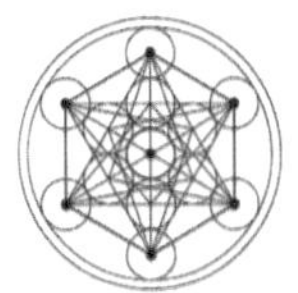

SIXTY-EIGHT

TICKS AND TOCKS AND TACHYONS

When Morna was all cried out, she must have passed out, because as she woke up, she assumed it was in time for the Big Show. She didn't want to open her eyes, but the familiar voices all around were definitely not acting like it was the end of days. Well, actually, when she cracked her eyes and saw Creak doing a keg stand with the help of Hildi in HQ, she considered she may still be totally out cold! There's no way they all gave up and decided to party with what little was left of time.

I mean, she thought, *not that it would be the worst plan.*

"Morna," Creak yelled from his inverted position as soon as the tap left his foamy maw. "She's up, guys. SHE'S UP!" Creak alerted everyone in HQ to Morna's awakening.

In seconds, Morna was surrounded by all of her newfound friends, and two very old ones, who were sitting directly across from her on the opposite jewel-toned sofa in HQ.

"Morna, are you OK?"

"Does it really matter?" Morna answered flatly. "We failed… I failed."

"No, Morna. We won. You won."

"What, how?" Morna asked, still not certain she was conscious. "The Pale has the God key! Even if Torquemada can't get through 9.999's gates, he still would have burned through an infinite amount of mass on his way there. Way more than the omniverse could handle processing. You told me that yourself, Cradle. No God key, no Tachyons, therefore all that burnt up energy!"

"Well," Karma interjected. "I may have had a little something to do with the tachyons. I slipped my spoon in Torquemada's chariot before we popped into the library, Morna."

"I don't remember that, Karma, and we were together."

"Ticks and Tocks and Tachyons, my dear."

And just like that, Morna knew it to be true. Karma had popped off for a millisecond before they made their way down the, now you see me, now you don't staircases into the library. Karma had come back different, lighter somehow.

"Karma, you can't give away your tachyon. You said it yourself, it's how you're built. You're not meant to stay in one place for long."

"I'd say giving up my role as Karma was a fair price to help stop the end of the world, don't you? Besides, the omniverse sorts these things out," Karma said before reaching to touch the necklace in the shape of a lucky horseshoe at Morna's throat.

"I'm Karma?" And just like that, Morna knew it was a tachyon-laced necklace, and she was now Karma, and the previous Karma was once again just an angel named Jane, just plain Jane who had done her time.

Now it was Morna's turn.

"What the actual fuck," Morna said, twiddling with the horseshoe-shaped necklace, reminding her. "But, the Horsemen have the God key! They will destroy everything!"

"No, Morna, they won't," Cradle said. "Bill and Steve never wanted to give up Mahjong night with Dorian, the Pale is happy to have an unlimited library card, and Lena never wanted to leave her horse Ruby, or Pythia, for that matter. You see, even if it's the tiniest of things, if you have something you love, it's worth living for. The Four Horsemen are quite content with their lot at the moment. Plus, no one will ever think to go looking for the God key in the corrals, so it's in as safe of hands as it could possibly be in, for now.

"Wow. How long was I out?"

"About fifteen minutes," Jane answered.

"Things sure do move fast around here," Morna said.

"Just wait," Jane said on a laugh that was quite possibly maniacal enough to land her in the nuthouse.

"Ticks and Tocks, huh?" Morna questioned.

"Yeah, Ticks and Tocks," answered Jane, who coincidentally looked very content sitting on Loki's lap.

"To the Ticks and Tocks and Tachyons!" Creak toasted before Hildi flipped him upside down for another keg stand.

"To the Ticks and Tocks and Tachyons!" Everyone toasted as Cradle bent Silla back over his knee for a kiss.

"What the fuc…? Never mind, just gimme a drink."

Morna looked on as her imaginary best friend and actual best friend just go for it, right there in HQ, in front of everyone. Everyone stopped what they were doing at the sudden knock on HQ's only formal door. The one right next to the nest of sofas everyone sat on, except Creak and Hildi, of course.

Everyone got really quiet, really fast, as Cradle went to the door. Before he could even get there, the security system gave a few beeps and a couple of clicks as heavy grinding gears parted the twelve-foot double doors, leaving Cradle with just one thing to say as he looked over his shoulder at his inverted friend drinking a gully wash of beer.

"Creak, I think it's for you."

ABOUT THE AUTHOR

J.K. Raymond received her Bachelor of Arts in 1995 from Fontbonne University, where she fell in love with everything in St. Louis-and under it.

J.K. also has the most amazing safety net in her tiny world, which selflessly helps her to continually heal. Her husband of twenty years, Matt Houser, her two sons, Aidan and Jace, her mother, JoAnn, and her grumble of pugs, Lollie, RueRue, and TukTuk.